Reviews from Park's earlier novel: *A Gift of the Emperor*

"A valuable addition to World War II literature…"
—*Kansas City Star*

"…a horrible story beautifully told, a graphic,
fictionalized account of Japanese brutality…"
—*Sojourner: The Women's Forum*

"She controls the story with magnificent restraint… She juggles the
responsibility of storyteller and historian with remarkable restraint…"
—*American Reporter*

"Lyrical bittersweet moments shimmer throughout…"
—*MSRRT Newsletter*

The Northern Wind

Forced Journey to North Korea

Therese Park

iUniverse, Inc.
Bloomington

The Northern Wind
Forced Journey to North Korea

Certain characters in this work are historical figures, and certain events portrayed
did take place. However, this is a work of fiction. All of the other characters, names,
and events as well as all places, incidents, organizations, and dialogue in this
novel are either the products of the author's imagination or are used fictitiously.

Photo Credit: Reproduced with permission of The Kansas City Star,
copyright 2011 The Kansas City Star. All rights reserved.

iUniverse books may be ordered through booksellers or by contacting:

iUniverse
1663 Liberty Drive
Bloomington, IN 47403
www.iuniverse.com
1-800-Authors (1-800-288-4677)

ISBN: 978-1-4697-6908-0 (sc)
ISBN: 978-1-4697-6909-7 (e)

Printed in the United States of America

iUniverse rev. date: 3/12/2012

To all Americans who fought the Communists to grant freedom to South Koreans in the 1950's;

To all South Koreans who participated in the *New Country Building Campaign* of the mid—1960's South Korea, including school children.

Chapter One

June 1967, Kanghwa Island, South Korea

THE STEEP TRAIL BELOW her feet was strewn with tree roots, weeds, and dwarf bushes, and Miyong swallowed. This wasn't the way she had come earlier that morning, but she had no time to find her usual path on the other side of the creek because she might run into the riflemen she had seen moments earlier. So she lowered herself to the trail, carefully and slowly, and began to descend. The breeze was cool, even pleasant to her lungs, but it tossed her shoulder length hair, blocking her view of the horizon below with soybean fields, rice paddies, and straw-thatched huts. But she couldn't give up. She must reach Hope Community at any cost and report to the new director what she had just seen in the woods. Suddenly her foot slipped on loose gravel and she let out a cry, but she didn't fall. Something, maybe a buried rock or a root of some kind, stopped her from falling, and she made it safely to the dirt road that ran through the village. She began to run.

In the morning haze, the soybean fields on both sides of the road were dotted with farmers, their backs bent. Somewhere, a dog barked ferociously as if it could see her, and other dogs responded in chorus.

She felt safe. She had been here a few times with the Community members during the rice planting season in May. Once, one of the girls had a leech lodged in her leg, and a farmer helped her loosen it with a burning cigarette.

Slowing her pace, she wondered how many men had been there. *Ten? Twelve?* Though they wore South Korean army uniforms, they were dirty and unkempt, as though they had been sleeping on the ground for days. South Korean soldiers would never look that filthy. And these men had distinctive Northern accents!

She had been at the creek, washing her clothes, sitting on a flat rock surrounded by low-hanging willow branches, when she noticed four soldiers passing her. Each had a load on his back, and they were headed toward the lower end of the creek, where the stream narrowed and the dry area with smooth pebbles and leaves widened, a spot twenty yards or more from where she sat. Within seconds, more men, maybe six or seven, joined them, but these men had rifles with them, besides the backpacks they were carrying. After a quick assembly, they scattered. A few of them lowered their loads to the ground, took off boots and socks, and headed to the water, chattering like kids; others rested, some smoking, their backs against rocks; and some tried to fall asleep, eyes closed. She thought a regimental training had just ended somewhere and kept washing. Since the country's political power had shifted from a civilian government to that of the military a few years earlier under the new president, President Park— a former army major who had succeeded in a coup d'etat— all sorts of training had been going on everywhere. Even civilians were rounded up on weekends and trained under military codes.

But it didn't take long for Miyong to become suspicious of the men she was looking at. They began singing a military hymn she wasn't familiar with. She knew many South Korean military hymns because every morning, the KBS (Korean Broadcasting System) radio station played them over and over. But the song these men were singing was totally new to her. The singing ended rather abruptly, and someone asked, *"Dongmu,* how much time do we have here?"

Miyong couldn't believe what she had just heard and cringed. Here in the South, no one addressed someone as *dongmu* (comrade) because North Koreans used that word to address one another. South Koreans called a friend *chingu*, never *dongmu*. *Did I hear it correctly?* she wondered.

Another man said, "Hey, how many times did I tell you not to call anyone *dongmu*, while we're on a mission?"

"Who can hear us?" the first man said. "The birds? The winds?"

Through the willow branches, she saw the side view of a stocky fellow approaching a young man with a shaven head sitting on the ground a few feet away from him. Grabbing the young fellow by the throat, the stocky fellow slapped him hard. "Are you a mule? I told you not to use that word, didn't I?"

The young man was surprisingly calm. "Yes, *dongmu* — I mean, sir. But I keep forgetting!"

"Forgetting? Do you know where we are and why we are here?"

"Of course, sir!"

"What's the security code for the night?"

"I'm not as stupid as you think, sir. I know exactly where we are and why we're here. And I know where we're meeting the others, too!"

"You'd better! Don't let me repeat it again, understand? If something goes wrong tonight because of your stupidity, I will shoot you myself."

"Understood!" The young man sat erect and saluted.

When the leader turned his back to him, the young soldier picked up a pebble and hurled it across the creek, muttering something Miyong couldn't hear. The water splashed as the rock bounced on the surface a few times before it sank, leaving ripples.

For a moment, her mind was blank. She didn't know what to do. She couldn't just get up and leave, without being noticed by them. She couldn't stay there either. What would she do when they found her? The better question would be what would they do to her? One woman against that many men was never a good combination in such a remote place as this. She carefully pulled her clothes out of the water, just in case, squeezed out as much water as she could, and dropped them in her wicker basket.

While waiting for her moment to flee, she regretted coming. She should have stayed at the Community no matter how much the idle girls gossiped about her old roommate Jongmi and other girls who were no longer with them. Miyong had joined Hope Community in March, and like everyone else, she worked alongside villagers from dawn to dusk, doing farm work. Some days they worked in a barn, replacing the hay or tending pigs and chickens, and other days they planted and weeded in the fields until her back ached. But this morning, the second Saturday of June, she came alone to the creek in the wooded area to wash her clothes. Not that she loved solitude, but she was tired of being with the girls and listening to their unintelligent conversations. It was true that Jongmi had been infatuated with the tall, handsome former director Captain Kim who was now in Seoul, but was she pregnant with his child?

Miyong didn't believe it. Even if the rumor was true, what did it matter, when Jongmi wasn't with them anymore? She couldn't make them stop talking; all she could do was move away from them. And she loved the mountain air early in the morning, and the cool water caressing her hands. *Now what should I do?*

"Attention!" the stocky man said, and all turned to him. "Get ready!" he said, picking up his backpack. It took a while for the men in the water to get out and put their socks and shoes on, and for those who had been sitting on the ground to rise and shake dirt off their pants. In two minutes, all of them gathered their belongings and retreated into the woods.

Miyong remained still until she heard no human sounds and saw nothing moving. Checking all around her, she leaped to her feet and headed in the opposite direction from where the soldiers had disappeared.

Ten minutes of running made her exhausted, but she couldn't stop. More farmers were working in this part of the field, appearing like some animals. A woman yelled, "Are you all right, miss?" but she couldn't reply. Another few minutes of running made her lightheaded, but she pressed on. Soon, the granite slab bearing "Hope Community" in Chinese letters became visible, so she slowed her pace and checked herself. Her shoes were caked with mud and her skirt had a rip near the hem on the left side, but she was presentable. She wiped the sweat off her forehead.

When she entered the lobby, the front desk clerk, a young man with a clean boyish face, sprang to his feet. "Miss Hahn, you have a letter!" he announced excitedly, lifting a white envelope from the counter.

Miyong had no time for interruptions. And this young man could hold her up for petty conversations. "I'll get it later," she said, and reaching the staircase at the corner, she ran up.

"Miss Hahn!" his voice rang behind her, but she didn't stop.

*   *   *

When he heard a soft knock on his door, Major Min Haksoon stopped unpacking the boxes and crates of his belongings and looked up. This was his second Saturday at Hope Community, and he couldn't think who might be visiting him on a Saturday. When he heard the knock again, he stood, shook the dust from his army T-shirt and pants, and walked to the door.

A young woman stood before him, her black shoulder-length hair clinging to her neck and her face covered with sweat. She looked as though she had just run a marathon.

She spoke first. "Good morning, sir."

"Good morning…" Min was suddenly aware of the T-shirt and work pants he was wearing. Had he known that he would be receiving a female visitor this morning, he would have changed into his uniform. "What can I do for you, Miss…?"

"I…I'm sorry to bother you like this," she stammered. "My name is Hahn Miyong, sir. I need to talk to you. It's urgent!"

"Come in." He stepped aside.

Her eyes shifted from his face to the bare wall behind him, and she walked in carefully.

The major winced when he noticed her canvas shoes caked with mud. He had been in CIC for too long not to notice her unusual appearance and the fear on her face.

"Sir," she said, stopping in the middle of the room. "I remember you telling us to report any suspicious person or people we see, and I think I saw a bunch of suspicious soldiers."

"Oh?"

"They might be *ganchup* [Communists], sir! I'm serious."

"Sit down," he ordered, pointing at the straight-backed chair facing his desk, and when she was seated, he sat in his swivel chair on the opposite side of the desk. This island, including many others along the coast, had been a stepping stone for the North Koreans to reach the capitol. During the war in the earlier decade, those fields outside his window had been cluttered with corpses in Red Army uniforms, in greenish American uniforms, and in white farmers' outfits. The villagers called this part of the mountains Skull Gorge, because about 200 villagers had been buried alive in a cave during a severe bombing. The war had ended more than a decade earlier, but no one had attempted to excavate the bodies or even to find the entrance to the cavern, fearing that the place was cursed with hundreds of angry ghosts.

In the middle of the night, he often heard some muffled noises at the beach, followed by the familiar sounds of the patrol boats. And now, here in his office, a young member was about to report on the "suspicious soldiers" she had encountered on the mountain earlier this morning. "Take your time," he said.

"May I have a glass of water, sir?" Miyong asked.

"Certainly," Min said, rising from his chair.

Min walked to his mini kitchen at the far end of the room, turned the water on, and taking out a clear glass from the overhung cabinet, he filled it and brought it to her.

"Thank you, sir," she said, before emptying it. For the next five minutes, he listened to her story—what she had seen and where, what they had looked like, what they had said. "I came as soon as I could, sir, to report to you."

"What were you doing on the mountain early on a Saturday morning?" he asked.

"As I said, I went there to wash my clothes, sir. On a Saturday, we can't fetch enough water from the well because everybody does her laundry." She couldn't tell him that she had been avoiding the girls and what they had been talking about.

"I see..." the major said, uninterested. Opening a drawer and producing a cigarette, he lit it and smoked. The gray vapor rose, obscuring his expression, and for a moment, she wondered whether he believed her story.

"The men you've just told me about...Describe them to me."

"They dressed like South Korean National Guards, sir, but they were filthy and untidy. They didn't look like our soldiers we see here. And one of them, a young guy about my age, called the older man who seemed like their leader *dongmu,* and the leader slapped him. I thought it was strange..."

"Go on."

"The leader didn't seem to trust the young man and asked strange questions: 'What's the security code for the night?' 'Do you know where you are and why?' The young man said something about 'meeting others' tonight, sir."

"Meeting who and where?"

"He didn't say. Immediately, they left the area."

Min dropped the burning cigarette onto the brass ashtray in front of him and reached for the phone. He dialed a few numbers, and when the muffled voice of a man came through the receiver, he turned to the window and began talking softly.

Miyong couldn't understand a word he was saying, yet she could sense the intensity in his whispers. She was now convinced that this director took her report seriously. Compared to tall and good-looking Captain Kim, whom her friend Jongmi had been madly in love with and followed to Seoul, this new director was short and had no particular physical attraction except his fierce dark eyes that reminded her of black diamonds she had heard about. But he was stricter with the house rules and members' conduct than Kim ever had been. And he had his own philosophy about certain things: for instance, he disliked the weeping willows in the courtyard and had the garden crew replace all twelve of them with blue spruce, for blue spruce, according to him, was for young people with energy and new ideas, while weeping willows were for older folks who lived in the past world. He also had the crew fill the well that had been on the side of the property and dig a new one in the back, because water was the blood vessel of the earth, and the original well had not been aligned with nature's rule.

The major hung up the phone and turned to her. "You might be right about the men you saw," he said, talking fast. "The Coast Guard I've just talked to said that they spotted a suspicious vessel near the beach at dawn, but they lost it in the fog."

"What does it mean, sir?"

"They think the men you saw might have come in that boat. Stay in your room today, Miss Hahn, just in case. In other words, you're excused from the fieldwork. Thank you for coming!"

On the way to her room, Room 205, on the second floor, which she shared with three other girls, she remembered the letter the front desk clerk had mentioned earlier, and stopped to get it.

"Too busy even to pick up your letter, Miss Hahn?" the clerk teased, smiling crookedly. She didn't respond, and he handed it to her.

The letter was from her brother, Jinwoo. He had been demonstrating against deployment of Korean troops to Vietnam since the beginning of that year, along with thousands of others, and as a result, he had been battered by policemen many times. She hurried to her room, sat on her bed by the wall, and opened the envelope.

Dear Sister,

It seems as though it was only a couple of days ago I saw you leaving for Kanghwa Island, but it's been three months. I am glad you're doing well, in spite of the hard physical labor you're enduring. Many things have happened here in Seoul, since you left. Though you've urged me not to get involved in the student demonstrations against the government's troop deployment policy, I have been, and to make a long story short, I spent three nights with other troublemakers in a jail cell last week and just returned to my apartment on College Boulevard. We've been beaten and tortured, some more than others. The recent news revealed that our President received an undisclosed amount of money and military supplies from the American government, in addition to 150 million dollars he received a year earlier, in exchange for another 100,000 troops to fight in Vietnam. Now Americans couldn't do without ROK soldiers in Vietnam. There's no telling what our President will do.

The more our President uses his well-trained Special Troopers to crack down on us with teargas bombs, water hoses, and clubs, the angrier we get, and we fight, on behalf of our brothers falling fast in Vietnam. The casualties among Korean troops in Vietnam rose to two thousand as of yesterday, the KBS [Korean Broadcasting System] announced. Think about their widows and fatherless children! Think about their parents, siblings, friends grieving for their loved ones killed in a foreign land! It's sad that demonstrating is all we Korean boys can do. One of these days, I too might be in Vietnam, whether I like it or not. In my humble opinion, a president selling his countrymen to die in a foreign land is worse than a cattle owner taking his herd to a market. He should be shot for sure. But who can do the job?

When are you coming to Seoul? Let's get together soon. You are all I have in this hostile world. Just remember!

Your brother, Jinwoo.

Miyong muttered, "Why do you always have to be so brave, *Oppa* [Brother]?" The thought that he had been beaten savagely by policemen brought tears to her eyes. The two of them had been sent to the South with their trusted neighbors, Uncle Hong and his wife, Auntie Moon, during the war, when the American troops occupied Pyongyang. Thousands of North Koreans had fled then. She was only four and her

brother seven. There were so many things she couldn't understand—
why her father had them go with their neighbors, without him, and why
her mother hadn't been there the chilly morning when he handed them
over to Uncle Hong and Aunt Moon as if they were packages. She still
dreamt about that morning when she had been awakened by a distant
siren and her father's voice ordering, "Get up, children, get dressed."

"Where are we going?" she asked, in a sleepy voice.

"You're going for a trip with Uncle Hong and Auntie Moon."

"Are you not coming with us, Father?"

"Not today, but your *Omma* and I'll find you shortly, okay? Hurry,
they're waiting for you."

It seemed odd that they were going with their neighbors, but when
their father looked tense, like he was now, she knew better than to ask
many questions. Then it happened fast. Bundled up in wool coats and
hats, and each with the backpack their father loaded onto them, they
walked out the back door to find Uncle Hong and his wife waiting for
them under the early morning stars.

"Be good to Uncle and Auntie," their father said, his voice cracking,
and she and her brother responded by wailing. Uncle Hong tore them
from their father and forced them to walk. "Come, children, the guides
are waiting for us!"

Their father's last words resounded loud and clear, "Brother Hong,
take care of them as your own! And children, be good to Uncle and
Auntie!"

Chapter Two

AFTER MIYONG LEFT, THE major picked up the half-burned cigarette from the ashtray and began to smoke again. *Hahn Miyong...* He might have seen her at Monday assembly, but wasn't sure. All eighty women looked alike when he faced them from the podium in the courtyard, and some were in their mid-thirties, with families somewhere, but only a dozen were Miyong's age. Remembering the file cabinet in the corner, he dropped the cigarette butt in the ashtray, and walked to the cabinet and opened it. Finding a file with Hahn's photo stapled on the cover, he brought it to his desk to look through. On the first paper, at the bottom of the application form to Hope Community, he read the handwritten note:

The applicant grew up in Good Shepherd Orphanage operated by American missionaries in northern Seoul and speaks some English, she says. Her parents are believed to be alive in the North. Shy yet expresses herself clearly and seems enthusiastic about the program. I give my full approval.

It was signed by someone in the Department of the Urban Development Program at City Hall. Included in the file were her high school transcript, three recommendation letters — two from her teachers, and one from the director of Good Shepherd Orphanage in the northern part of Seoul — and a couple of awards from her high school. He read everything. Nothing impressed him because most recommendation letters didn't say anything important. But the fact that she had lived in an orphanage caused him to think about his own life.

Aren't we all orphans? he thought bitterly. In his case, his father harmed him more than helped, by forcing him to marry a girl whose father had been their landowner. Min had been only eighteen, then. His father offered his son to the landowner like a sacrificial animal to wipe out his accumulated debt, and at the same time, to gain a servant for a lifetime. That was the Korean custom, then. Min had despised his father for his calculated evil deed, which eventually ruined a young woman's life, besides pushing him away from the home where he had been born and raised. His now-estranged wife had been only fifteen, and had never crossed the threshold of a school. She worshipped Min as if he were her deity. He paid no attention to her, yet at night, he turned into an animal, devouring her piece by piece until he was filled. A year later, he was the father of a little sickly boy. How much he resented himself for his ability to plant a seed of life in a woman's body! He couldn't look at the infant sucking his wife's swollen breast. After that he never touched her and never spent a night in the same room with her. Luckily, the baby died of some contagious flu before he turned six months old, and Min left home for good. When he returned a few years later, for his father's funeral, he learned from his mother that his wife was in a sanitarium.

That was eleven years before. So many things had happened, but military life suited him just fine. To a soldier, he always thought, his country was a god. He looked at his watch. 8:20 a.m. He thought about going back to the boxes he had been unpacking earlier, but he didn't feel like it. He pulled out another cigarette from his cigarette case, lit it, and began to smoke again.

On Sunday morning, Miyong picked up *Dong-ah Daily News* from the newsstand at the entrance of the cafeteria. The caption on the cover page gave her a slight shiver: **President Park escapes assassination attempt!**

"Saturday around twenty past eleven p.m., Sergeant Chung Il-moon of Central Police Station #24 saw a regiment of National Guards passing by and halted them, demanding the security code for the night. Instantly, the National Guards took a defensive position and began firing. Having been informed of suspicious men in National Guards' uniforms sighted on Kanghwa that morning, 200 policemen had been waiting in combat position nearby and counterattacked. All thirty-one commandos were killed, except one, who is being interrogated. No policeman was injured. CIC reported that the commandos were handpicked and sent by North Korean premier Kim Il-sung to assassinate President Park. CIC is further investigating the incident."

It was unbelievable. She could have been the only person who saw them and reported to the authorities. As she looked at the girls passing her and walking toward the cafeteria, chattering, she felt as though she was no longer one of them. They seemed innocent and naïve, while she felt aged.

At about ten till nine, as Miyong stood in line with others at the entrance of community, waiting for the truck to take them to a nearby farm, two dozen reporters and TV crews passed them and entered the building. They each carried a briefcase or a movie camera marked with *Dong-a Daily* or *KBS* [*Korean Broadcasting System*] or *Chosen Daily*.

Miyong knew why they had come.

"Miss Hahn, Major Min wants to see you right away," Major Min's secretary, Private Shim, a man with pale skin, showed up at the doorway and announced.

"Why does he want to see me?"

"How do I know?" he said, with a crooked smile. "Be glad that you don't have to go to the farm and sweat all day. Hurry! He's waiting."

Noticing the girls' eyes glued on her face, she followed Shim, wishing she could go with them.

Sitting at the table, the major seemed in a good mood. She bowed to him deeply.

"Did you have a good dream last night?" he asked, rising from his swivel chair and walking toward her.

"Good dream, sir? If I did, I don't remember."

"A press conference is set for nine in the meeting room downstairs," he said. "Those reporters never give you any advance notice. You're not nervous about it, are you?"

"A press conference, sir?"

He smiled widely. "You're a celebrity today, Miss Hahn. You saved our President's life by alerting me about the commandoes on the mountain. Come, I'll introduce you to the reporters."

Miyong wasn't a bit glad about a press conference. *Probably they'll take pictures and ask questions.* She checked herself. She was in her work clothes—a light blue cotton blouse and gray corduroy pants. She would rather be in the field with the others, no matter how much she'd have to sweat, than facing the reporters and cameramen. "Do I have to be there, Major Min?" she asked.

"Of course. They didn't come to see me! Let's go!"

The conference room, with its white plastered ceiling and walls, was jam-packed with men with notepads and cameras, and when Major Min and Miyong entered, everyone stood up and applauded. The major sat behind the long table facing the reporters, motioning Miyong to take the chair next to him. Bright lights flashed, and she blinked. She was nervous and her mouth felt dry.

Major Min welcomed them and said, "Gentlemen, meet our member Hahn Miyong. As the director, I am very proud of what she has done. It took some courage for a young woman to report some strange fellows she saw on the mountain, wouldn't you say? She was scared, of course. Let us give her a hand to welcome her!" He clapped loudly, and the crowd applauded again.

Her throat was tight, as though she were about to cry. A prayer came to her lips. "Help me, Lord. I'm scared! I've never been interviewed before, but here I am, facing a roomful of men…" She noticed her hands shaking in her lap.

"Miss Hahn." A young man about her brother's age, with a pleasant-looking face, rose from the first row. "Please describe the men you saw on the mountain on June 12th."

She told them, as she had told Major Min. Telling the major had been easier than speaking to these strangers, but she pressed on. Her voice sounded alien to her and she heard herself stammering and repeating the same words. *These men are only reporters,* a voice whispered in her ear. *After this, you'll never see them again. And they're humans… None of them is perfect.*

She heard her words articulating as she concluded her story. "When I saw them marching away toward the woods, I had only one thought in my mind: to report them to Major Min. He told us many times to report any suspicious men, and those men certainly behaved suspiciously, in my opinion."

A gray-haired man with a Stalin moustache in the second row rose and cleared his throat. "Miss Hahn, you said that the men wore our soldiers' uniforms. Did they look exactly like our soldiers?" He looked stern and merciless.

"No, sir. They were filthy, dirt all over their uniforms."

"Were they wearing the same hats, the same uniforms, and the same boots as our soldiers?"

"Yes, except the boots. They wore canvas boots, the kind the Japanese wore in movies."

A few men chuckled softly, but she paid no attention to them.

"What made you certain that they were North Koreans?" the man with the moustache asked again.

She said the same thing she had told Min, that one of them called the leader "*dongmu*" and that they talked about "security code" for the night and meeting "others."

"I thought it was strange."

The reporters scribbled fast on their notebooks, while cameras flashed over and over.

"Would you recognize them if you saw their pictures?" another man, who wore thick-rimmed glasses, asked, rising from the back row.

"I think so."

A stack of photos in his hand, he approached the table and spread them in front of her. "Tell us, are they the same men you saw on the mountain?"

Miyong cringed. One photo showed the young man who had been slapped by the leader. His eyes were wide open and his nose and mouth were bloody. In another picture, a man looked directly at her as if he were alive, but his forehead had a dark spot that seemed to be a bullet hole. Still another picture showed another young fellow whose mouth was wide open as if the camera had caught him while he was screaming in pain. She turned her head away.

"Are they the same men?" the same reporter pressed.

"Yes, they are."

Major Min unexpectedly rose from the table. "Thank you, gentlemen," he said. "I believe Miss Hahn provided you enough information for the news articles. If you have other questions, I'll answer them for you individually. Thank you for coming."

Then, he did something Miyong had never expected. Producing a silver pendant from his pocket, he reached to her and placed it around her neck. Turning to the audience, he said, "Gentlemen, this piece of metal is called the Medal of Courage, the highest recognition a civilian can receive from CIC. Normally, our director should deliver it himself, but he had urgent business to take care of, so I have the honor of presenting it to Miss Hahn, our model citizen."

The room shook as the men applauded again. Then, opening a document, he read aloud: *In recognition of your remarkable courage to protect your country from the North Korean terrorists, I, Kim Chang-Kiu, the director of the Central Intelligence Corps, hereby name you, Hahn Miyong, an Exceptional Citizen of the Republic of South Korea. Please continue to serve your country..."*

Standing awkwardly, Miyong was numb. It felt as though she were watching a scene in a movie. It couldn't be herself, standing in front of all these reporters and cameramen. Bright lights exploded again, and then suddenly the ordeal was over.

"Thank you for coming, gentlemen!" the major said, and then led her out of the room.

That evening, with about a dozen others in the lobby, Miyong watched the whole news conference through the Sony television. She heard her own name several times through the lips of the anchorman and watched herself smiling nervously as Major Min placed the pendant around her neck. How ridiculous it was that one could be famous for something that happened accidentally!

"You're a celebrity," the girl next to Miyong said, turning.

"They should make a movie about you," another voice said from the back.

"I'm sure, they will!" still another said.

Miyong rose and headed for her room.

*   *   *

On the first Monday of July, around eight a.m., Major Min sent Joongsoo, the front desk clerk, to the cafeteria to fetch Miyong. When she entered his office, Min was pacing back and forth, his hands locked behind him. "Sit down," he ordered as usual. Seeing that she was seated, he said, "I have a proposition to make."

"A proposition…?"

"How would you like to be my secretary?"

"What about Private Shim?"

"He's not with us anymore. He's in jail with a misdemeanor charge."

"What has he done?"

The major turned to face the window, as if he found the topic uncomfortable to talk about. "His drinking problem finally cost him his job. This time, he beat up a bar girl, and he'll be locked up for some time." He turned toward her. "Going back to my proposition…

Normally, I'd have Headquarters fill the position, but if you want the job, it's yours."

"I've never worked as a secretary before, sir," she confessed. "Don't you need someone with experience?"

"Let me ask you this, then. Can you type and take shorthand dictation?"

"We learned the basics at school, sir. How fast should I type?"

"As fast as you can."

Miyong couldn't help but laugh. "Yes. I want the job more than anything in the world!"

"Can you begin tomorrow?"

"I surely can, sir."

He produced a small ring of keys and handed it to her, explaining which key belonged to which door. "Don't lose them," he said, and looked at her to make sure she heard him.

"I won't."

"Security is most important," he said.

Until late that afternoon, Min personally trained her, taking her around and showing where things were, how to answer the phone, how to use the American- made typewriter with "Remington" printed on in English, and how to make coffee with powdered coffee. While she was typing, he stood behind her, watching, and she smelled his shaving cream, the same kind her brother used, which had the faint aroma of an almond cookie.

"You'll learn as you go," he said when the session ended.

"I'll do my best, sir."

The next morning, Miyong took a long time to get dressed. It was her first day in Min's office and she wanted to look her best. She skipped breakfast because she was too nervous about her new job. Before leaving her room, she checked herself in the oval wall mirror by the door and was pleased by the way she looked. In her navy-blue two-piece dress that her brother had bought for her after her high school graduation, she looked as good as any office girl she had seen on the streets of Seoul.

On her way to Min's office, Miss Yang, the program director, who always wore a tight sweater over her tight skirt, noticed her. "Well, you're all groomed up this morning. What's the occasion?"

It was too early to brag about her new job, so Miyong said, "No particular reason, really. Major Min wants me to work for him until he finds a new secretary. It's only temporary."

"Good luck to you! I hope he hires you as his permanent secretary."

"Thank you!" With a quick nod, she headed for Min's office.

"You look lovely!" Yang said to her back.

Min looked at Miyong when she entered, but didn't say anything about her appearance, which she was glad about. She was never comfortable when people commented on her looks. Though she enjoyed dressing up, she didn't do it for others. She felt good when she looked decent.

"Shall we begin?" Min said.

Another day of learning and lots of typing! After lunch, the major got busy with some village leaders in the meeting room downstairs, and she saw him only before she was done for the day.

That Thursday morning, Major Min was looking at the papers in front of him and when she entered the office, he said, "I will be leaving for Seoul around noon today for a three-day meeting, returning on Sunday evening. There are some letters I want you to type while I'm gone."

"Yes, sir."

"The rest of the papers are about a five-year New Country Building project the government is launching at the beginning of next month. The weekend meeting is about this plan. To give a short description: by 1972, every dirt road in the major part of the island will be replaced by a paved road, and each home will have running water, a sewer system, and a slate roof. The beauty of this project is that the government is encouraging each citizen to get involved in improving the country they live in. We, the government, will provide everything to them— material and trucks and tools — in exchange for manpower. We're about to teach every citizen how to 'catch fish' with his or her own hands, instead of merely waiting for the government to deliver it to them. Does it make sense?"

"Yes, it does!"

"The greatest reward for the workers is to recognize their own abilities and be proud of what they can contribute. By the end of five years, we'll either be proud of ourselves as a nation, or feel that we failed. Time will tell." He stopped briefly to gather the papers, and handed them to her. "When I return, I'll conduct a meeting with village leaders about the project, and I could use some flyers. Read the material I gave you carefully, and condense it into a few pages so that the villagers can understand."

"Yes, sir."

On Friday, Miyong sat at her desk all day, summarizing the contents of each paper she read, underlining important points, and then typing them neatly and carefully. It was a long process, but she enjoyed the work; mostly, she wanted to impress her boss. Also, by making these flyers, she was making a difference to her country's future. The phone rang often, and each time she told the caller that Major Min wasn't available until Monday. Around noon, Major Min called to see how she was doing.

"I'm doing fine, sir."

"Were there any calls for me?"

"There were quite a few, but none of them left their number for you. I told them that you're not available until Monday."

"Good. I'll see you Monday morning, then."

"Have a safe trip, sir."

By four-thirty, she felt the temptation to run out of the building and stroll on the beach. About this time of the day, the sand was toasty under her bare feet and the wet seashells glistened in the late sunlight like jewels. But she couldn't afford such leisure. She had to finish her work.

A few minutes before five, as she began to clear her desk, the phone rang loudly. She almost wanted to ignore it. It was time for her freedom. But she picked up the receiver anyway.

"*Onni* [Big Sister]?" the caller said before Miyong said anything. Miyong held her breath. No one called her *Onni* but Jongmi. She was only six months younger than Miyong, but she persistently called her *Onni*. Jongmi had been popular for her movie-star face and her singing ability, and everyone missed her since she followed the captain to Seoul. Had Jongmi not been popular, perhaps the girls wouldn't have talked about her that much.

"Are you there, *Onni*?" Jongmi pressed, as if she thought Miyong had vanished.

"I'm here. Where are you, Jongmi?"

"I'm only two miles away from you. Can we have dinner together?"

"I'd love to. Come join us here."

"No, let's go somewhere. I'll pick you up, say, in ten minutes?"

"Fine!"

The phone clicked. As Miyong cleared her desk, a scene floated into her mind. It was about six weeks earlier, in mid-April, before Jongmi's departure to Seoul. When the Community members returned from a rice paddy at two-thirty instead of five due to a storm warning, their work clothes sodden with mud and filth, a thick and round woman and a broad-shouldered man stood in the lobby, inspecting everyone walking in. Miyong didn't know who they were until she heard the woman's high-pitched voice calling, "Jongmi-*ya!* Why did you run away?"

Jongmi headed for the door, like a rabbit at the sight of a wolf.

"Get her, *Kisa* [chauffeur]. Quick!" her mother ordered.

The man ran after Jongmi, bumping into some girls filing in. Jongmi tripped on something and fell on all fours, and the chauffeur picked her up, slinging her over his shoulder like a sack of potatoes. Jongmi fought like a child, kicking, hitting, and screaming at the top of her voice, "Let go of me! Let go, I say!" but the chauffeur ignored her. Returning to the lobby, he dropped her onto the floor.

The woman came over, grabbed Jongmi's arm and forced her to stand, and then began to slap her, yelling at the same time, "Why did you run away? Tell me!"

Jongmi cried, "Didn't you know why? I'll tell you then! I hated you, that's why!" Sobbing, she sank to the floor.

The woman pounded her daughter with her fist, heaving like a wrestler.

Miyong stepped forward and pushed the woman away from Jongmi, but two arms grabbed her shoulders and spun her around. It was the chauffeur. "This is a family matter, miss. Leave them alone," he said.

Something thumped on the staircase, and everyone looked up. Captain Kim stood there, silently. He seemed to be expecting a report from someone, anyone, but when no one volunteered, he asked in a controlled voice, "What's going on here?"

The mother let go of Jongmi to look up. "Who are you?" she said, acting annoyed.

"I was about to ask you that, lady," he said, shifting his weight to one side. "I am the commander here. And tell me who you are and why you're assaulting one of our members."

"Commander, eh?" she said boldly. "I'll tell you who I am and why I'm here. This is my daughter and I came to take her with me. I want you to stay out of it."

Kim was calm. "All right! I'll stay out of it," he said but didn't move. "Call security!" he roared to the front desk.

"Yes sir."

There was a quiet stir in the room as everyone let out a sigh of relief, but no one said a word.

Two security guards rushed in immediately and escorted the woman and her chauffeur out of the building. Something must have changed in Jongmi at that moment, because she acted rather strangely. She laughed hysterically first and then wailed, covering her face, still sitting on the floor.

"Don't just stand there," Captain Kim roared to the crowd again. "Go back to where you belong. Now!" He then disappeared.

After that day, Jongmi was a different girl. Not only that her eyes always followed Captain Kim whenever he appeared, in the hallway or in the cafeteria or in the courtyard, but she was also in a dreamlike state. According to the gossip, Jongmi went to his room every day after dinner. And as if to prove it, she returned to the girls' shared bedroom late at night, with the smell of alcohol about her. Once, Miyong asked, "Where have you been, Jongmi? You've been drinking, too."

"Mind your own business," Jongmi snapped, sounding like a drunkard. "I was with Captain Kim. Is there something wrong with that?"

"It's past midnight. How long were you with him?"

"Don't talk like my mother," Jongmi said. "I can't stand it. As far as I know, she's dead! So please don't talk like her."

"You know that Captain Kim is a married man, don't you?"

Jongmi stared at her with hate in her eyes. "Thank you for telling me that. But I don't care."

Two weeks later, Captain Kim left the Community, driving his military Jeep himself, and later that afternoon, Miyong found Jongmi packing her suitcase, dropping tears on her hands.

"Are you leaving?" Miyong asked.

Jongmi kept throwing her clothes into her suitcase without a reply.

"Where are you going?"

Jongmi said nothing, as if silence were the most effective punishment for her nosy friend. The next morning, she was gone. Miyong sometimes wondered whether she had been too harsh on her, but now, at the prospect of seeing her, she was happy. Changing quickly into her summer dress with the sunflower print, she ran downstairs.

The front desk clerk looked over her from head to toe. "You look gorgeous in that dress, Miss Hahn. Going out for a date?"

"Yes, but not with a gentleman."

"That's good! I'd be jealous if you were. Someday I might ask you to go out, and please don't say no."

"You're too young for me," she said with a straight face. "I prefer an older, mature gentleman to go out with."

His smile vanished. "Darn, my grandpa just passed away," he grumbled.

Miyong exited through the glass-paneled door quickly, without a word. *A tiresome insect!* she thought. She paced in the courtyard back and forth until a blue taxi crawled into the courtyard.

"*Onni!*" Jongmi called out from the back seat, waving her hand through the open window.

Miyong ran to her. Jongmi wasn't who Miyong remembered: She now had short straight hair barely reaching the ends of her earlobes, instead of long braided hair. She had lost weight, too, but in her red dress with tiny white dots, she was still pretty and looked considerably younger than her eighteen years.

"You look terrific!" Miyong said.

"Is that supposed to be a compliment?" said Jongmi, squinting into the setting sun.

"Of course!"

"I don't like compliments. They don't mean anything. Get in!"

Miyong got in and sat next to her. "You haven't changed a bit, still arguing as before."

Jongmi giggled like a small child.

"Where are you going, ladies?" the driver asked, turning.

"To the Pelican Café!" Jongmi said.

The taxi made a full circle in the courtyard before swerving into Ocean Boulevard. The broad view of the ocean unfolded before them. With multi-colored clouds hanging over the red sun on the hazy horizon, the water's surface sparkled as if gold dust had been sprinkled on it. It was the same body of water she saw every day, yet it was never the same. This evening, waves were dancing with joy and the gulls seemed happy as they glided through the air.

"I missed you." Miyong said.

"I did, too," Jongmi said in a tiny voice. "I read about you in the paper. Congratulations!"

Miyong merely shrugged.

"I read every word in the article and said to everyone I know, 'She used to be my roommate!' I'm so proud of you, *Onni!*"

"Let's talk about something else," Miyong said. "Where have you been all this time? Why didn't you even drop me a note?"

Jongmi drew a long sigh. "It's a long story, *Onni*. So many things have happened to me since I left here. I could write a book about it. But let's skip it for now. Do you remember the day I made you cry?"

"What are you talking about?"

"It was the day you and I hiked all the way up to the rest area with totem poles where we could see the 38th Parallel, remember?"

Miyong remembered. It was such a clear day that they saw the Han River at their feet, flowing westward like a blue strip of a fabric, and the 38th Parallel was a long green belt before it merged with gray mountains and vague and empty space farther away. Jongmi had been silly and bossy that day. "I see Pyongyang way out there," she had said, shading her eyes with her hands. "Call your mom and dad, *Onni*. I bet they can hear you!"

"Don't be silly," Miyong had replied.

"But look. From here, North Korea is so close. I could even jump over the river and run on that pasture." She then cupped her hands and shouted, "Dear Mr. and Mrs. Hahn. Can you see us?" Her voice fading away to the open field before them must have triggered Miyong's longing for home. She found herself shouting too, through her cupped hands, "*Abuji* and *Omma* [Father and Mother], can you see me...?" Her voice cracked and before she knew what was happening, she was crying violently like a child. It still puzzled her how suddenly she had turned into the small girl she once had been.

"I'm sorry, *Onni*, I didn't mean to upset you," Jongmi said, as if she thought Miyong were crying now.

"Don't be silly," Miyong said. "We saw snow cranes migrating to the South that day, didn't we?"

"Yeah, we did. Now that no one lives along the 38th Parallel, the whole area has become a wildlife sanctuary!"

The taxi turned into a parking lot and parked in front of a white one-story building with a huge picture on the front wall of a pelican standing in water. Inside, a man was pecking at the keyboard of a baby grand piano, blocking the view of the sun setting over the ocean. A young hostess in a long red dress led them to the table in the corner, away from the piano. As soon as they were seated, Jongmi ordered beer for herself and green tea for Miyong, without even asking.

When the waitress walked away, Jongmi said, "I've changed a lot, haven't I, *Onni?*"

"Maybe a little. You still look great."

"I feel I'm ten years older than when I last saw you. I didn't know what I was doing when I left here. You knew that I was carrying Captain Kim's child, didn't you?"

Miyong was surprised that Jongmi could talk like this about such a sensitive issue as her pregnancy. "I heard rumors, Jongmi, but I didn't believe it. It was true, then!"

"Of course."

"Why didn't you tell me about it? Everyone knew except me!"

"Well, it's over now." She cut Miyong short. "I was crazy enough to follow him to Seoul, hoping that I could be with him. I was too naïve and stupid. I showed up at the CIC Headquarters every day, but he never came down to see me. Not even once! One day, I suddenly understood everything,*Onni*; he didn't care about me at all, although I was carrying his child. That's how men are. As soon as they learn that the woman they were sleeping with is pregnant, they lose interest in her. When I realized this, I felt sick! Can you understand what I'm talking about?"

"Why didn't you come back to the Community, then? We missed you."

"Are you kidding?" She rolled her eyes. "What do I have at the Community, other than the memory of the creature I detest? Besides, I was big with his child! No, I couldn't do that!"

"What did you do, then?"

"I went to a clinic one morning and aborted the baby. It was after the guard at the CIC building told me that I was wasting my time with a married man. He was about fifty, or maybe older. I'm sure he felt sorry for me. Once my mind was made up, no one could stop me. I just walked into the clinic and told them I wanted an abortion, and they took care of it, free of charge!"

Miyong cringed.

Jongmi stared at her coldly. "What's wrong?" she asked, but she didn't wait for Miyong's response. "I had no choice. What else was there for me to do with Kim's baby?"

The drinks arrived on a tray. Jongmi waited until the beer was served, and then emptied the whole glass, as if it were water. She ordered another.

Miyong couldn't touch her tea.

"It was the turning point of my life," Jongmi continued, wiping the foamy film from her mouth. "When I got rid of the baby, I could live again. My life as Jongmi ended on the table in the abortion clinic. You have to live, you know. So I changed my name too. *Shin Yonghee* is my new name. Don't I look happier now, *Onni?*"

"You're the same girl I used to know, except for your new hairstyle. I like the *old* Jongmi just as much as the *new* one I'm looking at."

"Don't say that!" Jongmi frowned.

"Jongmi, you can't be someone else no matter how much you want to forget what happened to you. You're who you are from birth to the end."

"That's not true!"

"If you could change that easily, this world would be like a zoo full of monkeys, everyone pretending to be someone else."

"Whatever," she said tartly. "You're not me, and why should I expect you to understand what I've gone through?"

Jongmi dug into her purse and produced a gold cigarette box and a lighter. She lit the cigarette and began smoking.

Miyong had never seen her smoking before but didn't say anything.

After a few seconds, Jongmi said, "I have some news for you."

"What news?"

"Tell me: If someone walked in here and told you that he had news of your parents, what would you say?"

"What are you getting at? Don't you know they're in the North?"

"Take it easy, okay?" Jongmi said, acting like an older person. "Going back to that article about you in June…I showed it to my boss at the nightclub in Itaewon, and he said he knows you. 'That's impossible,' I said, but he was dead serious. He explained it this way: Your family lived in the same commune in Pyongyang, where he and his mom lived, and your mom and his mom were good friends."

"I left Pyongyang when I was four okay? I don't remember any woman my mom was close to."

"He said that you look so much like your mom. He said the kids in the commune, including you and your brother, called him 'Uncle Bear' because he was big and wore a moustache. Back in those days, he said, most of men were dragged to the Red Army except government employees and invalids, so the residents were mostly old people and women with children. He lived there because he failed the Army physical exam."

Miyong didn't want to hear more. "It's getting late, Jongmi. Can we go?"

"My boss wants to meet you!"

"Are you out of your mind?"

"No, I'm not."

Miyong looked at her straight. "Tell your boss that I can report him to the police for talking about my parents in the North. One other thing, Jongmi: It's about time you and I get serious about anti-Communism, too."

Jongmi clicked her tongue. "You're so paranoid."

"Take me home."

Sleep didn't come easily for Miyong that night. She tossed and turned endlessly on her sleeping mat. *What if there were such a man as Jongmi described? And what if this man really knew my parents?*

Chapter Three

MONDAY MORNING, MAJOR MIN sat at his desk, reading the newspapers, just as Miyong had imagined. "How was your weekend, sir?" Miyong asked.

"Good. We were busy, as usual, but we got a lot done. Have you finished typing those letters I gave you?"

"I did, sir."

"Thank you." He nodded. "I have more for you this morning. Tell me when you're ready."

"Should I make your coffee first?"

"Yes, please."

Walking to the mini kitchen with a portable stove and a sink next to it at the far end of the room, she filled the teakettle with water and put it on the stove. While waiting for the water to boil, she swore she'd never see Jongmi again. Who'd have thought that she'd bring such disturbing news, news of her parents whom she had not seen for sixteen years? The authorities had never been kind to those from the North, especially whose families still lived in the North. *I could lose my head, if Major Min found out about Jongmi's visit and what she and I discussed.*

The teakettle began to whistle, and she turned the burner off. Reaching into the overhanging cabinet, she took out Major Min's favorite ceramic mug with an image of a long-necked crane, and dropped two spoonfuls of Maxwell House Instant Coffee and two squares of crystal sugar into it. She then filled the mug with steaming water, stirred, and took it to the major.

"Thank you."

"Are the papers ready, sir?"

"Yes." He handed her a few sheets.

"Oh, I have the flyers ready for you to inspect, sir."

"Good. I will look at them later. Bring them to me when you can."

Miyong went to her desk in the adjacent room, found the flyers in her center drawer, and brought them to Min. "Is there anything else, sir?"

"That's all for now."

Miyong came back to her desk and began to type the new documents Min had handed to her. But the tiny words seemed to escape her attention no matter how carefully she typed. Jongmi's words kept ringing in her ears in fragments: *My boss has recent news of your parents…He said you look like your mother in her younger days…He wants to meet you…*

Miyong wanted to go to Seoul and talk to her brother as soon as possible. She had not seen him for more than two months. She kept hitting wrong keys, but kept on typing.

At three-thirty, as she delivered the flyers to the Conference Room, she saw two dozen farmers in loosely fitting work clothes standing and talking amongst themselves. She saw the village elder, too, who always walked with his long bamboo pipe in his hand, and others she had seen in the rice paddy while her group planted rice in early spring.

"Are they serious about paving the roads and building a water purifying plant, sir?" a young man asked the elder, showing respect.

"I'm as puzzled as you are," the elder replied with authority. "Let's wait and see what happens."

"I don't think they're lying," said another young man, who wore a dirty shirt and mud-caked sandals. "It's been broadcast on the radio loud and clear. Our President grew up on a farm and he knows what hunger is."

"Yeah, I know," the young man said. "I think he wants to make life better for poor folks like us."

"That's for sure," the elder said. "Our President isn't like any other presidents we had before. He was a soldier before he became the president."

"Shhhh," someone hissed.

Miyong saw Major Min entering, and the villagers taking seats, making banging and rustling noises.

Miyong seated herself in the back row, close to the door. If she were lucky, she might squeeze through the door without being noticed by her boss, and maybe catch the five o'clock boat. The only problem was that she had to run to her bedroom and get her purse before leaving for Seoul. What could she do in Seoul without money? She doubted that Major Min would look for her after this late-afternoon meeting.

Major Min began talking, and a hushed silence fell in the room. He talked about the same five-year project the government was launching in the remote areas that he had told her about earlier.

As time passed, she kept looking at her watch. At four-thirty, she casually rose and exited through the back door. Closing the door carefully behind her, she ran for her room. Two minutes later, she was on her way to the port. When she reached the port, the forty-seat steamboat was half-filled with men and women taking sea produce to a market in Seoul, and some dirty children, who seemed to belong to the merchants or the boat crew. She seated herself on the wooden bench in the middle section, next to a young woman nursing her infant. A young woman wearing a wide-brimmed bamboo hat and a red sleeveless dress was singing a song Miyong wasn't familiar with, holding a microphone. The ocean breeze was pleasant to her lungs, but some old passengers were fanning themselves with bamboo fans or wide-brimmed hats.

Its horn blaring, the boat began to move. Five minutes later, it passed a rock island where hundreds of seagulls had gathered and then an old lighthouse casting a purplish shadow onto the trembling water. She had not known that such a lighthouse existed on Kanghwa Island. With dark, thick green vines crawling on the exterior and some bricks missing on one side, it seemed deserted. She wondered if the Communists would use such a ghostly place as a hideout from the Coast Guard.

About an hour later, the boat swerved into the channel where the Han River drained, and a few miles west and three songs later, the bright city lights poured onto the water's surface. The boat reduced its speed and glided into a long box-like structure standing in oily water. Seagulls emerged from the dark and flew toward the twilight, chattering.

The dock was crowded and the air stifling with the smell of rotting fish. Finding a public phone mounted on a wall full of graffiti, Miyong dialed the number of the family whose children her brother tutored.

The housekeeper, who had a Southern accent, picked up the phone. "Your brother is teaching now," she said. "He won't be done before nine. May I take a message?"

"I must speak to him. Tell him it's urgent."

"Wait then, please."

After the noise of a sliding screen door and muffled voices, Jinwoo's voice came on the line. "Are you all right?" he asked.

"I'm fine, *Oppa*, but I need to see you. I'm in Seoul. Can we meet at the Corner Teahouse in your neighborhood?"

"Why didn't you tell me you were coming?"

"I had no time. I'll tell you all about it when I see you."

"I'll see what I can do. It might take a while until I can get away."

"I'll wait."

She took the bus, Bus 56.

The Corner Teahouse bustled with men and women smoking cigarettes and talking, overpowering the jazz ensemble in the background. Miyong sat at an empty table next to a window, overlooking the busy street lit with bright lights. The waitress, wearing a red apron, came over and handed her a menu. "What would you like to drink?"

"I'm waiting for someone," Miyong said.

"I'll be back." The waitress left.

Jinwoo arrived within twenty minutes. "What's the matter?" he asked as soon as he sat opposite her. "You didn't get kicked out of the Community, did you?"

"Of course not. In fact, I'm now the director's secretary!"

He raised his eyebrows, surprised. "Then why are you here?"

Miyong called the waitress back and ordered two green teas. She began cautiously. "Do you remember my friend Jongmi I wrote about? Well, she suddenly showed up on Friday. She told me that her boss at the nightclub where she works has news of our parents and wants to meet me. I said no way, but something kept bothering me after she left. It's like a big joke. I don't know what to think. That's why I'm here."

Her brother said nothing, only watched her, so Miyong continued. "I'm scared, *Oppa*. What if my boss finds out about Jongmi showing up at the Community, and what she and I have discussed? He works for CIC."

The tea came on a tiny wooden tray, but neither of them could touch it.

"How well do you know this Jongmi?" Jinwoo asked. "Is she someone you trust?"

"We were close before she left the Community," she said. "We did some hiking together and ate practically every meal together, too. But to tell you the truth, I can't say that I trust her. I don't know anything about her, really. It's silly, isn't it, *Oppa*; that I'm all stirred up because of what she said? Maybe I should forget about the whole thing. Maybe I should never speak to her again."

"Not so fast," Jinwoo said. "I know some risks are involved here, but suppose you meet Jongmi's boss face-to-face and see what he has to say? You can tell whether he's telling the truth or not when you face him. What can you possibly lose by meeting him?"

"It's not that simple, *Oppa*," Miyong said. "I work for a man who was once an important man at CIC. I could get in trouble by meeting this guy, if he has a bad record with the police."

Jinwoo clasped his hands and lowered his eyes to the table, as if he might pray. After a lengthy silence, he looked up. "You're only confirming Jongmi's message, that's all. Who'd know about it? I'm sure Jongmi wouldn't tell. If we're lucky, we might hear news of our parents. If you do nothing, they'll forever remain only in our memories."

Miyong drew a long sigh. "Tell me, *Oppa*. If you were in my shoes, what would you do?"

Jinwoo stared at the corner of the table for two seconds, and then said, "I think I'd meet the guy. Why not? We're talking about our parents here, aren't we?"

Chapter Four

ON THURSDAY, RAIN POURED down hard from the charcoal sky. While checking his mail, Major Min had a feeling that his secretary was not quite herself this morning. Could it be the rain? Women go through monthly cycles men don't, but serving him coffee without sugar and not bringing him the newspaper from the front desk downstairs? Miyong had never done it before. Then, unexpectedly, she had opened the folding door between her room and his, asking, "Did you call me, sir?" When he said no, her response was, "I thought I heard you calling me," and then she closed the door. An hour later, she was back, her eyes wide, not focusing on anything. "Did I leave the memo you gave me yesterday on your desk, sir?" she had asked.

He thought she was either losing her mind or was nervous about something. But what? He had been in CIC for too long to ignore it. And now, he could hear her dialing some numbers on her phone. On a dreadful day like this, no villagers came to ask questions, and the members idled in the building, gossiping, or doing laundry on the covered porch. Where was she calling? Who was she calling?

Then, there was no sound coming from her room. A minute

stretched to three or four, but still no sounds. Then, he heard the receiver dropping on the phone cradle. A second or two later, her phone rang and it seemed she was picking it up, carefully and slowly. Then silence again.

According to the report of the front desk clerk, Miyong had gone out on Friday evening with someone that had come in a taxi, not returning until past nine. Miyong had not said anything about it. *How strange…*

He signed the papers waiting for his approval and then called the Division of Urban Development in the Capital Building in Seoul and ordered material and equipment for the new road construction project. When he finished, he reached for his cigarette box next to the ashtray.

Miyong appeared, wringing her hands. "Sir, can I be excused for the afternoon? I'm not feeling very well."

"What's wrong?"

"Maybe I'm catching the flu, sir. I just feel sick."

"Take care of yourself."

"Thank you, sir. I'll be back in the morning. Oh, the letters…I'll finish them tomorrow when I get back."

"No problem. I hope you feel better soon."

After she left, the lunch bell rang loudly, so Min headed to the dining room adjacent to the cafeteria. He sat at his usual table by the window and read the newspapers until his lunch came on a tray. While sipping the steaming tea from a white porcelain cup, his eye caught something he wished he had not seen. Running like a marathoner toward the entrance of the property in the pouring rain was none other than his secretary. He couldn't believe it.

By the time Miyong reached the port, the rain had stopped and patches of blue showed in the sky. Finding Choi's Noodle Parlor, which Jongmi had mentioned, she relaxed. This was where Jongmi would find her when she came to fetch her. She sat on a bench to catch her breath. It bothered her that she had lied to Major Min, but all had gone well so far. She had called Jongmi early that morning, and when Jongmi picked up the receiver, she said nothing. Jongmi kept saying, "*Yoboseyo* [Hello]? *Yoboseyo?*" but Miyong kept her silence for a long moment and then hung up. It was the only thing she could do to indicate that she wanted to talk; since Major Min was on the other side of the louvered door. As bright as Jongmi was, she could figure out who might be calling and would try to call her back. And the plan worked. She talked fast: "Wait for me in front of the noodle shop at noon. I'll be coming in a white speedboat. You can't miss it." Then she hung up.

A beggar boy, about ten years old, came over, bowed, and thrust his dirty hand toward her. "Give me a coin, Sister," he said in a demanding voice.

It's not a time for charity, Miyong thought. And there were too many beggars! *I'm hungry too, you know? But I can't worry about it now.*

A bright white speck on the ocean caught her attention just in time, and Miyong sprang up. The white speck grew in size by the second, and she recognized Jongmi behind the steering wheel, wearing sunglasses.

"Here, here!" Miyong shouted, waving.

Jongmi maneuvered the boat skillfully to the dock and cut the engine. Miyong ran to her. "I didn't know you could operate a boat," she said.

"Small boats are easy," said Jongmi, showing her confidence. "I once handled a sixteen-footer with ten passengers by myself."

"I'm impressed."

"Get in!"

Miyong did as told, but the boat rocked wildly under her weight. Jongmi grabbed her elbow to steady her friend, and when she sat on the wooden bench, steered the vessel back to the open sea. The misty wind slapped Miyong's face. She must have shrieked because Jongmi said, "Is this your first time on a speedboat, *Onni?*"

"Yes, it is."

"Interesting!"

They passed a school of white fish in a jumping contest, their scales glinting white and bright against the slanting sun. Two minutes later, a group of dolphins appeared before them. Jongmi reduced her speed. Rolling on their backs and splashing with their fins and squealing, the dolphins seemed to be having the best time of their lives. Within moments, they too were gone, and the boat regained its speed. A mass of black kelp, the size of a comforter, surfaced, and Miyong watched for otters that might pop up from beneath, but they never did.

In ten minutes, they reached an area with many small and large rocks, some as large as a schoolhouse, surrounded by white foams. The boat merely crawled, puttering. Soon, a dome-like structure approached.

Bird deposits plastered the surrounding rocks. A dozen seabirds were preening or napping on the rocks, their necks severely twisted. The boat glided into the tunnel-like structure, moss-covered rocks on both sides. With another turn to the left, the sunlight dimmed, and Miyong felt cool air on her skin. There was the smell of rotting fish. The water beneath the boat was dark and solid, like a sheet of slate.

"Jongmi, I don't like this place," Miyong said. "Why are we here? I thought we were going to Itaewon to meet your boss."

"I never said that."

"Why did I get that idea, then?"

"I don't know, but look! Isn't this a neat place? Listen!" Letting go of the steering wheel, she cupped her hands and yelled, *"Yoboseyoooo-Hello!"*

Her shrill voice echoed through the walls, giving Miyong chills down her back.

"Stop it, Jongmi."

Jongmi laughed.

The motor's dull rumble grew louder as they approached a dark wooden structure, whose shadows were somber and eerie. A faint shaft of sunlight descended through the staircase connecting the upper part of the structure. Countless oysters clung to the moss-covered legs of the building.

Jongmi picked up a bundle of rope from the bottom of the boat, tied it around the wooden frame, and killed the engine. "We're here, Mr. Ho," she yelled toward the staircase.

"Is she with you?" a man's baritone voice rumbled.

"Yes, she is."

"Come on up, then."

Jongmi stepped onto the staircase and began to climb. The boards groaned under her weight. "Be very careful, *Onni*," she cautioned without turning. "It's slippery."

Miyong found the staircase not only slippery but unstable, too. "How deep is the water here?" she asked.

"No one knows. Just be careful."

Halfway up, where the staircase made a sharp turn to the right, Miyong saw a man in his forties in a wrinkled khaki shirt and matching pants, standing without expression. "This is my friend you've read about in the newspaper, Mr. Ho," Jongmi said. "And *Onni*, meet your old neighbor, *Uncle Bear*."

"*Anyong-haseyyo* [How are you]?" she said mechanically.

"Welcome!" he said. "Did you have a pleasant boat ride?"

"Yes."

He thrust his hand toward the ascending staircase on the right. "Please!"

Jongmi climbed the staircase first, and Miyong followed.

The rectangular room was the size of her bedroom at the Community. On the wooden floor sat a short-legged rectangular wooden table and four square bamboo cushions, two on each side. Looking up, she saw a poster with an image of a hammer and sickle, the symbol of Communism. She was rather calm, though her heart pounded. *I was right about him! No South Koreans would display such a poster.*

On the first day at Hope Community in March, she and a dozen newcomers had watched a film titled *North Korea Today,* narrated by a handsome Army captain. He talked at length about that very same logo hanging before her, saying that Kim Il-sung's North Korea was modeled after Adolph Hitler's Nazi Germany, and that the symbol represented Kim Il-sung's Workmen's Party, as the logo of an eagle over a swastikas represented Hitler's Third Reich. The narrator also had pointed out that Kim Il-sung's title as *Great Leader* came from Nazi salute "Heil, Mein Fuhrer (Hail, my leader)". Miyong looked at Jongmi.

"What's wrong?" she said with a straight face.

"Did I say anything?" Miyong asked.

"You look nervous."

"I'm perfectly calm."

"Please sit down," Ho suggested, seating himself on the cushion on one side of the table; Jongmi and Miyong sat on the opposite side, each on the bamboo cushion. Miyong wished she hadn't come, but what was there for her to do now? *Stay calm,* she told herself. *Panic makes things worse.*

"I feel I've known you all my life," Ho began. "I read every word in the recent article about you. I must admit, it takes a certain quality of woman to do what you've done for your country."

Miyong wasn't impressed. *You're a Communist. Make your speech short! Let him talk,* her brother's voice said in her mind. *See where he's leading you.*

Ho went on. "CIC wouldn't have caught the Commies without your prompt action, but your President didn't reward you for saving his neck, did he?"

Jongmi said, "She's been promoted to the director's secretary. It's better than a piece of paper saying how great she is. Someday, we'll read about her again."

He and Jongmi exchanged a secretive smile. Ho said, "The more the public hears a story like yours, the more popularity the Park administration gains. It all boils down to one thing — politics!"

A teenage boy with a shaven head appeared at the doorway, with a tray loaded with food balanced on his palm. He stood there as if waiting for an order to enter the room.

"Come in, Yongdu," Ho said, and the boy walked in. He unloaded three bowls of steaming rice, a large plate of boiled crab legs, and a steaming pot with reddish soup.

"Enjoy!" Yongdu said, giving Miyong a quick glance.

"What about *soju* [rice wine]?" Ho asked Yongdu.

"It's coming, sir. Will the ladies drink too?"

"Of course," Ho replied.

"No problem!" Yongdu went out, and in less than two minutes, he returned with a long-necked white porcelain jug and three tiny matching teacups.

Ho dismissed Yongdu with a quick nod, and after the boy left, he filled all three teacups with the clear gingery liquid. He gave one teacup to Miyong, one to Jongmi, and then lifted one. "To us!" he said.

Miyong wasn't comfortable drinking wine with a man she had just met. "I don't drink, Mr. Ho," she said.

He acted as though he were insulted. Dropping his wine cup noisily on the table, he said, "A young person must never refuse a drink from an older person. If you were a man, I'd teach you a lesson for such bad manners."

Miyong looked at Jongmi for help.

"Come on," Jongmi said, nudging Miyong's elbow. "One drink won't hurt your pristine reputation, *Onni*. Don't insult your host on your first visit."

"But I don't drink."

"Just one sip!" Ho said. "You must. It's the custom."

Check him out, her brother whispered again. *Ask him some questions.*

"Mr. Ho, Jongmi said that you have news of my parents — is that true?"

"Of course!"

"I'll drink it if you tell me what kind of information you have of them. How did you meet them, when, and where?"

Ho's glee faded from his face, and he swallowed. He picked up his wine cup and emptied it in one gulp. "I was fifteen, just about Yongdu's age. It was before the war...My mother and I had just moved into the commune where your family lived. Ask your brother. I'm sure he'll remember us."

"When did you last see them?"

"I…saw them two weeks ago. When you attend the Neighborhood Criticism Meeting, you see everyone. I went to see my mother, who still lives in the same commune where your family used to live. They're fine."

Miyong still didn't believe him.

"I have pictures to show you, if you want."

"Pictures?"

"Yes. But you have to drink first!" Ho said, pushing her drink toward her. "A promise is a promise."

Miyong picked the teacup and took a sip. A warm sensation came over her instantly, and she coughed.

"Try some crab," he said, lifting a copper-red crab leg from the tray and dropping it into Miyong's rice bowl. "You have to always eat when you drink wine. Otherwise the wine will consume you before you know it."

Miyong began to eat.

"They're delicious, aren't they? They're the best kind of crabs you can get. Do you know where I got them?"

"Where, Mr. Ho?" Jongmi asked.

"In Haeju Bay, about sixty miles north of here. These crabs are so tasty that the Japanese crab boats swarm in that area. In Tokyo, a plate of sushi made of these crabs costs as much as an ounce of gold! I'm not exaggerating!" Grabbing a crab leg, he sank his teeth into it and chewed, making crunchy noises.

"An ounce of gold!" Jongmi echoed.

"Haeju is north of the 38th Parallel," Miyong said. "How did you get crabs from Haeju?"

"Easy! Haeju is only an hour away from here by speedboat. You can even swim there, if you're a decent swimmer. You might think the border is sealed off, but who can divide the ocean, eh? And who can divide the sky?" He laughed, *ha, ha, ha…*

Miyong blinked to stay alert, as her eyes were losing focus. Ho's face began to swell up like a balloon, and then shrank back to its original size. The wall behind him moved in a few inches and retreated back. She noticed that one corner of the ceiling was about to cave in, but when she blinked, it was perfectly straight. She began to sweat. *Am I losing my mind?* Remembering what Ho had said, Miyong said, "Mr. Ho, you said you had pictures of my parents. Can I see them now?"

Turning to the wall, Ho yelled out, "Yongdu, bring the slide projector."

"Yes, sir."

Yongdu showed up in the doorway again, with a black box in his hand as wide as a small trunk. He moved quickly. He set the box on the floor and cleared the table to make room for the projector. He then plugged the cord to the receptacle on the wall, and left the room.

Ho took over and with a click, he began the slide show.

Blinking hard, Miyong couldn't make out the blurry images on the screen at first, and then the images became sharp.

"Do you remember this place, Miss Hahn?"

The place looked somewhat familiar. *Yes…it's Grandmother's house in Kaesong.* This photo had been taken on her father's birthday, in the courtyard, some months before they were separated. At the center of the picture sat her grandmother, smiling just as she always had, and on her right was her mother, not smiling, and on her left sat her father, who wasn't smiling either. He looked sad, although this was his birthday. *Did he know he'd lose his kids shortly, never to see them again?*

Tears trailed down fast, and Miyong brushed them away. *Wait, didn't he say that he saw them two weeks ago?* "Mr. Ho, I thought you saw them recently. Do you have their recent photos?"

"I do, but they are blurry. Wait, I'll show you."

Clicking the remote control, he caused an image of an old man and an old woman sitting on a bench to appear, but she recognized neither of them. She couldn't even distinguish their ages. Was it because she had consumed alcohol? Disappointed, she just sat there.

"They're not that far away, you know," Ho said in a strangely soothing voice. "Going to Pyongyang from here takes only four hours by car — so simple, so easy."

Miyong's throat ached. *It's been so long, Father and Mother.*

"You miss your parents, don't you?" Ho said.

Miyong nodded like a child, tears streaming down her face.

"Do you want to see them?"

She nodded again.

"I'd be more than happy to help you, Miyong," he said, switching to her first name. "Can you trust me?"

Again, she nodded.

Chapter Five

AT EIGHT THE NEXT morning, Major Min opened the manila envelope from CIC Headquarters and was surprised to find five glossy black and white photos. Captured in the prints was Miyong, sitting with another young woman her age on a boat. She had left work early yesterday, claiming that she wasn't feeling well. What disturbed him the most was the scribbled note attached to the photos. "Hahn Miyong and Shin Yonghee sighted five kilometers east of Kanghwa Port: 7-11-1967. Please inform your secretary of my visit sometime today." It was signed by Captain Yoon, a detective at CIC, whose nickname was Tough Nail. Once, while Min had been the chief investigator, he had interrogated Yoon for his aggressive methods, which had cost a man's life.

Min had trusted Miyong. He had even appointed her to be his secretary. *Why is she betraying me like this?* The old Korean proverb *"Your trusted dog can bite you"* rang in his mind with a new meaning. She had not told him of her evening outing with a woman who came in a taxi the past weekend while he had been in Seoul; he had heard it from the front desk clerk. Then on Monday, while he was conducting the meeting with the village leaders about the five-year government project,

Miyong walked out through the side door, right before his eyes. It was her duty to attend every meeting, dictate what was discussed, and type and file it. Then yesterday, how did she behave? She asked permission to leave, complaining about flu symptoms, and then ran out of the courtyard like a marathoner, full of energy.

The air in the room was so stifling with summer heat that he rose, walked to the window, and opened it. The cool ocean breeze comforted him. He thought about smoking, but did nothing. He wanted to enjoy the ocean view for a moment. The seabirds gliding through the dusty blue expanse seemed happy, and he looked at them for a long moment.

The phone rang, jolting him. He went back to his desk and picked up the receiver. "Major Min Haksoo speaking," he said.

"Good morning, sir," Yoon's husky voice boomed in his ear.

"Yes, Captain?"

"Have you received the photos yet?"

"I did, Captain. When will you be coming?"

"Is ten okay?"

Ten o'clock was only one hour and twenty minutes away. "Captain, I haven't told her about you coming yet…"

"It's only preliminary questioning, sir, to ask about the photos. It won't take long."

"Fine, then."

Hanging up the receiver, Major Min scratched the back of his head. Things were getting out of hand, and he didn't like it. Rising from the desk, he walked to the door, swung it open, and yelled downstairs. "Send Miss Hahn to work. It's almost nine!"

*　　*　　*

A soft knock on the door awakened Miyong. *Where am I? How did I get back?* The brownish water stain on the ceiling confirmed that she was in her room, still in bed. The stench of rice wine was strong on her breath. *What time is it?* She had been dreaming of home, a sense of warmth all around her. It was a vague, yet strong feeling, like the time when she had curled up next to her mother's warm body back in Pyongyang. There had been that smell of soap, too, the clean smell, the smell of home. Another knock on the door yanked her out of the sense of home and she shivered. "Yes?"

"Miss Hahn, the major is looking for you." The front desk clerk's voice resounded from behind the closed door.

Instantly she grabbed her comforter and pulled it to her neck, as if Major Min were standing before her. "Tell him I'll be there in a few minutes."

"You better hurry, miss. He's in a foul mood!"

She looked at her watch. *Five till nine?* She sprang up, but instantly fell back onto her pillow. She was dizzy. The ceiling before her turned like a merry-go-round at a carnival. *How can I face him like this?*

"Are you coming or not?" the clerk urged, annoying her.

"I'm coming!" she snapped.

When his footsteps moved away, she rose again and forced herself out of her sleeping mat. Now, she wasn't as dizzy as before, but a pang of hunger stabbed her stomach. But she couldn't worry about it now. *Major Min is in a foul mood!*

She hurried. Ten minutes later, she walked into Min's office. "Good morning, Major. I overslept. I'm sorry."

From behind his desk, Min's expression was icy cold, as he flipped some white papers in front of him.

"I went out with a friend last night and we each had a glass of rice wine. That's why I overslept. It won't happen again, sir."

Still, he said nothing, his gaze still on the papers.

"I'll make your coffee, sir."

Finally he lifted his face. "Never mind the coffee. Captain Yoon will be here shortly."

"Captain Yoon? Who is he?"

"A detective. His full name is Yoon Kiwon, but you may call him Detective Yoon."

"Why is he coming here, sir?"

"He wants to talk to you."

"Me?" Her legs felt weak. "Why?"

"If you don't know why, you better come here and look at these photos. They'll refresh your memory, I'm sure."

Her heart palpitated as she stood next to him and saw the photos he was holding. She had an urge to run away and hide like a mole, never to be found again. But it was too late. In the first photo, Jongmi sat behind the steering wheel of the speedboat, just like the previous evening. The sunlight had been so bright that Jongmi's sunglasses had white spots on them. In the second photo, Miyong herself was getting into the boat, her arms outstretched, trying not to lose her balance. The third photo was blurry, probably due to the ocean spray, but she and Jongmi were talking to each other. She couldn't look at the rest of the photos anymore. Three were enough for now.

"Well?" the major said, not turning toward her.

She wrung her hands, searching for words. "I don't know what to say, sir."

"Who's with you in the photo?"

"My friend Jongmi," she said, not certain whether she should tell the whole story. "You didn't meet her, sir. She left the Community before you came."

"I know who you're talking about. Where did you two go?"

"We went for dinner."

"Dinner in the middle of the ocean?"

She felt sick, being caught like this. But confessing everything right now didn't seem to be a good idea. "Not exactly in the middle of the ocean, sir," she said, trying to be calm. "We went to this cozy little place on the other end of the shore, famous for clam stew. It was pretty good, sir."

A crooked smile spread on his face. "I am glad you had a good time. What's the name of that restaurant? I might try it sometime." His casual manner told her that he had dealt with liars before and that he could play any game she wanted for as long as she wanted to.

She felt sweat on her palms. "I...I don't remember the name of the place. By the way, thank you for letting me off yesterday…I felt better when I got home, and we…"

"We're not getting anywhere here, are we?" he said coldly. "Either you tell me the truth, or make up something convincing. Don't waste my time or yours."

A tall officer wearing sunglasses and a well-pressed uniform walked in without a knock on the door, a briefcase in his hand. "Good morning!" he said pleasantly.

Major Min walked to him, and the two men shook hands without a word. Then, Major Min walked out, without even introducing Miyong to the intruder.

Miyong bowed to the detective.

Captain Yoon came over, sat in Min's swivel chair, and thrust his name card toward her. Miyong took it. *Yoon Kiwon, Investigation Specialist.*

"You don't know me, but I read about you," he said. "I will do my best to make this as painless as possible, Miss Hahn; that is, if you cooperate with me. The man you met with last night is a North Korean agent named Ho Suknam. During the past two years, he went to North Korea a dozen times, using a different name each time. He's also the leader of a gang of twelve named *Black Python* that bombed two government facilities last year, a concrete factory on Ulsan Island and a fertilizer warehouse in Chunju City. Where did you meet this man and his mistress last night, and what did you three talk about?"

Mistress? Is Jongmi…

Yoon fidgeted. "Let's understand one another correctly, shall we?" he said in a sarcastic tone of voice. "You're a government employee and so am I. Our time is money for the government. Tell me, just as it happened. After you left the port with Shin Yonghee at noon in her speedboat, where did you go?"

She told him. There was no reason to make up a story. *I'm trapped!* When finished, she added a line. "I had second thoughts about meeting him, but it was too late. I never thought my friend would betray me like that."

"Why did you agree to meet in the first place?"

"I wonder about it myself, sir. I guess I wanted to know whether my parents were still alive."

The detective showed no emotion. "What disturbs me the most, Miss Hahn, is that you trusted a total stranger who lied to you, saying that he had recent news of your parents in the North. Imagine what could happen, if every South Korean did what you've done? There are millions of South Koreans who have blood relatives in the North, as you know."

"Wouldn't you want to know about your parents, if you were in my shoes?" she asked.

"That sort of mentality is dangerous! Let me ask you this, then: would you have gone to the North to see your parents, if Ho offered to take you?"

I would have, she thought, but she couldn't say that to this detective. Feeling helpless, she said, "All I wanted to know was whether or not they were still alive. I am their daughter. I had to know!" Hot tears stung her eyes.

"We're in an ideology war with our other half," the captain lectured. "Communism is a disease that's eating away people's minds and hearts. If we lose this ideology battle with the Communists, we lose our country, and if we lose our country, what could happen? Tell me!"

Miyong stared at the floor. What was there to say?

"There are two kinds of people we are looking for," Yoon said, "Communists and potential Communists. How do you judge yourself?"

Miyong knew what he was getting at. She lifted her face and looked directly at him. "Captain, is my filial love toward my parents a crime?" she asked, noticing her sharp tone of voice. "If my parents lived here in the South, of course I wouldn't have to do what I did. Who divided our country, sir, and why? I'm not sorry for what I did!"

Major Min was restless as he paced in the courtyard. *Why is Yoon taking so long?* he wondered. He looked at his watch for the third time. Captain Yoon could eat a thing like Miyong alive without thinking twice about it. Miyong had disappointed him by lying about meeting with Ho Suknam, but now he was worried about her. He wanted to get her out of the detective's claws. Once she was labeled as a "potential Communist" by Yoon, there was little he could do for her, though he was a major and Kim only a captain. Then, he heard footsteps approaching. He turned to a blue spruce, acting as though he had been inspecting it.

"There you are!" Yoon said in his husky voice.

"What did you find out, Captain?" Min said, turning.

"Everything," Yoon said, touching his uniform necktie. He was at least a head taller than Min himself, and he loved to show it, straightening his back. "The next step is to make sure she isn't playing games with us. I'll go with the Coast Guard this afternoon to find the location where the meeting took place. You'll hear from me soon."

"I'll be waiting!"

Yoon saluted and headed to his military Jeep parked at the curb.

Min had known Yoon for at least fifteen years, first in the artillery unit on Chiri Mountain during the war where Min had been his trainer, and later in CIC, until Min's recent transfer to the Hope Community. As his nickname "Tough Nail" implied, Yoon had been a good detective with mercilessly accurate investigative skills, but he lacked human warmth. "Captain!" Min suddenly called out.

"Yes, sir!" Yoon turned, squinting in the sunlight.

"Let me give you a piece of advice."

"Please, sir."

"The laws are made to serve people, not to break them. Don't enjoy your job too much."

"Pardon me, sir?"

"You heard me, Captain. Don't let your ambition turn into a bloody hatchet." Without waiting for Yoon's reply, he turned his back to him.

"Bloody hatchet!" Min repeated under his breath. Dark anger

seared in the depth of his soul. He could have died long ago under the "bloody hatchet," like his older brother had. Min had been in his second year of high school, innocent and green, when he had been tortured for the first and last time in his thirty-eight years. He still dreamt about the bamboo needle piercing into the flesh under his fingertips at night, waking him up sweating. The pain was like nothing he had experienced. The worst of all was the stream of water forcing its way into his nose and then into his stomach. The helpless feeling that had come over him before he passed out was something he could never forget. It was a chaotic time, after Korea's liberation from Japan in 1945, three years before the Republic of Korea (ROK) was born under Syngman Rhee's leadership. His older brother, a schoolteacher, had attended a teachers' conference in a theater in Taegu, not knowing that the organizer had come from the North to establish an underground Communist network in the South. Min had heard from eyewitnesses that the lights went out in the middle of the meeting and dark figures rushed in and smashed everything they could land their clubs on.

That night, when the policemen found Min at his home, at his desk, doing homework, he learned that his brother had been slain at the conference, along with two other teachers. During the months that followed, Min faced his torturers daily, a few times everyday. This was when he learned that the truth had no power before any police badge; and that his scream resembled that of a pig in a slaughterhouse. He vowed to himself that if he ever walked out of the police station, he would become a soldier, so that he could find all those who had beaten the life out of his brother and others at the conference, and blast their brains out. He had done his job while he had been the Chief Investigator at CIC; half a dozen men were now serving life in prison.

When he returned to his office, he found Miyong sitting in her usual wooden chair, crying. Coughing gently, he walked to his desk and sat.

Seeing him, she quickly brushed her tears away. "I...I should have told you the truth," she said in a congested voice. "I made a stupid mistake, sir. Had I known better, I would not have met with Jongmi's boss."

Producing a cigarette from the box, he lit it and puffed. The smoke soaked into his lungs, and he was comforted by its prickly sensation. The last thing he wanted to do was scold his secretary when she was broken like a small yelping animal. "What stupid mistake are you talking about?" he asked gently.

"You know what I'm talking about, sir. I didn't know Jongmi's boss was a Communist. How would I have known? No one told me."

He didn't say anything.

"And this morning, sir, I kept lying to you because I didn't want to get in trouble." Her hand touched her eyes again.

It was indeed a stupid mistake on her part. But Min knew better than to lecture her when she was confessing like a sinner. "I know you didn't mean to lie to me but you had to. What's going on here in our country today isn't ordinary. Don't you agree?"

She looked at him but said nothing. Her eyes were red and watery; she looked tired.

"Think about it for a moment. Our land was divided two decades ago by other nations, and five years later we were at war with our other half, brothers killing brothers. The war lasted three long years, during which time much of our verdant land was gone, three million were dead, and ten times more were injured and homeless. Worst of all, the 38th Parallel is still in the middle of the country, and the hostility between the two Koreas is uglier than ever. At such a time, how can we expect a peaceful, ordinary life?"

She didn't seem to know where his lecture was leading. She kept blinking, as if trying to understand what her boss was getting at.

"There's nothing wrong with what you've done, Miyong," he said, switching to her first name. "No one can blame you for wanting to hear about your parents. In fact, only ill-bred sons and daughters would look away when someone brings news of their parents with whom they have had no contact for years. Even animals would do better than that."

"That's exactly what got me in trouble, sir," she said defiantly, her voice cracking. "Look at me and tell me what I've done wrong. I'll soon be punished for my attempt to hear about my parents. It's confusing, sir. I was only four and my brother seven when we last saw them. Do you know what it's like, growing up in an orphanage when your parents are alive somewhere? Captain Yoon asked me if I regret coming to the South, and I said 'no' out of fear. But to tell you the truth, yes, I do regret it. I should have lived with my parents in the North, or anywhere in the world. Don't you agree that the best place for a child is with her parents, sir?"

"I hear you," Min said. "You and I are individuals with feelings and thoughts, yet we each are components of this huge machine called a nation. Sometimes, a nation cannot honor each individual's feelings and needs. If we can't unite within the nation and defend ourselves against our enemy, we'll lose our country. That's where we stand, Miyong. Inside, we're humans with feelings and thoughts, but on the exterior, we must be tough against our enemy."

She lifted her head and looked at him. "How long can we live like this, tough on the exterior, like a tank shell?" She bent and sobbed.

If Yoon had been here, Min thought, he would have a field day with what she had just said. He didn't blame her for the way she felt, and yet she could get in serious trouble by talking like this.

"Miyong?"

"Yes, sir."

"Why don't you take the afternoon off?"

"Pardon me, sir?"

"Go on. You need it!"

Chapter Six

DAYS PASSED SLOWLY AS Miyong awaited word from Captain Yoon. It was as though she were a convict waiting for her sentence to begin. People at the Community were watching her. When she sat at her usual table in the corner at the cafeteria, a security guard would walk in and stare in her direction until she'd lose her appetite. When she was in the bathroom, a woman would come in and use the next stall. Sometimes she had a feeling that someone was following her in the hallway or courtyard, so she would turn around quickly, but there was no one. She thought she was turning into a paranoid lunatic.

Not being able to speak to her brother was torture: she couldn't use the phone at her desk, afraid that Major Min would hear every word. She couldn't use the phone at the cafeteria, for it was always busy. Her brother would be dying to know about the meeting between Ho and her. He would have no clue what she had gone through and what she was dealing with now. On second thought, why should he know? He'd be worried to death if he heard all that had been going on with her. Who said that ignorance was bliss?

Major Min's attitude toward her had changed somewhat since

the day Captain Yoon had interrogated her. He was still kind, yet she had noticed his icy glance glued to her while she dictated his letters. He had taken back the keys to the file cabinet and vault, blaming the Community's new security policy, but she knew better. He talked to her less and less, although he still drank the coffee she made for him, just the way he wanted.

One Friday morning in early August, Major Min dropped in.

"Captain Yoon wants to see you in his office at three this afternoon. It's on the third floor at CIC Headquarters, Room 305."

"Why, sir?"

He avoided eye contact. "You should know why he wants to see you. It's about what he and you talked about last week, remember?"

She dropped her gaze to the desk. Of course, she had known he'd contact her sooner or later.

"To get there in time, make sure you leave by eleven, considering the busy season at the port."

At ten before three that afternoon, she got off the bus on Jongno Third Avenue and headed to CIC Headquarters, half a block down the road. The summer heat was so intense that her cotton blouse began to stick to her back as if it had been glued on. Passing vehicles of all kinds honked loudly, as they always did, and pedestrians on the sidewalk bumped into her. But once she entered the lobby with glass doors, cool air enveloped her.

The young sentry wearing a holstered sidearm gave her no trouble when she handed him her photo I.D. He even smiled when he handed it back to her. It was her heart that couldn't be calm. *They'll question me again! What was that ruthless investigator's name?* She couldn't remember.

The door of Room 305 was marked with a nameplate that read "Yoon Kiwon, Chief Investigator," and she was relieved that she had come to the right place. . She had been anticipating this moment, even imagined walking in, trying to smile, but now, standing here, before Yoon's nameplate, she wanted to vanish as quickly as she could.

She knocked on the door.

"Come in!" a tenor voice resounded, and she entered. The smell of cigarette smoke mixed with some other scent, leather or ink, invaded her, although all three windows facing the street were open. Sheer curtains were dancing in a joyous rhythm in the summer breeze, not knowing her hidden thoughts and fear.

Four men sat behind a rectangular table, each with some papers in front of him. Captain Yoon was on the far left, two men with dull expressions in the middle, and a young man with a crew cut at the far right.

She bowed deeply.

"Good to see you again, Miss Hahn," said Captain Yoon cheerfully, as though he were talking to a distinguished guest.

"Good to see you, too, sir," she lied.

"Please meet my colleagues in my division." He introduced Lieutenant this, Lieutenant that, Sergeant something. "Please make yourself at home."

How could I, sir, standing here?

"I'm pleased to inform you that your description of the place where you met Ho Suknam was quite accurate. Thank you. However, the structure has already been destroyed and everything was gone, including the occupant."

"Sir," the young man with a crew-cut interrupted Yoon. "We did find some valuable artifacts, sir, which we're grateful for: half-burned books, maps, human bones, gold bars. Miss Hahn's information opened doors to some unsolved mysteries, particularly the disappearances of our early CIC members."

Yoon's expression turned cold. "Lieutenant, I'll get to that. First, let me finish what I have in mind."

"Yes, sir."

Turning to her again, Yoon said, "It's not uncommon for the Reds to destroy evidence that would lead to their tails, but we'll continue our search until we locate them. Before we reach our final decision, we have a few more questions today, if you don't mind."

"I don't mind."

"Did you reveal any information on the New Country Building project or the new security issues to Ho Suknam or your friend Shin Yonghee the evening you met them?"

"None, sir."

"Did you give him any papers containing classified information?"

"No. Where would I get such papers?"

"You have keys to Major Min's file cabinets, vault, and desk drawers, don't you? You're the only person in the building who can go in and out of his office at any time of the day or night. Am I correct?"

Now she understood why Major Min had taken all his keys from her. It might not have been his decision.

"I returned all the keys to Major Min."

"When was this?"

"After you came to talk to me."

"I'm talking about earlier. I don't suspect that you'd give papers to outsiders while you were on surveillance. That seldom happens. Let me rephrase my question: Have you taken any document from Major Min's office without his permission?"

"Are you accusing me of stealing, sir?"

"Please answer the question," the officer sitting next to Yoon interjected.

"I've never stolen anything in my life."

"That's not the answer to my question. Please say yes or no. Have you taken any papers from Major Min's office?"

"No! I grew up in a Catholic orphanage, sir. I know what's right and what's wrong."

"You know that the Republic of Korea ended all contact with the DPK [Democratic People's Korea] at the end of the war, in 1945, don't you?"

"Yes, sir."

"Are you aware that North Korea has enforced their anti-South Korean policy since the beginning of the year?"

"I'm not aware, sir."

"They've increased their Special Purpose Forces [SPF] to 120,000 members this year from 80,000, for three purposes: one, to destroy our command posts, including naval posts and airfields; two, to cut off the supply of food and other essentials reaching the DMZ zone; three, to abduct and assassinate government officials and senior military officers. As you know, our military power is divided at the moment between Vietnam and the mainland. At such a time, you had a secret meeting with an active Communist sent by Kim Il-sung himself!"

She only stared at her hands.

He seemed to be waiting for her response, but when she said nothing, he said, "People do make mistakes. We're human. We're not here to condemn you for your innocent mistake, but rather to decide what we should do about it."

"Please get to the point, sir. What are you going to do about my mistake?"

"Considering your age and the anti-Communist spirit you've shown in June," Captain Yoon said, "we have a recommendation for you. You can either go to prison for violating the national security law or help us capture Ho Suknam and his accomplice."

"How could I help you capture him or others?" she said incredulously. "I am a girl who's only eighteen."

"We'll educate you. It's all mapped out for you. Ho's not taking you to the North out of kindness, you know. Think about it: Why would a Communist spy want to help you see your parents, unless he'd gain something from it? What is his motive? Have you ever thought about it?"

Miyong was tired. She wished she could sit down.

"It's obvious that Kim Il-sung ordered Ho to bring you to the North for propaganda purposes. Once you're in the North, you will have no control over yourself. But there is an alternative that will save your neck as well as help your country capture the Commies. So many young South Korean agents are now working for us in the North. They'll help you once you're there."

Yoon picked up a blue booklet in front of him and shook it. "This booklet will explain everything you need to know. Read every word in it. And included is the application form for the espionage school *The Pigeon's Nest*. Fill out the form and mail it to us as soon as possible."

Application form?

"That's all for now," Yoon said. "Thank you for coming."

Outside, the heat was so intense that she felt as though she had just walked into an oven. The sidewalk seemed to be melting; it felt softer under her shoes than it had earlier. She looked for a telephone booth. It was a perfect chance to talk to her brother, away from the Community, though she might not be able to talk to him. The last time, two months ago, she had met him in a tea room, seeking his advice on what to do after Jongmi had dropped a bomb on her, saying that her boss had recent news of her parents. It seemed an eternity had passed since that evening. He would be glad to know that she was all right.

Finding an arrow sign with "Telephone" written on it, thirty feet away, she headed in that direction. The street was even more crowded than it had been earlier, as if a parade had just ended here. As she was about to enter the phone booth, she heard a man's voice calling, "Miss Hahn!" Turning, she found the young man with the crew cut, whom she had seen in the interrogation room, walking toward her. He was now wearing lightly tinted sunglasses that reflected a tall building and the sky above. The last person she wanted to see now was a man from CIC. *What does he want?*

"Let me introduce myself," he said, taking his glasses off. "I'm Lieutenant Lee Dongwoo. I used to work with Major Min Haksoo before he took the director's position at your Community."

She nodded to him.

"Major Min asked me to make sure you understand everything that went on today. Do you have any questions I might be able to answer?"

What's the use? she thought. The only thing she wanted to do was to call her brother and tell him what was happening. "I have the booklet, sir," she said, her eyes lowered.

He dug into his shirt pocket and took out his name card. "Call me, if you have any questions about the espionage school or anything. I'll do what I can to help. Good day!" Touching his hat quickly, he turned around and moved away in the direction he had come.

Miyong walked into the stall and dialed her brother's number, but he wasn't there. Walking toward the bus station, she opened the booklet.

The first paragraph read, "The Pigeon's Nest, a three-story building with a traditional Korean-style roof, sitting on the outskirts of Seoul, was built as a Japanese officers' bathhouse, 'Water Lilies,' in 1920, in the early phase of the Japanese occupation of Korea. After the liberation in August 1945, it turned into an American military officers' cocktail lounge, 'Venus and Mars.' American entertainers such as Marylin Monroe, Benny Goodman, Louis Armstrong, and Frank Sinatra performed there. It has had its current name, The Pigeon's Nest, since 1951, when an American Navy major, Albert Boyle, gathered starving Korean boys and trained them to fight for their country. Our grateful president, President Rhee Syngman, awarded him the building to use strictly for espionage purposes."

Chapter Seven

"YOU CAN'T SEND THIS to your brother," said the major, sitting at his desk and lifting the letter Miyong had written to her brother the night before. It was a big day for her, the moving day to The Pigeon's Nest. The taxi could show up at any moment, and she had been summoned here, to the director's office on the second floor. What bothered her most was the fact that her letter had been opened and obviously read!

"When did you tell me I couldn't write to my brother, sir?" She noticed a sharp edge to her voice.

"It's common sense, isn't it?" said the major with militaristic contempt. "We're not sending you on a picnic, you know. Such classified information as where you're going and what you'll be doing should be kept from outsiders." He dropped the envelope into the trash basket next to him, two feet from her.

"The training takes six months, Major. Are you saying my brother shouldn't know anything about where I am or what I am doing for the next six months?"

"I don't make rules for CIC."

"My brother is the only family I have here, sir. Do you know what that means?"

Major Min sat back in his chair, looking frustrated, even angry. "You should know better than to tell him every little detail of what was discussed between you and CIC officials. If this was disclosed, I'll be blamed. I'll write to your brother and let him know you're away for training."

Miyong stared at him and then at the envelope in the basket. She wasn't sure whether she could write her brother another letter while she was in the espionage school. She wasn't sure whether she could see him again. Who could predict the future?

Min suddenly rose, as if eager to lose her. "Good luck with your training," he said, articulating each word. "I have to meet the road construction crew downstairs in five minutes!" Walking to the door, he took his hat from its peg, put it on, and checked his appearance in the mirror, turning this way and that.

Quickly, Miyong reached for the trash can, retrieved the envelope, and put it in her skirt pocket, without making any noise.

"Coming?" the major said. He was looking at her, holding the door knob.

She managed to look sad and walked to the door, and when he opened it, she slipped out.

"I'll get in touch," he said, as he locked the door behind her.

Hahn Jinwoo is my brother, sir, not yours, she wanted to shout. *My brother will die if he doesn't know where I am, so forgive me for disobeying you. Luckily, you'll never find out what I've just done.*

Walking into her room, Room 215 on the second floor, which was now empty of her roommates, occupied only by crumpled comforters and women's sleepwear, she moved quickly. She went to the desk by the window, which she shared with her roommates, took out the glue stick from the center drawer, and resealed the letter, neatly and carefully. It bothered her that she had not told her roommates where she was going and why, thanks to Major Min! She had told them she was going back to Seoul to find another job. But here again, the girls were her roommates, and Major Min had nothing to say about what she *could* or *could not* tell them. She had lived with them in the same room for one third of a year, sharing life stories, face powder, or lipsticks, and other things only women shared with one another.

She heard the honk of a car and suddenly remembered the taxi she had ordered earlier. Walking to the window, she saw the blue box-style vehicle parked at the curb, and the driver standing next to it, looking around as if waiting for her to show up. She put her letter into her purse, checked around to make sure she had not left anything that shouldn't be left behind and hurried to the door.

Up close, the driver was an older man in his fifties with a balding head. He took her suitcase from her without a word, put it in the trunk, and locked it. He then walked to the passenger's side of the car, opened the door for her, and then went to the driver's side. The taxi was in motion. As it moved out of the courtyard, the events of the last few months passed through her mind. *How many times have I passed this entrance with the granite bearing those Chinese letters? Where will I be six months from now?*

Around eleven that morning, Miyong stood by the window of her second-floor bedroom at the Pigeon's Nest, a building surrounded by a wrought-iron fence amidst young trees, bushes, and greenhouses. She was watching the busy Tong-il [Unification] Highway in the distance where cars, trucks, and huge construction vehicles whizzed by, confirming how far she had come from Hope Community on Kanghwa Island and where she stood now. She couldn't help but smile as she remembered dropping the letter in a mail deposit box on a busy street in the eastern part of Seoul. She had thought about asking the driver to please stop the car in front of a post office, but she couldn't, because of the rush hour traffic. Unexpectedly, the driver pulled over to the side of the road and parked in front of a tobacco shop, saying that he had to buy cigarettes, and a few feet away stood the black metal box with "Mail Deposit Box" printed in gold. She couldn't have been luckier than that.

Upon arrival, she had picked up an armful of manuals and folders from the office downstairs, which had been waiting for her in a tote bag with her name on it. But she wasn't eager to read any of them now. It pleased her to just stand here and look out the window, without any particular thought in her head other than the fact that she was in a new place. Once the class began the next day, she would be too busy to enjoy anything at leisure.

Many homes in this area looked primitive with mud-plastered walls and straw thatched roofs. Some had chicken coops, some had barns, and a few had hog houses next to the houses. The land was scattered with mostly boulders, creeks, small rice paddies, and patches of crop land. Like everywhere in the country, the mountains here were bald, too, because, during the Japanese occupation of Korea, the tyrants chopped down all mature trees, shipped them to Japan, Manchuria, China, and the Pacific islands and produced battleships, military huts and brothels, and airplanes with them. Still, Japanese lost the war to the Allied Forces.

Beneath her bedroom lay a spacious courtyard with gingko trees and a long flower bed along the wrought-iron fence. Under a gingko, she noticed a pond in the shape of the map of Korea, without a line in the middle. Red, yellow, and white fish were swimming in it, freely up and down, without worrying about barriers or checkpoints. *Who made that pond in that shape?*

Late that afternoon, Min was in his swivel chair next to the window, smoking again. *A hypocrite*, he muttered to himself. He had scolded Miyong for writing to her brother that morning, which he himself would have done had he been in her shoes. Without the drone of the typewriter from behind that folding door, he felt empty and aged. Since he had learned of her departure for espionage training, which could last at least six months, he had thought about taking her to a nice restaurant for a dinner, to thank her for hard work and maybe encourage her to come back. But it wasn't a practical idea, the two of them dining in a restaurant. What would the members say about their director sitting in a restaurant with his young secretary? What would the villagers say? Gossip traveled fast when people lived a simple life. This morning, he unexpectedly found her letter to her brother sitting on his desk and read it. She had told everything: the trouble she had gone through during the past week and what she was facing now, concluding, "At the end of this long tunnel I'll see our parents. *Oppa, I wish you could come with me. I'm so scared.*"

He had done what he had to do as the director of the Community, but sitting here alone, he felt empty and aged. He could not deny that it was *he* who was to blame for all the trouble she had gone through for the last couple of weeks and was going through now. He had exposed her to the public after the incident with the North Korean commandoes in June. Now she was in the hands of CIC, and soon would be in the North, perhaps with Ho and her friend. Once there, Ho Suknam would use her, like a trophy, to show off to his Party members that he had brought with him the girl responsible for their thirty-one slain comrades.

"My brother is the only family I have..." Miyong had said that morning.

Remembering what he had said to her, he picked up a pen and began to write on a notepad:

Dear Mr. Hahn,

As the director of Hope Community, I hereby inform you that your sister Hahn Miyong has been sent for training and cannot be reached at this location for a few weeks. Your correspondence with her can be achieved only through this office. If you have any questions regarding this matter, please don't hesitate to contact me.

Sincerely,

Maj. Min Haksoon,

Commander of Hope Community, Kanghwa Island

Chapter Eight

AT NINE THE FOLLOWING morning, Miyong sat at a long table with five others she had met the previous day. Everyone sat quietly at his or her chosen seat, waiting for the instructor to arrive. A motto was scribbled on the blackboard, and Miyong read it: "Leave your personal life outside these walls." She looked around. Everyone seemed to be thinking what she was thinking: that this place was like a prison and that they would have to live like inmates, not being able to see anyone or talk or write to anyone outside this place.

Lieutenant Larry Tompkins, a tall lanky American Army officer wearing gold—framed glasses she had seen at the orientation briefly the day before, walked in and looked around the room with authority. "Good morning, everyone!" he said. "Did you sleep well?"

"Yes!"

"That's very important for aspiring spies." He smiled. He seemed eager to break the uneasiness everyone felt as a first-timer here, yet he exuded the same confidence Major Min often had shown, except this man was a tall westerner with curly brown hair.

He lectured, "Your work is important for your country, regardless of the reasons that brought you here. I will do my very best to help you learn the art of espionage and everything you need to know before you're assigned to the enemy territory. Since your group spirit is vital to your success as secret agents, let's go around the table and talk about why you're here. You go first, Sangpil." He pointed to the bushy-haired young man sitting in front of him, to his left.

Sangpil blushed. "Uh…I'm here because I want to help make our country a better place to live, free of Communists."

"Very good," Tompkins said. "I understand that your father was one of the KLO [Korean Labor Organization] members some years ago, wasn't he?"

"Yes…he died during a mission when I was only three. The plane was shot down, killing all six men… By following in my dad's footsteps, I can continue the work he couldn't finish…"

The room became deadly quiet, as Sangpil bent his head and said nothing.

The man with a crew-cut sitting next to Sangpil, who had called himself an "ex-cop" earlier, volunteered. "I served in the Army as well as on the police force, so I'm aware of the danger we're facing against our 'other half.' What can be better than to live and die for your country?"

"Me, sir?" said a middle-aged woman who had introduced herself as the mother of five the day before, who was now sitting next to the ex-cop. "I'm here because I want to make money. I don't mind doing some dangerous work, if I can feed and clothe my five children better." She then complained about the moldy long grain rice and the clothes too large for her and her children, which she received from the church she attended.

When it was her turn, Miyong told them that she was one of the eighty women involved in a government rural development program on Kanghwa Island, and that not long ago she had had a brief encounter with the Communists on a mountain. "I thought it was a time for me to do something positive for my country," she concluded.

"You're a perfect candidate for this," one said.

Returning from lunch at the cafeteria downstairs, they watched two documentary movies about World War II, one after another—the first one had been taken during the Pacific War and the other during Hitler's ruling of Europe. Then they visited the library, after passing a long corridor facing the courtyard with a fish pond surrounded by tall shady trees. The bronze bust of the slain American president, John F. Kennedy, welcomed them from the pedestal. Tompkins explained that Kennedy was the first U.S. president who had attempted global peace by suggesting complete disarmament. "His idea was that," Tompkins said, "by surrendering arms, each nation could suppress its attempt to threaten others, and eventually the world would unite as a whole."

After a quick tour of the library, they met the director, Albert Boyle, in his office on the third floor. He was a heavy-set American in his fifties, with sandy hair, and had a strong American accent when he introduced himself in Korean: "I am the mystery of the attic," he said, trying to be funny. "You won't see me every day, but I'm always here. If you have questions or complaints about your instructors, I'm the one you should come and see." He turned to Tompkins, and they exchanged a warm, trusting smile.

Every day, the students learned the aspects of espionage from textbooks, films, and lectures. Miyong studied documents and reports from actual spies and learned coding and decoding, along with how to operate a machine called Lodestar. It was a machine similar to a typewriter, except that tiny lights blinked in the middle of it when it was in operation. The magic of this machine was that messages sent to a certain place could not be read by another, unless the receiving party had the coordinating keys. It was mind-boggling for Miyong to master the use of the device at first, but after one-on-one instruction and practice, she became familiar with it.

The weekly visit to CIC's "Special Room," in the basement of a nearby warehouse, was most engaging for everyone. It was where North Korean infiltrators were interrogated daily, Tompkins had told them.

On the first day there, Miyong smelled caustic soda mixed with blood in the air, as though someone had just bled or even died. Under the dim fluorescent ceiling light, the thick ropes hung from the wood ceiling at the corner, each held by a rusted metal hook, and against the wall sat two wooden chairs studded with nails, whose sharp ends protruded ferociously. At the other end of the room sat a long wooden table with two matching chairs.

Mr. Tompkins led the class past the table, into a spacious closet-like space with a large tinted window to look into the room. "Please be quiet when the session begins," Tompkins said. "No one on the other side can see you, but they can hear you. We'll be witnessing a few actual interrogations shortly, and I advise you to listen carefully. Someday it might be you who will stand before the interrogators you'll soon see."

Two men—one in a black suit, and another in a plaid shirt and dark trousers—walked in and sat at the desk.

A hefty guard escorted a thin, scrawny man in blue prison inmate's overalls into the room. His feet were in shackles. The guard positioned the prisoner before the interrogators, and with a quick nod to the men, he left.

"State your name," one of the interrogators, the man in black, said when the prisoner faced him.

"Hong Gyusuk, sir," the inmate said in a flat voice.

"What was your position in the military at the time of your arrest?"

"A drill sergeant in the Eleventh Battalion in the Blue Dragon Division, sir."

The interrogator read the charges against him: "Defendant Hong Gyusuk is accused of crossing the border on April 16th of this year, to see his brother Hong Pilsun, who was sought by the South Korean police in connection with the disappearance of two South Korean military officials last year. The two brothers are believed to have plotted the kidnapping and possible murder of the military officials on duty in Taebaek province." Lowering the paper, he said, "If you confess your crime, we'll consider a lighter punishment."

"You've got the wrong man!" the prisoner said defiantly. "I have no brother and I was never in the North! My family is from Kyongsang Province near the South Coast, and still is. What're you talking about?"

"You're seen in these photos," the interrogator said, thrusting two photos in front of him.

The prisoner gave the photo a quick glance and said, "I don't see myself in the photo. You've got the wrong man!"

"Then why were you in the heavily wooded area three miles north of the 38th Parallel in Kangwon Province on April 16th?"

"I'm a drill sergeant, as I said. It's my duty to investigate the area for regimental training. Passing the border and going beyond the restricted area wasn't my fault. I saw no markings anywhere, to show where our territory ends and where North Korea begins. Check for yourself! That area is an endless field of tangling vines, shrubs, and tall weeds."

"You're a military man responsible for training our troops. If you don't know your regimental boundary, how can you expect the inexperienced boys to know?"

"They don't!"

"The report says you ignored the MPs' warning shots and kept running, further into the North."

"It was difficult to know where the shots were coming from, so I just ran for cover."

"Couldn't you tell the difference between the Russian rifles and the American?"

"Of course I can. The Russian rifles make stiff noises like the German rifles — *tan,tan,tan,tan,tan* — but the American ones make smoother sounds – *dararararara…* But that day, I only heard the Russian rifles firing, not American, so I ran. It was a foggy morning. The visibility was poor."

"You'd been missing three days from your post prior to that incident. Prove that you were inspecting the area only for regimental training purposes, instead of trying to defect to the North."

"Ask my boys. They'll tell you. They've been camping only four miles south of where the MPs found me. They know."

The interrogators conversed with one another, their heads almost touching. The man in black straightened himself and cleared his throat. "Very well, Sergeant Hong. We'll investigate further and let you know."

The prisoner bowed to the interrogators deeply before he was led out of the room.

A small and short woman in an oversized inmate's outfit entered the room, following the guard. After her name was confirmed and the charges were read, she began weeping. "I'm very sorry, sirs!" she squeaked through her tight throat. "I...I made the terrible mistake of keeping my uncle in my house. We didn't know he had been in the North all these years. When he showed up at our door one evening, he told us that he had been living in Japan since the war ended, and that he was passing through on his way to Seoul to see his wife's family. We believed him…" She kept talking.

The interrogator in black pounded the table. "You can talk only when I ask you, understand?"

"Yes, sir…I'm trying to explain why…"

"Wait until I ask you to speak!" he shouted.

"Yes, sir."

"Are you telling us that you didn't know your uncle moved to the North during the war and had served in the North Korean government ever since?"

"No, sir. I've already told you. Many of our relatives, including my parents, died during the war, and I thought my uncle did, too, because we never saw him again. How was I supposed to know he was lying to me when he showed up and said that he had been in Japan? I'm not educated; I quit going to school after my parents passed. Besides, our country is big, with thirty million people. I'm just a country woman. Please let me go home! My kids need me." She began weeping.

The two men exchanged a quick conversation. The man in the plaid shirt raised his arms into the air to motion the guard to take the woman. As she followed the guard, the woman kept turning, saying, "I'm telling the truth, sir. I'm serious!"

The next prisoner had purplish circles around his eyes; his lips were crusted with dried blood, and his mouth was stuffed with something that had been white. His eyes shifting in all directions, he seemed as frightened as a caged animal. He coughed a nervous cough. He then shifted his dark eyes to the window, through which Miyong and her classmates were watching him. His gaze lingered there as if he suspected eyes behind the glass panel. The guard spun him around, forced his mouth open, like a veterinarian handling a dangerous dog, and pulled out the saliva-soaked handkerchief. Now, realizing where he was and why, he coughed again, straightening, making him taller than when he had walked in.

"State your name," the interrogator in black ordered.

The young man did not respond.

"State your name!" the interrogator repeated.

The prisoner said nothing, his mouth tightly sealed, his gaze lifted to a corner of the ceiling.

The interrogator hit the table. "Did you hear me?"

The prisoner smiled, showing his missing front tooth.

Miyong wondered whether he had lost his tooth during torture. She had heard too many stories of men and women who had lost eyesight or the ability to walk after severe torture.

The interrogator's eyes flashed maliciously. "All right, then. If you forgot your name, I'll remind you. You're Shin Sangwoo, born in Chongjin City in Hamkyong Province on February 19th, 1940, and you lived there until age fifteen. Some time in 1955, you joined The Youth Red Army, infiltrated to the South and lived in a safe house in Taegu until the beginning of this year. You're here with the charges of murdering two police officers during a student demonstration, disguised as a student. Is it true?"

"Yes," the prisoner answered in a rusty voice. "I'm indeed Shin Sangwoo, born in the Year of Metal Dragon. I was sent here with our

Great Leader's direct order to liberate my South Korean comrades under the atrocious policemen…"

"Answer yes or no!" the interrogator said in a composed manner. But his hand holding a pen trembled noticeably.

"*Dongmu,*" the young man said, louder this time. "What I've done is to save my brothers from their brutal assailants. The South Korean policemen are known for their iron hands. Our *Suryingnim* [Great Leader] is losing sleep worrying about his young men dying and being bitten by Park's hound dogs. I did what I had to." He then began singing, at the top of his lungs, calling out "Liberty!" and "Our Leader, Our Father" as if he thought he was in the middle of a performance.

The interrogators stood up. The guard came, collected the prisoner — who was still singing — and dragged him out of the room.

Lieutenant Tompkins dismissed the class, and went out to shake hands with the interrogators. While the three men engaged in a friendly conversation in Korean, Miyong left with others, feeling drained and sad. It was an intense session, in which right and wrong were judged by something called "ideology." From what she had seen, the young man wasn't at all guilty of what he had done. He acted as a hero who had tried to save the South Koreans from the brutal policemen. But the young woman accused of sheltering her uncle, not knowing he had been a Communist, was guilty of her own ignorance and was dragged out. How confusing *life* was!

Two weeks later, each student was assigned to a personal trainer. Miyong's was Moon Hyunja, described as "a seasoned agent with eleven missions under her belt." The note Tompkins handed to her had Moon's phone number and address. She lived in the Hannam (South of Han River) area, the only area in Seoul that had newly built tall apartments whose windows deflected violent sunlight during the day, altering the view of the old city's skyline.

Miyong took the bus that Saturday to meet her trainer for the first time. Stepping into the spacious lobby, as spacious as the gym at her high school, she was bewildered. The gold-framed mirrors on the wall reflected a row of gilded chandeliers, making the space seem larger. A tall white porcelain vase with colorful freshly cut flowers stood on every corner table she could see. The rust-colored carpet with abstract designs was soft and cushiony under her feet, as though no one had stepped on it before. A pair of American Army officers passed her, nodding quickly.

A slender Korean woman wearing a pearl necklace over a tight leaf-green silk dress, and matching high-heeled shoes, walked toward her, smiling. *This can't be Miss Moon!* She looked beautiful. She must be wealthy, too, to be able to afford an apartment in a place like this.

The woman came right up to her, with a waft of lilac about her. "You must be who I'm waiting for. Aren't you Hahn Miyong?"

"Yes, I am. Glad to meet you, Miss Moon."

"Miss Moon?" she said, furrowing her brows. "It sounds too formal. Call me Hyunja."

"But…" Miyong hesitated, noticing that she was at least three or four years older than herself. "I must call you *Onni*, at least."

"Please don't," Hyunja said firmly. "Calling me *Onni* makes me feel like an old maid. We Koreans always recognize one's age, but let's don't. You and I are friends. Miyong and Hyunja, how's that?"

"Fine! Hello, Hyunja," she said, thrusting her hand out to Hyunja.

They shook hands.

"Come! I'll show you my place," Hyunja said.

They took the elevator. Hyunja's spacious apartment on the ninth floor displayed elegance and wealth, with traditional Korean furniture inlaid with mother-of-pearl, scrolls with ink paintings, and a black lacquered folding screen showing a pair of long-necked cranes glaring at one another. But the picture window in the front room was priceless, with a view of the Han River and a panorama of new and old buildings along the embankment boasting their vantage points.

"Make yourself comfortable," Hyunja said, as she sat on a long plush white sofa that divided the large space into two: a living room and a dining room. When Miyong sat next to her, she asked, "A drink? I have soda pop and red wine."

"I'll drink water," Miyong said.

Hyunja disappeared through the door frame they had walked through earlier, and soon a clatter of glasses and the faucet spewing water followed. A moment later, Hyunja came back, a glass of water in one hand and a glass of wine in the other.

While drinking, Miyong thought Hyunja seemed to have everything a woman could want: beauty, elegance, wealth, and a taste for nice things. But there was something peculiar about her. She seemed nervous; her eyes blinked fast as she sipped her wine.

"If you can live like this," Miyong said, "working for CIC must not be so bad."

"CIC…?" She laughed. "I have a boyfriend in Japan, who pays my rent and buys me things, but my salary takes care of the utility bills and other essential things women can't be without—cosmetics, clothes, and small things. I'm not complaining, though."

Miyong wasn't comfortable knowing that Hyunja had a Japanese boyfriend, rich or not. Most Koreans would be hostile to the idea of a Korean female having an intimate relationship with a Japanese male, due to Korea's 36-year-long slavery to the Japanese Empire that ended at the end of World War II. *Why is she dating a Japanese, when there are so many Korean men, as many as the fish in the ocean?*

"See this pearl necklace?" Hyunja said, grabbing it and pulling it toward Miyong. "Ryutaro brought it to me on my twenty-fourth birthday in June. It's from the Nohoku, a region known for oyster farming in northern Japan."

"Very nice."

"How about you? Do you have a boyfriend?"

"No."

"I don't believe you."

"It's true."

Hyunja was a nosy type, Miyong decided. In the following two minutes, she asked a stream of questions: Do you go to school? What school? Where do you live? Do you have brothers and sisters? Miyong had no choice but to answer all her questions, revealing why she ended up coming to The Pigeon's Nest.

"You're from the North, too!" Hyunja exclaimed. "I didn't know that!" She volunteered her story: she had been a "noticeable child" both in school and in her neighborhood in Pyongsong, a town Miyong wasn't familiar with.

"Every adult in my neighborhood turned toward me when I passed them, saying, *Isn't she so adorable?* or *She's the kind of child I want to take home with me.* At school, I was the leader of my class and wore a mini button with Great Leader's face on it. Once, a very important group from the Central Workmen's Party in Pyongyang came to town, including Great Leader himself. For this occasion, we practiced the song 'Our Father, Our Leader' every day for a month. The song goes like this." Hyunja began singing:

Shining like a lighthouse on a vast sea
You led your flock to the path of hope
Without your courage we're lost forever
Ten thousand years for you, Our Father!

You shed blood to grant us freedom!
You drove the enemy out of this land!
All heads and knees are bent before you.
Ten thousand years for you, Our Leader!

"That day *I* presented Great Leader the flowers and ended up sitting next to him for the photo session afterward. Can you believe it?"

"Wow! Do you still have that photo?" Miyong asked.

Hyunja didn't answer, her bright expression dimming.

"What happened to it?"

"I'd rather not talk about it, Miyong," she said. "I'll change and we'll go to the gym downstairs." She disappeared.

Miyong couldn't figure out why Hyunja's mood suddenly changed.

Now she was more curious about the photo. *She'll have to tell me, someday,* Miyong thought.

Hyunja returned, wearing a tight silky black jogging suit and matching shoes, the kind available only in the stores in Itaewon that sold strictly American merchandise. She avoided Miyong's eyes as they walked out of the apartment together.

All that afternoon, in her private "workroom" in the basement of the apartment complex, Hyunja was a difference person: she was a merciless instructor whose only goal was to teach her student the basic aspects of self defense, including shooting and martial arts.

Miyong was eager to learn, too. For the first time in her eighteen years, Miyong discovered that she was clumsy by nature and could not think quickly enough.

"You must think yourself as one of these machines, Miyong," Hyunja lectured, pointing at several pistols on display. "Each of these has to do a certain job. For instance, look at this one." She picked up a pistol from the display case and held it. "When you aim at your target accurately and pull the trigger, the bullet will obey you and hit it. Let your hands and fingers see your target the way your eyes do. Precision is the keyword in the espionage business. If you lack precision, your chance of survival is slim."

Hyunja then dropped the pistol in Miyong's hand, startling her. Miyong couldn't believe that she was actually holding a real "killing machine." Yet, she was thrilled, like the day she had held a whole Hershey bar in her hand for the first time when she had been small. Hyunja demonstrated what she called the "Tae-kwon-do trick." Positioning herself onto the center of a room-sized rug, she suddenly rose toward the ceiling with a sharp, determined cry, and as she came down, she opened her legs like scissors and kicked the post in front of her. Then, landing onto the floor lightly and gently, she performed two somersaults, like a boneless creature, before jumping up to her feet.

"Wow," was all Miyong could say.

Hyunja then moved to a small table next to the wall, fitted with two solid boards, breathing deeply. She paused, facing the boards, concentrating as if her enemy was about to lurch. Then, yelling *Yahhh*, she broke the boards with two quick consecutive blows. "You must be quick on everything," she said, beads of sweat on her forehead. "You either kill someone or get killed. There's no middle ground."

Miyong admired Hyunja. She was a step ahead of her in every aspect of life. She was a shrewd, merciless trainer, yet once in a while, she turned into a warm, kind individual. One day after another strenuous session, Hyunja offered Miyong some of her clothes to take home, opening her closet door wide. "I have way too many clothes."

"No thanks," Miyong said. It hurt her ego to get free stuff, especially from her friend who had a rich Japanese boyfriend.

"If you don't want them, they'll go to charities," Huynja said, as if she could sense Miyong's hunger for what she didn't have.

Her spirit was weakening before a long line of fancy women's clothes neatly hung on hangers, some with the price tags still on. While she lived at Good Shepherd Orphanage, Miyong wore used clothes donated by Americans, often too large for her, and after she left the orphanage, she was too poor to buy anything in a department store. These were expensive clothes, something she could never touch! But she didn't want Hyunja's stuff.

Walking away from the closet, she politely thanked her.

"You sure?" Hyunja said.

"Yes, because I don't have anything to give you. Instead of those clothes, maybe you can let me ask a few questions."

"Of course," she said.

"How long have you been in the South?"

"Two years."

"Only two? I thought you worked longer, more like five or six years. Mr. Tompkins called you a 'seasoned agent with eleven missions under her belt.'"

"If I must include the time I worked for the DPRK [Democratic People's Republic of Korea] Intelligence Agency, it's eight years."

"You mean, you were…?"

"I was. I don't know how I got into such a mess, but I learned my job from both sides. It's scary when I think about it. Once I was Great Leader's pet, and now I'm his enemy. I'll do anything to destroy him, even if I die."

As youngsters we believed that we belonged to Great Leader, who owned our country. In our second year of middle school, in 1956, we began military training. We walked ten miles a day, shouting slogans, besides rope climbing, obstacle jumping, and shooting with real rifles. Our drill instructors told us that we were preparing for another war against the Capitalist South, to free our brothers and sisters from the imperialistic Americans. About that time, China was boiling over with Red Guards hunting for Class Enemies—landlords, intellectuals, and the foreigners who were "sucking the blood of the Chinese"—and Kim Il-sung, too, saw a chance to lock up his rivals and landlords and businessmen and sweep up the wealth they left behind. Often, we kids were sent to large homes with carved wooden doors and cabinets to steal whatever we were told to steal and beat whomever we were told to beat, and we obliged without thinking twice about what we were doing. Then, in the first year in high school I was selected for the "Exchange Students Program." That year, I spent my summer vacation in Beijing, learning Chinese society under Mao, and the next year, I was in Okinawa Japan, learning Japanese and studying how the American Imperialists had brainwashed people of this ancient island, and whether or not our comrades were striving within the foreign occupation. The following year I was in Seoul with a dozen selected students, in a safe house hosted by a Seoul University professor named Suk. The city was bustling with pedestrians, vendors, and all kinds of vehicles, which we didn't have in the North. What impressed me the most was that giant machines were doing everything at construction sites, from breaking the ground to scooping up the dirt and carrying it across the field and dumping it. It seemed that the South Koreans were happier than we North Koreans. In Pyongsong where I lived, for instance, the buses ran across town only a few times a day and we walked to school, to the market, to the district office — but here, in Seoul, the buses were waiting for people, the attendants calling out their destinations. All you had to do was get on the right bus. And every store we passed was packed with food, clothes, appliances, cigarettes, candies, and other essential things. In the North, we would stand in line in front of the Distribution Center for hours to get even a bag of low grade rice. Once I asked our director, the professor, "I thought South Koreans were starving, but the stores had all kinds of stuff we don't have in the North," and he said, "Don't be fooled by what you see. It's for display only. In this large city, tens of thousands of people are starving."

Teamed up with our comrades already living in several different towns in the South, we students were put to work immediately. On the first trip to Inchon Harbor, where the Americans had mass murdered the North Korean troops during the war, we blew up a U.S. cargo ship waiting for inspection, killing a few Americans and destroying undetermined amounts of military goods. At Panmoonjom, where the armistice was signed by the world leaders at the end of the war, we killed South Korean guards on duty and blasted their equipment. We recorded our daily activities, printed them, and passed them to our secret agents to be sent to the Central Workmen's Party in Pyongyang for their approval. In the evenings, after a successful mission, we always feasted at the professor's large home, drinking makoli [a mild alcoholic beverage] and singing Youth Red Army songs. I was turning into a devil, Miyong, but I wasn't aware of it; in fact, I was more determined to help South Koreans end their miseries under the American Imperialists, by bombing and killing their enemies. The following year, I received a gold pendant sent by Great Leader, engraved with "Notable Revolutionary." I was thrilled. Great Leader himself acknowledged my efforts and awarded me this pendant. I wrote him to thank him.

A few days later, in the evening, an old man came to see the professor. The two men talked for a long time in the professor's office. You would never guess who that old man was, Miyong. He was a seasoned spy who came to select his assistant for his next mission—the bombing of the Ginza Hotel in Tokyo.

When the professor sent for me and I walked in, the old man acted as if he had known me all his life. "I want to work with her," he said to the professor, smiling, loud enough for me to hear. The professor introduced him as Noguchi-san, whose Korean name was Kim Chul. "How would you like to be his granddaughter for the next few days and tour Tokyo?" he asked me, his eyes playful.

"I don't understand," I said.

"He'll explain the details when the time comes," the professor said. "For now, just remember that you've been selected to do very important work for the future of the People's Republic of Korea."

Later, as Noguchi walked me back to my room, he informed me that the South Korean Minister of Foreign Affairs was visiting Hayato Ikeda that week, the prime minister of Japan, to open the dialogue between the two nations that had been closed during the Rhee regime. He said, "Now that South Korea is under Park, the former army major who succeeded in coup d'etat earlier this year, the South Korean leaders want Japan to help them to grow economically, so that they can trade with other nations around the world. Our Suryongnim [Great Leader] doesn't want this to happen. If Japan and South Korea join hands in coalition, his reunification plan would go down the drain. Make sense?"

"Yes, but what are we supposed to do in Tokyo?" I asked, but he brushed it away.

"You'll soon find out." The next day in the afternoon, we flew to Tokyo and checked into the Ginza Hotel. Our room was on the fifth floor, Room 523, with a view of tall buildings and the sun setting in the sky above.

That evening around seven, a hotel employee walked in and delivered a large package to Noguchi and left. Without a word, Noguchi handed me the box. I opened it. Do you know what I found? A blue silk dress, matching high heels, and a purse made of alligator skin. I looked at him in disbelief, and he said, "There's more!" Digging further, I found an envelope with 2000 yen, and a velvet box containing a pearl necklace, pearl bracelet, and matching ring.

"Who's giving me all these?" I asked.

Noguchi chuckled. "You didn't expect to do such dangerous work for nothing, did you?"

Dangerous work? "What kind of dangerous work am I supposed to do?" I asked.

Again, he said, "You'll find out tomorrow. Until then, enjoy your life as much as you can. Put on your new clothes, and let's go out."

Noguchi took me to a fancy restaurant with a dance floor, and I felt as though I were dreaming. It was the first time I watched men and women dancing fast Western dances, arm in arm, their bodies touching. Noguchi asked me to dance with him but when I said no, he danced with a young Japanese woman whose face had been powdered ghostly white.

The next day we toured the city. With a camera hanging from his neck, Noguchi was a typical tourist as he showed me around the town, sometimes in a taxi, other times in a horse-drawn carriage. We ate lunch in another fancy restaurant specializing in sushi made of bluefin tuna, the most expensive sushi of all.

When we returned to our hotel room, Noguchi turned into a different man, edgy and nervous, his forehead showing deep lines. He told me to change into "casual clothes," and come join him at the table in the corner of the room. When I did, a small palm-sized Sony transistor was laid in front of him.

"I'll explain what we're going to do now," he said, without looking at me. "Listen carefully. This transistor has a time bomb inside. We'll go to the ninth floor, to Room 913, where the South Korean foreign minister is staying, and leave the transistor and walk out. While I set the timer, make sure no one walks in, understand? When I'm done, we get out through the window to use the emergency staircase leading to the alley. Remember, we only have five minutes to do the job. Five minutes!"

My heart pounded so fast that I inhaled deeply.

"Once we hit the alley, we split. Don't wait for me, hear? In case I slip and fall, just keep going until you find a place to hide. You can fool anyone as Japanese, so don't panic. And you learned enough Japanese during training, didn't you?"

"I was in Okinawa for one year."

"You're set, then. Meet me the next day in front of the Ichiban Train Station at eight sharp," he ordered. "If I don't show up after fifteen minutes, you're on your own. Find a way to get back home."

He asked me if I had any questions, but I couldn't think of any, and we left our room together, with him in the lead. We took the elevator to the ninth floor. The corridors were lit brightly but were deadly quiet, with no one in sight. Noguchi turned to me and smiled. "Just in case something goes wrong, take this…" He grabbed my hand and dropped something tiny and smooth.

"What is it?" I asked, opening my palm. "A red capsule?"

"Shhhh…Use it when you feel you have no chance of survival. Come, let's go before they return!"

The door was locked. He took out what seemed to be a pocket knife from his pants pocket, and drilled the blade into the keyhole and twisted it. It opened. He closed the door behind us and turned the ceiling light on. He moved quickly. While I stood by the door, my legs shaking, he sat on the bed and opened the back panel of the transistor. I kept saying, "Hurry, hurry!"

The light went out, leaving us in total blackness. I've never been so panicky. The door burst open, almost knocking me onto the floor, and black figures rushed in, and suddenly the light was on. "Down on the floor, or we'll shoot!"

Five Japanese policemen stood before us, each with a rifle. While Noguchi stuttered incoherently in Japanese, begging them not to shoot, I crawled on the carpet until I found a dark corner between the wall and the sofa. The next few seconds seemed surreal, Miyong. Men were yelling, Noguchi crying, and feet were marching around me for what seemed like an hour. Remembering the capsule Noguchi gave me, I quickly threw it into my mouth. A foot kicked my face, and I was numb. I couldn't decide whether it was the blow to my face or the capsule working on me, but I felt as though I had just been sucked into a dark tunnel.

Later, waking up in the hospital room with white walls, I learned Noguchi had died. One of the men wearing dark suits told me in Korean. I wasn't a bit glad that I was alive when he was dead. Men were asking questions all at the same time: What were you doing in Room 915? Who sent you? What's your relation to the old man? How long have you known him?

But my mind wasn't able to process the words I was hearing. All I could dwell on was that the old man had died and I'd be next. A few days went like that, men coming in and asking questions, nurses forcing me to swallow pills and sometimes sweet liquid, and doctors forcing my eyes open and pointing bright flashlights into them. Then, I was lifted on a stretcher, hands and feet bound and mouth stuffed with something soft, and was loaded onto an ambulance. After a long ride, I was on a large ship, as large as a schoolhouse. Three Koreans, two men and one woman, were watching me closely whenever I opened my eyes. It didn't take a genius to figure out who they were and what they might do to me once I landed in South Korea. They were CIC agents!

After the longest night on the boat, I was in Seoul. Oh, how dreadful the interrogation was! It went on night and day, the same questions over and over, each time by a different interrogator. Out of everything, the court appearances were most trying. Sometimes the spectators threw shoes, coins, eggs, and books at me while I stood before the three judges, my hands bound behind me and feet shackled. I responded to them by singing the "Great Leader" song at the top of my voice, just to show my defiant spirit, and more than twice, the judges walked out, announcing a recess.

One day, after another court hearing, a Catholic priest came to see me in my cell. He was an old man, a grandpa type. He made me cry. This was when I realized that a man's kind words spoken in a gentle voice were far more powerful than all the violence in the world. He said that he had been in the courtroom since the preliminary hearing and that he wanted to do something for me. "Even when you're found guilty by the court, God will never punish you for your mistakes. In fact, He will draw you closer to Him, to open your eyes to see His Kingdom…" By the time he finished his sermon, I was weeping and begging him to help me. I told him everything—about my childhood in the North and my life in the South as a terrorist until a very important man in the North sent me and Noguchi to bomb the hotel room where the South Korean Foreign Minister would be, so that Japan and South Korea could never join hands as business partners. Would you believe that Father Lee pulled me out of the prison, like a magician pulling a rabbit out of a hat? He conducted many prayer services in his church, and the whole congregation stood behind me; they petitioned to the court, *saying that I was too young to commit such a horrific crime alone. They even demonstrated in front of Blue House and the courthouse, holding signs that read, "Moon Hyunja deserves freedom" or "Don't punish innocence!" Every newspaper in Seoul printed my story, and I responded with a public apology. I was on the public radio six times, apologizing over and over, always with Father Lee next to me. Three years ago, on August 15th, on the 19th anniversary of Independence Day, President Park pardoned me, along with a dozen others. It was the turning point of my life, Miyong. CIC not only provided me a place to live, but also paid me when they had me speak in schools or for private organizations.*

"What a story!" Miyong said.

Hyunja didn't smile. "I'll give you a piece of advice: As an agent, you must never expect so much from anyone. Your *life* isn't really yours, because someone else controls it. But in a big picture, you are a small cog in a big machine called a *nation*. The leaders of that nation can turn you into a devil or an angel. They decide, not you!"

Chapter Nine

THE SKY WAS LIT with the half moon and thousands of bright stars, but the air was humid. From her transistor radio on the nightstand, the newsman was reporting. "The native Vietnamese in Hoa Province are grateful for our troops, the White Horse Division. Today they destroyed 300 Vietcong, but there were only a handful of casualities on our side. Our allies, the Americans, consider South Koreans 'exceptional soldiers' and praise their perpetual devotion to kill enemies and to show their loyalty to those who saved their country from the Communist North during the earlier war."

Miyong turned the radio off, moved to the window, and opened it. "A handful of casualties means a handful of deaths," she said to herself. Frogs, crickets, and other insects she couldn't identify were singing. It was pleasant music to her ears. Far away, on the Tong-il Highway, cars and trucks whizzed by, as always, but tonight their headlights seemed brighter. She wished she could get on one of those moving vehicles and go somewhere, not to Hope Community on the island or to the orphanage, but somewhere unknown and far away.

A "click" on the window startled her, and she moved away from the window, to the left. Then, she thought it could have been a twig blown into her window, or a bird that had lost its sense of direction and hit the glass pane. *Poor thing…* Another click on the window confirmed that it wasn't a twig or a dumb bird. It was definitely louder this time, more like a small rock hitting the glass pane. *Who's doing this?* Noticing the ceiling light still on, she quickly moved to the switch by the door and flipped it off. In the dark, she slowly moved back to the window. She could make out only the outlines of trees, the wrought-iron fence, and the pond reflecting the moonlight. Then, she froze. Under the canopy of the ginkgo branches toward the entrance stood something dark and solid. An intruder!

A crow squawked loudly three times from the gingko tree, overpowering all the noises of the summer night. Strangely, the sound was familiar: it didn't sound like a real crow. It was different, yet familiar. She waited for another round of three squawks. And they came! She couldn't help but laugh. *Oppa. You've come.*

While living in the orphanage, her brother had shown many talents: he had been a soccer player, basketball player, and was a choir member, too. But his imitation of a crow earned him respect among other boys his age. Whenever all eighty kids poured out to the playground after lunch — the only time of the day Miyong could see her brother — there were those squawks blaring like a trumpet, always three times, and she would run to him.

Carefully, she looked down. The dark shadow had now moved out of the canopy and was standing under the faint moon, like a stone statue.

She waved.

He waved back.

Darting quickly to the door, she quietly slipped out of her room and walked down the staircase, careful not to make any noise. At the landing, the old guard sat at his usual spot behind a small desk, his head nodding. She tiptoed to the back door behind the utility room, and stepped out.

The night was full of the pungent smell of a countryside summer

— hay, weeds, cow patties, and other scents she couldn't name. Noises of frogs and summer insects were loud and cheerful. She took small, uncertain steps toward the front, where she had spotted her brother. At the corner, she saw a silhouette of a man approaching. "*Oppa*, is that you?"

"Hey, it's me!" her brother said.

The next moment, Miyong found herself in his two strong arms. "What are you doing here, *Oppa*?" she asked.

"Happy Birthday, kid!" he said, hugging her tighter. "It was two days ago, but it's never too late to celebrate, is it?"

"My birthday?" she said. "I forgot my own birthday. How did you get in? We have tall iron fences all around."

"I climbed over the fence. I'm in the boot camp four miles south of here. Can you feel the Army fatigues on me?"

"Is that what this is?" Miyong asked, touching his sleeve. "It feels stiff, like tent material."

He laughed. "At first I felt like a walking tent myself, but gradually it got better. How did I get here? I bribed the delivery truck driver with a pack of cigarettes. But I have to go back on foot."

"How can you walk four miles in the dark?"

"Let's not worry about it, okay? I'm here with you, and that's all I care about now."

She didn't say anything, and the two sat in silence.

"I have something to tell you, sis!"

"What is it?"

"I'll be in Vietnam in six weeks."

"In six weeks?" she cried. "You can't be serious!"

"Not so loud," he cautioned.

"But six weeks is less than two months!" she said, softer this time.

"Don't lose sleep over it yet, okay? Our Basic Skills instructor doesn't think we'll be ready in six weeks. But the government is itching to send us there as soon as possible. It all began about three weeks ago, when we were on the Yonsei University campus in Shinchon District, demonstrating, and armed policemen marched in and beat us like dogs and loaded us onto trucks. More than a thousand guys spent two days in jail, sitting on the concrete floor, shoulder-to-shoulder. Then, the next thing we knew, we were heading to the boot camps, in several different trucks."

Miyong felt a sudden chill in the breeze and wrapped her arms around herself. "I'm scared," she whimpered. "What am I going to do without you, brother?"

"Hey, a guy going to Vietnam is no big deal today, here in Korea. Ask anyone on the street: One out of five will say *I have a brother or cousin or a friend in Vietnam.*"

"I will have no one here after you leave…" She fought not to cry, not in front of him, but tears flowed down her cheeks anyway.

Jinwoo said nothing for a long while and then said, "You're an adult now. I can't protect you like I did when we lived in the orphanage. You'll be fine. Be strong, promise?" Heavy silence fell between them when Miyong didn't respond. The noises of the frogs and cicadas and other insects got louder, as if they understood the conversations between the two siblings.

"When are you leaving for the North?" he asked.

"I don't know. The training will end in December."

"Be careful, okay? If I don't see you go…"

"I'm not going to a war, like you are, *Oppa.*"

"I know that. But who can tell what's worse, going to fight in Vietnam or in the North? In every spy movie I watched, the female agents were hookers. I don't know of any spy movie that doesn't use women as bait to get what the spymaster wants."

I'd rather die than sell my body, she thought, but didn't say anything.

"I'm just telling you what can happen."

"I know, but don't worry." *What would it be like when he was gone? What if I never see him again?* She didn't want to show tears at a time like this, but she felt a hot sting in her eyes.

Jinwoo produced an object from inside his coat and handed it to Miyong.

It was heavy in her hands, and was the size of a pocketbook. "What's this?" She shook it, and something made a dull *clink* inside.

"It's the bamboo trinket box that was on Mother's dressing table, remember? Father packed it for me in my backpack."

"What's in it?"

"Our birth certificates, your necklaces, the family photos, including their wedding pictures…I think there were a couple of gold rings, too, but Auntie Moon might have taken them when I was asleep on the road. Anyway, I want you to keep it until I come back. They'll be safer with you than with me."

Strange noises in the air startled them both. Looking up, they saw lights shining in the attic and pigeons flying out, one after another. But the birds didn't fly away. Cooing and squawking, they kept making small circles in the dark sky.

"*Oppa*, you'd better go," Miyong whispered. "Our director lives there and he must have heard us."

He talked fast. "You'll be notified through the mail, here or at Hope Community, about when we'll be deployed. And in that box, you'll find some cash. I emptied my savings account for you. There's enough money to put you through a two-year college."

"College? Why would I want to go to college when you're in Vietnam?"

"I'll come back for your graduation, remember that!" Without waiting for her response, he walked away.

Miyong stood there until his dark silhouette disappeared completely, feeling empty. Lifting her head, she looked for stars or the moon, but the sky too was empty.

Chapter Ten

Jinwoo

THE SLOPE OVER WHICH Jinwoo had come an hour earlier was deadly quiet, except for insects chirping and toads bleeping. Getting into the courtyard surrounded by an eight-foot-tall wrought-iron fence hadn't been easy. On his first attempt to climb it, something sharp pierced his little finger and it bled. But on his way out, he found a stump leaning against the fence, and the rest was easy. He stepped onto it, pulled himself up as he had learned in boot camp, and then jumped off to freedom below. After such strenuous gymnastics, walking in the dark was nothing, except for the eerie rustling of the trees and bushes on both sides of the road.

He would be heading to Vietnam in a few weeks, whether he liked it or not. He knew the Southeast Asian jungles were densely populated with beasts — not only the four-legged kind, but also two-legged ones called "Vietcong." The Vietcong, he learned, were geniuses in setting up underground booby traps fitted with bamboo spikes so sharp that they could drill into a hefty American, killing him instantly. During the training, he had seen a photo of a big American hanging on a tree, as if he were trying to dry his wet uniform, except that the man was lifeless. Everyone at the camp talked about how agile the Vietcong were, suddenly lurching out of vast green vegetation like monkeys, stabbing anything they saw. Jinwoo wanted to think about them now, without fear of being actually killed. Didn't Confucius say, "Fear is a man's worst enemy"? He had just lectured his sister to act like an adult, hadn't he?

He imagined that those somber shadows were Vietcong aiming firearms or daggers at him, and every step could lead him to a pit that would suck the life out of him. His drill sergeant, named Chang, came to his mind. Chang was a fearless bastard with rock-like muscles and a metallic voice that could break a man's spirit like a twig with one spiteful word. He could kick, beat, and stab, knocking down any man as easily as a cat knocking down a mouse. Everyone in his group feared him.

"When you're in a Vietnam jungle, boys," Chang once had said, white foam gathering at the corners of his mouth, "you'll remember how religiously I tried to teach you about survival. When you realize that you learned something from me, don't write me thank-you notes. Instead, kill those gooks for me. Got that? You'll never regret following my instructions. Now, move your asses, boys!"

Jinwoo began to sweat, as he walked, imagining Chang's staccato voice ringing in his ear, *"Hana, dool, set, net...One, two, three, four...."*

His sister's face loomed in his mind. *"How can I live without you, Oppa?"* she seemed to say. *"It's not that I can't take care of myself, but not having you around would be like losing the whole world..."*

He had sounded rough, which he regretted now. Ever since he and his sister left home in Pyongyang that cold, cold winter morning, he had feared losing her. Growing up in the orphanage, he was her protector. Whenever any boys bothered her, he ran to rescue her, often getting bruises on his face. Tonight, he shouldn't have revealed his feelings about going to Vietnam — the fear of dying, more than anything. But there was nothing he could do now, on this lonely road, except find his way back to the camp. A faint light showed up ahead, and then he heard the noise of the passing cars. He was close to the highway, which would take him to the camp within two hours. He began to whistle "Amazing Grace."

Miyong couldn't fall asleep that night. The bamboo box contained so many memories of her family and her childhood. Her parents' yellowed wedding photo and her glass necklaces were her new treasures. The thought that she'd lose her brother soon was so unbearable that burying her head in her pillow, she began to sob. Memories rushed back to her mind.

One summer, when she was seven and her brother ten, Miyong had been ill with typhoid fever. She still remembered the white walls, a window fan that blew in warm air, and two American nurses, one skinny and another medium-sized, dressed in white gowns and white gauze masks, coming in to take her temperature and force her to swallow white pills. She had been bored, listening to the whining kids all around her, complaining about thirst and the summer heat. One day, she heard someone crying. Forcing her eyes open, she caught a vague glimpse of her brother standing next to her, wiping tears with his fist.

"What's wrong, *Oppa?*" she asked in a tiny voice.

He nearly jumped — for joy or in terror, she still didn't know. "Miyong-ah, are you okay?" he said cautiously, his voice congested from crying. His eyes were full of tears.

"I'm tired." She barely mouthed the words.

"The nurses brought me here because you didn't wake up for two days. They said that if you keep sleeping like that, you might die!" He bit his lips to fight back tears, but they kept coming, and he wiped again. "They told us to pray for you every day..."

"I'm not dying."

"You have to live, kid. You can't die, understand? I can't leave here all alone!" With that, he fell on her and bawled.

Then, a year or so later, on a bitterly cold night, a fire started in the orphanage, in the poorly built kitchen, and spread to the west side of the building. While a fire chief stood on the fire truck, ordering the firefighters and the grownup onlookers to pass buckets of water and pour it onto the flames, two Army trucks rolled into the courtyard and began loading the children. Not finding her brother anywhere, Miyong kept screaming, "My brother is in the building! He's inside! I'm not going anywhere without him!" As everyone stood there merely watching the flames dancing and licking the building, a fireman carried her brother out and dropped him onto the truck. For days following, lying in their temporary residence, an empty schoolhouse, Jinwoo coughed like a honking goose. Every kid made fun of him, imitating his coughs, but to Miyong, it was like music. She was glad that he was in one piece and had received no serious burns.

Now, ten years later, she was about to lose him to Vietnam, where he might die. She needed him and he needed her. They had been together all these years, without their parents, denied of comforts and privileges most kids took for granted. *How can I lose him?*

Chapter Eleven

Sorak Mountain

A TWO-WEEK-LONG INTENSIVE SURVIVAL Training began on a slope of Sorak Mountain, on the property of an old Buddhist temple that overlooked the seashore in the front and a steep pine forest in the back. Arriving on a Friday afternoon, Miyong thought it was a worthwhile trip. She liked everything she saw: the green pastures, the long curling trails connecting the fields with the surrounding mountains, the deep purplish valleys, and the ponds reflecting the cloudless sky.

Each student pitched a one-man tent on a clearing, according to Tompkins' instructions: the male students on one side, the females on another, and Tompkins himself in between. After a simple dinner of military ration canned food, they sat around a bonfire they had built with broken branches and twigs. It was a perfect evening, Miyong thought. The sun went down slowly behind distant mountains, turning the sky from pink to lavender and then to gray. Frogs, birds, and insects began to show their talents, bleeping or droning or chirping. On such a night, the girls at the Community would tell one another stories —

their own life stories, or those of others, or ghost stories. But here, with the future spies, the conversation was about spying.

"Did you read about the North Korean girl caught in Japan recently?" the ex-cop asked.

"You mean Yim Heesoon, the girl who tried to bomb our embassy in Kyoto?" Sangpil said.

"Yeah! The newspaper said that it was her first mission after a five-year training in Kim Il-sung's Foreign Language School, which serves as a spy training school. What got her in trouble was her fake passport." For the next few minutes, they talked about the North Korean teenager whose photo had been on the front page of the newspaper for several days, and who was now in prison waiting for a trial.

Tompkins commented, "It was a good report of a botched mission, I thought. By reading that article, you can learn what can actually happen in a mission."

Everyone turned to him. "What was the biggest mission you've accomplished, Mr. Tompkins?" Sangpil asked.

He had a vague, mysterious smile on his face. "I caught my wife using my credit card and reported her to my bank."

"No, seriously," Sangpil said. "Did you kill someone?"

"Of course! I was one of the Marines in Berlin in 1944, finishing up Hitler's puppets."

"Did you really kill Germans?"

"Of course."

"How many?"

Tompkins laughed a quick, dry laugh. *"How many Germans did I kill?* Perhaps more than two dozen. But my wife doesn't know that. If she finds out, she'll call me a murderer and file for a divorce. She doesn't know anything about what we Americans did here in your country, either, after the American military took over south of the 38th Parallel in September 1945, and occupied until August 1948. Let me give you a short history lesson here about your own country after liberation from Japan."

On September 9th, the first American GIs landed on Inchon Port. This was after we attended the Tokyo Bay Surrender Ceremony on September 2nd, during which time Japan officially apologized for her wrongs to the world and the documents were signed by both Japanese and American officials. It was a fine closure to those who fought in the war and to the victims of Japan's evil deeds to mankind, which had resulted in the mass destruction of a civilization, and 21 million deaths. General MacArthur's speech was powerful. He promised U.S. support of Japan until her complete recovery from the devastation and her conversion to a democratic nation, revealing his hopes for a better world, "a world founded upon trust and understanding, a world dedicated to the dignity of man and fulfillment of his most cherished wish, for freedom, tolerance, and justice."

The Inchon beaches looked deserted, with abandoned Japanese military equipment, driftwood, and dilapidated port structures. At one place surrounded by a chain link fence, about a hundred or more men with bare chests and shaven heads sat, their hands bound behind them, and a dozen men in navy-blue uniforms walked around them, yelling and striking them with whips. Though we didn't understand what they were saying, we understood the solemn fact that the Japanese soldiers were being held by the Korean guards. My impression of Korea at that moment was a crossroads where the conquerors and conquered had switched places. As we entered the capital on the military trucks, with our red, white, and blue flags flying on the hoods, we saw the buildings flying the Japanese flags at half mast, and thousands of school kids and adults lining the streets, welcoming us, shouting and throwing their arms in the air. It felt good. We were their new rulers.

We occupied JoongAng-Chong, the capital building, at the center of the city, with a large sign that read, "The United States Army Military Government in Korea" in the front. We soon learned that we American soldiers weren't made to administer a nation of 5000 years of written history, even though the people had been severely impoverished by their earlier tyrants and were powerless. Imagine a five-year-old boy trying to tell his eighty-year-old grandpa what to do! It was the same irony.

The first obstacle was the language barrier. No one told us to learn the native language, because we were the ruling power. Our arrogance was revealed in broad daylight when General MacArthur ordered through the radio that all Korean government employees, without exception, must learn English in order to communicate with the ruling party. Learning a foreign language isn't a small feat. It not only takes time, but also one must have the will to learn. You can't simply order someone to learn your language so that you can tell them what to do, can you?

The unfavorable political climate was another matter, as waves of refugees, who fled Russian-occupied North Korea, crossed the border and the soldiers from the Pacific War, who had fought for Japan against us Americans, returned. One of the serious mistakes our U.S. military government made was that they employed the men who had betrayed their country and collaborated with Japanese officials to work with us, to control the North Korean refugees and men returning from the foreign war. Not surprisingly, pro- Communist organizations began to mushroom in the midst of chaos.

The root of all the troubles surfaced from one thing: U.S. government control of rice, the White Gold. We Americans never understood what rice meant to the Korean people until then. During nearly four decades of Japan's ruling of Korea, the Japanese stole rice from Korean farmers and shipped it to Japan to feed the inland people, for the quality of Korean rice was far superior to theirs. When the food shortage hit the general public, they transported lower quality rice and millet from Manchuria for the natives.

We Americans first issued a free market system, but the ignorant farmers were ripped off by the brokers, who bought bulk from rice farmers at a hideous price and sold it to the Japanese at a huge profit. Wealthy Koreans were no better. They made a fortune by buying directly from the farmers and keeping it in their warehouses, selling only a small amount at the market when they needed money. Some greedy farmers kept their produce all to themselves, causing the price of the grain to jump. The Russians were sending their men, asking for rice, but we couldn't help them. As you know, the North is mostly mountains, and the soil is unsuitable for farming; thus for a long time the Northerners had depended on their

Southern neighbors for White Gold. When the shortage of rice became life-threatening, we changed the tactics. We did exactly what the Japanese had done, by demanding that farmers pay taxes with rice, up to 45% of their produce, leaving them a bare minimum to survive. When they resisted, we arrested them and charged them for non-compliance with the authority. This created a huge anti-American movement, forcing the leftists to organize guerilla armies to fight against us.

One particular incident I still remember was in Cheju Island. The island had been a secret stage for several guerilla forces trained by the North Koreans. For three days and nights we fought. We lost about thirty men altogether, but killed several thousand islanders who fought mostly with old, rusted Japanese rifles, or spiked bamboo poles, or farm picks and shovels. Oh, it was such an ugly sight — corpses all over the streets, women and children wailing over their dead fathers, brothers, teachers, and uncles...

When I look back, I realize that we failed as a temporary government, but we were there to help at the most uncertain time of Korea's history. One thing to remember, folks, is that you just do your best at the given moment, for you have no other choices. The only judge we have is history, or maybe God, who sees through everything.

He stopped and looked at each student closely to see whether they were still awake. No one said anything. The fire had died and thin strands of smoke rose from ash-covered black logs. With clap of his big hands, he said, "Well. It's getting late, folks! I have a surprise for you tomorrow morning, so get a good night's sleep. Try not to think about what I've just told you. Even good people with good intentions make mistakes sometimes. And that's life!"

The next morning, after another meal from the military cans, Tompkins ordered everyone to board his mini-van.

"Today, I'm taking you to a spot twelve kilometers north and will drop you off, one by one, and you have to find your way back."

This hadn't been discussed, and everyone looked at one another trying to figure out whether their leader was joking. But with his lips tightly sealed, he seemed serious.

"Twelve kilometers is a long distance," someone grumbled.

"I know," Tompkins said.

"What if it rains?" Miyong asked, looking up at the gathering clouds.

"God will help us," Tompkins said, and distributed a brown sack to each of them. He then seated himself in the driver's seat and turned the ignition. The motor growling, the van carried them out of the campsite to a winding dirt road lined with tall pines on both sides. It was a rough ride; everyone bumped his/her head on the ceiling or into one another. Thirty minutes later, Tompkins drove into a clearing with red clay dirt, and parked the van.

Everywhere Miyong looked, there were layers of hazy mountains, indicating how far they had come from the campsite.

"This is the first drop-off. Any volunteers?" Tompkins asked.

No one replied.

"Are you all cowards?"

"Yes!" everyone chorused.

Tompkins clicked his tongue. "If you're on a spy plane in enemy territory, your pilot might not be as patient or gentle as your instructor here. Come on, someone!"

Sangpil said, "I'll get off!" He crawled out of the van.

"I'm proud of you!" Tompkins said.

Sangpil said, "Hope to see you all later."

"Good luck!" everyone said.

The van moved to the next stop. When they reached another empty, deserted area next to a wide, clear stream, the ex-cop volunteered to get off. Methodically, Tompkins got rid of three more in the area of two square miles, and drove Miyong to a clearing surrounded by scraggly bushes and tall grass and parked the van. "Good luck to you, my dear," Tompkins said sweetly when she got out.

"Thank you for your kindness," Miyong said as sweetly she could manage.

"You're very welcome!" Smiling, he drove away, honking his horn three times.

Surely, he would worry about the safety of his students dropped off in a remote place like this. *If we don't show up at camp in time, he will drive up, looking for us,* she thought. She began walking. There was not a single human form as far as she could see, and the only sound she could hear was the gurgle of a stream somewhere. There was not a single bird in sight! It comforted her. Many poems were wrtten about streams, bamboos, winds, and stars. It was a time to imagine what it would have been like before God created people and animals. At one spot, however, on a slope, she was looking down at a deep valley where cows grazed in a plush green field, and a dozen miniature homes lay like matchboxes. She was glad that people lived here, after all. *If I ever get lost, I'll run down there and ask for help. They might even take me back to the camp.* She tried to find a trail leading to the valley, but amidst thorny shrubs and tangling vines, there was no hint of a walking path.

An hour of walking made her hungry and her legs achy. She sat on a large rock in the shape of a humpbacked turtle and, opening the brown sack Tompkins had provided for her, she found a can of Coca-Cola and crackers wrapped in clear cellophane. *I deserve at least this much!* With a quick prayer, she began eating. The sky turned dark and within seconds, raindrops began to fall on her. She gathered her food, thew it back into the sack, and ran for a cover, while the merciless rainfall beat on her like bamboo sticks. By the time she stood under a tall pine with spreading branches, thunder boomed like a timpani solo in a band performance. Lightning blinded her. She was soaking wet. The color of the landscape was now somber gray, black clouds hovering overhead. In a panic, she thought about finding the valley with homes and cows she had seen earlier, but going back there was out of the question, even if she could find the trail. And even if she made it down to the valley safely, how would she know the people would help her? She might walk into a lepers' colony or a home of Communists disguised as farmers. The only sensible thing to do now was wait until the rain stopped and find her way to the campsite. She was sorry to find herself in this dreary, primitive land, soaked to the bone, but this was a part of training, which she must endure. Her brother would soon be in Vietnam fighting for people he didn't know or care about, and this was nothing. Only a training. And it would be over soon, and everyone would laugh about it when they were together again.

Her wet clothes were stiff and uncomfortable against her skin. She hoped that Tompkins would drive up soon with some towels. A pot of hot tea would be nice…And maybe he'd bring some snacks, too, crackers and peanuts.

Finally, the rain stopped, and the dark clouds dispersed, showing thin patches of blue here and there in the sky. She began walking again. She kept sneezing. Two hours of skidding on the slippery wet dirt and shivering in her wet clothes, she walked into the campsite. No one came out to greet her, not even Mr. Tompkins. She crawled into her tent, found a towel in her bag, and began to dry herself. She was tired. Using her bag as her pillow, she lay herself on her sleeping bag.

As tired as she was, sleep didn't come. Her mind was like that of a newborn, content for no reason at all, disconnected from all worries and anxieties. Then came the noises that she had heard before, the same muffled screams of a woman, something falling, crashing, banging. This happened only when she was alone, as she was now. Then, she was with her brother Jinwoo, in their parents' bedroom in their old home in Pyongyang. Just the two of them. Since lunch that day, bombs had been exploding and a man's voice had been blaring through the commune speaker, which they couldn't understand. A dull siren rose and died down. A blinding light lit the rice-screen door before them and disappeared. They knew their father was at the district office as always, but why wasn't their mother home? "*Oppa*, I'm scared," Miyong whimpered.

"*Omma* will be back, soon!" her brother said, trying to comfort her. "She went out to talk to the neighbors."

Their mother had never been gone that long, leaving just the two kids at home. *Something is wrong*, Miyong thought. But her brother didn't do anything, probably because he didn't know where to find their mother when bombs were dropping like this. They skipped dinner that night. When their father returned later, the three of them searched and found her, in the cellar, all alone, delirious and talking gibberish. Their father carried her home but quickly sent the two children to bed, without dinner. The next morning, she was gone. "Your mother went to see your grandma in Kaesong," said their father.

* * *

On the last day of training, the group visited Panmunjom, where the final documents of the truce had been signed by the UN delegates and the Chinese military officials on July 27th 1953. Their guide was a tall man with an American name, Johnny Kim, who had been waiting for them in a vacant lot by the Tong-il Highway. Tompkins introduced him as the South Korean Special Forces' Reconnaissance officer, adding that he had lived in the U.S. as a child.

While driving Tompkins' van, Kim explained in his accented Korean that the area they were visiting today was the most heavily armed border anywhere in the world, and that even fourteen years after the war ended, the 155-mile long and 2.5 mile-wide patch known as *No Man's Land* was lined with checkpoints and embedded with land mines. Before the war, he said, that area had been a peaceful farming community where cows were fattened and children roamed about, but in the fall of 1945, shortly after the 38th Parallel moved in, the area turned into a combat zone between American-occupied southern Korea and Russian-occupied northern land. Farmers vanished. Two decades later, only two tiny villages existed there, one immediately north of the 38th Parallel, and another on the south side. The village on the north side was called Freedom Village, and the North Korean government used it strictly for propaganda purposes. The South Korean government, however, maintained the small town named *The Place Under a Big Star* to guard their territory against the North.

"While we're there," Kim said, "you'll hear messages coming through a hidden speaker on the North side, denouncing American imperialists and their *puppets*, meaning us South Koreans, and asking them to defect to the North."

Tompkins, sitting in the passenger's seat, turned and looked at each of the students. "Has any one of you thought about defecting to the North?"

"Me, me…" Three men raised hands, acting silly.

"I know of at least four American GIs who defected to the North while they were on patrol duty," Tompkins went on. "Two of them fled to North because they were sought by the U.S. military police for raping local girls, one was angry at his sergeant and defected as revenge, and the other was simply tired of being an American. If you're thinking of defecting today, I have some helpful advice."

"Please," Sangpil said.

"Prepare your will before we get there. You have only thirty minutes to do it."

"*A will?*" all three men echoed.

"Yes, a will," said Tompkins. "There's a strong chance that South Korean guards might shoot you when they see you crossing the boundary line. You're their enemy! Don't forget that."

"In that case, I won't do it," Sangpil said.

"Me neither," another said.

"And even if you succeed," Tompkins went on, "and get there without a scratch, don't get the idea that the Communists will treat you like kings. About 90% of defectors have either died or are locked away, and the rest are in labor camps."

No one said another word for a long moment.

The House of Peace wasn't anything impressive in Miyong's mind. It was merely a cluster of crudely built rectangular structures sitting in an undeveloped flat area full of tall weeds growing from the red dirt. Several groups of Japanese tourists were following their guides, like children following their teachers on a field trip, while reporters with cameras busily moved about, taking photos. In the lobby, an armed South Korean soldier stood in each corner, their eyes on everyone stepping into the building. In a large framed photo mounted on a wall, a bunch of soldiers — some American, and some Chinese with red stars on their hats — sat around a long table, staring somberly at the papers in front of them.

Following Johnny Kim to the conference room, Miyong saw a white line on the floor in the middle of the room. On each side of the line stood an armed soldier — a South Korean on the South side, a North Korean on the other — their expressions rigid.

"This room is the womb that nurtured the peace you're enjoying today," Kim lectured. "Please be advised not to turn abruptly or look into your purse or pocket. To the guard on the North side, everyone in the room is a potential terrorist who might shoot or throw a grenade at him. Any questions?"

"What if we sneeze?" one of the male students asked.

"Do it quietly if you must," Kim said.

"What if someone has to burp?"

"Don't be silly," Tompkins snapped. "It's a serious matter. Pay attention."

Kim went on. "Altogether, 1076 meetings between UN delegates and Chinese leaders took place here between June 1951 and July 1953 to draw up a peace agreement. Do you know what the troops of both sides were doing during those twenty-six months? Fighting! About ninety percent of casualties on both sides occurred during the last two months of the war, while the ceasefire agreement was in progress."

At the five-minute break, Miyong eased away from the group, with a new realization that this place had so much to tell. Each of those walls seemed to be a witness to those historic days when the killing finally stopped and prisoners returned to their homes. She had learned of the war and the armistice, but actually being in this room was like stepping into a history book. Seeing a long telescope fitted at the window facing north, she looked through it. At first, everything was blurry. By adjusting the control knob at the top, she was suddenly looking at a dozen houses with straw roofs, and in the very center stood a tall flagpole flying the North Korean flag with a red star and two blue stripes. *What would it be like standing over there, looking in this direction?*

Chapter Twelve

ON TUESDAY SEPTEMBER 8ᵀᴴ at ten a.m., the city square in front of the main train station buzzed like a marketplace on a Saturday. On one side, men, women, and children had gathered and were shouting goodbyes to their fathers or uncles or brothers leaving for Vietnam. On another side, a large battalion of students waited for action, holding banners and placards, whispering and fidgeting. The policemen, each with a club, were behind the students, watching every move the students were making. Close to the entrance, a row of military trucks stood, probably blocking civilians from getting too close to the troops.

Miyong had never imagined that such a large crowd would gather at the station. The postcard from the ROK, which Major Min had forwarded to her, didn't say much — only the date and the location from which her brother's infantry division was departing. She tried to squeeze through the wall of people in an attempt to get a glimpse of her brother, when she heard an angry chorus shouting, "Stop selling men to the international market!" "They're not cattle!" "Let them die at home, not in a jungle, like beasts!"

Some policemen blew whistles and others shouted at the men

and women to stay back. But the chorus didn't subside. Instead, it got louder. Then a group of armed soldiers wearing masks walked in, their military boots thumping against concrete. Stones began to fly. The chorus grew angrier, more ferocious. "Don't kill the fathers of the next generation!" "Stop selling men for stinking American pennies!"

Tear gas bombs exploded. White smoke rose. Clubs clattered. Screams erupted. People ran in every direction.

In a stupor, Miyong merely watched students falling as troopers struck them with rifle butts. A hand roughly grabbed her elbow. A policeman wearing dark safety glasses was shouting in her face. "Don't just stand there. Run!" He pushed her. But a gang of students blocked her way, and she was suddenly trapped. Several policemen encircled the students, striking them with clubs. She found herself crouching. Between the pant legs dancing before her eyes, she saw a space opening up on her left, and, like a dog, she scurried away on all fours. There was a burning smell, and she couldn't breathe.

A man's booming voice froze her stiff. "Dear students and fellow citizens, I am your president, whom you elected three years ago." Feet stopped moving. Voices halted screaming. Moans of pain subsided. Everyone turned around to see from where the president was speaking. Miyong too looked around.

"Who's mimicking his voice?" a young man next to her shouted, and another voice replied, "It's a recording! Can't you hear the buzz?"

Miyong recognized President Park's voice coming through the speaker mounted at the entrance of the station she had passed earlier.

"My fellow citizens," the voice went on, "this is a solemn moment we all have been waiting for. Those who are leaving us today heard a call to help our neighboring nation fallen prey to the Communists' aggression. At such a time, can we sit idly and watch a distant fire, clicking our tongues and saying, 'It's too bad. God help them'? Let us not forget, students and fellow citizens, that a number of years ago, the United States of America helped us when 95,000 Communists launched a surprise attack on us, with Russian tanks and ammunition. 54,000 American soldiers died during the war and are still buried in our soil. How could we ever forget who delivered us the peace and freedom we're enjoying today? How could we turn our heads away when the Americans are again fighting at the cost of their lives — this time, to deliver peace and freedom to our Vietnamese brothers and sisters, who are in the same situation as we were only a decade earlier?"

Faint applause erupted from where the troops waited. Some men's voices called out, "We'll fight, President! We'll bring honor and glory to our motherland!"

The President's voice continued. "As we send our beloved sons and brothers to the faraway front today, let us wish their safe return and bless them with our love, instead of showing our doubts and fear. We must show a sign of unity to our sons and brothers leaving their homes for a greater purpose..."

Loud band music exploded, with a tune of the military hymn called "Sons of Tangun [Korea's mystic father]", and then soldiers behind the trucks began marching toward the station entrance, singing:

By the will of the Heavens and seas
We're called to the distant front
We'll return, singing hymns of glory!
Mothers and fathers, wait for us.

Flying Taeguki high in the air
We fear no enemy, nor death
Let there be joyful songs, friends
We're the invincible sons of Tangun.

Teary-eyed spectators watched in silence. Students began to scatter, one by one. The special troopers marched out of the square as quickly as they had entered.

Miyong watched the thinning crowd, fighting back her tears. Her legs felt weak. A city of eight million seemed empty all at once. *Oppa, I didn't even say goodbye to you...*

Jinwoo's letter found her two grueling weeks later.

Dear Sister,

Eight p.m., Thursday, rainy and cold. We're in a small town in Quang-nam province near Hoi An, fifteen miles north of China Beach. It was raining when we got here two days ago, and it still is. The two dozen guys are packed in our tent like sardines in a can. Leaving Seoul without having a chance to say goodbye to you was the most difficult thing I have endured in the recent past. We not only left a week ahead of the schedule, but weren't even allowed to see our families! We, the ill-fated 2400 ROK soldiers, boarded the USS Patch in Pusan and headed south the night you last saw me in Seoul. In the cabin, we slept in the triple-tiered bunks.

But the good news is I'm in good spirit, considering the circumstances. All day today, we dug six-foot deep trenches around the camp, so my hands are covered with blisters. We hear shots fired occasionally from the wooded area near us, but we aren't fighting yet. Lucky, I guess.

Someone told me a long time ago that you don't really appreciate your country until you lose it or you're away from it, and I'm discovering that to be true. Everyone in my unit is homesick. Some guys are writing letters, like me; some are trying to sleep in their bunkers, in spite of the noises the poker-players are making; and two guys are arguing about something, calling each other names. But we're all missing home, that's for sure.

We'll stay here for a few days, but we don't know what comes next. That's the life of a soldier. But I'm not worried. I'll take one day at a time. I'll write as soon as I can, but I can't promise anything. Who can?

Take care, my dearest sister. I'm missing you so much. Keep me and my buddies in your prayer.

Your brother

That night, a phone call awakened Min. He picked up the receiver from his bed.

"Sorry to wake you, *Hyongnim* [Brother]." Lieutenant Lee Dongwoo's voice rang in his ear. Lee had been Min's assistant at CIC Investigation Division until Min moved to Hope Community. Lee was like a younger brother to Min. Lee's father had been Min's company commander who was killed in action during the early phase of the war, and Min had helped the fourteen-year-old boy to grow up. After his graduation from high school eight years earlier, Lee chose a military career, and ever since, the two men had worked closely together.

Min looked at his watch. Five past midnight. "Dongwoo, do you know what time it is?"

"Sorry, *Hyongnim*! Something urgent came up. I'm at Headquarters. I have something urgent to tell you."

"I'm listening."

"I'd rather talk to you in person."

Agitated, Min said, "Why can't you talk about it on the phone?"

"It's a long story, *Hyongnim*. Do you remember Miss Watanabe, the Japanese spokeswoman for the royal family?"

"Of course."

"She phoned me this afternoon to tell me that Prince Koo has been missing for two weeks. I guess she waited this long to break the news because they thought he'd show up. She said that the prince's mother has not touched food for days…"

Min sat up and scratched the back of his head. Prince Koo was the nephew of Sunjong, the last emperor of the Yi Dynasty, which was eradicated when Japan colonized Korea in 1905. Koo was an American architect, who taught at some university in California. He and his American wife had been in the news in May, when they just arrived to visit Koo's ailing father, who was the only surviving prince of the fallen dynasty.

"He wouldn't just disappear from his father's palace like steam," Min said. "They have security guards."

"Your guess is as good as mine, *Hyongnim*. All I know is that he's in Camp 14 in Kaechun, in the North!"

"What? How do you know?"

"I have a photo and a handwritten note from our friend Lee *Bujang* at the camp, right here in front of me. Are you coming or not?"

"I'll be there."

After Min hung up the phone, he thought about phoning Private Kim to tell him to drive him to the Headquarter, but he decided against it. This was big news. If he accidentally revealed it to his chauffeur, there was no guarantee that the private would keep his mouth shut. Kim had an army of drinking buddies here on the island. Min had to drive himself to the Headquarters at this hour of the night.

Lee Dongwoo was waiting for him in his office, sipping tea. When Min walked in Lee produced a book-size photo from a pile of papers on his desk and said, "Take a seat and look at this."

Min took the chair next to Lee's cluttered table and looked at the black and white photo in front of him. A young man looking back at him, wearing a gray inmate's quilted coat, in front of a dilapidated shack, was definitely Prince Koo. Min had met him briefly last May, at the banquet hosted by the President and the First Lady at Blue House, the presidential mansion in Hyoja District. More than five hundred people including diplomats, entertainers, politicians, and Army officers had gathered there. In this photo, the American architect looked haggard and dirty, not at all like the clean young man with whom Min had talked briefly that night. "It's him all right," Min said. "What are we going to do now?"

That Saturday morning, Miyong stood under a ginkgo tree, a teacup in her hand, admiring the leaves turning lemony yellow against the cobalt blue above. She missed her brother. He was thousands of miles away, unable to enjoy this splendid fall color, but more than anything, she couldn't see him or talk to him, even if she took the boat and went to Seoul. The last meeting she had had with him was something to cherish. Before he left, she had never paid attention to the news reporting the number of the injured or dead, but now it was different. Every evening, she listened to the news. And she often wondered, *How's he doing?*

A military Jeep showed up in front of the wrought-iron gate, honking its horn twice. The stooped old gatekeeper sprang out of his box-like stall and swung it open. The Jeep crawled into the courtyard and stopped a few yards away from her.

Her eyes widened. It was Major Min and Lieutenant Lee, the investigator. She ran to them, hoping they had the news of her brother. "What brings you here, gentlemen?" she asked cheerfully. Major Min was still the same — serious, short, and skinny — but Lieutenant Lee had gained some weight.

"You look good, Miyong," Major Min said, as he stepped out of the passenger's seat. "How's the training going?"

"Not bad. It's so good to see you, sir."

"I've received good reports from your instructor and Miss Moon," Major Min said, pinching off a yellow leaf from a low-hanging ginkgo branch, as he walked toward her.

"I'm glad that I didn't flunk the tests. Would you like to come in for a cup of tea?"

"We'll pass this time. We have some urgent business to discuss with you."

"With *me?*" Her gaze shifted from Min to Lee.

"Yes, Miss Hahn," Lee replied. "We'll bring you back before noon."

"Where are you taking me?"

"CIC Headquarters."

Her jaw dropped. It was the last place Miyong wanted to be on this beautiful autumn morning. "Why? Am I in trouble again?"

They both laughed. "You're in big trouble," Min said, his eyes playful. "Two army officers came to get you!"

"No, you're not," Lee said. "We'll explain when we get there. It's only a twenty minute ride."

Miyong checked herself. She wasn't at all presentable. The thin gray sweatshirt showed stains from *Kimchee* casserole from last night, and her sneakers were caked with mud. And no makeup! "Would you give me five minutes to clean up? I'll be right back."

"Don't worry," Major Min said in his non-negotiable manner. "You're not going to a party. We don't care how you look. Let's go!"

"But…"

Lee said, "You look lovely, as always."

This angered her rather than comforted her, but what was there for her to do? She walked ahead of the two officers, and reaching the jeep, she climbed into the back seat as if she had done it all her life.

Lieutenant Lee drove.

"Sorry for kidnapping you like this," Min said dryly, as if reading from a book, while the Jeep sped toward the main road, raising dust. "You might as well get used to the fact that we CIC men aren't a polite bunch!"

The Headquarters was quiet on this Saturday. The sentry wearing white gloves at the front door saluted the two officers when they walked in, instead of demanding their IDs. The front lobby and the staircase with its gleaming banister were empty, and other than the noises of Army boots thumping on the concrete floor, the building seemed deserted.

Room 227 on the second floor was stifling with the smell of men, summer heat, and dust churning in the light filtering through the window. It was similar to a small classroom, except that only six large desks and matching chairs sat in two rows, three on each side, and in the front hung a blackboard bearing some chalk-marked numbers and letters, and a Sony television sat in one corner.

Lieutenant Lee led Miyong to a desk against the wall and motioned for her to sit in a wooden high-backed chair, seating himself in the armchair on the opposite side, but Major Min walked to the window and opened it. The noise of the traffic was loud, accompanied by honks of horns. Turning to face them, Min took out a cigarette from his coat pocket, lit it, and smoked.

Lee produced a square letter-envelope from his desk drawer and handed it to Miyong. "Major Min received this from your friend Shin Yonghee," he said, using Jongmi's new name. "Read it, please."

Miyong took it, noticing a slight tremor of her hands. It was definitely Jongmi's handwriting: she always wrote neatly, each line perfectly spaced and aligned. Miyong was uneasy. Jongmi had given her so many headaches before. What was she up to now? Opening it, she read:

Skipping greetings... Mr. Ho and I are finally going. Meet us on Tuesday SEPTEMBER 24th at 5 p.m. at the same place. Hope you can make it. We'll talk then. Don't tell anyone about it, especially you-know-who. Jongmi.

"How did you get this, Major Min?" she asked.

"Shin Yonghee called last week, asking for you," he said. "I knew she'd call, so I told Sunhee to pay attention. You remember Sunhee, don't you? She has taken your place. She talks much like you; her voice is soft, and she has patience like you do."

"Jongmi doesn't know I moved," Miyong said defensively. "I haven't spoken to her since in June. What did Jongmi say? Did Sunhee tell you?"

"Sunhee said that Shin Yonghee only wanted to find out if you were still working there. When Sunhee said, 'Of course I am. Did you think I'd get fired?' Yonghee quickly ended the conversation, saying she'd write to you. Then, I found this letter on my desk yesterday."

It was a convincing story, Miyong thought. Jongmi never liked long phone conversations. She had a chronic fear that the line was bugged and every word she uttered would haunt her later. Out of fear, she might have believed that the woman on the other end of the line was Miyong herself. "You mean, this letter has something to do with why you brought me here?"

Major Min closed the window. He joined Lee and Miyong, seating himself in an armchair across the aisle.

In the next thirty minutes, Miyong learned from both officers why they had brought her here on a Saturday. The CIC had been struggling for more than a month with a highly classified national emergency: the sudden disappearance of Prince Koo, the nephew of Korea's last emperor, Emperor Sunjong. After confirming that the prince was in a North Korean detention camp, CIC had been looking for someone who could help them bring Prince Koo back to the South — someone they could trust, someone who had not been exposed to the North Korean Intelligence Network. Then Jongmi's note found Major Min's desk.

"We need your help, Miyong." Min said.

"You can't be serious, sir!" she said. "You know I have no experience in such work. I'm not even finished with training."

Major Min picked up Jongmi's note from the desk, and said, "This is one reason we chose you, Miyong, among other things. This is our ticket to the North, to the prince, and we want to take advantage of it. Are you with us?"

"Let me explain why Major Min and I got involved in this case," Lee said. Using some military vocabulary unfamiliar to her, he explained that he had accidentally opened an envelope addressed to his boss who was in Vietnam to be with his injured son, and learning what was in the envelope, he sought Min's advice on what to do. "I couldn't let others see it," Lee said. "It would endanger the prince's life and we might never see him again. After investigation, we had some clues as to what might have happened to him."

Lee said that after the prince's American wife returned to the States weeks earlier, Prince Koo had too much time on his hands after his daily visit to his father at Seoul University Hospital. To kill his boredom, he often snuck out of his residence at the old palace and walked next door, to the main palace, which was now open to the public. He would spend hours there, striding in the spacious park adorned with fish ponds, old gazebos, and the statues of warriors and kings.

Miyong had read about Price Koo in the spring when he and his pretty golden-haired American wife arrived in Seoul to visit his ailing father, who had recently regained his Korean citizenship, abandoning his identity as a Japanese citizen after sixty long years. Every newspaper nationwide had printed a long article recounting the final day of the Yi Dynasty in the fall of 1905, the day a battalion of armed Japanese soldiers marched into the royal palace and forced the king to allow the Japanese military full use of the land without restrictions, killing hundreds of court employees. Miyong had been saddened by the Yi Dynasty's tragic end that led the prince and his two dozen siblings to a long sorrowful life as Japanese citizens.

"This is Prince Koo's photo," Lee said, handing her a yellowed black and white picture. In it, a scrawny man in his early thirties wearing a mud-colored quilted coat was staring at her, standing in front of what seemed like a battered tool shed. Though he looked more like a beggar she had often seen on the street, his facial features were those of the Prince Koo she had seen in the newspapers. Why did they kidnap the prince, instead of a rich businessman? In reality, it was as though she were watching the old dynasty's tragic end with her own eyes.

As if encouraged by her silence, Major Min moved to the blackboard, picked up a piece of chalk from the chalk tray, and explained the plan. A few names of men and the names of places were scribbled quickly, and a few lines were drawn between them. He talked fast.

"You're going with Shin Yonghee and Ho Suknam to the North by boat, and will stay in a small village named Yonghwa-gun three nights, where you'll meet with your parents."

"My parents, sir? So they're actually alive! How are they?"

"We'll get to that," he said, agitated. "Let me finish first. On the fourth day, a day before the National Workman's Annual Conference at Kim Il-sung Stadium in Pyongyang, our agent 'Red Snake' will snatch you from Ho Suknam and his girlfriend, and hand you over to our friend Lee *Bujang* in Camp 14, in Kaechun." He circled the word Kaechun with the chalk. "We don't want Ho to expose you to the Communist assembly, so we want Red Snake to get you out of Ho's hands at any cost on that Thursday. At Camp 14, you'll be known as Lee Soonok, a runaway inmate caught by the Chinese guards while attempting to enter China through the swampy end of the Yalu River for the third time. The rest of your stay in the North should be arranged after you get there. Lee is your local director."

Major Min then talked about a Catholic priest named Father Sohn who'd actually help the prince escape the camp and get out of North Korea, adding that, over the past few years, Sohn had helped nearly 200 North Koreans escape to the South, through China. "If you can hand the prince over to Father Sohn, your job is done. He has done this many times."

It seemed easy enough, Miyong thought. "How can I communicate with the prince, assuming that I get there safely? I thought he speaks only Japanese and English."

"He does speak some Korean, maybe like a four-year-old child. You can't have a long conversation with him; only short ones." He then looked at her, his forehead pinched. "I thought you spoke and understood English. You wrote on your application that English is your second language."

Miyong blushed: she felt as though she was caught while lying. "I do speak some, mostly from what I learned in the orphanage. But Prince Koo is an American citizen. That's a different story."

"Well, if you grew up around American missionaries, you shouldn't have any problem communicating with the prince."

"I'm not sure, Major Min."

"Worrying doesn't help," he said, in a businesslike manner. "If you don't have other questions, I'll show you some slides."

He's going too fast! she thought. "Why did you choose me when you have so many others to choose from?" she asked. "I mean...I don't know if I can handle it. I've been in the espionage school only a few weeks."

"We're not sending you to a desert to die, my friend," he said mercilessly, "if that's what you're worried about. We'll be working with you until you return." Abruptly turning to Lee, he told him to show the slides. "I'm taking a short break," Min said, and left the room, probably to smoke.

Lee smiled at her uncomfortably, obviously feeling sorry for her. "It's a scary thing, going to the North. But think of it this way: we've sent thousands to the North last year alone, and 99% came back without a scratch on them. And also, Major Min wouldn't send you there unless he felt that it was a safe mission. Know what I mean?"

"I don't, sir."

He stifled a smile. "He has talked to me so much about you: how courageous you were when you reported the commandoes you saw on the mountain, how hard you worked when you were his secretary, and so forth. He has absolute confidence in you! May I go on?"

Miyong shook her head. She didn't need to listen. They were sending her to the North, the forbidden place, talking as though it were an honor for her. "Show me the slides," she said.

Lee turned a switch on the machine on his desk, and an image of an old fishing boat with a white flag at the stern appeared on the television screen. "Probably Ho Suknam will use this vessel to take you to the North," Lee began. "It resembles the Japanese fishing vessels that steal crabs and squid from our waters, so it's safe for him to make it look like he is another thief. The Coast Guard will ignore it because there are so many boats like that." Skipping a few slides of the countryside with shacks, parks with giant-size Kim Il-sung statues, and a wide, empty highway, he produced the photo of three men wearing Mao-style uniforms with dozens of buttons on the front. "These three are the guards in Camp 14, where you'll be going. Look at the gentleman in the middle: he's our man, Lee *Bujang*. I want you to look at him carefully, because you'll be working with him, in Camp 14."

Lee *Bujang* wore dark-rimmed glasses and was significantly better- looking than the other two, who seemed uneducated, more like common peasants, except for their uniforms.

"Lee *Bujang* has been working with us for many years now," said the lieutenant. "He's originally from the South."

"Why is he in the North, then?" Miyong asked.

"That's the tragedy of being a Korean at the wrong time, I suppose," he said vaguely, not answering her question. "There're thousands of men in the North who're originally from the South. Actually I am from the

North, too; our family lived in Sokcho, while my father was in Seoul. And you…You too are from the North."

"Yes."

He produced another image on the screen, the image of men, women, and children working on a vast field. "These are people in Camp 14… All labor camps are similar. They have a compound for families, another for single men, still another for single women…"

The door opened, and Major Min returned with a tall frost-covered bottle and some plastic cups. "I brought some cold barley tea," he said. "Let's take a short break."

While the two men sat comfortably in their chairs and began to drink, Miyong was worried. *How could I be a spy and bring the prince back from the North Korean labor camp?* It was like a fairy tale. In a fairy tale, everything was possible. A prince could turn into a frog by a curse from a mean witch, and turn back into human by the sweet kiss of a girl. If this were a fairy tale, she'd turn into a snake and slither away without the men noticing her.

Major Min asked the lieutenant, "Did you show her the photo of the old man who knows her father?"

"My father?" Miyong sat erect. "Who knows my father?"

"I guess you didn't," Min said to Lee.

"Not yet."

"Show her," Min ordered.

"Are you sure…"

"Why not?"

"I thought…"

"That's okay. Knowing is better…"

What are they talking about?

The lieutenant pressed on a button on the projector and a humming noise filled the air.

An old Korean man with impressive whiskers appeared on the screen.

Major Min said, "This gentleman is the village elder in Yonghwa-gun, where you'll be staying. This man knows your father and will arrange a meeting for you to see him."

"I'm confused. You said only minutes ago that I would see both of my parents, but now you talk only about my father. What's going on, sir? Isn't my mother with my father?"

Major Min looked uncomfortable, like a child that had accidentally spilled a glass of water and couldn't decide whether he should cry or laugh about it. He looked at the lieutenant as if asking for help.

"You might as well tell her the whole thing, sir," said the lieutenant.

"What whole thing?" Miyong asked.

Major Min touched his chin. "I'm afraid we have some bad news for you."

"Bad news? Please tell me."

"First, your father is in a special camp near Yonghwa-gun for elderly people with physical limitations. Unfortunately, we know nothing about your mother at this point, other than the fact that they're not together. It's not uncommon for married couples in the North not to live together. Maybe it has something to do with the fact that your father lost his sight."

"You mean he's blind?"

Min's expression turned cold. "I didn't see him with my own eyes, so I can't tell you much. What we know is from what Lee *Bujang* wired to us. The best thing to do for you is to wait until you see him for yourself."

"When did you find out?"

"Some time after you met with Ho. We did our own investigations to see what Ho had in mind when he met with you. It's our job."

Miyong could not look at another slide. She had no more questions, either. She wished she could talk to her brother about this madness.

"If you help us bring Prince Koo back," Min said in a businesslike tone of voice, "I'll have my men bring your parents here to the South and help them settle in a town of their choice. It can be done, trust me. And nowadays, blindness is not a big problem as it used to be. Did you know that our eye surgeons can restore sight to the blind? Last year alone, our doctors' team at Seoul University restored sight to more than 200 blind people…"

She could listen no more. *Oppa, Father is blind!*

Chapter Thirteen

THE DAY BEFORE HER departure to the North, Miyong moved back to Hope Community at Min's request. "In case Jongmi has a last-minute message for you," he had said on the phone, "it'd be better if you were here to answer it." Miyong had agreed. It was an opportunity for her to see her old friends as well as to see the ocean again, which she had missed so much. As she climbed the staircase leading to Major Min's office that morning, it seemed that an eternity had passed since she left this place. She knocked on the door three times, and when she heard his usual "Come in," she walked in.

"Glad to see you," Min said from behind the desk and then, rising, he walked toward her.

"Good to be back, sir." She bowed.

He shook her hand. "Come and have a seat."

Looking around, she thought nothing had changed. The room was the same: the smell of the cigarette permeating the air, and the window full of the ocean view, the blue water dancing and the seagulls gliding in the sky. Here in this office, she had heard lectures on the New Country Building project, taken dictation of nearly a hundred letters for him, and made coffee every morning — sometimes after lunch, too.

"You look well," Min said, a faint smile on his determined lips.

"Thank you, sir."

"The reason I wanted to see you before your departure to the North is because I wanted to update you on Ho Suknam and Shin Yonghee, so that you know what's been going on."

"Yes, sir."

"They've been sighted on remote areas of the shore a few times, one day here, and another day there, but we told our agents not to trail them, just to observe them. We didn't want to lose them, of course. So, when you're with them tomorrow, act casual. You're going with them to see your parents. That's all you want them to know, understand?

"Yes. But does Ho know about my father being blind and alone? I don't want to say anything unnecessary."

"I don't think so. Otherwise he might have said something to you. Anyway, all you have to know is that he's doing a big favor by taking you to your parents, understand? Don't forget to thank him."

"I will, sir."

"All is arranged; our Coast Guard might stop the boat for a routine check, but nothing will happen, and don't worry about anything. Any question on that?"

"No, sir."

He picked up a blue pouch the size of a pocketbook from his desk and handed it to her. "Open it."

The bag was made of thick, rubbery material and was heavy. Opening it, she saw a small transistor, a tiny handgun, a bottle of multiple vitamins, and two stuffed envelopes — one white and the other blue. She looked at Min for an explanation.

"That transistor can also take pictures like a camera. Using the earpiece, you can hear the KBS news. It looks like cheap transistors common in the North, so no one will be suspicious when they see you carrying it around. See the gun?"

"Yes."

"That's for an emergency. I hope you don't have to use it, but when you smuggle the prince out of the camp, for instance, you might need it, just in case… The good thing about that gun is that it doesn't make any noise when fired, and it's very light."

Miyong swallowed. Light and tiny, it felt like a toy gun in her hand, but it could kill.

"The bottle contains special vitamins," Major Min explained. "Two a day will help you maintain your metabolism, in case you have to skip a meal or two."

"Thank you, sir. But…what are these?" Miyong pulled out two pen-shaped sticks.

"They're special markers. Only those with special infrared lenses can see the markings they make, and all our agents own the glasses made of those lenses. In a simple explanation, it's similar to the lens that captures the images of human bone structure but ignores anything else — skin, organs, and water."

"Amazing!"

"Yes, indeed! We should all be proud of our own scientific team at Seoul University. They discovered it for the military, for espionage purposes. It only works on wood, metal, stone, and fabrics, but not on paper or plastic. Please remember it. Those markers are identical — just in case you lose one, you'll have another."

"Does it work at night, too?"

"Good question. Under normal daylight, it turns luminous green, but in the dark it looks red. It's a marvelous tool you can carry around to leave messages, without worrying about others reading them."

"And these two envelopes?" Miyong lifted them both.

"They're money."

"Money, sir?"

"The blue one has North Korean money. Use it for anything, to bribe the locals or to buy things you need. Remember, people are starving in the North, so they'll do anything for you for a few coins. Don't offer too much, though: they might get a hunch that you're not

one of them. Some of our agents never made it home for that reason…
Oh, that white envelope? It has South Korean currency."

"Why do I need South Korean money, sir?"

Major Min looked away. "Just take it," he said, his hand fumbling
through some papers on the desk as if he were looking for something.

"I don't understand, sir."

"It's your salary while you're in the North, and a bit of extra for
your good work. I advise you to deposit it in your bank account for
later."

"I don't know what to say, sir."

He finally looked at her and smiled.

"When you come back, will you work for me again?"

"Of course. I'll be more than happy to."

"Well then, it's settled. I'm sure you have a lot to do before
tomorrow."

"Thank you. I have something to ask you."

"Go on!"

"If my brother writes to me, who'll keep his letters until I get
back?"

"I've thought about that too, Miyong. I'll tell Sunhee to keep an eye
on them. When you come back, they'll be waiting for you here."

Unexpectedly he rose, came over, and wrapped his arms around
her shoulders, his cheek gently touching hers. She didn't know how to
react to him. His hands on her back were warm.

"I will be waiting, Miyong…" he said, his voice barely audible.
He remained in that embrace for a long moment, and then, suddenly
loosening his arms, he walked back to his desk. Miyong felt warm all
over, as if she had been suntanning all day. She didn't know what to
say. *Thank you, sir? I promise I'll be back?*

Chapter Fourteen

AT FIVE O'CLOCK ON Tuesday September 24th, the dock was particularly crowded with workers shuttling crates and large boxes back and forth. With a tote bag in her hand, Miyong waited for Jongmi and Ho in front of Choi's Noodle Soup restaurant, but they were nowhere to be found. The Japanese boat she had seen in the slides wasn't there either. *Did something happen to them? Did they cancel the plan?*

A small beggar boy, about eight or nine years old, showed up, thrusting his hand before her like a tax collector. "Give me a coin, Ajima [auntie]!"

"I have no money," she said, her eyes looking for Jongmi and Ho and their boat.

"Fine. I'm not going to give you the note, then!"

She looked down at him. He was smiling now. "What note?"

"A tall and handsome *Ajushi* [uncle] over there told me to give this to you." He opened his palm holding a folded white paper, and then closed it quickly. "He said I shouldn't let anybody see it. He gave me a coin, too!"

Miyong doubted that it was for her. It could be a love letter from a heartbroken soul confusing her with his secret love. Still, she couldn't let the boy keep the note. Reaching into her purse, she took out a coin and handed it to the boy.

"Only a quarter?" the boy said obnoxiously.

"Okay, here's another. Now give me that note."

"That's better!" he said, as he exchanged the note for the coin. Then he was gone.

She opened it: It was Jongmi's handwriting.

We're waiting behind the docking area to avoid you-know-who. As soon as you pass the Pacific Seafood Trading Company on your left you'll see an old Japanese-style fishing boat with a picture of a carp on both sides. See you! Jongmi.

Miyong checked around to see if anyone were watching her. The area was still busy—men were still shuttling crates back and forth, and peddlers with trays of goodies were still pestering passengers waiting for their boats. A few old men were merely killing time, their hands locked behind them, walking aimlessly about.

Miyong headed toward the Pacific Seafood Trading Company. Within five minutes, she spotted the boat. Standing on the wooden vessel and shading their eyes with their hands against the afternoon sun, Jongmi and Ho Suknam appeared to be looking for her. In his light gray suit and the typical Japanese wooden sandals, Ho had camouflaged himself as a Japanese businessman who frequented the area, but Jongmi, wearing a cheap yellow cotton dress and a matching hairpiece, was a typical Korean vendor heading for an evening market.

Miyong ran to them. Without a word, Jongmi helped Miyong board the boat and led her to the middle bench, and Ho Suknam quickly maneuvered the vessel away from the densely crowded dock and then steered it to the open sea. The sea was calm today, but whenever a speedboat passed by, tall waves danced on the surface, sending cool mist in their direction.

"Here we are again!" Jongmi said finally, seating herself next to Miyong on the middle bench.

Miyong smiled. Words seemed powerless at a time like this. It felt as though years had passed since she had last seen them both at that strange place in the middle of rock formations. *You'd never believe what I have gone through because of you!* Miyong thought.

"Are you excited about the trip?" Jongmi asked.

"Are you kidding?" Miyong said. "I couldn't sleep last night. I'm so excited."

"Tell me, were you gone for a while?" Jongmi asked.

"No. Why do you ask?"

"Because I called you two or three times before we finally connected. I was worried that you got in trouble for meeting with us in June."

"Trouble from whom?"

"The CIC pigs, who else? I'm glad if they left you alone."

Ho turned to Jongmi. "Why can't you keep your mouth shut?" he said and leered.

"Don't tell me what to do!" Jongmi snapped.

Ho gave Jongmi a long glance, but said nothing.

Jongmi waited until Ho turned back to the steering wheel to continue, this time in a softer voice. "The patrol boat kept showing up every day, and he blew the place up with dynamite. And ever since, we've moved around like gypsies—a couple of nights in his clubhouse, another few nights in a warehouse by the train station, another few in a motel...I hated it. We thought we would never find you again."

Ho turned again. "Miss Hahn, I heard that your brother left for Vietnam. Is it true?"

"How did you know, sir?"

"Didn't I tell you I have connections in the South?" he said and grinned.

What else does he know about me or my brother?

"How do you feel about it?" said Ho, probably disappointed that she didn't volunteer her anger toward the South Korean government.

"How do you think I feel?"

"If you care to know what I think, your president deserves to be shot and hanged in the town square for everyone to see! He's selling his countrymen for stinking American money!" He shook his head.

"Your brother and many others protested the government's man-selling enterprise, but what happened to them? Where are they? They are in Vietnam, offering their necks and blood like sacrificial animals on an altar table."

Miyong remembered the handgun Major Min had given her. It was in the pouch, inside her bag she was holding on her lap. She imagined herself suddenly rising to her feet and ordering, "Raise your hands, Ho Suknam!" and actually pulling the trigger. *I could do it.*

He went on: "In addition to the policemen cracking down on the demonstrators, your president recently ordered the special troopers to shoot demonstrators, didn't he? And the police didn't disclose who the victims were, making more people run to the street and demonstrate— professors, religious leaders, parents, women's organizations, and even high school kids…"

"You talk too much!" Jongmi said, probably sensing that Miyong disliked listening to him.

"Do I?" he said, not looking at Jongmi.

"Yes. Tell her about what we'll do in the next few days instead," Jongmi ordered. "We didn't tell her anything about the trip."

"True," he said. "Let's see…Tomorrow afternoon is secured for you, Miss Hahn, so that you and your parents can spend some time together…"

"Will I actually see them tomorrow?" Miyong said, faking her excitement.

"As far as I know," he said, not turning to her. "And the next day…"

"Please tell me how they are. Are they well?"

"To tell you the truth, all I know is what I heard from the village elder I've been corresponding with. You'll meet the old man as soon as we get there, and he'll tell you everything about your parents."

Miyong had a strong urge to confirm whether or not her parents were together, but she resisted, remembering what Major Min had said about talking too much.

"We have a few options for Thursday, Miss Hahn," Ho said, finally turning to her. "We can go to an ancient temple called 'The Gate to Eternal Freedom' on the Five-Peak Mountain, and then attend the country fair nearby. If we have time, we can go to the Korean War Memorial, about a two-hour drive from the fair. The next day, on Friday, we'll go to Pyongyang for the National Workmen's Annual conference."

Miyong acted surprised. "I thought I was coming to see my parents. I didn't know we had other plans besides…"

Ho avoided her gaze again. Turning back to the steering wheel, he mumbled, "We haven't seen you for a while, so we had no time to communicate about the trip. You don't have to go, if you don't want to, but since you're here, I thought you might enjoy visiting the capital city of your old country."

My old country? Why does this sound so strange?

The boat chugged along painfully slowly.

Part Two

Chapter Fifteen

AM I IN THE *North?* Miyong wasn't sure. This room looked different from the one she had boarded in the night before. *And who're those men wearing mud- colored quilted coats and matching hats?* Two were moving about, and the other four sat on a bench, talking or sleeping. There had been loud clatter and rumbling footsteps on the spiral staircase during the night. *Yes...I remember now.* Jongmi had stood by the cabin door, telling her that they were changing the boat to avoid the checkpoint. Miyong remembered walking on a flat rock glistening like polished granite under the bright moon, shivering in the cold breeze and listening to Jongmi's warnings to be careful. "It's very slippery," she had said. They walked down some squeaky steps to this dark, dank place filled with the smell of tar and burning oil. Yes, Miyong remembered everything now. Jongmi leading, they had found this bench by the wall and sat together, side by side. Miyong had been sleepy, but not sleepy enough to ignore a strange conversation she heard from those men in mud-colored quilted coats she was looking at. They had been talking about a CIC agent she was familiar with. If what she had heard during the night was true, Agent Kim Changyong was in their custody now.

They talked roughly, using the vocabulary men could employ only when no women were around.

Agent Kim Changyong had a bad reputation even in the South for his bloody ambition to capture, torture, and execute North Korean infiltrators. It was hard to believe that he was now in the Communists' hands. Not long ago, the newspapers reported another of Kim's success stories, exposing how "Scorpion X," under Kim's command, had destroyed two dozen armed North Korean infiltrators in a remote fishing village. But it turned out that the men "Scorpion X" had executed were not North Koreans but South Koreans, mostly ignorant peasants. It was unclear how men under Kim Changyong could make such a grave mistake, but the peasants were dragged to a remote shore, forced to wear North Korean guerrilla uniforms and kneel on the sand, and were shot — all two dozen innocent civilians. In a way, Miyong was glad that Kim Changyong would no longer torture and murder innocent South Koreans, only to get recognitions. He was the enemy of both sides. How could a man be so cruel to his own kind?

Jongmi whimpered. Turning, Miyong saw Jongmi still asleep, her lips slightly parted, her arms hugging her knees drawn to her, and head against the wall, two feet below Kim Il-sung's portrait. If the boat caught the wind and rocked, the picture would surely land on her friend's head.

Miyong shook Jongmi's arm. "Where's Mr. Ho?" she asked.

"I don't know," Jongmi mumbled sleepily. "You didn't see him?"

"No. I barely remember getting onto this boat."

"He was with some guys I don't know, but he said that he'll join us when we land."

About twenty minutes later the boat began to lose its speed, and after a few minutes of puttering and spattering, it pulled into a dock. All the men were on their feet, and began to move about.

Miyong and Jongmi followed other passengers to the deck. It was windy. *The Northern wind*, she thought.

A thin layer of fog had blanketed everywhere—the surrounding mountains, the long piers hanging over the water, and a dozen fishing boats strewn about the beach. The scene was no different from what she had been accustomed to on Kanghwa Island, but the wind was ferocious, whistling and pinching her skin.

She turned to face the South and she could feel the wind whipping her back like thin bamboo sticks. She was cold. Her hair danced wildly and she could feel the goosebumps rising on her arms.

It was a strange feeling, standing here on the deck and taking the beating of the wind, while the scenery before her was not much different than what she had seen on Kanghwa Island.

"There you are," Ho Suknam said, suddenly appearing next to her, a black leather bag in his hand. Wearing a greenish Mao-style uniform with matching pants and a cap with a Red star, he was a Red Army officer. "We're getting off here, *Dongmu*," he said, calling her "Comrade" for the first time.

"I'm ready!"

"Good!"

Jongmi stood behind Ho, looking tired, with dark circles under her half-open eyes. "Are we getting off now?"

"Yes, babe," Ho said. "Are you ready?"

"Of course I am."

The men in trench coats came out and headed to the ramp, and they followed them to the boarding dock. Ho headed directly to the parking lot, where a few pickups and cars were parked.

A man in a gray uniform next to a sleek black sedan noticed Ho and bent his head in greeting. Ho waved, walking faster. "Good to see you, Yu *Dongmu*," Ho said, as he shook Yu's hand. "Have you been waiting long?"

"Not at all, Comrade. How was your trip?"

"A pleasant one. No storms, no headaches." Ho introduced Jongmi and Miyong to Yu.

"Welcome, Comrades!"

"Good meeting with you, *Dongmu*!" Jongmi chirped.

Miyong nodded to Yu.

They got in, and the sedan left the beach area. Before long, they were on a straight four-lane highway lined with tall poplars. This scene was quite different from what she had seen in the South. In the South, the highways were busy with all sorts of vehicles — semi trucks, pickup trucks, construction vehicles, passenger cars, trailers, buses — but on this highway, their sedan was a solo runner. Occasionally, men in loosely fitting Korean outfits with huge knapsacks on their backs and women balancing bundles larger than themselves walked along the road, but as soon as they saw the sedan, they stopped walking and lowered their heads. It felt strange for Miyong to see people bowing in her direction.

The signs of severe poverty were everywhere. One area was completely bare of trees and bushes, but cornstalks, rows of soybeans, and cabbages were growing in terraced land. The surrounding straw-thatched homes reminded her of chicken coops or barns in the Southern countryside.

In half an hour, the sedan passed through a tiny village whose entrance was marked with two totem poles, one in the form of a female god with an enormous bosom, and the other an armored warrior holding an oversized sword. After another five minutes on a dusty narrow road, they entered a village with identical authentic Korean-style homes. The car stopped in front of a home with a heavy wooden door decorated with a metal door knocker in the shape of a tiger's head.

They got out of the car. A brown dog leashed to a rusted metal post next to the gate barked and growled, jumping and twisting its body, showing all of its teeth.

"Calm down!" Comrade Yu ordered, and the dog immediately sat, without another bark, sweeping the dirt with its bushy tail. The chauffeur walked up to the door and banged on the knocker three times. Muffled footsteps approached, before the door swung open.

An old man wearing a traditional Korean ash-blue vest over white baggy trousers and a matching tunic greeted everyone with a solemn nod. "Kwon Sang-hyun here," he said, in a low, dignified voice. "Welcome to my humble home!"

"Hello, Kwon *Dongmu*!" Ho said, grabbing the old man's wrinkled hand with both of his and shaking it.

Miyong recognized the old man: his picture had been on one of the slides she had watched at CIC headquarters. This was the man who was supposed to know her father. She looked at him carefully, hoping he'd say something to her, but he only said to the group, "Come in, come in!" motioning with his hand.

Ho approached the old man and whispered.

Miyong overheard the old man saying, "Yes, he's here!" Her heart fluttered.

The courtyard was decorated with dwarf red maples and cypresses, a fish pond bordered with a narrow flowerbed, and a long line of round stepping stones leading to the living quarters. The front room was elegantly decorated with wall hangings and paintings, like many homes in the South. One of the scrolls read, *"Seeing once is better than hearing a hundred times."*

The old man directed everyone to sit on the cushions surrounding a short-legged black lacquered table. When he saw Miyong standing, he said, "Lunch will be served shortly. Please take a seat."

"I think my father is waiting for me."

"I know, but wouldn't you like to have lunch here, with everyone, before you see him?"

"No. Please take me to my father."

"Follow me, then." He excused himself from the guests and led her out of the room. "I'd better explain before you see him, Comrade," he said as they walked on the squeaky hardwood floor side by side. "You see, your father has had some misfortunes and is now blind. He'll tell you more when you see him."

"Really?" Miyong faked her astonishment. "No one told me that!"

He nodded at her solemnly, as he stopped in front of a twin screen panel. "Go in. He's waiting for you." He then said louder, "Hahn *Dongmu*, the guest you've been waiting for is here. I'll leave you two alone, all right? Enjoy your visit!"

"Thank you, Kwon *Dongmu*. We'll talk later," an old man's coarse voice replied from behind the screen panel.

Miyong slid the screen panels open and entered. On a gray square cushion against the opposite wall sat an old man, facing her. He wore a Mao-style quilted coat and matching trousers. His legs were crossed like those of Buddha in pictures. *Father...?* Her father was only forty-six, but this man could be easily sixty, his cheeks hollow under the solid dark glasses, which only the blind wore. Her eyes filling, she didn't know whether she should meet him or run away.

"*Agha* [Little Girl], are you here?" he asked cautiously, tilting his head as if trying to see her. He had always called her "*Agha*" and hearing that word again brought tears to her eyes. She bit her lips.

"*Abuji* [Father], I'm here," she said, and bending her knees, she sank to the floor and bowed to him until her forehead touched the floor. She knew he couldn't see her, but did it matter? He was her father, and she his Little Girl. Rising to her feet, she bowed two more times, just the way her mother had taught her to do when she was a child.

He didn't stir, as if trying to decide how to cross the invisible boundaries that had separated them all these years-—the boundaries of time, space, and what's called "ideology." In the sunlight filtering through the window next to him, the scars around his sunglasses and on both cheeks resembled the texture of a walnut shell.

He extended his trembling hand toward her, as if asking her to take it. "You've come! My little girl is here to see me!" His voice quivered.

Miyong grabbed his hand and the next thing she knew, she was in his bony arms, sobbing. The familiar smell of his hairstyling oil was still about him. She was indeed his Little Girl he used to toss into the air and catch, like a ball.

Her father too was crying and talking at the same time. "You're here, *Agha*! I didn't believe Comrade Kwon when he dropped in and told me that you were coming. But it actually happened. There was not a single day I didn't think of you two children..." He sobbed, holding her tighter.

"Father, we missed you so much, *Oppa* and I... We waited for you and *Omma* for so long. Whenever we were on the street, we looked for you..."

"It wasn't possible, *Agha*...the secret policemen were always sniffing around us after our neighbors vanished with you two. So many people were arrested, for the simple reason that their relatives left the North..."

It was strange, she thought, crying with her father in a place like this. It was like the day she had last seen him as a child, that freezing winter day when he placed her and her brother in their neighbors' hands. She wished her brother were here with them. But he was thousands of miles away, in a strange place called Vietnam, fighting for strangers... Just imagining him and her father reuniting, hugging and crying, like she was now, brought more tears, and she sobbed uncontrollably. It didn't seem that she was actually with her father: it seemed more like she was witnessing someone else's tearful reunion. At the same time, it seemed they had never been apart. He still wore the same men's hairstyling oil, and she was still his little girl crying in his arms for comfort. Beyond that, nothing mattered.

"Talk to me, *Agha*," he urged in his congested voice, loosening his embrace. "Why didn't your brother come with you?"

"He couldn't, because of school," she lied. "He asked me to send you his love." How could she tell him that his only son was fighting in Vietnam?

"Is he all right? I mean, is he healthy?"

"Yes, Father. You should be proud of him. He's supporting himself through a four-year-college by tutoring two elementary school kids."

"*Ummmm,*" he said. "Then, what I heard on the radio wasn't true."

"What did you hear, Father?"

"They said that the South Korean president is selling young men as mercenaries to the international market, and tens of thousands are already fighting in Vietnam."

Miyong swallowed. "Some went voluntarily. But as I said, *Oppa* is home, studying to be an economist."

"Economist, eh?"

"Yes. He has a good future, Father."

"I'm glad," he said, touching his fast-thinning gray hair. "I've been having terrible dreams about him lately. I must be getting old."

"What were your dreams about?"

"In one dream, he was on the train, going somewhere, but I couldn't get to him. I called out, 'Jinwoo-ya, let me come with you,' but he didn't hear me. I was panicky, trying to get to him… And in another dream, I saw him lying on a railroad track and I was worried that the train would run over him. Again, I kept calling him, but he couldn't hear me. Why do I dream such awful dreams?"

Miyong was uncomfortable. *Who can truly understand one's dream?* "I don't know, Father. You might be still hurting for sending us to the South, but as I said, *Oppa* is fine. Tell me, why are you blind, Father? And why isn't *Omma* with you?"

Min had informed her of his blindness and that her parents weren't together, but she wanted to hear it from her father.

He drew a big sigh. "War is hard for everyone, but it's harder for women."

"What do you mean?"

"How can I tell you all that happened to your mother and other women in our commune during the war, in a way you can understand? While the Yankee troops crossed the 38th Parallel and were advancing to Pyongyang in late October, 1950, Great Leader released all prisoners from the city jails and labor camps, so that the enemy wouldn't use them as their slaves. But where can these criminals go when the town is occupied by the enemy? No food distribution centers or homeless shelters were opened anywhere, and bombs were dropping. They went around the town, hiding during the day, showing up in residential areas at night, to find food and shelter. It was a time when most of the men were away, fighting somewhere, leaving their wives and children behind. The rest is easy to imagine, isn't it? One day an old woman in our commune found a male corpse wrapped in a blanket in a crawl space under the house, and the police were called in. The detectives identified the body as one of the prisoners recently released from the city jail, and conducted a broad investigation. Since there were no eyewitnesses, the interrogators depended solely on rumors. The old woman claimed that she saw your mother coming out of the crawl space with a fire log in her hand before the corpse was found. The policemen took her in for questioning."

Sweat glinting on his forehead, her father stopped to catch his breath and to wipe the perspiration. "As you know," he continued, "your mother was the commune leader at the time, and when the gossip-hungry residents learned of the dead body and your mother's arrest, everyone had something to say. No one actually believed that your mother could commit a murder, yet everyone agreed that your mother had done something to conceal the body. Your mother was locked up. I had no choice but to send you and your brother away. I didn't want you to hear the ferocious gossip about your mother. It was the only thing I could do at the moment."

"Is she still in prison?" Miyong asked.

"She was released five years ago, *Agha*. She's now remarried, and they live in Pyongsong."

"Remarried?"

"Don't judge her," he said in a stern voice. "It's the system. It's not her fault!"

"What system are you talking about, Father?"

"While your mother was serving her eighth year in prison, the Party Headquarters in Pyongyong wrote me a long letter, suggesting that, in order to keep my pristine record with the Party and not to jeopardize my chance for promotion, I should divorce your mother before she was released."

"That's absurd!"

"That's exactly what I said. I was beside myself. I protested to the Central Party in writing, saying that the government had nothing to do with one's marriage, and that a married couple is joined until death parted them. The only thing I received from them was notification a month later, that the divorce was finalized. The next morning I was in Pyongyang, at the Central Party Headquarters on Taedong Street. Do you know what I learned there?"

"What, Father?"

"Your mother consented to the divorce already! The clerk showed me the papers with your mother's signature on them. I lost my temper that day and was arrested. The charges were 'insulting' and 'threatening' a public officer and 'destroying public records.' It took me a while to figure out that your mother might have been forced to do what she had done, probably in exchange for a shorter prison term. You understand the system I'm talking about?"

"I don't! How could they do such a thing?"

"Now, about my blindness…" He stopped, touching the frame of his dark glasses. "It was a stupid accident. We call it 'Baptism in the Leather Tannery,'" he said, and for the first time, he laughed, making a squeaky noise through his throat. "It happens here all the time. In my case, a careless lad dropped a huge bolt of leather into a tub of boiling dye, and it splashed all over. I'm not the only victim. About four others were burned like me. That boy…" He clicked his tongue. "The poor lad was beaten so severely for what happened that he limps now. I feel sorry for him more than I'm sorry for myself."

"Father, your eyesight can be restored," Miyong said.

"What? Blindness is a permanent human condition."

"Not anymore, Father. Please listen to me."

Miyong told him what Min had told her at CIC Headquarters, that restoring eyesight was no big deal in the South. "South Korean surgeons can successfully operate on blind people…"

Her father turned pale. His hand went up to his face and covered his mouth. After a long moment of silence, he suddenly raised his voice and began to talk in a manner as if he were addressing an audience. "Oh, yes — Restoration Camp is godsend to folks like us. Great Leader makes sure that we have enough to eat and good clothes to wear. On his birthday every year, each man gets a new outfit like this." He grabbed his left sleeve with his right hand and shook it. "We even have a game room where we can play chess all day…we also have our hands on small carpentry projects or basket weaving, too…all you have to do is ask."

Miyong mutely watched him. *We're in two different worlds, Father,* she thought. *Who has built this thick, invisible wall between us?*

He went on for a few more seconds and coughed a dry cough. Lowering his voice, he said, "Tell me, *Agha*, why are you here?"

Suddenly her mind went blank. *Why didn't I prepare an answer for such a question?* She lied, "A few South Korean women, including myself, are invited to the National Workmen's Party in Pyongyang this Friday, Father. The two countries have decided to open a dialogue… and our group is the first…"

"Don't lie," he said coldly. His dark glasses glared at her maliciously and she wanted to hide somewhere, anywhere. "In my forty-six years," her father continued, "I have gone through much, but I never expected my daughter to come back to her father's country as a South Korean spy! I could never accept such a reality, even if my eyes are filled with dirt."

"Father, please let me explain …"

"Don't bother, child. I know! I'm blind, but not stupid. I've heard of too many youngsters raised in the South returning home to spy on their parents and relatives. Every year, those sons of dogs blow up bridges, overturn Army trucks, and distribute anti-government flyers to people who can't even read, endangering them. I don't need to tell you more, do I? Do you know what could happen to me if the secret police find out about you visiting me?"

This wasn't in the script, Miyong thought. It was supposed to be a peaceful reunion between a father and daughter after a long separation. What had gone wrong?

"Miyong-ah!" her father called.

"Yes, Father."

"I'll never see you again, so listen to me carefully. Once they label me a traitor, I'm finished. There are camps designed for what they call 'dog-eating dogs,' and that's where they'll send me. It's a place without three daily meals or the comfort of beds. And think about your mother for a moment. She deserves a decent life after years of imprisonment! There are far worse things in life than a country split apart and people losing all contact with their family and friends."

"Father, I never thought our meeting would come to this. I thought…"

"Don't say any more. Just remember one thing: we each have a given fate, no matter where we are. We must accept it. Go back to where you belong and stay there. Goodbye." He rose with much effort, and then, a hand stretched in front of him, he headed toward the door.

"Father, please don't leave yet," Miyong said, crying. "I have so much to tell you. Did you know that *Oppa* and I lived in an orphanage for fourteen years, after Uncle Hong and his wife got arrested for drinking too much?"

He stopped in the middle of the room, his back turned to her.

"It's true, Father. Uncle Hong and his wife couldn't raise us. When we lived in the refugee camp in Seoul, they kept fighting like a dog and a cat. The police was called in…It was terrible, so we ended up in an orphanage…"

"Why are you telling me this?" he asked, still not turning toward her, his voice cold and flat. "You've survived and come back as an enemy spy. Do you want me to feel sorry for you? Do you want me to apologize for your hard life in the South?"

"Of course not! I just thought you might want to know how we survived without you and Mother. Don't you want to hear more?"

"Save it for someone else," he said heartlessly. "I can't regret what I've done. War was going on, and we had to stay alive as best as we could, your mother and I. Considering how many people died during those three years, you and I are lucky. Let's leave it at that." He resumed his walk, and reaching the paper screen door, he opened it roughly and shouted, "Kwon *Dongmu*, please take me home!"

Miyong couldn't let him leave like this. "Father, there's more…I lied about *Oppa*. He's in Vietnam," she said as heartlessly as she could manage.

He froze, his hand still on the door as if he didn't know whether he should believe it or not.

"I didn't want to tell you, because I didn't want you to worry about him."

Chapter Sixteen

RETURNING FROM THE ROAD construction site near the port at five p.m. on a sweltering day, covered with sweat, dust, and dirt, Major Min thought about going to a public bathhouse for a good scrub and a long massage performed by local teenage girls. But he remembered his appointment with Lee at Strictly Dumpling on Jongno Street in Seoul at seven, and settled for a quick shower in his own bathroom. This was his favorite time of the day, when his work ended and he could enjoy his freedom. While drying his hair with a towel, he walked to the stereo sitting on his bookshelf, and turned it on. The air was filled with Mozart's lively *Jupiter Symphony*, and he headed for his corduroy sofa to rest and to enjoy the music. He noticed several letters sitting on his desk but wasn't in the mood to check them. He wasn't on duty. But the letter at the top of the stack had a few unfamiliar stamps. He looked at them closer. They were Vietnamese stamps, and the letter was addressed to Hahn Miyong, his old secretary who was now in the North. He opened it.

Dear Sister,

Today, our group spirit is deflated. It's raining in this cursed jungle, and we're stuck in foxholes. We've been fighting (I mean, killing, with real rifles and grenades) since yesterday, and the rain is spoiling everything. The foxhole, which I share with four other guys, is muddy, and when I move, my boots stick to the glue-like mud, and I feel exposed to an enemy that might attack me from all directions like leopards. Writing to you is the only thing that makes me feel connected to civilization. Get the picture?

We have two local people, a man-woman team, helping us to find snipers. They do everything with us: patrolling, interrogating prisoners, and eating and sleeping, too! Though their English is limited, we can communicate with prisoners through them. Two nights ago we caught four Vietcong in the jungle, and as we escorted them to the camp, one guy exploded himself with a grenade, killing himself and one of our patrolmen nicknamed Cutthroat (he was excellent with his dagger). The thought that "I" could have died gives me the shivers. We should have stripped the Vietcong naked when we caught them, as we had learned in boot camp. Why didn't we? Why did we let them kill one of us? If we had followed the rules, our buddy Cutthroat would be here with us today. I finally learned not to treat the enemy like human beings. "Thou shalt kill!" is my new resolution. The sad reality is that I can do it.

When are you leaving for You-know-where? If you're reading this letter, please send my love to Mother and Father. And if you can, drop me a note. And be careful no matter where you are!

Love,

Your brother.

Major Min folded the letter, put it in a manila envelope, and sealed it with a piece of Scotch tape. He then wrote Miyong on the front of the envelope and dropped it into his bottom desk drawer on the right.

He relaxed in his chair, his feet on the desk. By now, Miyong was preparing for the big day, the day Red Snake would steal her from Ho

Suknam and take her to Camp 14. *How did the meeting with her father go?* he wondered. Yesterday, he had confirmed that Ho Suknam's boat had been spotted by the Coastal Tower's radar, but passed without an incident. All he had to do now was wait to hear from Red Snake.

The road construction was advancing as planned, which he was glad about. Villagers worked vigorously, sometimes spending extra hours to earn extra money. Of course, his presence at the site, working with them in his civilian clothes, seemed to boost their team spirit. In the beginning, they had little trust in the program. Besides, most of the young men didn't know how to work harmoniously with one another and fought almost daily. Some showed up dead drunk, which Min couldn't tolerate. With time, though, they began showing some improvements. He now believed in them. They had been so poor for so long that they were obedient to their given fate, but now they knew they could do hard work with their own hands.

The restaurant Strictly Dumplings, sitting in a narrow alley between two large buildings in the Jongno District, was so small that it contained only a dozen tables. As the name of the restaurant implied, their dumplings were known for taste and quality.

At ten minutes past seven, Strictly Dumplings was half empty. Min found Lt. Lee waiting for him, sitting at the table by the wall under a dim lamplight. Two empty rice wine jugs in front of him and his droopy eyes told Min that Lee had already consumed a considerable amount of alcohol. As soon as Min seated himself, Lee ordered toward the wall, "Bring us another jug. My guest is here!"

"Yes, sir," a young woman's voice resounded from behind the wall.

"Never mind another jug!" Min said loudly, too. "We don't need more drinks."

A girl wearing a light-blue traditional Korean dress rushed in with a jug in her hand and a puzzled look on her wide face. "Did you want more *soju*, sirs?"

"Yes! Leave it!" Lee said.

"No, take it back," Min said, "but bring us dinner. The grilled beef dinner is fine for me."

The girl just stood there, looking at Lt. Lee and then at Min. "What do you want for dinner, sir?" she asked Lee.

"The same thing," Lee blurted out. "Whatever my superior officer wants, I want too, *ha, ha, ha…*"

Bowing quickly, she left.

Min said, "I hope you have something important to tell me. I don't particularly enjoy watching a drunken man."

"Of course, *Hyongnim*," he said, blinking hard to stay awake. "The reason I wanted to talk to you is because Miss Watanabe called. Remember her? She's the secretary to Princess Masako, the prince's mother. She wanted to let me know how the old lady is lamenting these days over her son's disappearance, and asked me why CIC aren't doing anything about it. 'How long must Princess Masako suffer like this, Lieutenant?' she said in a scolding tone of voice. 'The poor lady can't eat, can't sleep, and can't even take care of her husband…' She went on and on. To say it mildly, that Watanabe is a typical Japanese bitch!"

"What did you tell her?"

"The truth, of course. I told her there's nothing to report at this moment and that we're doing all we can to find the prince, so please do us a big favor by not calling."

"Was she okay with it?"

"Of course not. She snarled at me, saying, 'Lieutenant, do you realize who you're talking to? I could report to Princess Masako how rude you are.' So I said, 'I don't know what else I can tell you, ma'am, besides the truth,' and she said, 'I must remind you that I'm calling on behalf of Princess Masako. It's been more than two weeks since her son disappeared, but you haven't done anything, absolutely nothing! You must be ashamed of yourself!' She then hung up on me. Then, to my dismay, Princess Masako herself called."

"What did she want? She can't even speak Korean."

"She kept crying, saying, *Dozo, dozo,* [please, please] and I kept repeating myself, *Sumimasen, sumimasen,* [I'm sorry, I'm sorry]. It was the longest phone conversation I've ever had with anyone. *Hyongnim*, we need to tell her something."

Major Min took a cigarette from his uniform shirt pocket, and Lt. Lee lit it for him. "Somebody has to, I think."

Min said, "There isn't anything to tell her until we hear from Father Sohn, is there? We can't make up stories just to please the old lady. You've done exactly what I'd have, Dongwoo."

"Write a note to Princess Masako then, *Hyongnim*. Even if it's the same thing she heard from me, she'd feel better about getting an official letter from you."

"It's the director's job," Min said. "Not mine!"

"But the director isn't here; he's with his son in Vietnam. Somebody has to do the dirty work."

"Just wait. Sometimes, silence works magic."

"Whatever you say," Lee said. For a moment, they just sat there, Min smoking and Lee watching him smoke. "Oh, there's something else I must tell you," Lee said.

"What?"

"I overheard the director's secretary, Captain Chung, talking at the lunch about the American ambassador, what's his name…?"

"John Porter."

"Yes, Porter. He called to ask about the prince."

"How does he know about the prince?" Min sat erect.

"That's what everyone asked, and Captain Chung said that the ambassador received a call from the prince's wife in California, asking him to find out what happened to her husband. My guess is, when she called the palace, the prince wasn't there and she couldn't talk to anyone, because the prince's mother doesn't speak a word of English. So she called the ambassador to cry about her husband's disappearance. It's getting very complicated, *Hyongnim*!"

"What does the ambassador want us to do?"

"He wants only one thing: to know where the prince is. The secretary said that the ambassador was mad that he wasn't informed about the prince being missing. You know, the prince is an American citizen, so the ambassador feels that it's his responsibility to do something about a missing U.S. citizen in a foreign land, but he wasn't even informed about it."

"How did the secretary respond to him, I wonder?" Min asked.

"Captain Chung told the ambassador that the director would call him when he got back, but the ambassador started to yell. So the captain hung up, because his English isn't good enough to argue with an angry American".

Min laughed. "There isn't anything for anyone, including the ambassador, to do but wait!"

"Exactly."

The food arrived and they began to eat.

Chapter Seventeen

North Korea

THE FIVE-PEAK MOUNTAIN WAS much taller than any mountain Miyong had visited, and here, too, was evidence of Japanese thievery of Korean natural resources. Some areas of the mountain were brown and gray, only rotted stumps and upturned saplings and mounds of bare dirt filling the vast space.

"The Americans bombarded this area during the war," Ho said as they drove up a steep road. "See how empty the field is? Our rangers still find duds around here from time to time."

Miyong thought it was odd that Ho blamed Americans for these bald mountains. In the South, people still hated the Japanese for stealing trees from their mountains and using them to build kamikaze planes, ships, and brothels during the war. She had not been aware that the U.N. troops had bombarded this area. Some other areas were still forest – green, with tall pines.

The Buddhist Temple, overlooking a vast field of crudely built shacks and crop land, wasn't all that impressive in comparison to the temples in the South. Kim Il-sung had banned worship of any gods since he rose to a deity figure after liberation, banishing all clergy and believers to labor camps and destroying every Christian church and Buddhist temple throughout the country. And this temple too was mostly closed off, except the Main Hall known as "Shin-Jun" (God's Chamber), which was in need of repair. The walls and floor were dirty, and even the ceramic woman god glazed in tacky yellow sitting on the altar table, showed no signs of dignity or piety, for the tips of her long earlobes had chipped away.

Miyong felt compassion toward this woman god. If this god could talk, what would she say? That she was doomed in this prison, without any soul seeking her guidance? And that she was broken-hearted, because people were starving to death, not only from lack of food but deprivation of freedom and God's love? On second thought, this was a manmade figure. How could she have feelings? How would she know anything about people? *How silly!* Miyong walked out of the room.

Outside, the sunlight was warm and pleasant. But she couldn't enjoy the warmth, because she suddenly remembered Red Snake. He could lurch out at her from anywhere at any time now. She checked her bag. Seeing that it was still against her side, secured by a shoulder strap, she relaxed. Earlier, before they left the old man's home, Jongmi had asked, "Why are you carrying the bag with you? We're staying here another night, you know."

"It's not heavy."

"It's safe here, if that's what you're worried about."

Miyong had ignored her, and she was glad that the bag was with her.

Looking around, she noticed that most of the tourists around her seemed like North Koreans, except a few Westerners and a few Japanese here and there. Two dark-skinned soldiers passed her, nodding, and she wondered if they too were Communists.

When would Red Snake show up? Was he already here, looking for her? He could be that stocky guy at the far left end of the courtyard, wearing dark sunglasses and a gray suit, a camera dangling from his neck. He looked more like a Middle Easterner, with brown skin. Not knowing that he had an audience, the man studied the roof that was lined with wooden statues of animals, the protectors of the temple, shading his eyes against the sun. A woman wearing a black all-weather coat showed up next to him, and the two walked away, talking.

Two minutes later, another man, shorter and smaller than the earlier one, appeared from the gift shop on the left. He walked toward the stone ledge on the right, which overlooked a peaceful village below. He stood there for a moment and then lifted himself onto the ledge, crossed his legs, and sat still, merging with the countryside landscape.

Miyong hoped that he wouldn't fall asleep and end up in the valley hundreds of feet below.

Jongmi showed up from nowhere, saying, "How did you like the temple?"

"I liked it. I can't say I was impressed."

"Me neither, but the wood carvings in the doors were beautiful."

Ho, the old man Kwon, and the chauffeur joined them. Ho said, "Let's go. If we don't get to the fair in time, the restaurants might be too crowded."

In the car, Ho asked Miyong the same question Jongmi had asked. *How had she liked the temple?*

"I wish more buildings were open. I didn't see much of it." Miyong couldn't say that the temples in the South were better.

"I know what you mean," he said, eager to talk. "The Central Party is divided on the issue of restoring historic treasures such as that temple. Lack of money is one thing, but the older members are afraid to say anything against Great Leader, like subjects of a warlord in the olden days. But men like us with younger blood hate to see such ancient treasures sit and collect dust and grime, so we urged Great Leader to do something about it."

"Are you able to discuss such issues openly with Great Leader?" Miyong asked.

"Openly...?" Ho shook his head. "If you're asking whether we can argue about it at the assembly, the answer is no. But one of the party members wrote an article about it in *Pyongyang Daily*, and Great Leader responded to it positively. It might take a while, but someday those ancient temples might get a facelift."

The scenery changed, and rows upon rows of crudely built booths made of khaki canvas showed up on the side of the road. "This is it," Comrade Yu said, pointing at an arched gate with "Country Fair" written on it. When they got out of the car in the parking lot adjacent to the entrance, the air was filled with the shouts of vendors advertising their merchandise and the aromas from sizzling grills.

As they walked through the aisles, Miyong saw a woman pan-frying what looked like beef strips and sliced vegetables on a flat cooking surface. Miyong's mouth watered. She wished she could sink her teeth into those beef strips seasoned in a mixture of soy sauce, ginger, and sugar and cooked until the edges were crispy. But looking closely at the strips, she decided that they looked different. Instead of turning dark brown, they were turning pinkish red. "Is this beef?" she asked the vendor.

The woman gave her a crooked smile through her decaying front teeth. "Beef, *Dongmu*? Where can we get beef?"

Miyong quickly reminded herself that she was in the North. "That's why I'm asking, *Dongmu*. I haven't seen beef for a long time."

"Who has?" she said. "Beef is a rare commodity since the last flood, when we lost 30,000 hectares of farmland. This is opossum meat, *Dongmu*. The animal looks ugly, but the meat tastes good. You want to try one?"

Finding a chance to get away, Miyong said, "No thank you! I prefer dog meat over opossum meat."

"Good luck finding it!" the woman said.

Miyong found the rest of her group watching the men and women making pots and plates with wet clay behind potters' wheels, and joined them. Several painters were near them, capturing the surrounding scenes on their canvases. But Jongmi quickly got bored.

"I have no artist's blood in my veins," she said. "I'm looking around."

Miyong saw Jongmi stop at the booth selling women's jewelry

made of seashells and bleached animal bones, and she too browsed alone. Across the narrow aisle, an old man was sitting like Buddha on a straw mat, his legs crossed, and weaving a basket and chanting at the same time, "Baaaskets! Baaaaskets!" A handful of women had gathered there, touching the finished baskets hanging from a short post.

"How long have you been weaving baskets, *Dongmu*?" Miyong asked the old man.

"Since I was six," said the old man, forming dimples in his leathery cheeks. "We've been weavers for several generations."

"Your baskets are beautiful," Miyong said.

"Thank you, *Dongmu*. My grandfather considered basket-making an *art*. His name is recorded in the textbook called *Korean Art History*. He was a proud man, my grandfather. He said to me, 'We basket weavers don't make money, but we're rich in our hearts.' It's true, *Dongmu*; I get much enjoyment out of…"

A sudden blow on her back felled her onto the mat, inches away from the weaver. She screamed. The onlookers vanished quickly. The weaver, dropping his basket, babbled unintelligibly, and to her horror, her bag was slipping away from under her arm. "My bag, my bag!" she cried, but it was too late.

She saw the thief — a teenage boy, no older than sixteen, running away with her bag. He wore a mud-colored shirt and matching pants.

Springing to her feet, Miyong ran after him. A sharp pain stabbed her upper back where the blow had landed, but she couldn't lose the bag! Everything she needed was inside: her mini gun, the camera, the money. Losing it would be like losing her head. She could do nothing without it.

The boy zigzagged through the crowd faster than a dog. She followed him with all the speed she could muster. He turned to his left where two women stood arguing, and she followed him, but as soon as she made another corner, the boy vanished. She was alone in an alley between two mud walls lined with tall trash barrels on both sides.

Carefully she walked along the barrels, checking each one. They were tall and wide, and each of them stank like an outhouse. But she couldn't give up. The thief was here somewhere and she must find him.

A thundering clatter startled her. The boy lurched from behind a trash bin like a flying monkey, knocking over an empty barrel, followed by another man wearing a red headband. They grabbed her elbows from both sides and forced her to walk. She screamed. A big, smelly hand covered her mouth. "*Mmm…*" she heard her own moan.

"Don't make any noise!" one of them said, pinching her elbow. She fought, twisting and squirming and crying out, "Help! Help!" But all she could hear was her own whimpering.

There were footsteps and voices. "Let go of her, or I'll shoot!" a man's voice resounded in the alley.

Suddenly she was free, and she heard feet running away. A hand spun her around. Ho stood there, silently, holding a pistol and looking at her. Comrade Yu and the old man were there too, but Jongmi wasn't there. "My bag," she cried.

"Here!" Comrade Yu said, picking it up from the ground two feet in front of him. He shook the dirt off before he handed it to her.

"Thank you!"

"Are you all right, Hahn *Dongmu*?" Ho asked.

"I think so…"

"Stay close to us, please," Ho said. "We don't want to lose you."

"Sorry, *Dongmu*! They were trying to take me with them. I don't know who they were."

"Probably some hungry kids trying to steal. There are too many!"

Jongmi suddenly showed up. "What happened?" she asked, looking at Miyong and then at Ho.

"It's your fault," Ho said.

"What have I done?"

"If you hadn't made us wait, this wouldn't have happened."

"How sorry I am!" Jongmi said sarcastically.

"Please…" Miyong said. "I was watching a basket weaver when a boy snatched my bag and ran away."

"Didn't I tell you to leave the bag at the house?" Jongmi said.

"What can I say except sorry." She lifted her bag. "See, it's here now."

"Let's go back, shall we?" Ho suggested.

"Already?" Jongmi said. "We didn't even have lunch."

"Lunch can wait, can't it?" said Ho. "Hahn *Dongmu* needs a rest after what she's gone through, and so do we. Tomorrow is a big day!"

"What about the Memorial?" Jongmi asked.

"We can see the Memorial any time," the old man said.

Back in the car, Miyong forced herself to relax, leaning back into the seat. *It could have been worse. At least I have the bag, thanks to Ho.*

The highway was still empty as they drove north, except a few bicyclists and rusted military trucks passing by. After a while, the four-lane highway turned into three lanes, and then two, and trucks and bicyclists began to slow down.

"Road construction again!" Yu muttered, reducing his speed.

Behind the barricades, the construction workers were busy, some digging with shovels, some mixing concrete in a large tub, and a few carrying buckets or planks of wood. As the car moved on, she realized that some workers were teenagers wearing adult army uniforms. In the clouds of dust, a table stood in the middle of nowhere and two boys seemed to be preparing lunch, one of them stirring a steaming cast-iron pot with a wooden spoon, and the other setting the table.

"They're only children," Miyong said.

"Not ordinary kids," Ho said. "They're from correction facilities. They're paying for their crimes."

"You mean they're juvenile convicts?"

"Exactly. They deserve what they do. Work is good for them."

As the sedan passed them, the boys stopped what they were doing and bowed deeply.

Ho nodded to them, smiling.

Miyong was not comfortable being the recipient of their bows, whether they were convicts or not. She wondered whether the South Korean juvenile convicts were forced to do adult work like these youths were doing. She was glad when their car passed the construction area and regained full speed.

Again, she thought of Red Snake. *Why hasn't he shown up yet?* She had forgotten all about him. If she returned to the old man's house, it meant only one thing — she'd have to go to Pyongyang with Ho and Jongmi. *Where will I be tomorrow about this time of the day? If I'm in Pyongyang, who will help Prince Koo to escape? Never mind Prince Koo... What will happen to me? Will I ever go back to the South?*

The driver was muttering, "They've built a new checkpoint here. How about that!"

"A new checkpoint? What do you mean?" Ho asked.

"Look over there. I never saw it before."

"Security gets tighter and tighter all the time," said Ho. "Probably nothing to worry about."

The car slowed again. On the right shoulder of the road, before a wooden stall, stood a guard, signaling the cars to stop and blowing his whistle.

Two cars, both old and rusted, were ahead of them. Miyong pulled her bag tightly against her side and nervously watched the guard speak with the driver of a car a few yards ahead. The driver handed a paper to the guard, and the guard motioned him to go. The next car passed, too, without fuss, and it was now their turn.

The guard with dark eyebrows studied the paper Yu handed to him. Then he lowered his head and counted heads inside the car. "Where are you going, *Dongmu?*" the guard asked Yu.

"Can't you recognize the vehicle, *Dongmu?*" Yu spoke with an air of arrogance.

The guard looked at the hood of car and then the tires. "What about it?"

"Don't tell me you're new at this? This *Dongmu* here," Yu quickly glanced at Ho and turned back to the guard. "He's a member of the Central Party!"

The guard looked at Ho, unimpressed. "Comrades, have you been listening to the radio?" he asked to no one in particular.

"Radio? What're you talking about?" Ho asked.

"National security law was enforced at twelve noon today after the South Korean terrorists bombed a district office building in Pyongyang. All vehicles are subject to inspection."

Yu stammered. "We…we have been on the road since nine."

"Then go home and listen to the six o'clock news," the guard said. His gaze shifted to Miyong's face and lingered. "*Dongmu*, what is in your bag?"

Miyong froze. "It's…my clothes and cosmetics."

The guard's dark eyes narrowed. "Cosmetics, eh?" he said contemptuously. "Thousands of our comrades are starving every day, and you have money to buy cosmetics?"

Miyong realized her stupid mistake. She knew that no women here wore makeup. "It's not mine! It belongs to…" *Another stupid mistake!*

"Pass the bag to me at once!" the guard ordered, extending his long arm into the window, forcing the chauffeur to bend forward.

"I can't!" she cried, hugging the bag.

The guard walked to her side and opened the door. Reaching for the bag, he yanked at it, and the bag fell out of her hands. Miyong watched the guard unzip the bag and prayed, *God, help me!*

"Come with me!" he said, grabbing her elbow and forcing her out of the car. "Move it!" the guard yelled at the driver.

Ho emerged from the passenger seat. "Wait, *Dongmu*. You can't hold her in custody without proper procedure!"

A flicker of hope passed through Miyong. *Please do something, Mr. Ho.*

"*Proper procedure?*" the guard mimicked Ho's voice as he said those words. "Back into the car, or I'll shoot!" The guard placed his free hand on the pistol on his side.

"I can have you arrested if you don't let her go!" Ho said with authority.

A loud rumbling noise intruded. A military truck braked to stop behind their sedan. Two more guards leaped out from the truck and came toward them. "What's going on here?" one of them, the taller of the two, said.

Ho acted as if he were glad to see the new arrivals. "Comrades, check to see that this young guard has proper identification. He behaves inappropriately, searching my car and interrogating my guest."

Instead of turning to the guard holding Miyong, the two men dashed to Ho, and while the short man yanked Ho's elbow, the tall one punched and kicked him, causing him to lose his balance and fall like a tree, on his belly.

Yu shouted, "Get in, Ho *Dongmu*! Let's get the hell out of here!"

Ho didn't move. The two men lifted him to stand, forced him to walk to the car, and threw him onto the passenger's seat through the open door. The sedan lurched forward and drove away, all four wheels screeching, the door to the passenger seat still ajar.

Miyong was scared. To make the situation worse, her captor let her go and returned her handbag back to her. The two men each shook hands with the guard, congratulating him for something Miyong couldn't understand. Then, the shorter man turned to Miyong and said, "Welcome to the North! I'm Red Snake."

Chapter Eighteen

IN THE TRUCK, SITTING between the two men, Red Snake on the driver's seat and the other on her right, Miyong didn't know whether she should cry or laugh. She had never imagined that she would be "snatched" from Ho and land in Red Snake's hands in such a dramatic fashion. *At least I'm in good hands!*

"We've been following you around since nine this morning," Red Snake said. It was clear now that his companion, the man who was sitting next to her, the man who punched and kicked Ho mercilessly moments earlier, was Father Sohn. With a new awareness, she studied his profile. With high cheekbones, jet- black hair, and a determined mouth, this priest could pass as a Communist soldier, she decided.

As if sensing her gaze crawling on the side of his face, the priest coughed into his cupped hands and then chuckled soundlessly, heaving his shoulders. Then, both men laughed aloud.

She laughed, too, without knowing why.

"How do you feel, Miss Hahn?" Red Snake asked.

"I'm not sure… I feel okay, I suppose."

"You look fine after all that drama," he said warmly. "We could have gotten you earlier at that alley at the market, but your company spoiled it. Anyway, you're with us. Let me introduce my friend, Father Sohn. We've been working together for two years."

"Who said I'm your friend?" Father Sohn said, his eyes playful. "You're a spy and I am in the business of saving souls."

"But we work together, Brother. We're doing God's work!"

Father Sohn laughed loudly, but Red Snake didn't. Turning to Miyong, Red Snake said, "Father Sohn here works directly with God. Even the Pope in Rome can't order him around. He came here two years ago, because he heard a call from the Almighty Himself to save His forsaken flock, and ever since, he has been going from one village to another, baptizing, healing the sick, and comforting wounded and broken people. He performed many miracles!"

"That's enough," Father Sohn said ruthlessly. "Miss Hahn needs rest. You talk too much, Brother!"

This suited Miyong just fine. In two or three hours she'd be at Camp 14. Being snatched by Red Snake and Father Sohn from Ho had been stressful, although it was a happy ending. She had never thought that a happy ending could be exhausting, but she knew better now.

"Let me tell you a bit about Lee Soon-ok, the inmate you're replacing," Red Snake said, ignoring Father Sohn's suggestion. "It's important that you know what she was like when she lived at Camp 14. She was about your size and looked demure like yourself, but she was quite feisty. I picked her up at the border and took her to the camp the last time she was caught, and did she put up a fight with me! I was scratched up so badly that I tied her hands up before loading her onto my truck. She kept screaming..."

Father Sohn turned to Red Snake and nodded.

Red Snake stopped talking and reduced the speed.

Father Sohn removed his hat and topcoat quickly and placed them under his seat, exposing a dirty khaki shirt with holes in the sleeves.

"Miss Hahn," Red Snake said in a solemn voice. "We're approaching a checkpoint, a real one this time. I want you to know that you and

Father Sohn are prisoners returning to Camp 14. Did Major Min explain it to you?"

She remembered. "Yes."

"Don't volunteer anything. I'll do all the talking."

"Fine with me."

Father Sohn took out two sets of handcuffs from his pants pockets, handed one to her, and kept one for himself. "Put these around your wrists," he ordered. "They have a magnet at each end, and all you have to do is to make the two ends come together." He then handcuffed himself, to show her how to do it.

The polished metal was cold and heavy against her wrists. Twenty yards ahead of them stood a stall similar to what she had seen earlier. Red Snake stopped the truck right in front of the bony guard, lowered his window, and handed him two yellow papers. "Good day, Comrade," Red Snake said politely. "I have two inmates in my custody."

The guard looked at the papers, one after another. Lowering his head, he looked into the car.

Father Sohn bent his head, as if studying the floor.

Turning to her right, Miyong saw her reflection in the windowpane, next to Father Sohn. In the bright afternoon sunlight, the image stared back at her. *Lee Soonok… You're a feisty little bitch that ran away from the camp twice, each time caught by the Chinese guards. You have records of prostitution and illegal border crossing. What can you tell me about Camp 14?*

"Destination?" the guard asked Red Snake.

"Labor Camp 14."

"Your ID?"

Red Snake produced a card from his uniform shirt pocket and showed it to the guard.

Blowing his whistle, the guard handed the yellow papers back to Red Snake and motioned him to go. The truck lurched forward. When they merged with the highway and regained their earlier speed, Red Snake produced a small radio from the glove compartment, turned it on, and began talking to it in a soft voice.

A road sign that read *Labor Makes Our Nation Greater* passed the window. Several men, each carrying boxes or large bundles atop his wooden frame called a *jige* passed, too. Miyong was tired. It had been a long day. Leaning her head onto the back of the seat, she closed her eyes. The rumbles of the motor beneath her were louder now. Red Snake's voice was diminishing, turning into mere murmur. Jongmi's face appeared in her mind. "Where are you, *Onni?*" she seemed to ask, but before Miyong could answer, her eyelids felt heavy and she drifted away. Then, she was at the orphanage in Seoul, looking out through a window.

Boys are jumping up and down, playing basketball, and the small ones are prancing around, pretending they are horses. Some boys are hanging on the gym set, like monkeys at the zoo. Her brother isn't there, not playing basket balls, not on the gym set. Looking around, she finds him on the ground under the window, only a few feet away from her. He's pulling something black and long from the dirt in the flowerbed. Anything slimy fascinates him, especially snakes. Did he forget the old saying that says, A snake tail can lead you to a dragon's den? "Let it go, Oppa!" she shouts, but her voice doesn't come forward. "Leave it, I said," she screams, and this time, her brother lifts his face to her and smiles as if to say, "Don't worry, kid, I'm okay. It's just a snake."

"It can bite you!" she yells.

Her own voice awakened her. She was still on the pickup, but the seat next to her where Father Sohn had been was empty.

"You were sleeping soundly," Red Snake said when he saw her stirring. "I've been trying to wake you for the last few minutes. We're approaching the *In-min Bowiso* [People's Reeducation Center] 14."

A watchtower overlooking hundreds of gray rectangular buildings on her left caused cold sweat break out on her forehead. Some buildings were spewing gray smoke through the chimneys, like the concentration camps in Germany, which she had seen in movies. "Where's Father Sohn?" she asked.

"I dropped him off about ten minutes ago," said Red Snake. "He's visiting a widow who just lost her husband to cancer. He didn't want me to wake you, but he wishes you the very best and said he'll see you soon."

She vaguely remembered the two men whispering and a door closing, but she kept on sleeping. She wished she had spoken more with the priest, since he would be the one who would actually get the prince out of the camp and out of the country. She had many questions to ask but she had lost the chance.

"In a few minutes we'll get there," Red Snake said, not knowing the thoughts in her head. "I wish you my best, too! Once we're in the camp, I'll have to treat you like an inmate, so please understand."

Suddenly afraid of what was coming, she said, "Will I see you again?"

"Most definitely. I can't tell you exactly when, but we'll be seeing one another again."

They passed through the camp's arched gateway, where Red Snake presented a paper, and then drove to a parking lot encircled by several buildings, each with bold black letters that read, *People's this or People's that*. Red Snake parked in front of a two-story white building marked with "Administration" in black on the front.

Then everything happened very fast. An old guard who limped rushed over, opened the door, grasped her arm, and pulled her out of the truck. He never loosened his grip, as if he thought she might run off. He forced her to walk with him. Over her shoulder, she saw the truck making a full circle and driving back toward the gate they had just come in.

Chapter Nineteen

Camp 14

THE OLD GUARD LED Miyong through a long corridor, making uneven noises with his shoes on the hardwood floor, and then stopped in front of a double wooden door. He pushed it open and pushed her into a square room that could have been a classroom at one time or another, where an interrogation was in progress. Four men in uniforms sat at a long table in the center of the room, listening to a woman in front of them, and on the facing wall hung Kim Il-sung's portrait, looking directly at Miyong. She dropped her gaze to her feet.

"Go over there and wait until your name is called," the guard instructed her, pointing to about ten women sitting against the opposite wall. Miyong wondered if they were newcomers like herself.

The guard then left the room.

Clutching her bag, she crossed the room and sat next to a teenage girl whose hands were trembling. Miyong recognized Lee *Bujang*, the man sitting at the right end of the table, writing something on his notepad. Although she could see only his profile from where she sat, he was the best-looking of the four men. The man next to Lee was a thin fellow with an exceptionally large mouth, and the one next to him wore gold-framed glasses as if to camouflage his unattractive beady eyes.

"Get to the point," the man with beady eyes said, interrupting the woman being interrogated. "Did you kill your husband or not?"

"I did, *Dongmu*," said the woman in a sinking voice, her head bent. "Everything the report says is true. Why would I want to hide anything now, when my days are numbered?"

"Why did you kill him?"

"He was drinking too much… He cheated on me, too, but that's not why I killed him."

"How did you kill him?"

"Doesn't it say on the report?"

"Never mind what the report says. Just answer the question!"

"I made a pot of cabbage soup with caustic soda. He was hungry and he ate it to the last drop…" Her voice quivered, but she continued. "Then he began to vomit, screaming like a woman giving birth…rolling and kicking, too… I smothered him with a pillow. He died quickly, maybe in about five minutes."

"Where were your children when this happened?"

"My two boys were at the Youth Red Army camp on Kumgang Mountain. I planned it that way — and my little girl was with my mother."

"Why did you wait until the next day to report it?"

"I didn't want to disturb everyone in the building. It wasn't a pleasant thing to deal with."

"You premeditated the murder! You killed him in cold blood."

"But *Dongmu*, I didn't kill him out of hate. I wanted him to stop drinking, but instead of listening to me, he drank more, to prove his point. And he often beat me in front of my kids. I had no choice… I wanted to save my boys from becoming like their father. Doesn't the old proverb say, *The upper stream must be clear to expect the lower stream to be the same*? In a sense, I saved the future generation from corruption."

The four men leaned toward one another and whispered. Then, the same man wearing the gold-rimmed glasses spoke. "What do you think would be a fair punishment for a woman who murdered her husband?" He was calm, as though questioning someone who had confessed to breaking her neighbor's window.

"She deserves to die," the woman said with stony expression. "But in my case, I honored our Great Leader's *Juche* [self-reliance] philosophy. He teaches us that the consumption of alcohol is a fast way to corruption, doesn't he? I eliminated a social enemy, *Dongmu*! Now my boys will grow straight and strong to carry on Great Leader's *Juche* philosophy. I might be locked up behind bars, but someday, someone will realize that I've done something right for my boys."

"Tell us, then." This time, Lee *Bujang* spoke. "How can you repay your country, if we decide to give you another chance?"

Here, she acted as though she were on a stage. Sinking to her knees, she bowed deeply and said, "How could I ask you to spare my life after what I've done? But if you would consider, Respectable *Dongmu*, I've lived a clean life and was a loving mother and a diligent wife. In fact, I'm a good weaver, too. My scrolls, tablecloths, and pillowcases sold well to Japanese tourists before this tragedy ruined my life. If I am worthy of Great Leader's mercy, I'll work until my fingertips bleed a thousand times!"

The four men again talked among themselves. Then Lee *Bujang* picked up the wooden mallet in front of him and hit the table three times. "*Dongmu*, your correct thinking and humble manner have spared your life. We order you to serve ten years in the tapestry factory! Make many, many scrolls, wall-hangings, and other artwork in Great Leader's name!"

"Praise Great Leader!" she said, and bowed until her head touched the floor.

The same guard came in, helped the woman to her feet, and escorted her out of the room.

While the men were busy rearranging the papers and talking to one another, the woman sitting ahead of the teenager with shaky hands turned. "Hey, kid, they'll ask you to do only three things," she said in an all-knowing manner. "State your crime, confess your wrong, and promise to reform. The best thing to do is tell them everything and agree to do whatever they ask you, you understand?"

"But I didn't steal anything," the teenager said nervously. "The district clerk lied; he falsely accused me of stealing because I refused to do what he asked me to. He was as disgusting as an old goat! After I bit his arm instead of...you know, he wanted to punish me. I wish he were dead!"

"I'd be careful, if I were you. *Truth* doesn't matter here! He's a district clerk, and you were the errand girl in his office. Who do you think these men will listen to, you or their colleague?"

The teenager said nothing, biting her lips.

"The important thing is, these guards want to hear that you know what you've done wrong and are willing to learn from your mistakes. That's how the system works here. You want to walk out of here alive, don't you?"

"Of course I do."

"Then kneel and beg!"

"But...I didn't do it. I swear."

"Don't be stupid."

Another name was called. A woman in her forties approached the table. She acted as though she had been practicing from a script as she made a quick confession that she stole government goods from the distribution center where she had been working. "*Dongmu*, I am willing to pay the price for my mistake."

Lee *Bujang* hit the table with the mallet. "You've committed rather a grave crime against your country and your people. We recommend eight years in labor camp to produce a thousand times what you've stolen."

The woman bowed and exited with the guard.

One by one, they all admitted their wrong, some shedding tears and some straight-faced, and the mallet landed on the table powerfully, before the guard came in and led them out of the room.

Things didn't go well for the teenager. First, she admitted to stealing a watch from a district clerk, but then added stupidly, "Comrades, I'm only fifteen and my parents are waiting for me at home! They're heart-broken…I was sending them money from what little I earned at the district office as an errand girl, and if I'm found guilty, they'll be starving…Great Leader said that our filial duty is a God-given privilege…I won't do it again."

Lee *Bujang* hit the table again, much louder this time. "You want to go home, eh? Do you know why you're here?"

She began to stammer. "Actually, no! Comrade, I…I didn't steal anything, and that's the truth! I lied because she…" She turned to point at the woman who had been sitting before her and said, "I lied because she told me to agree with the charges, saying that it's the only way I can walk out of here alive. The truth is…the clerk made a false report on me after I refused to do what he wanted me to… It's something I can't talk about here…"

Lee *Bujang* looked angry now. "Are you accusing a public employee of falsifying a document?"

"I…I don't know what you mean…" The girl's voice quivered.

"Stealing is one thing and falsely accusing a public servant is another. In the olden days, people lost their heads on both accounts. Do you realize that?"

"No, Comrade!"

"All right, we'll fix you so that you'll learn something today. You'll be admitted to the clinic this afternoon and a doctor will remove your right thumb, so that you'll never steal again! Case dismissed!"

The girl's knees seemed to buckle, and then she was on the floor, crying hysterically.

"In addition," Lee continued, "you'll work in a quarry for five years! You're young and it's better to learn the lesson now than later. Learn your lesson well!"

The guard came and took the wailing girl out.

"Lee Soonok, step up!" the clerk shouted.

Miyong rose and approached the table. She looked at Lee *Bujang* for moral support, but he didn't even make eye contact with her. *If I mess up here,* she thought, *the prince will never get out of here. And how about me?*

"State your name!"

"Lee Soonok, *Dongmu*."

"State your crime!"

"Respectable Comrades, I have no excuses for escaping to China twice, breaking the laws. I've shamed my nation and our Great Leader, and I swear before you that I'll never repeat the same crime as long as I live. But one thing I want to call to your attention is that I didn't sell myself to those Chinese men as the papers say. I was forced..."

The guards were losing interest: they looked tired. One of them scratched his head and another yawned. She knew that they would rather be at their office, playing chess or smoking.

She continued as earnestly as she could. "Those Chinese men on border duty have been away from their wives and mistresses for so long that when they see someone wearing skirts, they lose their minds..."

"Get to the point," Lee *Bujang* grunted, not looking at her.

"The point I'm trying to make is that the patrolman who caught me was the worst kind you can imagine. When he had his fill of me, he went out and brought two more men, and all through the night..." Miyong stopped, and lowering her face, she pretended she was wiping her tears.

Hushed silence followed, except for her sniffles.

"But you signed the paper," Lee said, lifting the papers in the air. "You acknowledged the charges against you by signing these documents."

"I didn't do it voluntarily, *Dongmu*. If I couldn't prevent them from raping me, why do you think I could prevent them from forcing me to sign? Besides, I don't read Chinese. I didn't know what I was signing; all I could think at the moment was that my ordeal had ended, although I was still bleeding and the pain was..."

"That's enough!" Lee *Bujang* snapped. "We'll investigate further and let you know."

Miyong bowed. Walking back to her spot, she grabbed her bag to leave.

"Bring that bag here!" Lee roared.

You can't be serious, she thought. *Whose side are you on?*

He hit the table again. "Bring that bag!"

Miyong felt blood rushing to her head. *What should I do?* Biting her lip, she took the bag to Lee.

Lee took it and motioned to the guard at the door to escort her out. In the hallway, the guard said, "Wait here. I think Lee *Depyo* wants to talk to you."

Miyong was puzzled about Lee *Bujang*. He had treated her roughly. Even Ho Suknam had treated her better. *He might go against me and maybe against CIC, too.* She was now worried.

About five minutes later, Lee *Bujang* walked out, and seeing her standing in the hallway, he nodded in her direction, and walked toward the entrance. She followed him. He unexpectedly stopped at a small window, where a young girl about fifteen years old sat, and Miyong too stopped, about five feet away from Lee.

Lee *Bujang* questioned the girl at the window in a quiet voice, producing a small note, and the girl handed him a square cardboard box with "New Inmates" written on it in bold black ink.

"Thank you," he said. Then he said more, pointing to the floor.

"This one, *Dongmu*?" the girl said, lifting Miyong's bag.

"Yes, that one," Lee said louder, so that Miyong could hear. "I'll drop it off at the inspector's office, since I'm heading that way."

"Sure thing!" the girl said as she gave it to him.

"Thank you," Lee said, and carrying it in one hand and the box in another, he headed to the door. Miyong followed him.

In the parking lot, he moved fast. He loaded the bag and the box onto the back of his pickup truck that Miyong had seen in the slide, and returned to the driver's seat. He opened the door to the passenger's side for Miyong and told her to get in. When she seated herself, she noticed the strong smell of fuel but didn't say anything. This was a Russian truck. *At least it's running*, she thought. As they drove out of the parking lot, Lee said, "Welcome to Camp 14!"

"Thank you, Lee *Dongmu*!"

"You did very well at the interrogation."

"I did?"

"I was impressed. You never know how things will turn out at the preliminary interrogation. If you can do what you've done just now, I'm convinced we can get the prince out of here!"

"How is he?"

"Better. I moved him to the guest house yesterday. He still babbles in Japanese and in English a lot, but luckily, the guest house is not bugged. In other words, people can talk and no one can listen to their conversations. We've been lucky so far. But please be careful. Don't talk carelessly, just in case."

"I'll be careful!"

Now they were on a curvy road that divided the vast brown field, which was dotted with small discolored structures and inmates in mud-colored outfits moving about.

"We have to get him out of here as soon as we can, possibly within a week. Otherwise, he'll be assigned to a permanent barracks with common laborers. In his state of mind and without proper language skills, he'll go crazy in a barracks surrounded by peasants and common laborers. At the clinic, there was a doctor who spoke some Japanese, but he's been transferred to another clinic."

Miyong couldn't help but notice Lee's mouth and neck twitching as he spoke. *Why is he doing this?* she wondered.

"When can I meet the prince?"

"I don't know yet," he said, glancing at her quickly. "I'll have to talk to my co-worker Kim Yongsoon about using you as one of her maintenance crew in the guest house. I'll let you know tomorrow or the next day. Until then, think about how you can convince him of why you're here and who is behind you in this operation. It might not be easy, but a woman can do impossible things sometimes. And I'm convinced that you can do it, too."

They passed a junkyard on her left, where a handful of small children wearing dirty clothes were rummaging through a heap of debris with rusted scrap metal, wooden sticks, and torn tires. Miyong wondered why no adults were watching them. At the next corner, behind barbed wire, a group of men in rags sat in several rows on the bare ground, their heads lowered, while two guards, each with a stick, walked back and forth through the aisles, yelling and landing the whip on them.

Miyong wanted to ask why those men were being punished, but she didn't. Didn't Major Min say not to talk too much? Lee *Bujang*'s profile in the slanting sunlight was somber, as if he too were thinking about those men.

They drove past a vast wheatfield turning gold in the wan sunlight. A few magpies were feasting in one spot, maybe on fallen grass seeds, and two crows on a tree branch seemed to be laughing at them, squawking and flapping their wings. She had heard that birds were rare commodity here in the North, because starving people caught them and ate them. But it seemed that some lucky ones were still around.

A rectangular barracks with *Women's Reeducation Center* written on the wall appeared on their left. Lee *Bujang* stepped on the brake pedal. With the brakes squealing, he parked the truck in front of Unit 264 and killed the engine.

"This is your temporary home," he said. "Seven girls will share this place with you. They're at work now."

"Will I be working with them too?"

"Your unit leader will tell you where to go until I assign you to the maintenance crew." He turned to her. "A few things to remember."

"Yes, Lee *Bujang*."

He frowned. *"Lee Bujang?"*

Puzzled, she only looked at him.

"'*Bujang*' is a title that exists only in the South. If you call me *that*, you're labeling me as a South Korean pig! You must change the habits you've been accustomed to in the South as quickly as possible. Every small error, like calling me *Bujang,* could cost your life as well as mine. Please be careful."

"What should I call you, then?"

"People here call me Lee *Depyo* [Deputy], but you can call me "Lee *Dongmu*. It's safe. Everyone calls everyone else *Dongmu*."

"I'll be careful."

"Another thing: Avoid conversations with the inmates as much as you can, understand? Don't volunteer any information. I'm smuggling you in here, risking my neck."

"Yes, *Dongmu*!"

"That's better. If you need to contact me, use the utility shed over there." He pointed to a box-like wooden structure wedged between Unit 264 and Unit 266. "It's strictly for the maintenance crew, so it's safe for you to leave me messages on the wall. Use the Magic Pen. I assume you have one."

"Yes, I do."

"When you go in, make sure no one is watching you. Here, every inmate is trained to watch every other inmate, so extreme caution is important. Also, guards on the watchtower can see everything that moves in the camp, and I do mean EVERYTHING!"

"When is the safest time to go in?"

"After sundown. One last thing. Pay attention to me when I'm in the field. On the spur of the moment, I may signal you something, and I want you to understand what I'm trying to convey; for instance, when I scratch the back of my head, know that I'm coming to talk to you. But don't look me in the eye! In fact, you should never look any guard in the eye. When I bend and act as though I'm looking for something on the ground, know that other guards are near me, so don't try to talk to me. Any questions?"

"No."

"Let's stick with those rules for now. If I tell you more, you won't remember." Picking up the cardboard box from the floor between the two seats, he handed it to her. "You'll find a few essential items you need in here: an inmate's uniform, a comb, a toothbrush, a set of work clothes. If you don't have questions, I will let you go."

She got out of the car, carrying her bag and the box.

Lee *Bujang* drove away, before she could say "Thank you."

Chapter Twenty

Camp 14, Unit 264

UNIT 264... MIYONG DISLIKED the room number. The number "4," pronounced *sah*, the same pronounciation as "death", was an unwanted number in the South. This was the reason Number "4" was never used for house numbers or room numbers or group numbers in the South. *Why would North Koreans use this cursed number?* She couldn't understand. Stepping inside, she cringed. The smell of mildew and rotten vegetables was strong. It was dark, too, at four-thirty in the afternoon, only a dim light entering through a single window at the far end of the room that seemed to be a sleeping area. Everything — the mud walls, the dirt floor covered with rotting straw mats, the stump of a tree serving as the base of the washbasin, and the table and six chairs — was an ugly brown. It seemed the clock had turned back and she was in 19th-century Korea, poor and primitive. A few discolored potatoes in a straw basket on the floor hinted at the food shortage the inmates were suffering. *What would it be like eating such ill-looking potatoes day after day?* But Kim Il-sung's smiling face in the framed portrait hanging on the wall before her seemed to say: *They don't deserve much. They're criminals. And you…you're a capitalist! Why are you here?*

She remembered her pistol in her bag. *I must hide it somewhere!* she thought. *What if one of the girls goes through my belongings and finds it? Women are curious animals whether they are Communists or capitalists, rich or poor…*

She was glad that she remembered it now rather than later. But she didn't know where to hide it. The only place safe might be under her clothes, right under her belt. As she opened her bag, reaching for the pistol buried at the bottom, a whimpering noise startled her. Quickly pulling the pistol out, she secured it under the elastic of her underpants.

What was that? A cat? The noise ceased abruptly, but not for long. Now, the sound was definitely coming from the sleeping area at the other end of the room. It was too dark to see anything on that end, except the military cots, but the sound came clearly now, and it seemed that a woman was weeping softly. She thought about turning around and leaving the room. But she didn't know who would be watching her outside those mud walls.

She did nothing for a long moment. *Stay calm,* she told herself, but it was impossible to be calm when her heart palpitated so fast.

The whimper soon became incoherent mumbling, and she found herself walking in that direction, slowly, holding her breath, one step at a time. The straw mat under her feet made squishing noises. And there, on the third bed from the wall, lay a girl about fourteen, with pallid skin and dark half-circles under her eyes. A military blanket covered her from the waist down.

Miyong got closer. The girl's face was skeletal under a thin layer of skin. Miyong touched the girl's forehead. It was hot, and clammy with sweat. As if she could feel Miyong's hand, the girl rolled on her side, allowing Miyong a full view of her feverish face smeared with tears. The girl's arm, half-buried under her pillow, was no thicker than a bamboo flute.

"My baby…" the girl mumbled weakly.

Miyong stiffened.

"Don't kill her! Please..." the girl went on. "I must feed her... Please bring her to me..."

Mustering some courage, Miyong touched the girl's shoulder. "Are you all right?" she asked cautiously.

The girl sprang up, wide-eyed, a few strands of her hair glued to the side of her face. "Where's my baby?" she shrieked.

"I didn't mean to frighten you," Miyong said, scared. "You kept crying so I...woke you."

The girl stared. "I know you," she spat her words out. "You were there this morning at the clinic. You took my baby and the baby before mine, and the one before that one, too. What did you do with my baby?"

"I don't know what you're talking about!"

The girl burst into tears, covering her face with her hands that were nothing but bones and skin. Then she lifted her face and screamed, "Bring my baby! If not, I'll kill you!"

Miyong felt blood draining out of her face. "You...you're confusing me with someone else. I'm new here. I've just arrived two minutes ago."

"I'm not confused!" the girl screeched. "It was you, I swear! Remember me saying that my mother could raise the baby, and you said you'd think about it? Well, did you? I don't remember who brought me here but I *do* remember you."

The girl abruptly pushed away her blanket, exposing her thin gray hospital gown and her naked belly. "See? It's gone now. My baby isn't here anymore, hear that?" She pounded her swollen belly as if it were a drum. In the dim light, a dark spot between her legs seemed to be growing like some hairy creature, and Miyong pulled the blanket over her belly in attempt to cover it.

The girl angrily pushed her away. "Bring my baby. Now! If you killed my baby, you deserve to die!"

"Didn't I just say I've just arrived here?" Miyong said in a scolding tone. "I don't even know where the clinic is!"

Leaping to her feet unsteadily, the girl grabbed Miyong's hair with both hands and pulled at it, crying, "I hate you! I hate you!"

Miyong couldn't help but scream. *How can you let a crazy girl hurt you like this?* her brother seemed to say. *You have things to do here, Sis...* She pinched the girl's hands on her head as hard as she could, and suddenly she was free. Rising to her feet, she slapped the girl as hard as she could.

Stunned, the girl mutely stared.

Miyong had never struck anyone in her life, but she didn't regret what she had just done. "Good meeting with you, kid," she said. "Thanks for showing such hospitality to your new roommate!"

*   *   *

"Are you our new roommate?" a woman's voice asked.

The ceiling light had come on, and Miyong found herself squinting into the milky light, her head resting on her arms that were on the table. She hadn't slept, but she hadn't heard the doorknob turning or footsteps approaching. Sitting up, she said, *"Anyong-haseyo* [How do you do]? I'm Lee Soonok. Just got in this afternoon."

"We skip greetings here," said the oldest of all the six women who were standing in front of her. She had a round face and all-knowing eyes, besides looking healthier than the other five. "It'd be a curse if we welcomed you here, wouldn't it?" she said. Before Miyong could answer, the five others giggled. Two of them had puffy eyes and their faces were covered with brownish spots, one had an eye patch on, and the other two were thin and sickly looking.

Miyong didn't know whether she should laugh or cry.

"You can call me Ajima [Auntie], since I am older than all of you," the same one spoke.

"Hello, Ajima."

"I'm Yonhee," the tall and skinny girl said. She had freckles all over her, even on her exposed arms, and though she looked sickly, she seemed educated and friendly.

"Soonyi here," the girl with many ugly pimples introduced herself. "You have pretty skin," she added.

"Thank you."

The girl with an eye patch said, "My name is Yongok, but you can call me Pellagra. I don't mind it." In addition to her eye patch, her skin was an ugly yellow and her uncovered eye was watery. Miyong learned about Pellagra at The Pigeon's Nest; it was the common disease among starving populations worldwide. The symptoms of pellagra included depression, skin inflammation, memory loss, and ongoing diarrhea that caused weight loss and delusion.

"Let's not volunteer personal information, girls," Ajima cautioned the girl with an eye patch. "If you do, our new roommate might feel that she has to also." Turning back to Miyong, Ajima asked, "What happened to you? Your forehead is all scratched up."

Miyong had not been aware that the girl she had struggled with had left claw marks on her forehead. Miyong wasn't proud of what she had done to the delirious teenager, yet she didn't regret it. "What's wrong with that kid over there?" she asked. "She was crying and whimpering in her sleep, so I went to see her if she was okay. And she attacked me like an angry cat."

"She's crazy," the tall girl said. "Stay away from her."

"You're lucky she didn't scratch your eyes out, like she did to me," the girl with an eye patch added, touching the gauze.

"It's the abortion," Ajima explained. "Poor kid... When she found out that she was pregnant, she did everything to lose the baby; she ran around the camp until she fainted, she jumped off of a moving delivery truck, almost killing herself, and she even drank the solutions the doctor gave her. But the baby wouldn't die!"

All six women pitched in, and Miyong received a lesson on baby-killing in the camp. Consorting with the opposite sex was prohibited, and when camp officials learned that a girl was pregnant, they assigned her a doctor to help her lose the baby naturally, by jumping off of a moving pickup or running until she fainted. When all attempts failed, they forced her to drink saline solutions, which would get rid of the baby. But when that also failed, the girl was admitted to the abortion clinic and the doctor removed the baby piece by piece.

"The poor kid lost her infant daughter two days ago," Ajima continued, "but she's still having nightmares about it."

"What's going to happen to her?" Miyong asked.

Ajima said, "I'll report her to security tomorrow, and they'll move her to the mental ward. You're the third person she attacked since she got here. I don't want to be blamed for endangering others." She then clapped her hands three times. "Okay, girls, let's get moving. The light will go out in two hours, and we have things to do!"

Everyone scattered. One took down a dented cooking pot from the shelf in the corner, filled it with water from the barrel, scoop by scoop, and put it on the rusted wood-burning stove in the middle of the room. Another produced a match, ignited it, and threw it onto a loose bundle of twigs in the stove, causing a tiny orange flame to bloom like a flower bud amidst gray smoke. Within seconds, the walls began to glow with multi-colored light.

It's been a long day, thought Miyong. *Where are Jongmi and Ho now? Where's Father?* Her eye began to water, maybe because of the smoke and she blinked. *I'm actually in Camp 14!* Through the thin wall behind her, the noise of the wind was audible, chasing something metallic, maybe an empty beer can or a tin bucket. *The Northern Wind!*

Chapter Twenty-One

Kahn Hoa Province, Vietnam

THE AIR WAS THICK and sticky in his lungs like pasty glue as Jinwoo ran for his life toward the woods at the foot of the purplish mountains ahead. *I could die at any moment...* It wasn't a good thing to think about, but he was afraid of falling, never to get up. He wished he could find a clear stream and drink and drink, and then lie flat on a wide rock for a nap. But the mountains seemed to move further and further away with each step he took. The blazing sun was so merciless that he thought it could melt his helmet and the molten metal would drip and burn his eyes. Everything he saw was blurry and hazy in the heat and humid air. *At least I'm still alive,* he comforted himself. *Just a little longer...* His uniform felt heavy on his shoulders, back, and around his thighs, and it was difficult to run any faster than he had been. Again, he wished he could rest, only for five minutes.

My left foot! What's the matter with it? He couldn't feel anything from that foot. He felt no pain, no discomfort of any kind, but it kept dragging behind him. Either a bullet had entered there, or he might have stepped on something sharp that had pierced through his flesh and killed the nerves. Amazingly, he could still move forward without falling. He must get away from this merciless sun and the Vietcong killers, and find an old tree with thick leaves that would cool him off and maybe rest for a few minutes, flat on his back — only a few minutes. Just thinking about it gave strength, and he pressed on. He hadn't slept for days, maybe a week, except for a catnap here and there, in the bunker or on the road, while guns droned on like a witch's lullaby.

He kept licking the sweat dripping down to his lips — maybe there was blood, too. Every time he grimaced or frowned, he felt his lips cracking, and there was that acrid, nauseating taste of sweat mixed with blood.

God, I'm thirsty!

Columns of sickly orange-red rose from the mountains beyond the woods ahead, twisting, rolling, and squirming like devils in the Bible, which he had read in the orphanage where he spent two-thirds of his twenty-one years. Where the hell was everybody? Private Kim, Private Yoon, and at least two other guys had been in the bunker with him after a pack of Vietcong jumped in like some limbless beasts and cut three men's throats in the blink of an eye. His memory was hazy. He couldn't remember how he escaped. Was it when the lieutenant blew whistles and ordered, "Retreat! Retreat!"? Or was it when he knocked down one guy that was on top of the lieutenant? He cringed. *He died, too, the lieutenant, the shrill of his whistle still echoing thought the valley. What was his name...?*

Now, Jinwoo wasn't sure if he had dreamt this. But it wasn't a dream. He saw human body parts flying everywhere like birds of all sizes, and the spray of blood was cool on his face as he fled toward the green pasture ahead of him. *No, it wasn't a dream! It was real. I was there.*

He spat as he remembered men's heads separated from their bodies and rolling on the ground. Men shouldn't die like that, like chickens on a cutting board. They should die with honor and dignity, surrounded by their loved ones and flowers and candlelight. Then they should be buried on a sunny spot on a hill, where birds nestled nearby and brooks murmured ancient melodies, a place their loved ones could visit and leave flowers.

Vietnamese men and women were running alongside him. The men were pushing wagons loaded with boxes, bundles, and children; the women were carrying babies on their backs. A young woman wearing a blood-stained *aodai*, the one who had had a tiny baby strapped on her back, was still running, but the infant was missing – there was only the quilt strap hanging loosely around her slim body, but she kept running. This told Jinwoo that something had happened to the baby. But what? *Did she lose the baby? Did she abandon it?*

A gently rolling pasture with hundreds of green mounds presented itself before him without a notice. A cemetery! How glad he was to find *this*. Thank God! There must be a brook somewhere, because he could hear the gurgle of water.

Everyone, adults and children alike, ran in that direction to quench their thirst, some skidding and stumbling on the grass. Children wailed, *Mamaaa, Mamaaa,* the universal name for "mother."

Jinwoo took time while walking in the same direction, making sure not to fall down because of his bad foot. The headstones made of marble and limestone glared at him as he passed. Reaching the tiny brook, only about five feet wide, he knelt down on a smooth rock, lowered his head to the stream, and sprinkled water onto himself. *Ahhhh...* It was as though he were a newborn being baptized. Whenever he had watched a child being baptized, he or she always wailed, but he couldn't understand them now. The cool water on his head was heavenly.

Bending and lowering his mouth to the water, he drank and drank, stopping only briefly to take a breath — and then bending again, he drank until he was lightheaded. A few women and children were washing and drinking near him, each babbling in Vietnamese. An old man wearing a Chinese-style vest had stretched himself out on the bank, as if he thought it was a hotel room; he was snoring like a cicada.

Jinwoo savored this moment, his feet soaking in the water shaded by the leaves and his tummy was filled. He imagined every nerve and fiber in his body stretching and ticking with renewed vitality. A prayer sprang to his tongue. *Thank you, Lord, for leading me to this stream. Look over me and protect me for my sake, as well as my kid sister's.* Making a quick sign of the Cross on his chest, he lifted his troublesome left foot onto the rock to examine it. A blob of dirt clung where his big toe had been, and it was bloody mess. *Have I been walking like this all this time?* He couldn't believe it. A bullet had struck the toe, leaving a hole; dirt and blood had plugged it up. He carefully touched the dark spot, making himself scream. Clenching his teeth, he moaned.

He sat erect. *What was it?* He thought he heard something besides his own moans – maybe human voices. The only noises he could hear now were from the leaves above him swishing in the breeze. He put his hands behind his ears to retrieve the earlier sounds, the sounds of men's voices. His heart suddenly raced. *My fellow Koreans! They're talking in Korean.* Then, his shoulders slumped. He wished he had not heard them.

"Shut up, whore!" the man's voice yelled. "Make a choice: do you want a bullet in your head instead of this?"

A woman's desperate cries, begging and pleading, followed, but another male voice silenced her. "Shut up, whore. Do as he says!"

Forgetting the pain, Jinwoo rose. He was dizzy, as though all of the blood in his brain were draining away. Still, he swore he'd rather die than sit and pretend he was deaf, when a local woman was being raped by his fellow Koreans.

There had been too many complaints from the villagers that the Taihan (Korean) soldiers had snuck into their villages at night and raped their wives and daughters, but their regiment commander, a tall man whose ego was as great as his height, retorted in their faces, "How do you know they aren't Americans? Can you prove it? We're here to fight for you, and you're blaming us for something we didn't do! Go ask the Americans! They did awful things to our mothers and sisters during the Korean War." The natives never returned.

Jinwoo looked for his M1 carbine, but it wasn't there — not hanging from his shoulder, and not on the ground next to him. Where had he lost it? In the bunker? He removed the Colt .45 worn at his hip and, limping, he advanced toward the wooded area next to the creek where the noises were coming from. It was a long, painful walk, a distance that would have taken him only a few seconds, before his injury.

In front of a square hole in the ground covered with a bamboo grill, he stopped. The men's voices were coming directly from below, louder than earlier, and there were other noises, panting sounds, the kinds of sounds only a crazed man would produce on top of a naked woman. Suddenly, an ear-piercing woman's voice burst out: "Help meeee!"

Hueh! In the dim light escaping from somewhere down below, he saw a jagged side view of a man lying atop a woman, his bare bottom exposed and his pants hanging around his knees. At least two men were helping him, one holding her arms over her head and the other her legs that were twisting and kicking. *Those sons of bitches are raping our local helper!*

Jinwoo was beyond himself. He quickly calculated his chance of saving her without violence, but it was slim. He was up against at least three men, maybe more. He fired his pistol into the hole. The bamboo splintered and a spray of dirt flew up, producing a hole in the grill. "Raise your hands, all of you!" he yelled in Korean. Through a film of dust, he saw the two men letting go of the woman and raising their hands, but the guy on top of her didn't move, as if pondering what he should do.

He descended as quickly as he could, making more noise with his boots than necessary. The guy on the top of the woman finally raised his hands and slid down. It was dark, but he caught a naked woman's back flitting away toward the cave wall ahead.

"What's with you, buddy?" one of the two helpers said, suddenly appearing on his left. "Put that thing away!"

"Private Yoon!" Jinwoo muttered sadly. "What are you doing here?"

Yoon was in his patrol team under Corporal Chang. He might

not be the brightest man in the world, but Jinwoo had never imagined him seeing here.

"Take it easy with that thing, buddy," Yoon pleaded. "We weren't doing anything wrong, I swear!"

"Don't call me 'buddy,'" Jinwoo blurted out. "You and I have nothing in common! Never say that word again!"

"It's not what you think," Yoon said defensively. "We were hiding here and…the girl came down alone. We thought she was a Vietcong… Hey, what do we care, eh? When the war is over we'll go home and won't even remember what happened in this stinking place. It's the war that's making men do things they don't normally do, you know."

"It's not the war," Jinwoo said. "It's your decaying soul that turns you into an animal."

"Soul?" Yoon said. "Are you a preacher or something? Show me where your soul is! What does it look like?"

A dark figure leaped at Jinwoo at the same time his pistol blasted. As he struggled with the man who had pinned him against the wall, Jinwoo heard something heavy falling next to him. *Yoon? Did I kill him?*

"Hand me that pistol!" the figure barked, spitting on his face.

Corporal Chang, the squad leader!

Whenever Chang had had a chance, he had talked about the Vietnamese whores he had been with in numerous brothels. According to him, they were easier to handle than Korean whores. "They'll do anything you want them to do, for next to nothing," he had said.

"If you give me that pistol," Chang said, his hand almost touching Jinwoo's right arm, "I'll forget what you've just done. My lips are sealed. I promise you, man to man."

Man to man? Jinwoo landed a hard blow on the corporal's crotch with his knee, and when the corporal yelped like a dog and bent double, he pushed him to the ground and landed on top of him. Pressing the barrel of his pistol to the man's chin, he said, "Corporal, you've told us to live as true soldiers of Korea and here you are, raping an innocent local woman who was helping us! Does that mean anything to you?"

Chang spit at him. "You Vietnamese-lover, do whatever with me! When you go back, you'll be court-martialed. My men are watching this, you know." Jinwoo pulled the trigger. The gun blast echoed through the cave walls, and at the same time Jinwoo was covered with something warm and wet. *The corporal's blood!* He wiped his face with his sleeve, muttering, *You'll curse me forever from hell, but I can take it, Corporal. The world is better without you.*

Something knocked the pistol from his hand, and it flew away like a bird. Suddenly he was struggling to breathe, his back against the wall. Two hands were squeezing his neck like a vise, and he pulled them as hard as he could. They didn't budge. Strange colors began to swirl in his eyes and it was deadly silent. Am I dying here?

Oppa, you can't die here, Miyong whispered. *What about me?*

He threw his neck to his left as hard as he could, and when one of the attacker's hands slipped, he threw his fist into the dark figure. Then, a gun blasted and the hands on his neck fell away at the same time. *Who's shooting? Another corporal's buddy?* The gun went off three more times. Something thumped in front of him, something heavy. *Who was shot?*

Farther away, machine guns were droning, *tararararara, tararara, tararara...* like modern percussion music. His knees buckling, Jinwoo landed on the ground. *Why are the walls turning around?* Tasting something salty on his lips, he slipped into blackness.

Corporal Chang is yelling at him to stand, kicking his injured foot. But Jinwoo feels no pain. A laugh bubbles up and he says, "Corporal, didn't I just kill you? You were screwing a local girl... Don't lie! I can't stand a man who has no conscience..." The corporal's face melts down like candle wax, disfiguring his face, and Private Yoon is laughing like an idiot. "See what you've done, Private Hahn?" Yoon says. "I can't go home now: I'm stuck here forever, in this stinking cave..." "Hey, I didn't mean to, buddy," Jinwoo says. "Don't call me 'buddy'!" Yoon snaps. "You and I have nothing in common. You're alive and I'm dead!"

Strange noises woke him. Somewhere, a woman was sobbing softly, and before him lay three corpses, each with a dark stain next to him, as large as a cushion. Goose bumps rose on his arms and neck. He felt sick. *I've murdered my fellow Koreans!*

He looked for Hueh. Against the opposite wall, in the dim light, she sat with her knees drawn up to her and was crying, her face on her raised knees. At her feet was his pistol. *Was she the shooter?* He rose, but a sharp pain in his left foot stabbed him. Limping, he walked to her. "Are you all right, Hueh?"

She didn't move, nor did she say a word.

He waited for her to say something, but she didn't, so he said, "Hueh, I know how you feel, but whatever happened, it's not your fault."

After a long moment, she lifted her face to him. She wasn't crying anymore. "Let's get out of here," she said brightly.

"Fine with me! But to tell you the truth, I don't know my way around here."

"*I* do," she said. "If you can walk for about ten minutes, we can find a place with food and medicine. You need medicine for your foot!" She pointed.

True... He looked at it. It was too dark to see anything below his knees, but it felt as though a thousand needles had lodged there. *How can I walk for ten minutes?* A bomb exploded somewhere above, sending rocks and gravel down on them. He cowered against the wall, his elbow covering his face, a few feet from Hueh. The blasts of bombs and the drones of machine guns lasted a few seconds and then stopped.

"Hueh, tell me. What were you doing here? Did they drag you down here?"

She paused for a moment as if collecting her thoughts. "I was hiding in that corner," she said, pointing, "and four men came down, talking in Korean."

"Four men? Not three?"

"Four men! I was glad to see them because I recognized every one of them. But it was my stupid mistake. When they saw me walking out of my hiding place, they turned into animals."

"Where's the fourth one? I saw only three."

"I don't know," Hueh said. "He tried to stop the others, yelling in Korean. But that one," she pointed at the corporal, "hit him, and I never saw him again."

"I'm sorry, Hueh, I'm very sorry that…they were Koreans…"

Hueh dropped her face again, and Jinwoo thought she was crying. But she didn't. "It's the war…" she said. "I just shot someone, too."

They sat quietly for a long time, listening to booming sounds of bombs exploding and guns chattering.

Jinwoo fought to stay awake, but his head kept tilting to one side without warning. At one point, he saw his sister sitting next to him, not saying anything, only watching. *"Why didn't you tell me you were coming?"* he asked. *"Oppa,"* she said in a clear voice, *"if you fall asleep here, I'll never see you again."*

He jolted awake, banging his head against the wall. Eerie silence surrounded him. He was wide awake.

"We can leave now," Hueh said. "No bombs anymore."

Jinwoo agreed. The hole through which he had descended earlier had been plugged by chunks of stone, branches, and dirt, so they took the narrow tunnel-like space with an ankle-high stream running through it. Water splashed as they proceeded. It was dark; only the vague outline of the space was defined by walls with dimly glinting stones. He accidentally kicked something, and to his dismay, it rolled.

"What was it?" Hueh asked.

"I don't know." He thought it could be a head that had been separated from a corpse, but he didn't say it. As if to confirm his suspicion, the stench of decaying flesh invaded his nostrils, and he bent double and gagged.

"There're dead bodies everywhere," Hueh said calmly as if talking about some stone common in the area. Then, something swooped past his back, screeching, and he let out a cry.

"They're bats," Hueh again informed him.

"They're vampire bats," Jinwoo said. He learned in boot camp that these bats carried rabies, and one bite could be deadly. "Walk behind me," he ordered her. When she did as she was told, he walked quickly, beating the air with both arms and imitating the squawks of crows. Ten minutes later, Jinwoo found himself looking up at a square of blue overhead, through which a shaft of sunlight descended. Birds were fleeing by in the square of blue. *How can we get up there?* By looking around, he found a cone-shaped heap of rubble and stone whose end almost reached the hole.

"Hueh, I think we can get out of here through that hole," he said, pointing. "What do you think?"

"It's too high."

"We have no choice. Do you want to spend the night here, with vampire bats?"

"No!"

It was steep, but the mound didn't crumble under their feet. After five minutes of skidding and losing a few feet here and there, they reached the opening. Jinwoo crawled out first, to the clearing with tall grass and wild sunflowers, and helped Hueh to do the same.

From there, Hueh led Jinwoo, and in a few minutes, they walked into a ruined village with half-burned mud houses, charred tree trunks, corpses of adults and children, and scorched military vehicles. Snaking through more debris and more bodies, they stood in front of a skeleton of a mud house without doors or windows.

"We can hide here," Hueh said, her eyes showing a glimmer of hope. "People leave rice and beans when they flee. We can stay here for a few days."

Jinwoo hesitated. Hueh reminded him of his sister, and he wanted to protect her from all danger, but a man and a woman hiding alone in a place like this could complicate matters. "Stay here, Hueh. But I must go."

"Go where?" she asked, disappointed.

"I should go back to the base."

"What base? Everything is gone! No base. See the smoke?" She pointed in the direction where the base had been.

The columns of charcoal-gray smoke were so thick that they obscured the view of the mountains and the sky behind them. If the whole company was hit, he'd have no roof over his head, not to mention the danger he might be facing. Vietcong could capture him at any given time.

"Okay, I'll stay here until I find my company."

Chapter Twenty-Two

Camp 14, Unit 264

"WE'RE LUCKY TO HAVE Ajima as our unit leader," Yonhee said, as she led Miyong to Construction Site 12, their assigned workplace where a new trout hatchery was being built. Yonhee had already informed her about the camp: that about six hundred occupied guard houses were spread across 5,000 acres of mostly hillocks and mountains, and that 15,000 inmates worked year-round, from sunrise to sunset, except four days a year: Great Leader's birthday, his son Dear Leader's birthday, the anniversary of Korea's liberation from Japan, and New Year's Day. Some worked in the field to fulfill the yearly quota of grain, except in the dead of winter, some in the textile and garment factories, and others in the coal mines or quarries to produce raw materials. Two thousand inmates died yearly from work-related accidents, or starvation, or illnesses.

Now, Yonhee volunteered information on their unit leader. "Ajima's boyfriend is the cook at Guard House Number Two, and she brings home leftovers. That's why we don't starve as much as women in the other units." She then studied Miyong's profile for a moment, and said,

"If I were you, I'd stay away from the cook I've just told you about. He's creepy."

"What do you mean?"

"Come on, get serious," she said, suddenly becoming playful. "It's no secret that men like young and pretty women, is it? What I'm saying is, he's awfully friendly to many women, not just to Ajima, and she gets jealous. The older women have a taste for men, too, you know, sometimes much more than we younger ones do."

Miyong's cheeks burned with humiliation. "I'm not that type. Men don't interest me."

"I'm trying to be helpful."

"I know."

About twenty yards away at the crossroads, a round-faced guard in his forties stood, looking this way and that, as if waiting for his ride. Seeing the two women approaching, he straightened his back as if trying to look taller.

Yonhee talked fast. "When you pass him, make sure to bow. Don't look him in the face."

It was difficult for Miyong not to look at the man as she was warned not to. Yonhee bent her head first, and Miyong followed her example, noticing his unusual moustache that tapered at the ends, like two cow-hair ink brushes. This was when she saw his boots marching toward them.

"What are you looking at, whore?" He stepped in front of Miyong and slapped her face.

Miyong looked at him, stunned. "What have I done, Comrade?"

Another blow landed on the same cheek, then another. "Are you deaf? You're still looking at me, whore! Don't you know your proper disposition before an officer?"

Yonhee stepped forward, bowing deeper. "Forgive my friend, Respectful Comrade. My roommate is new here and I haven't had time to teach her the camp rules. It's my fault more than hers. It won't happen again."

Miyong wished she had her gun in her hand. *I won't miss him!*

"If this whore looks at me again, I'll beat you both!"

"Of course, Respectful Comrade! We're very sorry. Please be reassured that it will never happen again."

"Get lost!" he ordered, throwing his hand toward them as if shooing away a fly.

As they walked away, their heads lowered, he spat a wad of phlegm in their direction. Miyong's stomach churned. She quickened her pace, as if running away from feces.

"What did I tell you?" Yonhee said.

"I did what you told me."

"Not soon enough," she said in a scolding tone of voice. "That guard is a dog, the worst kind. That's why we call him Pit Bull. Next time, don't look at him at all; bow quickly and more deeply, to save yourself from a beating."

"How can you put up with that kind of animal?"

"You'll learn in time. Give them what they want, and they will leave you alone."

A few more minutes of walking brought them to an area with a tall wooden post that read "Construction Site No. 12," and about sixty men and women in quilted inmates' coats were standing before a roughly dug hole about the size of a mini rice paddy. They were shivering. Some were hugging themselves against the early winter chill and others were moving about, taking small, fast steps. A guard wearing a red armband with a yellow star separated himself from a half dozen guards standing around, and climbed the crudely built platform next to the post and positioned himself on it, locking his hands behind him. He had a large mouth, compared to his beady eyes and small nose.

"Dearly beloved Comrades," he began in a high-pitched voice, spewing steam from his mouth. "We are gathered here again today to fulfill our daily duty to our Great Leader and our nation. As you know, he wants you to work hard and be cleansed of your past mistakes and return to society as contributing members. You're called here to show your undying loyalty to him and to your motherland! Remember, we can live only one day at a time, and the future begins today, not tomorrow, not ten days from now. Who wants to express his or her loyalty to your motherland this fine winter day? Any volunteers?" His eyes swept over his audience.

A woman's voice rose from somewhere Miyong couldn't see. "I pledge to our Great Leader my very best efforts today. My fellow inmates, let us be reminded that our labor is what makes our nation strong and shine above others, like a North Star in the galaxy. Today, Comrades, we must give everything we have for our country and our leader, without keeping anything for ourselves." She then shouted, "Ten thousand years for the Democratic People's Republic of Korea! Ten thousand years for Great Leader!"

The others followed: "Ten thousand years for the Democratic People's Republic of Korea! Ten thousand years for Great Leader!"

The guard smiled a victor's smile. "Comrade, your love for and devotion to your leader and your motherland are ringing true in your voice! Thank you for sharing your loyalty to your motherland with us. Anyone else?" He looked around again.

A man called, "I want to add to what my comrade said just now."

"Go on."

His voice rose like that of an opera singer. "Oh, dearly beloved father and leader, I'll work harder than I've worked in my thirty-six years, without temptations to rest and without impure thoughts. Great Leader, please guide us today with the lofty examples you've shown us since the birth of our nation, and help us to be dedicated to what we're called to do, as long as we live!"

A few applauded.

Miyong heard someone shivering loudly, chattering his or her teeth.

The guard asked, "Comrade, please elaborate on what you've called impure thoughts, not only for you but for others as well."

"Please don't make me say it, Comrade," he said sheepishly. "I'm not proud of what's in my head sometimes."

"I insist that you tell us."

"All right, then. My...my wife is pregnant again, and she wishes that

I'd come home. You know how women are when they're expecting… I told her that's impossible, but I can't help worrying about her, whether she's warm enough or she has enough to eat, etc. But don't worry, Comrade. It will not affect my work, I promise."

"There's a solution to every problem," the guard said.

"Solution, Comrade?"

"Yes. Have her abort the fetus!"

The audience was deadly silent. No one stirred or shivered.

"Our nation's future is in our hands, Comrade," the guard continued. "How can we afford to be distracted by thoughts of home when we have so much work to do? Your impure thoughts will eventually ruin the team spirit!"

There was no response.

"Come see me at lunch break," the guard ordered the man with *impure thoughts*. "I'll write a note to your district office so that your wife can get an abortion immediately." Turning to face his audience, he said, "Why don't we end the meeting with the song *Our Father, Our Leader* before we begin our day?" He began singing at the top of his voice, showing a protruding vein on his neck, and everyone sang.

A sickle in one hand and a hammer in the other
I follow Great Leader to the sunny path.
He's set examples for young and old
With his virtues, courage, and zeal.

Don't look for him in a green pasture
But on a rough terrain or on a stormy sea
He calls us to reform, to build the future
I follow Great Leader to the sunny path.

Time seemed to move slowly as Miyong merely mimicked the others. But the singing didn't last forever. The guard blew his whistle, and everyone scattered. Some men grabbed shovels or digging forks and jumped into the half-dug hole and began to dig, while others scooped up the loosened dirt and rocks and filled the empty buckets lying around the hole. The women's job was to carry the filled buckets to the dumping station 100 meters away amidst broken concrete, rocks, and other junk, and empty them for the next trip. *Easy enough*, Miyong thought.

Six armed guards, all male, walked back and forth, each with a thin bamboo stick in his hand, looking for lazy workers. Once in a while, one of them would lift the stick and lash out at an inmate who was either talking or catching their breath. The first victim was a shriveled old woman whose mouth drooped to one side. When the whip struck her back, she let out a sharp cry and tried to dodge away from it, but with more lashes falling fast on her frail body, she turned into a human ball, her knees drawn to her and her head buried in them. After a dozen or more times of the whip hissing in the chilly air, the woman uttered no sound and the guard moved away to find another to beat.

The second victim was a sickly-looking young male with an ugly scar on his forehead. When struck by the whip, he apologized, and continued apologizing until the guard grew tired of the man's submissiveness, and walked away, muttering to himself, "Pitiful swine!"

Miyong learned that day that only two kinds of people existed here in the camp: government employees trained to break people, and those accustomed to unlimited pain and fear. The lives of both were entangled tightly, forming a community. But she knew this was only the beginning.

After about ten round trips to and from the dumping station, she was tired, but more than anything, her urge to empty her bladder was strong. "Where's the bathroom?" Miyong whispered to Yonhee as they headed to the dumping station side by side.

"You can't go now!" Yonhee said.

"Why not?"

"We can go only twice a day — at the lunch break, and around four before going home. Why didn't you go this morning?"

"I did, but I need to go again."

"They won't let you. Hold it until lunchtime!" She walked away, afraid that a guard might be watching them talking and rush over with a whip.

Miyong endured until her bladder felt like a soccer ball, but luckily another whistle announced lunchtime. Dozens of women ran down the hill, and she followed. The toilet stalls were inside a hog farm behind a stockade fence. The wait was long, but what disturbed her most was the fact that the two-story shack was designed to serve two purposes: for humans to empty themselves and pigs to eat what humans dropped.

Miyong came out gagging, unable to shake off the image of the black beasts gathering under her, snorting and grunting, in anticipation of feasting on her waste. She was glad that the ordeal was done — but only until the next time she had to use the stall.

Everyone was running in one direction toward the blue canopy flapping in the chilly wind, so she followed them. Two male duty inmates wearing black aprons were lifting a scoop of yellowish porridge from a large cast iron pot and pouring it into the bowl each inmate was holding. When Miyong received her bowl of porridge, she looked for somewhere to sit. Yonhee showed up with her bowl. "Come, I have a place for both of us." She led her to a smooth rock under an acacia tree where the midday sun was warm. They sat and began to eat.

A skinny girl with ginger skin showed up and stood by them without a word. "Don't pay any attention to her," Yonhee warned.

Miyong kept eating the watery soup. There was no taste, but food was food. And she was hungry.

"Hey, girls," the skinny kid said.

"What do you want?" Yonhee asked.

"Did you hear what happened at the coal mine yesterday?" she asked. When no one volunteered, she went on, "The inmates blew it up with the dynamite they were using, killing themselves and two guards and injuring I don't know how many. It wasn't an accident: it was revenge."

"Who told you this?" Yonhee asked.

"We overheard the guards talking about it at the river bank. Me and two girls in my unit were collecting edible herbs inside the barricades behind their barracks, and we heard every word they were saying. They were shaken up, I'm sure. One of them said that they were going to beat the hell out of the rest of the inmates who got involved in blowing up the mine, but another said, 'Don't be stupid, if you don't want to die.' I think we'll hear about it today."

Yonhee said, "You shouldn't go behind those barricades, if you don't want to die. They can shoot you."

The girl laughed. "They can, of course, but it hasn't happened yet. But *living* comes first, you know, before you worry about dying. By the way, if you're interested in finding clean watercress and sweet, tender grass roots, come with me next time. There are plenty to go around."

"Not me!" Yonhee said.

The girl looked at Miyong. "How about you?"

"No thanks!"

Loud music burst from a speaker mounted on a light pole ten yards away.

The girl left quickly, saying, "Think about what I said. Live first, sisters, before it's too late!"

A woman's voice came on through the buzzing noises. "Dearly beloved comrades in Camp 14! It's the time for *'The Letters to Great Leader'* again. Our program has been so popular that each week we receive several hundred letters from all over the country. Unfortunately, though, we can read only three or four each day. Please listen to the messages of love and gratitude toward our Leader expressed by people like you serving time to reeducate themselves. The first letter I'm about to read is from a mother of three children who had been stranded on a rock island during a rainstorm, but was miraculously rescued by a team of Coast Guards."

Loud applause resounded from the speaker, as if it were a live program. When it quieted down, the woman read:

"Dear Comrades of the Democratic People's Republic of Korea, I am Kim Yonghyo, a mother of three children living in a fishing village named 'Rocky' off the east coast. I am here today to share with you my profound gratitude toward our beloved Great Leader who bestowed his fatherly love to an ignorant country woman like me. One bright day last summer, I was alone on a rock island, collecting mussels. The sea was calm when I got there, but around noon dark clouds began to gather, and soon rain poured down. The rock became very slippery, as the waves kept slapping me. I thought I would die at any given moment, leaving my poor children motherless." Her voice grew louder. "But lo and behold, a helicopter appeared overhead, and a man's voice called down, shouting, 'Don't be afraid, Kim *Dongmu*. Our beloved Great Leader himself ordered us to save you.' In no time, a soldier came down on a rope, hooked me onto his belt, and the next thing I knew, I was in the air like a bird. I was saved by Great Leader himself! That evening, I learned from my husband that he reported to the district office where I was, and they telephoned the National Emergency Rescue Squad working directly under Great Leader. Because of our beloved Leader, I'm alive today and my three children have a mother. Praise Great Leader!"

Applause burst from the radio and spread across the camp.

"*Dongmu*," the announcer said, "the second letter is from a male inmate from Camp 22 along the Russian border, the camp for very serious offenders."

She read, "I am Moon Kyorim, serving a life sentence here in Camp 22. Last year, we built a seventeen-mile dirt road between Mount Baikdu and Changjin-po and reirrigated countless creeks and brooks along the way. We also cut the crumbling slopes of the stony mountains overlooking a deep valley and leveled them so that a railroad could be installed there. One very cold night, huge rocks rolled down from above without a warning, and several men went down with them. An emergency medic arrived before dawn and rescued survivors, but two had died, and many were injured. To everyone's surprise, Great Leader himself came the next morning by a helicopter to visit the injured men in the hospital! We were so touched by his genuine fatherly love for inmates like us that we're working even harder today. As a result, we'll be able to complete 40,000 cubic yards of untamed land by next month!"

Applause exploded again but died down quickly as the woman read, "Wait! I'm not finished yet. 'Great Leader pardoned 200 workers from our camp, and we'll be released as soon as the project is completed.'" More applause resounded.

The next letter captured Miyong's attention more than the previous ones. It was from an artist, a painter who had painted Great Leader's portrait, which displeased Great Leader, and had ended up in a camp designated strictly for artists. He talked about how he had reformed and reeducated himself in the "Artists' Colony," and that his newly complete portrait of Great Leader was approved by the Central Workmen's Art Commission for the1969 exhibition in June, in Pyongyang.

The announcer said, "We'll deliver you more heartwarming letters to Great Leader tomorrow. Goodbye until then." The music returned at full blast.

Returning to Unit 264 with Yonhee that evening, exhausted, Miyong found the delirious teenager gone, but her possessions were strewn on her bed: a bamboo comb with a few missing teeth, a chipped palm-sized mirror, two books, and two pair of socks with patches. Miss Pellagra was alone in the room, sitting on the floor, inspecting the girl's belongings as if looking for treasures.

"What are you doing?" Yonhee said in a scolding tone of voice.

"Can't you see?" Pellagra looked up and sneered.

"You should leave the stuff alone, girl. How would you like it if someone went through your things when you weren't there?"

"I wouldn't mind," the girl said tersely. "Why should I, if I couldn't come back?"

"That isn't the issue here," Yonhee said sharply. "This is her stuff. Rummaging through someone's belongings when the owner isn't present is disgusting."

"What do you care? It's not yours. Why do you always have to act so high and mighty, College Girl?"

Yonhee's gaze held Miyong's for a moment, and returned to the girl. "If you call me *that* again, I will break your leg."

Pellagra pulled her skirt up, exposing a good portion of her thigh. "Go on, break it, College Girl!" she said calmly.

"You stay here!" Yonhee turned and headed to the kitchen as if she might find an axe.

The door opened and the three others walked in, spoiling the drama. Miyong was relieved and disappointed at the same time.

"Why are you all standing around?" Ajima asked.

"The *College Girl* is about to break my leg," Pellagra said.

"What have you done now?"

"Nothing. The right question would be, 'What is the College Girl up to?'"

Yonhee poked her head from the kitchen, and asked, of no one in particular, "Where's the hammer we used to have?"

"Hammer?" Ajima asked. "We never had one. What do you need a hammer for?"

"Ask the Pellegra Germ about it."

"*Tsk, tsk, tsk…*" Ajima clicked her tongue. "Were you going through the missing girl's stuff?" she asked Pellagra, who was sitting on the floor, holding her skirt.

"I was just looking at her photos. What's wrong with that?" Pallegra said.

Yonhee hurried back to defend herself. "I told her she should never touch someone's belongings when the owner isn't present, and she got mad at me, calling me College Girl. So I was going to teach her a lesson."

"Go on, I won't disturb you," Ajima said. "These young kids today never show respect for their elders."

"No kidding," said another.

"When are you going to learn some manners?" the third one said.

"*Manners?*" Miss Pellagra snorted. "Maybe when I'm in college."

Yonhee grabbed the girl's hair with one hand and slapped her with her free hand. "Next time," Yonhee said, "I will really break your leg. Be careful."

"Hey, aren't we going to lose electricity soon?" Miyong reminded them.

Everyone scattered. They moved fast to the kitchen to prepare dinner before the lights went out.

The next morning, a Sunday, around eight, Miyong followed Yonhee to the Assembly Ground Number 8 in the empty parking lot across from the main building for the weekly exercise session. Yonhee had been quiet since they left their unit, so Miyong didn't ask questions. Then suddenly, she said, "I don't mind if you ask me why a *College Girl* ended up here."

"That's none of my business," Miyong said.

"Don't you want to know how I ended up here?"

"Not really. If you tell me, then I might have to tell you about myself, too. I agree with Ajima. We shouldn't ask personal questions."

"It's like a novel." Then she began.

I spent most of my childhood in Cuba because my father was Associate Consul there for eight years. We lived in an old beautiful three-story Spanish-style stucco building that we shared with four other families from four different countries: China, Russia, Bulgaria, and Czechoslovakia. It had a balcony overlooking the courtyard with a trellis loaded with red roses, a fish pond surrounded by statues of Greek goddesses, and a small playground with a sand box, a swing set, and monkey bars. We ate toast and butter and hot cocoa in the morning instead of steamed rice and kimchee, and Spanish-style goulash for lunch. We ate Korean food only for dinner. But that ended abruptly in my second year of high school, because Father was appointed to the director of the Foreign Exchange Division in the Central Workmen's Party in Pyongyang.

It was such a big change for me, you know, coming back to Korea as a teenager. Being with the Korean kids all day and eating Korean food three times a day was my new routine, which I wasn't comfortable with. Bread and butter were rare commodities here in Korea. But the funny thing was, the teachers thought I wasn't like a typical Korean kid and thought I was interesting, even smarter than the rest of the class. They picked me for just about everything — to sing Cuban songs or to dance a Cuban dance or to read something in Spanish, which no one could understand, of course. They even enjoyed my Spanish accent when I recited the old Korean poems. I think the country was so isolated that anything from the Western world stirred their curiosity. My classmates stole my pencils, my plastic rulers, and even my notebooks! It was eye-opening…quality pencils and notebooks made of white paper were hard to find.

It went on like that for the whole year. At the national holiday celebrations, I was always a solo dancer, along with a handful of others whose fathers were important party members. Once, the six of us shook hands with Great Leader at a reception. I didn't wash that hand for a month! It sounds silly, doesn't it? But believe it or not, I enjoyed the attention I was getting. I was "somebody" that other kids couldn't be.

Two years later, I entered Kim Il-sung University. Although I was only a freshman, I worked at Kim Il-sung Library because my Russian was better than that of most of the students. I handled hundreds of volumes on Great Leader's battle history against the Japanese while he was a captain in the Russian military—his diaries, and the letters he wrote to men like Joseph Stalin, Nikita Khrushchev, Leonid Brezhnev, Chang Kaishek, and Mao Zedong, to mention only a few. The following year in April I received a strange invitation from Kumsusan Palace, Great Leader's private home. He invited me to his fiftieth birthday party, along with five girls from our school, out of four thousand students! No boys, only girls. I couldn't believe it.

When my father heard the news, he made a long face. He particularly disliked the fact that the party began at nine p.m. instead of seven, like most parties. On the day of the party, as I was combing my hair and powdering my face in front of our oval mirror we had brought from Cuba, Father came and said, "I don't want you to go. I just don't feel good about the whole thing."

I told him not to worry. "There will be hundreds of people there tonight. And we're not kids!"

"That's why I'm worried," he said. "It's not what you think, child.

Great Leader's taste for a party is different from most men his age. To give you an idea, he drinks a potion made of deer antlers and bear testicles! Do you get the picture, child?" He went on and on until my mom finally shushed him, saying that he talked nonsense to his young daughter. A limousine showed up just in time, and I left home. Riding in a limousine with five others, all in long, colorful dresses, I felt like a princess from a faraway land.

As we passed the arched gate of Great Leader's palace, every guard in his well-pressed uniform bowed to us. In the lobby, adorned with chandeliers, long mirrored walls, and giant paintings, a tall slender woman in a long black velvet dress met us and led us into a brightly lit room with mirrored walls, where about two dozen girls my age sat on leather sofas, smiling nervously. We were introduced, while a man wearing a tuxedo served us pinkish drinks in delicate crystal glasses. The woman handed each of us a small square bag tied with ribbons and told us to open them. Mine had a strawberry-colored bikini and a sapphire pendant on a gold chain! Others had similar things, only in different colors and styles.

"What are these?" I asked.

The woman smiled big, showing her white teeth. "Special gifts for special young ladies. Put them on, why don't you?"

"This is swimwear," I said, picking my bikini up by the strap.

"Yes, it is. It's called a bikini and was introduced in Japan a few years ago. You'll be swimming with brand new naval officers just graduated from the Academy. Great Leader wants you to look your best for his favorite sons."

"But why in these? Why not in regular swimwear?" I asked.

She laughed a nervous laugh. "Because Great Leader wants you to. This is a surprise pool party Great Leader is hosting for his sons, get it? He wants to surprise them." Pausing for a moment, she concluded, choosing words carefully, "A smart young woman must understand men's desires and help them celebrate their manhood. Now, girls, let's get ready. I'll be there myself!"

It sounded reasonable, I thought. No one asked another question as we changed into the bikinis and wore the beautiful pendants in the room with *tall mirrors everywhere. Then we followed the woman to the basement, and then to the enclosed pool room under the dome-shaped glass roof.*

The steam obscured the view of the night sky, but we could still see thousands of stars looking down at us. The "officers" were waiting in the Olympic-sized pool. The woman introduced us to them, and they applauded. We joined them.

It was a total shock, Soonok. They surrounded us like a pack of wolves at the sight of fattened rabbits. And they were all naked! Our shock turned to panic when the lights went out, leaving only a dim recessed red light at each corner of the pool. A hand touched me! Then suddenly, two arms wrapped around me and I was pressed against a meaty, slippery chest. His breath was reeking of alcohol and other smells — I didn't know what. He pulled me tightly to himself, as if he were about to bury me in his body. Then something hard dug into my lower abdomen. I pushed him, but I was too weak to do anything against the force of his arms. My arms and legs felt very heavy and useless. This was when I vaguely understood that the drinks we had had were making me lethargic. The sky turned pitch-black and I saw no stars. Then the man did something I can't describe. I bit his arm, and he slapped me. I bit him harder, and he hit me harder too. Water splashed everywhere and the girls were fighting desperately just like I was. Then, I couldn't breathe. He had pulled me into the water and was holding me there! I kicked and hit him. I have no recollection of how long I was underwater or what happened to me after that. I woke up on a hardwood floor without a stitch on me, shivering and bleeding, too. I was charged with assaulting, insulting, and disobeying a naval officer, and without even a trial I rode in a black sedan to this place. Two years went by very fast, Soonok, believe it or not, but I have three more years to live in this dungeon, this hell on earth...

"Three more years!" Miyong exclaimed.

"Yes. But I'm glad that I've met you, Soonok," Yonhee said. "One thing you and I have in common is that we have the same goal, the goal to *live*. Probably you've noticed that some of the girls here don't even have that, the goal to live another day. They only exist, not even knowing they're alive."

*   *   *

Assembly Ground Number 8 was crowded with nearly two hundred men and women in work clothes waiting for the exercise session to begin. Old people were there too, blowing steam into their hands or shivering like wet dogs rescued from a creek. After a long wait, the door to the Administration Building swung open, and a dozen guards in identical gray knit exercise uniforms marched out and fanned in front of them. Lee *Bujang* was there, too, third from the right.

Miyong flinched when she noticed Pit Bull among them, at the far left. She moved a few inches to her right to avoid facing him.

A man with broad shoulders wearing tight, tight knit pants climbed up to the platform. "How's everyone this morning?" he asked.

"Fine!" the inmates replied in chorus.

"Louder! I can't hear you," he shouted at the top of his lungs.

"Fine!" everyone shouted.

"Good, I like to hear your energetic voices, Comrades. Exercise not only boosts your energy, but also improves your brain activity. You can be more productive in your daily life if you exercise regularly. Let's begin." He began to blow whistles, as he jumped up and down, throwing his arms to his sides and then over his head.

Everyone followed his example.

"Jump higher," he shouted.

Miyong thought it was insane to jump up and down like this so early in the cold morning, after the thin breakfast soup. Her arms and legs felt heavy and her throat hurt from inhaling the cold air. She kept thinking about the steaming white rice, hot spicy beef soup, and crispy salted grilled mackerel she would eat at Hope Community before a long day at a rice paddy or a hog farm.

"Jump higher, at least a foot off the ground!"

Amazingly, everyone did as they were told, spewing white steam into the chilly air.

The instructor changed his motions into something that resembled Tae-kwon-do chops, kicking his legs over his head alternately and punching the air with his fists, one after another. "Legs higher and arms straighter!" he ordered.

Miyong began to pant, and thought she might expire shortly if she kept on doing this. A whip snapped in the air, startling her. But she felt no pain. *Who was hit?* Looking over her shoulder, she saw a middle-aged woman slumped to the ground. On her knees, she was wheezing and hacking with coughs

A duty prisoner with a white armband stood next to her, counting down, "Five, four, three…" The woman tried to lift herself up, but she couldn't. When she slumped back to the ground on all fours, two men with a stretcher rushed over and took her away.

With another shrill of the whistle, it was suddenly over. But they didn't scatter. Everyone stood around, wiping sweat and heaving their shoulders.

"What are we waiting for?" Miyong asked Yonhee, who was also wiping her face with her sleeve.

"He'll tell us," she said. "We might go to the amphitheater and watch a soccer game or a kangaroo court."

"Kangaroo court?"

"Line up," the instructor ordered.

They formed two long lines.

"March!"

Everyone dragged their feet, like defeated troops. Miyong noticed that the camp officials weren't marching with them; they returned to the building.

Miyong wished she could sit and rest, sipping hot tea or even plain water. Yonhee seemed to think the same as she walked beside her, her head bent. Even if they'd had energy to talk, what could they talk about?

"How much longer do we have to walk, Yonhee?" Miyong asked.

"Ten minutes!"

"Ten minutes?" Miyong said. "And we have to walk back here, and by the time…"

"I'll take it back," Yonhee said. "It's just around the corner. The best thing to do is not to worry about how long it will take to get there, but think of something else. Or count your steps. Time goes faster that way."

Yonhee was right. Before Miyong counted two hundred, a C-shaped outdoor theater opened up in the lower ground. It was packed with inmates bundled up in their mud-colored quilted coats, hats, scarves, and even tattered blankets. This structure reminded Miyong of a baseball stadium in Seoul, with terraced seats under a dome-shaped roof, but this one was smaller and had no roof. The group scattered to the empty seats. Yonhee and Miyong walked down a few steps to find seats in the center aisle, and they sat side by side.

"What's happening here?" Miyong asked.

"The way it's set up, we'll be watching an execution," Yonhee said casually. "See those wooden posts over there?" She pointed to the center. "That's where they tie the condemned and shoot." She showed no emotion, as if they were about to watch a dogfight, which was common in the South.

"They actually shoot people to kill?"

"*Shhh!* They are listening."

"Yonhee, I am about to watch people die, but you're asking me to be quiet?"

Yonhee pinched Miyong's arm. "Please don't get me in trouble," she said through clenched teeth.

"Look, they're coming!" someone behind them shouted.

Three camp officials, each with red stars on their shoulders, appeared from the side door, marched in, and positioned themselves with about six feet between them, facing the audience. A covered military truck crawled in from the opposite side and parked near the farthest post. A guard with a red armband got out of the driver's seat, moved to the back of the truck, and lifted the tarpaulin, and six handcuffed men jumped off. The guard had them line up, blowing a whistle, and the criminals formed a single line. Some of them had bloodstains on their striped prison uniforms, and others had bruised cheeks or swollen eyes or red welts on their foreheads. The guard walked the prisoners toward the posts, and tied each one to a post, taking time.

One of the three camp officials spoke into the microphone. "We're about to witness how justice is served to enemies of the Democratic People's Republic of Korea. Our Great Leader gave each of these men a chance to cleanse their crimes against our Great Nation and be reborn as a contributing citizen, but instead of repenting their wrongs, they spat in his face by deliberately committing more crimes."

The crowd responded, "Kill them! Kill them!"

The speaker waited until the crowd quieted down and continued, "The three men on your right are the South Korean infiltrators who, over the past two years, methodically lynched our military officials. The ones on your left are the foreign spies, two Americans and one British, who, like the South Koreans, did much harm to the Democratic People's Republic of Korea. Let me remind you, Comrades, that our Great Leader once said, *Dead branches must be pruned, before they claim the life of the tree.* What would be a fair judgment for these criminals?"

"Death!" the crowd said in chorus.

One prisoner shouted from the post. "You made up that story!" he said in his halting Korean. "I'm no South Korean – I'm a Japanese businessman! Your leader, Devil Kim Il-sung, lured me to come, promising that he'd help my business grow, but he stole everything and threw me in a prison. And now..."

The guard rushed over and slapped the prisoner across the face, but the prisoner didn't stop. "Deliver my message to your chief. Tell him I'll be waiting for him in hell!"

With a loud drum roll, a firing squad marched in and spread out, each shooter positioning himself about ten yards from the men on the posts. "Ready!" the leader yelled, his arm raised, and the men took a firing position, each dropping one knee to the ground, his rifle aiming at a prisoner.

The audience went wild, shouting, "Kill them! Shoot them!

"Fire!"

The rifles opened fire. The popping noises lasted a few seconds.

Miyong closed her eyes, but the noises of running feet forced them to open. Men and women were running to the front, yelling insults.

"What are they doing now?" Miyong asked Yonhee.

"It's a tradition here that the audience is invited to cast stones at the corpses. It's a symbolic gesture, telling the corpses that they don't deserve a peaceful rest. Let's go!"

"Go where?"

"We have to throw rocks at them, too. Otherwise, the guards will be suspicious of us."

"I'm not going!" Miyong said. "Go, if you want to!"

Yonhee ran to join the stone casters. While watching stones flying through the air and listening to the voices cursing, insulting, and spitting, Miyong shivered. *Why are people so cruel? Do they realize that they could be on the receiving end of such cruelty someday, too?* "Yonhee, come back!" she shouted, but the marching feet of the firing squad heading to the gate, and the accompanying drum roll, swallowed her words.

Chapter Twenty-Three

AT LUNCH TIME THE next day, as Miyong ate with Yonhee at their usual spot under an acacia tree, she saw Lee *Bujang* walking in their direction. He had a long bamboo whip in his hand, like other guards often had, but he wasn't looking at her. He seemed to be looking for someone to strike, turning his head this way and that. She had mixed feelings about seeing him here. He might have news of the prince, but why was he carrying that whip?

He abruptly stopped about ten feet in front of her, and scratched the side of his head. Pointing at her suddenly, he said, "You! Come with me!"

"Me, respectable *Dongmu*?"

"Yes, you!" Turning his back to her, he began walking toward where he had come from.

She got up and followed him, leaving her soup bowl where she had been sitting. They walked for about a minute or two, him leading, until they came to a vacant lot strewn with dried leaves, vines, and rotted logs.

Turning to her, he said, "Please lower your head while I'm addressing you."

She obeyed.

He said, "It took me longer than I thought, but I have finally created a spot for you on the cleaning crew at the guest house. Be there at seven tomorrow morning and report to Kim Yongsoon *Dongmu*. The guest house is the one facing the main building."

"Yes, *Dongmu*."

"Kim Yongsoon and I've been working together for more than three years but again, don't volunteer any information. In this place, blind trust can cost your life and others'."

"I understand."

"What you need to do when you meet the prince is to tell him who you are and why you are here. Convince him that you're on *his* side."

"What if the prince doesn't believe me? He might not trust what I have to say."

"Don't worry, he'll trust you," Lee *Bujang* said without hesitation. "When you're locked in, like he is now, you don't have the luxury of doubting those who bring good news. Doubts are for privileged folks, whose bellies are full and whose minds want to be entertained. Those who fear for their lives…they'll believe anything that gives them a bit of hope."

"But I am a total stranger to him."

"He can't afford to doubt your words or sincerity. He has no other choice than to believe your words. Trust me. Anyway, I'll be talking to you soon. Watch for me next time, will you?" He left.

Kim Yongsoon was about a head shorter than Miyong, a homely woman who carried with her a bundle of keys. She had been waiting for Miyong at the door, and as soon as they exchanged greetings, she led her to the utility room.

Compared to Unit 264 in the women's barracks, this place was a castle. The wooden floor shone like a mirror and the ceiling was white and smooth, without cobwebs. A life-sized color portrait of Kim Il-sung on the wall captured Miyong's curiosity. Even in the South, color photos were rare, and she was looking at one here, in a prison camp.

"You'll be cleaning six rooms today," Kim Yonsoon said when they entered the utility room, "so take all you need."

Miyong picked up an empty bucket and filled it with rags, a bottle of liquid soap, and a scrub brush. Kim Yongsoon handed her a bristle broom and a mop with a wooden handle.

Before entering Room 15, the nearest of the assigned six rooms, Yongsoon informed Miyong about the occupant. Mrs. Petkov was the wife of a visiting Bulgarian diplomat who had fallen ill with pneumonia while traveling with her husband and the Central Workmen's Party members. "Poor woman!" Kim Yongsoon said and clicked her tongue. "She can't understand a word we're saying. Twice, I found her crying, but what can I do?"

In the room, a dark-haired, middle-aged white lady with feverish cheeks lay in her bed. "Hello ladies," the Bulgarian said in English, in her congested voice.

"Hello," Miyong responded in English.

Kim Yongsoon's head automatically turned to Miyong, her eyes wide in disbelief.

"Oh, you speak English!" the white lady said, beaming. "This is first time I've heard someone speaking English since I got here. Come here, dear. Where were you hiding all this time?"

Miyong immediately covered her error by saying, "Yongsoon *Dongmu*, I can say only *Hello* and *Thank you,* in English. But how can I tell her that?"

Yongsoon laughed. "I can do *that* much myself. But seriously, I wish I could speak some Russian."

Seeing that Miyong had switched to Korean and was ignoring her, Mrs. Petkov seemed disappointed. She remained quiet, her eyes blinking.

"Let's skip sweeping," Yongsoon instructed. "Dust can bother the lady. I'll be back in twenty minutes." She left.

When Yongsoon was gone, the Bulgarian seemed hopeful again.

"You do speak some English, don't you? I can tell because you sound very natural."

Miyong didn't return her gaze, nor did she speak. She quietly mopped.

"It's been awfully lonesome here," Mrs. Petkov said. "I've been lying here for more than a week now. No one tells me where my husband is or what he's doing. They just bring me a food tray three times a day, and when I leave it untouched, they take it away. What kind of life is this?"

Miyong kept mopping, her mouth clamped shut. The worst thing she could do for this poor lady was give her false hope that someone could talk in English with her.

The Bulgarian didn't give up. "You see, my husband should have been back by now from the trip. I don't know why he isn't dropping me a note or sending someone to check on me. My hands are tied here, can't you see? I don't know what's worse, being physically sick or worried sick."

It took an enormous effort for Miyong to pretend that she was deaf. *Sorry, lady. I wish I could talk to you, but I'd better not. Please forgive me.*

The Bulgarian finally turned her back to Miyong, and remained in that position until Kim Yongsoon returned.

Kim checked everywhere, looking for dust and grime Miyong might have overlooked, running her finger over the windowsills, the bookshelves, even the floor. She then made sure that the trash basket had been emptied and the bedspread smoothed. "The only thing I want to recommend is not to use a wet rag on the windowpanes. It makes streaks. Use paper next time. It works a lot better."

"I'll do that, Kim *Dongmu*! Thank you for correcting me."

They left the room without saying goodbye to the Bulgarian.

Before entering Room 18, the prince's room, Miyong told herself to be calm. *Your big moment has come, Hahn Miyong. You can either do your job and help him out of this dungeon, or screw it. It's your choice! Take a deep breath before you walk in!*

Kim Yongsoon opened the door without a knock, and Miyong followed. The prince sat at a desk, scribbling something on a white paper, his back turned to them. He wore a fairly clean beige-colored Mao-style quilted coat, but his long matted hair indicated that he had not bathed for at least a week or two. *What is he writing?* Miyong wondered. He didn't stir, although the door had creaked.

Kim Yongsoon cleared her throat loudly and said, "Yi *Dongmu*, we have a new housekeeper this week. If you have any specific instructions for her, please tell her. Her name is Lee Soonok."

Prince Koo didn't seem to hear what Yongsoon said. He kept scribbling.

"See, he doesn't hear me," Yongsoon said. "He's far away. They say that he's crazy, but I'm not quite sure about that. Once in a while, I can tell he understands where he is or what I say to him. At least he isn't dangerous." She then turned to the prince again. "Well, Comrade," she said louder than before. "Tell me how you like your new cleaning lady when I'm back, okay? Don't be shy about it." She left the room quickly.

Miyong's heart fluttered in a nervous rhythm. She had anticipated this moment and even practiced her speeches in her mind. Twenty minutes were all she would have to explain why she was here and answer any questions he might have. But standing only a few feet from him, she didn't know how to begin.

Taking a deep breath, she said in English, "Your Highness, I have news for you."

The Prince stopped writing. He sat as still as a plant.

"Please listen to me, Your Highness. My real name is Hahn Miyong, but I came here under the name Lee Soonok. The CIC sent me to help you escape from here."

A deadly silence followed, as he did not stir.

"I can't tell you exactly when or how you will be rescued, because I don't know that myself. But please prepare yourself for the time when it will happen."

Slowly, the prince turned and studied her for a moment. His once

clean, handsome face was now that of a beggar: his skin rough like
the bark of a tree, his lips swollen and parched, his overgrown beard
matted with grime and filth. But his sunken eyes glowed furiously,
as if he didn't believe what he had just heard. "What are you saying,
Comrade...?" he said in a low, frightened voice. His first words!

"It's true, Your Highness. I'm here for you. In a few days, you'll
be rescued."

"How... how do I know you're telling me the truth, miss?"

"I wish I could show you my CIC badge or a letter from the
director of CIC, but carrying such papers with me could cost my life,
not to mention the danger you might get into. You have to make some
effort to trust me, although it's difficult." She told him how she got
involved with CIC, after her brief encounter with the North Korean
commandos, who unsuccessfully attempted to assassinate the South
Korean president. She told him why she had been selected for this
mission instead of experienced agents.

The prince's expression changed slowly, though he still looked
nervous. "You say that you're here to get me out?"

"Yes. What I need now is your trust in me."

"And you work for CIC?"

"Yes."

"May I ask who sent you here?"

Miyong told him about Major Min; that he had promoted her to
be his secretary from a common member of a women's community
involved in the urban development program on Kanghwa Island; that
he was the mastermind of this rescue mission. "Major Min told me that
he met you at the Blue House last May."

His eyes fluttered as he tried to remember who Major Min was.
But there was a hint in his eyes that told Miyong he felt safe with his
prospective rescuer. "Major Min...?" he said, tilting his head slightly
to the left. "The name doesn't sound familiar, miss," he said, talking
fast. "You see, there were about five hundred people at the presidential
mansion that day, all trying to talk to me and my wife, and asking us

to pose with them for photos. I'm sure I'll recognize him when I see him."

"I'm sure you will, too, Your Highness. Major Min said you and he talked in Japanese."

"I spoke mostly English and Japanese that night. To tell you the truth, my Korean is bad — so bad that I want to hide if someone tries to talk to me."

Miyong laughed, and he did too. Encouraged, she said, "If you'll allow me to express myself, Your Highness, your father's request for an amnesty from our government created a sensation in Korea. Seeing your father returning to our country is like seeing our beloved old dynasty coming back to life. I read every word in every article that talked about him! I am so honored to meet you and speak with you like this, in spite of this misfortune..." Her voice quivered, and she stopped.

"How's my father now?"

"I believe he's still in the hospital, Your Highness. Other than that, I know nothing about him or your mother. CIC kept your abduction secret from the public."

"That's a good idea. If my parents find out where I am, they'll probably die of heartbreak."

"I know. And maybe some older people who remember the elder prince might, too, Your Highness."

Prince smiled uncomfortably. "Miss. would you please drop that 'Your Highness' title? I'm a common man, not a prince."

"What should I call you, then?"

"Call me Edward. That's my American name: Edward Yi."

Miyong heard footsteps in the corridor. Quickly, she picked up a rag and rushed to the bookshelf. She began to dust.

Prince Koo resumed his writing as before.

Kim Yongsoon entered. "How's it going?" she asked Miyong.

"Very well, Kim *Dongmu*," Miyong replied earnestly. "But I didn't wipe the windowpanes yet because I don't have paper."

"I'll get you some," she said. Turning, she said the prince, "How's it going with you, Comrade?"

The prince didn't reply, just like earlier.

Yongsoon shook her head, and then left the room.

Prince turned back to Miyong. He was now a different man, his eyes showing a flicker of hope. "I don't know how to thank you for coming for me, Miss Hahn. I've been so moved by the Korean people's loyalty to my father, to my mother, and to me since the day I landed in Seoul. But…" He stopped, his voice cracking and his lips twitching. With a gentle cough into his cupped hand, he continued, "I'll do anything, Miss, anything at all. Please tell me what I must do."

"You can do one thing for now, Your Highness."

"What's that?"

"Don't insist that I call you 'Edward.'"

"But that's my name!"

"You know that Koreans don't call anyone older than themselves by his first name, Your Highness. Besides, 'Edward Yi' sounds so foreign, like the name of a star."

He burst into laughter, tilting his head back. Then, with Yongsoon's footsteps in the corridor, he became serious. "We'll discuss it some more."

After sundown that evening, Miyong entered the utility shed next to Unit 264 for the first time. Using her Magic Pen, she wrote on the back wall: "The Crane is ready to fly home."

Miyong didn't work in Room 18 the next day or the next. But she saw the prince when she passed in and out of the back door to empty the bucket or to fetch water from the well or to wash dirty rags.

He strolled across the parking lot alone, his hands locked behind him, stopping only to talk to a tree or to passing inmates who never acknowledged him in any way. Passing the parking lot, he kept walking toward a busy area where construction workers swarmed until she lost sight of him.

Chapter Twenty-Four

"SNAKE!"

A sharp shriek awakened Miyong at dawn. Beds creaked and blankets rustled. "Where?" said a voice.

"Here, in the kitchen. I saw it!"

"Don't let it get away!" another voice rang out.

Feet drummed the floor.

"Shucks! It got away. It was right here and I lost it."

"No, it's there! I see it under the stove!"

Feet drummed some more. "Give me the broomstick! Hurry!"

Miyong didn't get up. She was too tired to worry about a snake that might have made a wrong turn somewhere and shown up here in the women's bedroom. She had seen snakes in Kanghwa Island a dozen times, on the way to the mountain and while cleaning barn houses. The village folks welcomed snakes because they killed mice, squirrels, and other pests. Once, when Miyong had screamed her head off at the sight of a snake that was as long as her belt, an old woman clicked her tongue and said, "Snakes are more afraid of humans than we are of them, child. Don't pay any attention to it and then it will go away."

But her roommates were terrorizing the creature. After another long moment of shouting, banging, and whacking, a victory was declared. "We got it! We got it!"

"It's a good size for stew," a voice said.

Stew?

"It will feed all of us!"

"Oh, I can't wait!"

Miyong got up and moved to where the excitement was. In the kitchen, everyone stood on their bare feet, encircling the table on which there was a black snake with a yellow stripe, about two feet long, as thick as a small child's arm. A bloody spot on its head and a cast iron cooking pot next to it told her how it had died. Miyong remembered one of Larry Tompkins' lectures about the food shortage in the North.

"North Koreans eat anything that crawls or walks or flies or swims — except manmade things — to supplement their meager food allowances. They'll eat your leather shoes or purse or belt, too, if you let them. During the famine, small children became victims of cannibalism. The parents couldn't eat their own, so they traded them with those of their neighbors, to ease their conscience."

Back then it was just one of the horror stories she heard in the classroom, but standing here, in this kitchen, in front of the dead snake, Tompkins' lecture rang in her ears like a parable read by a priest.

Her roommates were now talking about how to prepare the snake. "Let's grill it on an open fire and have a feast," Miss Pellagra said.

"Are you out of your mind?" Ajima said. "The whole community will follow their noses and gather here, in this room. And if the guards find out, they'll confiscate it even before it's cooked. It's better to pan fry it in a skillet."

"She's right," Yonhee echoed. "I think making soup is better."

Ajima clicked her tongue. "Do you know how long it takes to cook a snake until it tastes good? We don't have enough fire logs."

"I'll get some driftwood on the way back from work."

"We need more than you can carry," said Ajima.

"I'll make two trips."

"Okay, but by the time the soup is ready, the electricity will go out, leaving us in the dark. Let's think about it some more." She then clapped her hands. "Time to get ready for work!"

That evening, returning from work, Miyong found her five roommates sitting around the table with long faces, not talking. The unit leader was absent. "What's going on?" she asked.

"I think Ajima did something with the snake," said Soonyi, her pimples redder than ever before.

"It's Tuesday, too," Miss Pellagra joined in. "Tuesday is the day Ajima works in the kitchen at Guard House Number Two. Remember?"

"What are you saying?" Miyong asked. "Are you implying that Ajima gave the snake to the cook?"

"You're brilliant!" said Soonyi. "If she sees something he might like, she takes it to him."

"Without asking permission?"

"Permission? What's that?"

"Shhhhh! She's coming."

The door flung open and Ajima walked in, balancing a stuffed burlap bag on her head. She dropped the heavy bag onto the table with a loud thud and let out a long sigh of exhaustion.

"What do you have in the bag?" asked Yonhee.

"Today is a lucky day for all of us!" Ajima said, while unfastening the twine on the bag. Nearly two dozen potatoes in all sizes rolled out, along with a few discolored cabbages.

"Where did you get these?" Miyong asked.

"They came from heaven!"

"But what about the snake?"

"I exchanged it for these! It just happened that Comrade Choi was looking for a snake or an opossum for his sick father, and I made a deal with him. The old man is dying with lung cancer, on top of the pellagra he has been suffering for a long time. He needs protein badly, to stay alive."

"We need protein, too," Soonyi said, touching her pimples.

"We all need protein," said Ajima without losing a beat. "But a tiny bite of a snake isn't going to fix your pellagra, Soonyi. Considering our food situation, I did the best I could for everyone. These vegetables will last for a while."

"At least we'll not be eating each other," Miss Pellagra said sarcastically.

"Very funny," said Ajima.

"I'm not trying to be funny," said Soonyi. "I'm trying to make a point about the food shortage here. That snake was big and healthy. It could feed..."

"Shut up!" Yonhee snapped. "You make me sick! Didn't you hear what Ajima just said?"

"I can say what I want to!"

Ajima clapped her hands. "Girls, if you keep arguing, I'll bring the snake back from Guard House Number Two. Comrade Choi is still there. I know he'll give it back to me. Should I do it?"

No one said another word. Miyong learned a new lesson here: the quantity of food was far more important than the quality of it.

"Okay, let's get busy before we lose electricity," said Ajima.

They got busy. Potatoes were sliced and greens were chopped, while the cutting board, which had survived many years of abuse, changed hands. Water splashed every time it filled a container. When potatoes and greens were dropped into the cooking pot and then the pot was on the stove, everyone sat in her usual corner and waited in anticipation.

Miyong fought a strong urge to offer them the vitamin capsules hidden in her bag. But the bottle was clearly labeled "Samsung Product, Seoul, South Korea." Another idea was that she could use the North Korean money Major Min had given her and buy chunks of ox tail or beef ribs and make hot beef soup for everyone. But who would take her to the market? Other than the delivery truck drivers and repair crew coming and going, everyone here depended on their feet. And some of the inmates didn't have shoes, and some wore torn canvas shoes showing their dirty toes. And even if she could buy meat somewhere and brought it here, how would she know Ajima wouldn't take it to her lover? It wasn't a practical thought.

The potato porridge served them well. Each of them had two servings and wiped their mouths in satisfaction. When the table was wiped and the dishes were washed and dried, they all found something to do while electricity lasted: some brought their torn skirts or socks to mend, some had books to read, and one began to sing a children's song Miyong was familiar with and they all hummed along:

Little Calf, little calf in the barn
Why do you cry every morning?
My mommy went away, so I cry!

Little Calf, Little Calf on the hill,
How many spots have you got on you?
As many as my mommy has on her!

Miyong couldn't help but smile. She felt connected with her roommates in a way she had never imagined before. The fact that they could still enjoy singing a children's song together while living in a dreary place like this seemed amazing. Now, she was eager to feed them a decent meal. She looked for Yonhee to ask her how she could go to a market.

Yonhee was alone, sitting on her bed, reading a book, her face almost touching the opened pages.

"What are you reading?" Miyong asked casually, standing by her.

Yonhee closed the book so that Miyong could read the cover.

"*Stone Pillow?* What is it about?"

"It's a biography of Great Leader based on his battle experience against the Japanese as a young man. Would you believe that he and his comrades slept in the mountains, using stones as their pillows and sky as their covers? It's quite inspirational."

Miyong was surprised that Yonhee was an admirer of Great Leader. "Do you think I should read it, too?"

"I highly recommend it." Yonhee's gaze lingered on Miyong for a moment or two. "You didn't come to talk about the book, did you? Is it about the pellagra girl?"

"No, it's about something else. Can you keep a secret?"

"Of course."

Miyong sat next to her. "I have some money, Yonhee, and I wonder if there's a place I can buy some extra food for everyone."

"How did you smuggle your money in?"

This was unexpected. "Well, no one said I couldn't."

"Keeping money in the camp is illegal," Yonhee said, her tone of voice dropping a notch. "It's not allowed. You should have declared it on your first day here. But then, the guards would have confiscated it and divided it among themselves. If I were you, Soonok, I'd keep my mouth shut about the money. An inmate buying food for others is unheard of here."

Miyong realized her mistake. "You're right, Yonhee. Thank you for your advice."

Yonhee studied her for a moment. "Keep my name out of it, if you get caught for keeping money, will you?"

"No problem."

The light went out, leaving them in the dark. Feet moved about and hushed conversations followed before they faded in the darkness.

Another night here, Miyong thought as she lay in her bed. She was wide awake. *Oppa, what are you doing now?* She tried to remember the contents of his last letter. He had talked about rain and how homesick everyone in his tent was. He had talked about digging trenches that gave him blisters on his hands. Then, a men's chorus resounded in her ear, and the scene at the train station flashed back, the crowd shouting slogans and the policemen cracking them with their clubs…and the smoke! She could even feel the hot sensation in her throat and lungs that gave her an urge to cough, but she resisted it.

"Are you asleep?" a voice whispered. It was Yonhee, talking from her bed against the wall.

Miyong did not respond. She wasn't in the mood for a conversation with her. It was the time to ponder on her brother.

"I know you're awake, Soonok. You've been turning and shifting ever since the light went out."

Miyong said nothing.

Yonhee came closer and sat on the floor two feet from Miyong. "I've been watching you, Soonok," she said, her warm stinky breath on Miyong's neck. "You're very different from the rest of us. I'm not just talking about your Southern accent, Soonok. You stand out like...a sunflower in full bloom in a field of wilted grass."

Is she trying to be poetic when I'm about to fall asleep?

Ajima yelled from the darkness. "Stop talking, whoever you are!"

But Yonhee didn't stop. Lowering her voice to a whisper, she kept on: "Actually, everything about you is different from what we're accustomed to here. Your teeth are white like pearls, and you move quickly and smartly, never dragging your feet like we do. And your eyes...They're alive; they're not dead like ours."

Miyong felt as though a hammer had just landed on her head. She had not worried about her Southern accent since she had lived in the North as a child, but somehow Yonhee had noticed! What else did she know?

"Another thing," Yonhee said, "about you keeping money... Do you know how thoroughly I was searched when I first arrived here? Two duty inmates took me to a room and had me strip. Why didn't they do the same to you?"

Miyong couldn't pretend any more. "Yonhee, you woke me up. What were you saying?"

"You heard me. I was asking why you weren't searched like I was, on the day you got here."

"How am I supposed to know that? I don't work here. A guard picked me up at the checkpoint and brought me here."

"Good try, but I don't believe you. They search everyone without exception. You somehow got in without being searched. That never happens here. And you want to feed others! Don't tell me you're Jesus Christ wearing a skirt!"

"That's not funny!" Miyong said, defenselessly. She felt cornered. *How can I keep her mouth shut?* "Hey, don't get me in trouble! If you don't tell anyone about the money, I'll split it with you. I have one hundred won in my bag, and fifty is yours."

Yonhee didn't respond.

"Well? Say something!"

"You're not serious!"

"I am serious. I don't want to be interrogated."

"Where did you get the money, anyway?"

Miyong lied. "I made it in Dandong, China."

"Doing what?"

"Do you have to ask for details? Just to give you a hint, Dandong is a heaven for women: there're night clubs, dance halls, public bathhouses, massage parlors, taverns…you name it, and Dandong has it. If you ever get out of here, go to Dandong. You'll have no problem getting a job, a well-paying one!"

"Your offer is accepted, Soonok. And no one will ever know what we've just discussed, okay?"

"Good!"

"But for now, keep the money until I ask for it. We'll talk more. Good night!" She slid away into the darkness, and Miyong heard the rustle of her bed covers.

The next morning, Wednesday, Miyong left Unit 264 early, alone, without waiting for Yonhee. She couldn't let Yonhee complicate her life, not with an important mission she must accomplish. The air was chilly. Since she had arrived here, the trees were losing their leaves fast, showing their barren branches. Winter was around the corner for sure. She knew it was October, and winter came early here in the North. At the crossroads, a rusted pickup truck was parked on the side of the path leading to the main area. She dropped her gaze to the ground and slowed her pace. This was the same spot where she had been struck twice by the guards — once for not bowing quickly enough, and another time for not waiting for a motorcycle to pass before she crossed it. She hoped that the truck would pull away before the driver saw her.

The truck's horn honked.

She couldn't help but look up. Lee *Bujang*, wearing sunglasses, sat at the steering wheel, motioning her to come near. She ran to the side of the truck and lowered her head. "I'm surprised to see you here, Lee *Dongmu*."

"Hop in. I have something to tell you."

She walked around to the passenger's side, and he opened the door for her. The truck moved. Turning right at the crossing, they headed straight toward the hill. When an empty brown field strewn with bales of hay and stumps of trees appeared on the left, Lee parked the truck.

"I got the message you left in the utility room," he said, looking at the windshield. "We're looking at Friday. Father Sohn will be at the cemetery on Friday with his crew, and he'll have a truck. It's a dilapidated Russian model with a cover, the same kind as the delivery trucks here. Can you get the prince ready at the lunch hour, on Friday?"

"Lunch hour? What should I tell Yongsoon *Dongmu*? She'll be there."

"Tell her you're taking him out for a walk. Lunchtime is when the guards are busy eating and paying little attention to what's going on around here."

"But if I take him for a walk at lunchtime everyone will see us. Male and female inmates never walk together, as you know. We'll draw attention."

"He's a sick man, and you work in the guest house. No one will be suspicious."

She still didn't feel comfortable with the idea. "We'll have a better chance when it's dark, and Kim Yongsoon is out of the building."

"Keep in mind that security is tighter at night, and the guards have permission to shoot anyone suspicious. That's the rule here. Besides, how can you get into the building without Kim Yongsoon? You need a key to get in."

"I'll tell the prince to meet me outside. By six o'clock, it's dark and there're places to hide."

"Are you sure?"

"I'm positive."

"Fine, then. I'll tell Father Sohn to be there at six in the evening. Play it safe, hear?"

"Of course."

He turned the ignition and then turned to her. "One other thing. Tell the prince to stay put in his room until Friday evening. I saw him wandering about the main area, mumbling to himself, probably in English." He shook his head. "If someone hears him talking in English, he's dead. Besides, I'll lose my head, too. All his papers in the infirmary and the guest house have my signatures on them."

"I'll deliver your message."

Lee *Bujang* steered the truck around and drove back to the crossing. Miyong jumped off, and the truck sped away, leaving the stink of gas in the air. *Friday!* She had only two days until Friday. Actually, she had only forty minutes, if Yongsoon let her work in his room both days. If Kim Yongsoon assigned her to another room on one of those two days, she had only twenty minutes. Her earlier meeting with the prince had been successful, which wouldn't guarantee anything. Today, she would tell him that it was actually happening and that he should be prepared. She began to run.

"When are they coming?" Prince Koo asked as Miyong walked in, showing wrinkles on his forehead. He seemed drained.

"They'll be here this Friday, Your Highness!" she whispered, excited.

"Friday!"

"Yes. Lee *Bujang* just told me. He's the officer who moved you here from the infirmary. Do you remember him?"

"No. All I remember is two men in white masks. It was at night. I don't remember how many days ago it was."

"Lee *Bujang* asked me to tell you to stay put in your room until you're out. If you don't, it could complicate things."

"How can I live in this hell for two more days?" he muttered, throwing his hands into the air, oblivious to her warning. "I haven't been able to sleep since you were here last. I can't eat, and can't sit still. Does the U.S. Embassy in Seoul know about this?"

Miyong was surprised that he mentioned the U.S. Embassy. At the same time, she realized that he still had an analytical mind. "Your Highness, I've told you that only a few CIC officials know about your disappearance. Even your parents don't know where you are, sir. How do you expect the embassy to know about it?"

"I'm not expecting my parents to do anything," he said, raising his voice. "But the U.S. Embassy should know where I am. I'm an American citizen. They can influence the Chinese government to put pressure on the North Korean leaders to release me. It's as simple as that!"

Now, Miyong was frustrated. "How can the Chinese government do anything for you? Mao Zedong hates Americans. He could hurt you more than help you if he knew where you are."

"Tell me then, who's going to get me out of here on Friday?"

"That's what I was about to tell you. Please sit down."

The prince sat in his chair like a child, his folded hands between his knees. Miyong briefed him about Father Sohn: that he operated a safe house for refugees near the Chinese border and that he had single-handedly helped nearly two hundred people to reach freedom in the South. "Father Sohn and his men have access to this camp as gravediggers and this Friday, they'll be here again with a truck. The next two days will be like the blink of an eye compared to the time you've spent here, Your Highness."

"Long enough for me," the prince said. "This Friday is my ninety-sixth day here: I've been here nearly one-third of a year."

"You've been counting!"

"Of course I have. Wouldn't a man on a death row count his

remaining days? Come, I'll show you something." He rose and moved to the bookcase against the wall.

Miyong followed him.

"See those notches? I made them with my thumbnail, one each day. It was the only way I could remind myself that I'm alive. I lived one day at a time until you came. It is very difficult to feel that you're alive when everything is dead around you. You know what else I did?"

"No, sir."

"I recalled every day how I ended up here so that I won't forget. I'm not crazy, as the doctors at the infirmary seemed to think. Some men brought me here, and that's the truth. Of course no one believes me. My memory of that summer evening is as clear as what happened yesterday." The prince began to pace, his hands locked behind him. "That morning, a very warm day, my mother left for the Seoul University Medical Center to be with my father, and I was all alone again, surrounded by the palace employees who spoke neither English nor Japanese. You see, my mother went to the hospital every day, staying there all day, but I went every other day, because my father feels awkward when I'm alone with him, mostly because my Japanese is poor and he can't speak any English but I was in America for about ten years before I came to see him. Anyway, after lunch that day, I snuck out of my parents' place that used to be servants' quarters, and entered the main palace that's now open to the public. I had a wonderful time, walking in the park-like courtyard with ancient gazebos, sculpture of gods and warriors, and ponds full of colorful koi and water lilies, besides watching tourists passing by, taking pictures. I caught some men talking in English and I chatted with them, too. There's something wonderful about hearing the language of your home when you're thousands of miles away, especially when you're locked up like I am now. At closing time, instead of returning to my parents' place, I exited through the main gate with the tourists, without any particular thought other than just to get away. And then I saw people boarding the bus, and I got into one of them. It was the bus heading to Inchon Beach. It was my grandiose escape from the palace employees, who were always bowing to me and speaking in

Korean. The beach was wonderful. I spent hours there, walking on the sand and buying snacks from the vendors, without worrying about who might take a photo of me with a hidden camera or try to interview me, speaking in Korean. It was freedom!

"After sunset, when I was about to leave, a small rowboat carrying a young couple, who were waving and calling, 'Yoboseyo [Hello]!' slid toward me. I stopped what I was doing and waited. When the boat was near, the man said in Korean, 'Sir, I'm looking for the park with General MacArthur's statue, but I can't find it. We're Japanese tourists. We'd really like to find that park!' He was a pleasant-looking fellow with a camera dangling on his chest, and the woman seemed educated, too. She wore lightly tinted sunglasses and a straw hat against the setting sun. I gave him the directions in my poor Korean, and they thanked me and rowed away. I dried my feet and put on my shoes, and began walking to the bus station. I heard the same voice again! When I turned, he said, 'Sir, would you mind coming with us? We're new here, and I'm afraid we might not find the park before dark. All we need to do is take a few photos.'"

"I told him I had to return to Seoul for a family dinner, and kept going. 'We're going back to Seoul, sir,' he said. 'I have a car and we'll give you a lift!' I couldn't find a good excuse not to go with them. And the thought of returning to the capital at rush hour on a bus was dreadful. So I agreed. But the man didn't steer the vessel the way I navigated for them; it went opposite direction, toward a landmass in the middle of the ocean! I began yelling to take me back to the beach in my poor Korean, and the woman stabbed my back with what seemed like a needle. I passed out. When I came to, it was pitch dark, and I was in another boat, much larger than the earlier one. I noticed that my hands and feet were bound with something rough, like heavy rope, and my mouth was stuffed. I'll never forget the helpless feeling that came over me as I lay on that dirty floor, breathing the sickening smell of tar, while my feet and hands were tied, like a pig heading to a market. I must have screamed or tried to get up, because I remember a sharp sting again, this time on my hip. After another long period of ambiguity, I woke up in a different room, with thumping noises of feet, and people talking in a strange tongue. Again I was sedated. I don't know how many times I woke up and passed out or how many days I was on that boat.

"Finally I was in a room with white walls and the clean smell of alcohol. I was glad that I was still alive, until I learned that the officials could hear any conversations that went on in the room, through the secret devices hidden behind the walls. Because of this, my doctor, a young man by the name of Chun, lost his job, and I don't know where he is now. He was kind to me; when I spoke in English accidentally, he'd actually cover my mouth with his gloved hand, pointing at the ceiling, while talking louder about my condition or giving me instructions. Soon after, they moved me here, and one day you came in with unbelievable news. Good news isn't always easy to deal with for someone who has been expecting the worst. In fact, I was terrified, not knowing whether I should believe you."

For the first time, he smiled and let out a long sigh. "Can you understand why I dread being here for two more days?"

Miyong too smiled. "I understand, Your Highness. But it won't be long until we'll both walk out of here. Please trust me."

"I trust you. What else is there for me to do except to trust you?"

"I must go now, Your Highness. Our time is up!"

"Are you coming back tomorrow?"

"I'm not sure. If Comrade Yongsoon lets me, I'll be here at the usual time. If not, I'll be here on Friday for sure! See you then."

Chapter Twenty-Five

MIYONG DIDN'T SEE THE prince all day the next day, which was Thursday. When she passed his door, she wished that he'd peek out so that she would know he was there, instead of wandering about the camp. But it didn't happen. He wasn't outside, either. She worried about him. Around two in the afternoon, Miyong was dying to ask her supervisor if she had seen him, but knowing that she might get a crazy notion in her head that she had some feelings toward a male inmate, she asked about the Bulgarian lady first. "How's Mrs. Petkov doing today?"

"Her fever is down, but she still cries a lot," Yongsoon said in a flat, all-business manner. "I think she misses her husband."

"So he hasn't come back?"

"No."

"That's too bad…I hope he's all right. And how about the guest in Room 18?"

"He's fine. Lately, he stays in his room all day for some reason. He doesn't act so crazy when I see him in the hallway, either. Yesterday, he even said, 'Hello, Kim *Dongmu*' when he passed me."

"I'm glad. I have to go. Talk to you later."

That evening, when Miyong entered Unit 264, Ajima was crying, her nose red, while slicing potatoes on a cutting board. The rest of the women moved about the room in silence as if someone had died.

"What happened?" Miyong asked.

"Did you hear the radio during lunchtime?" Soonyi said.

"No. I was at the guest house."

"Lucky for you. You should never believe what comes out of that stupid box anyway!"

"What are you talking about?"

Ajima blew her nose loudly into the hem of her skirt before she said in a congested voice, "The radio announced that six *escapees* were shot down at the restricted area at the riverbank. You know who the escapees are?"

"No."

"Six girls, and the teenage girl who beat you is one of them."

"You mean they were trying to run away?"

"Of course not. The girls were collecting edible plants to eat — you know, watercress, grass roots, and weeds. You see, the children and women going behind the barricades were ongoing headaches for the guards on patrol duty. What triggered them to shoot the girls was that two male inmates escaped through the same spot, wearing women's clothes and scarves, the night before. The guards blamed the women for supplying their clothes, and shot them all."

Miyong remembered the girl informing her and Yonhee about that spot, saying that clean watercress and other edible plants were plentiful to share with others. She wondered if she had been a victim of the shooting.

Ajima was inconsolable. "One of them is my old neighbor's daughter. Poor kid… How can I look at her mother when I go back to the village?" She cried openly.

"Look at it this way, Ajima," Soonyi said. "Those girls are free now, including the crazy teenager. They don't need to suffer from pellagra or starve or be beaten!"

"Oh, you think dying is better than living here, eh?" Ajima released her steam on the girl. "If you want to die, it's easy! Go behind the barricades at the river, and the guards will show their kindness!"

The light went out. Deathly silence filled the room.

Before Miyong could collect her thoughts on the girls killed by the guards, especially the *crazy girl,* a faint siren in the distance captured her full attention.

"That's fire engine," someone said in the dark.

"Fire?" everyone said as they got up and moved to the window facing the road.

Miyong too went to the window. Towering flames rose above the main area where all important buildings stood, and sparks of orange and yellow danced in the dark sky like fireflies on a summer night. The wind must be strong, because the flames grew taller and wider by the second. Trucks and motorcycles passed their barracks, their headlights bright and shiny, and followed the dirt road leading to the towering inferno.

At the watchtower beyond the main area, a twin beam rotated, one sweeping over the main area and the vast vacant land to the left, and the other over the river's edge to the construction sites, revealing the bleak structures in between. The siren sounded eerie now, like the voice of a mourning woman at a funeral.

"Who set the fire?" someone asked stupidly.

"Why do you care?" someone else said.

Friday morning at dawn, Miyong was wide awake. This was her last day here, as well as the prince's, if all went well. When Lee *Bujang* would confirm what he and Miyong had discussed on Wednesday, she'd meet the prince at the guest house at a few minutes before six p.m., probably near the back door, and wait for Father Sohn's truck to show up.

She carefully pulled her bag from under her cot, opened it, and fumbling through it, she found her pouch. She removed a few North Korean bills from it and slid them in her pants pocket, just in case. She took out her pistol from the bottom of the bag and secured it inside the elastic of her underwear, just as she had done earlier. If something unexpected were to happen, it might save her life. And this pistol made no sound, Min had said.

She ate her last breakfast with her six roommates, acting casual, while thoughts cluttered her mind. Yonhee kept looking at her as if trying to read her mind. This annoyed her. "Why are you looking at me?" she asked.

"I'm not looking at you; I'm looking at a grain of rice you're saving on your cheek."

Miyong laughed, brushing it away. "I thought you were about to accuse me of something I didn't do."

"You're so paranoid."

"Let's go!"

Thin layers of smoke mingled with white fog around the main area, obscuring the view of the tall mountains beyond. The smells of smoke and soot permeated the air.

"About the fire last night," Miyong began, "has it happened before?"

"Many times. Didn't I tell you that about 2,000 men and women die here every year? Most of them die from illnesses such as pellagra, pneumonia, cancer, dysentery, and malaria, but others die unexpectedly, like in a fire or from explosions at coal mines. Of course, some kill themselves, but that's rare."

"Do you think it was arson?"

"I'm almost positive. Life is never complicated here, Soonok. Men with power crush the powerless, and the powerless can't take it anymore and explode like a bomb. Do you know what can happen to so many inmates in connection with the fire?"

"No."

"Some will be executed in the woods, some will go to the mountain to finish the railroad their fathers' generation started, and some will end up in Siberian forests to log. This is according to the agreement Premier Khrushchev and our Great Leader made a few years ago."

"What agreement?"

"That the Russians could use laborers to chop down trees from their vast forestland, and our Leader could use money. The deal was 50/50. You don't have to be a psychic to figure out what can happen once you land in the frozen land. Most of them never come back."

"I didn't know they made such a deal. Who told you about it?"

"You don't think people talk? Like Ajima, some women have connections with guards or other inmates. There are no such things as secrets here."

At the crossroads, they split; Miyong walked straight to the guest house in the main area, while Yonhee headed toward Construction Site 12.

The main area was blocked off with orange-colored tape, and the half- burned administration building stood like a colossal skeleton, black everywhere, thick wires sticking out of the beams and broken concrete walls. Several armed guards stood around, smoking and talking, while inmates wearing masks pounded on the blackened walls with sledge hammers or shoveled debris.

In front of the guest house, a tall guard Miyong had never seen before stood, watching her. "The building is closed, except for employees," he said.

"I work here, *Dongmu*."

"Let me see your employee ID."

She had no ID. "I'm replacing someone only for this week. Ask Kim Yongsoon, *Dongmu*. She's my supervisor."

"What's your name?"

"Lee Soonok, in Unit 264."

"Wait here!" The guard turned and walked in. A few seconds later, he came out with Kim Yongsoon. She looked pale. "We don't need you today, Soonok. A guest had a massive heart attack during the night."

Miyong was stunned. "Who had a massive heart attack?"

"I can't tell you that; it's against the policy. Please go. The detectives need me inside." She hastily walked back in.

Miyong didn't know what to do. *What if it were the prince?* She looked at the guard, with a faint hope that he might divulge some information, but he dismissed her with a quick wave of his hand.

She couldn't just leave. She walked to the side and approached the window of Room 18 to get a glimpse of the prince. But the reflection of the sky with white clouds had taken up the windowpane, leaving her no room to peek in. She was about to tap the window when a guard on a scooter rounded the corner and came in her direction. As he stopped and parked his scooter against the side wall along with other scooters, he asked, "What're you doing here, Inmate?"

"I'm one of the cleaning crew here, but I can't get in."

"Don't you know the building's closed?"

"I do, but a guest is expecting me. I told him I'd be here this morning. If I don't show up, he'll be very upset."

"I see…" He had a queer, all-knowing smile across his wide face. "A special guest, eh?"

"Would you please let me in, for only five minutes?"

He paused, as if thinking. "Try later. I'll be at the back door from noon to six. I'll see what I can do."

"Thank you, *Dongmu*."

"I'm not promising anything, understand?"

"Yes, *Dongmu*." Miyong bowed to him and turned to leave.

"And keep it confidential."

"Of course."

At Construction Site 12, she didn't see Yonhee at first, but after a few minutes, she showed up. "Hey, did you notice that we have only two guards here this morning?" she said.

Miyong then looked around. Not only did she find just two men with rifles, one on each side, but they weren't looking for someone to strike with the bamboo whips; they were just standing. "What does this mean?"

"It means that the other guards are somewhere else, probably looking for the arsonist. I've just heard that several top-notch officers are being held in connection with the fire. One of the big guys is responsible. Get the picture?"

Thoughts crossed Miyong's mind fast. *Lee Bujang is in trouble! If he's locked in, how can I make the connection with Father Sohn? What could happen to the prince then? What could happen to me?*

"What's the matter?" Yonhee asked, studying Miyong's face. "Are you not feeling well?"

"Where's the cemetery?" Miyong asked.

"*Cemetery?* Who's dead?"

"A guest had a massive heart attack during the night, my supervisor at the guest house just told me. That's why I'm here, not at the guest house. I'm wondering where he might be buried when he dies."

"There're a dozen cemeteries here in the camp, but the closest one is over that hill." She pointed. Squinting in that direction, she said, "Actually, I see a truck going up there now. Maybe they got the order already to dig the grave."

Miyong saw an old truck with a cover lumbering up the hill, dragging clouds of dust behind it. Her heart pounded. "How long would it take to walk there?"

"Ten minutes? Fifteen at the most. Why do you want to go there?"

"I'll tell you later." Miyong grabbed an empty bucket and quickly filled it with dirt. "If I'm not here at lunchtime, go ahead and eat without me, okay? See you later."

"Are you out of your mind?"

Miyong carried the bucket to the dumping station and emptied it. No guard was on her tail, and all the inmates were busy doing their tasks, so she slipped into the woods and followed the trail. This vast property was all connected with trails, so if she kept walking toward where Yonhee had pointed, she knew she would find the cemetery. The question was how long it would take.

It was not an easy walk. In the area where grass wasn't growing, the hardened mud had created deep grooves, potholes, and bumps on the surface. After a few minutes of laborious walking, she came to a deserted, flat area with mangled bushes. On her left lay bales of straw, where several malnourished hens were pecking at the dirt, and on her right was a tree lot carpeted with long brown pine needles. Walking some more, she saw four scrawny boys about eleven or twelve years old looking for something on the ground, maybe pine nuts that had fallen during the night. In Seoul, boys their ages would be in school about this time of the day, and when school was out they'd file into the market, buying candy, noodle soup, and roasted squid from the peddlers. *Why are these boys searching for pine nuts, like squirrels?*

Then, she found what she was looking for: the same military truck she had spotted moments earlier. It was parked near the poplar trees that bordered the cemetery. She ran toward it.

The cemetery was large and well leveled. A white canopy was flapping in the wind fifty yards away, and four men in civilian clothes stood about, one smoking, two digging, and one merely watching the diggers. Miyong walked straight to them.

One of them, the one who was just standing and watching, turned around, and seeing her, he rushed over. "Hahn *Dongmu*, we've been hoping to see you," the man said.

"Father Sohn! How glad I am to find you here."

Father Sohn introduced the three others, calling each Peter this, Paul that, and John something. "This young lady is who I was talking about," he said, excitedly. "God heard my prayer!" Turning back to her, he said, "Did you hear what happened to Lee *Bujang*?"

"That's why I'm here, Father. He was supposed to tell me how I could meet up with you, but I haven't seen him since Wednesday. I heard that several high officials are locked in, in connection with the fire."

"That's right. He needs our prayer. But we're going ahead as planned. We can pick you and the prince up at six this evening at the guest house."

"The guest house is closed, Father. I was there this morning. A guard is watching at the front, and I believe one is in the back, too."

"Then bring him here at any time. We'll hide you and the prince both in the tool shed over there," he pointed, "until we're ready to leave."

Miyong looked at the wooden shack with peeling paint under one of the poplars. It was a rectangular-shaped shed, large enough for a dozen people to hide in. "I'll see what I can do, Father. I might be able to see the prince this afternoon for a brief moment, if the guard I've talked to doesn't change his mind about letting me in. But if you don't see us here by five, plan to find us at the crossroads at six, not at the guest house."

"God be with you." Father Sohn said in a solemn voice.

"God be with you too, Father," she said, and turning, she headed back toward the guest house.

As she passed Construction Site 12, she saw men and women gathering around the canopy to get their lunch, and she felt a pang of hunger stabbing her stomach. But it wasn't a time for thinking of food, no matter how hungry she was.

At the back door of the guest house, the guard was waiting for her, as he had said he would be. He had been sitting on a wooden stool, reading a magazine, and when she said, "*Dongmu*, I'm back!" he looked up.

"May I get in now?" she asked.

"Which guest are you going to see?" he said, closing the magazine.

"The guest in Room 18."

He took out a white paper from his back pocket and glanced through it. "Edo-ward Yi, the Korean-Japanese architect?"

"That's him."

"How long are you going to be with this architect?"

"Ten minutes."

"That long, eh?" He smiled, showing his yellowed, gummy teeth.

Miyong took out currency from her pocket and handed it to him. "This is from the architect. I'll tell him how kind you've been to me."

He took the money and quickly put it into his uniform-shirt pocket. "I'm sure you're worth a hundred times more than this to him."

Whatever you want to think! She entered the building. It was deadly quiet. She walked carefully, to avoid making noise, but the floorboards creaked louder than ever. At Room 18, she knocked.

The prince opened the door. "How did you get in?" he asked in a hushed voice. "I thought I might never see you again." He blinked nervously.

"The young man in the back let me in. I think money helped."

"Get in!" Closing the door behind him, he was eager to talk. "What time are we leaving? Is the truck here already?"

She told him everything: that she hadn't seen Lee *Bujang* for the last two days and that he might be tied up in connection with the previous night's fire. "But I've just spoken with Father Sohn at the cemetery, and he suggested that we should meet them there, at the cemetery, as soon as we can, and they'll hide us in the tool shed until they're ready to leave. The problem is, Your Highness, we might attract the guards' attention on the way there. As you know, no male and female inmates walk together here in broad daylight."

"What should we do, then?"

"You go first, and I'll meet you there later, when I'm done at the construction site."

"How long will it take to get to the cemetery?"

"It's about thirty minutes from here." She gave the directions. "It's easy to find. See those poplars on that hill?" She pointed through the window. "That's the cemetery."

"But how can we get there?" the prince asked nervously, like a child on the first day of school. "The guards are at both ends of the building. If I walk out, they'll stop me."

"Your Highness, I can occupy the guard at the back door for a few minutes, long enough for you to get out. I can't guarantee anything, but if you're careful, you might get there. We have no other choice."

He wasn't convinced. "The guard at the back... What does he look like?"

"He seemed harmless. He might not be very bright, but he was kind to me. I know I can distract him for a few minutes by talking to him."

"Please invite him for a drink."

"What?"

His eyes glowing, he said, "I have a bottle of whiskey that a Japanese guest gave me when he returned home a few days ago. I am willing to share with him."

"But why do you want to give a guard a drink?"

"I want to borrow his uniform."

"You mean, you want to steal it?"

"Simply put, yes."

"What if you get caught?"

"It's better to get caught in a guard's uniform than in this." He patted his chest. "In this, I am a human target, but in his uniform, I am somebody. I hope I'll have the time to tell you how I felt in the North Korean prison guard's uniform some day. It'd be an extraordinary experience for me! Go on! Just tell him what I said. I'll do the rest." He nodded.

She had no reason to argue. She bowed and went out to see the guard.

"Are you leaving already?" the guard asked. "It's been only five minutes."

"I'm here to deliver a message from the guest, the architect."

"A message for me?"

"Yes. I told him how kind you were to me and he wants to invite you for a glass of whiskey."

"Whiskey?" he asked, springing from the stool.

"Yes. He said that a Japanese guest gave him a bottle when he returned home and he would like to share with you."

"I'm never too busy for a drink, but whiskey? I'll be there shortly. We're not allowed in a guest's room, so please keep me out of trouble."

"My lips are sealed, *Dongmu*." Miyong returned to Room 18.

"Is he coming?" the prince asked, standing before the desk loaded with a bottle of Johnny Walker and three empty sake cups.

"Yes, he is. I guess I'll go back to the construction site."

"No, stay," he said. "Sit by me and pretend that you're drinking. Men always enjoy the presence of a lady, I'm sure you know that."

There was a soft knock on the door, and the prince opened it. Smiling like a little boy before a camera, the guard entered, took off his hat, and bowed deeply toward the prince. "Thank you for your invitation. I'm truly honored," he said in Japanese.

The prince shook the guard's hand, as if he were meeting a distinguished guest. "Please, have a seat," the prince said in Japanese, seating himself in a chair. Miyong sat next to the prince as she had been told, and the guard sat on the opposite side, facing the prince. He set his hat next to him, on the table.

The prince served the drinks. With a "clink" of the glasses, they each took a sip.

While pretending that she was drinking, Miyong didn't miss the guard's servile manner toward the prince. Was it because the prince was half-Japanese and an architect? Unlike other guards, this young man showed no contempt toward Miyong, an inmate, probably because he thought she was having an intimate relationship with this Japanese-American architect. This thought amused her rather than angered her.

The prince kept pouring whiskey into the guard's glass, and the guard kept emptying it. Soon, the guard's eyelids drooped, and his words lost articulation. He kept laughing, without a reason, his cheeks tomato-red, and the prince went along with him, acting jovial and sipping the whiskey, too. The guard's head went down toward the table, and when his head touched it, he remained in that position, mumbling incoherently. The guard sounded as though he were talking with his mouth full.

The prince tried to help the guard to stand, but he slipped onto the floor, like a huge sack of potatoes, and then giggled. While talking to him, the prince laid him flat on the floor and began to unbutton his topcoat.

The guard didn't seem to know he was losing his coat, and kept giggling. It took only a few seconds for the prince to get what he needed, leaving the guard on the floor in his underwear, like a sleeping child. The prince then moved to his own bed, grabbed the quilted comforter, and returning to the guard, he covered him with it.

"How do I look?" the prince said when he wore the guard's uniform over his inmate's outfit. The uniform was too big and too long for his bony frame.

"You can fool anyone as a Red Guard, Your Highness, but I think you need your hat." She handed the hat to him and he wore it.

"Are you still calling me 'Your Highness,' Comrade?"

"I don't know what else I should call you, sir."

"I've already told you. Call me Edward."

"Comrade Edward, it's time to go now!"

"That's better."

Walking out of the room together, Miyong leading, they tiptoed toward the back door. When they slipped out, the sky had turned gray and not a single soul was in sight. "I'll meet you at the cemetery, Comrade Edward, as soon as I'm done. Good luck!"

The prince's gaze lingered on her for a moment, and then he touched his hat in a salute.

Turning, she headed to Construction Site 12. This was a longer way through the grass field, but it was safer because no guard would stop her to question her. She abruptly stopped walking. *What's that noise?* Turning, she saw the prince pulling the scooter from the wall, making scratchy noises against the concrete.

What is he doing?

He turned the ignition on and the motor growled. The prince jumped aboard and the scooter lurched forward, and before she could think what to do, he passed the front of the guest house and rode up the hill, toward the main area. The front door sentry ran out, shouting, "Hey, stop!"

The prince didn't respond, nor did he stop. The front door sentry rushed to another scooter parked on the side of the building, and lifting himself onto it, he followed the prince.

Dumbfounded, Miyong stood and watched the racing scooters,

until they disappeared. She resumed her walk, only faster. The best thing to do for now, she thought, was to lie low until five.

The work crew at the construction site was busy: some digging, some gathering dirt with small hand tools and filling the buckets with it. Miyong quietly walked to her usual spot, a few feet from Yonhee, trying not to disturb anyone.

A guard came over, blowing a whistle with authority. She bowed deeply and said, "I am sorry; I'm late coming to work."

"Why are you late?" he demanded.

"I wasn't feeling well, Comrade. I rested for a few minutes on the way here. I'm sorry..."

"What's wrong with you?"

"I'd rather not discuss it here, if you don't mind, sir."

"What? You're twenty minutes late and don't want to tell me why?"

Dropping her gaze to her hand, she said, "You wouldn't understand it because men don't have any clue what we women go though every month. Please, don't make me talk about it!"

The guard laughed awkwardly. "You're not lying, are you?"

"How can I prove that I'm telling the truth? But I'm fine now. If you want me to do extra work for being late, I will."

He stood there for a moment, and said, "We're expecting rain this afternoon. Don't be late again!"

"I promise, *Dongmu*."

As soon as the guard walked away, Yonhee came closer and whispered, "Are you having cramps?"

Miyong nodded.

"Try to chew on juniper berries. That's the best thing. I'll find some for you on the way back from the dumping station."

"Thanks, Yonhee!"

As the guard had said, it began to rain, accompanied by roar of thunder. *Forget juniper berries, Yonhee,* Miyong thought. Within minutes, the rain turned into a downpour and everyone was soaking wet. Dirt turned to clumpy mud, and digging or scooping became laborious. But no one dared to quit and no bells buzzed to liberate them. Miyong shivered in the cold. *Such hateful weather! What has happened to the prince? Did he make it to the cemetery before the rain? Did the guard catch him...?*

A loud siren wailed in the midst of thunder and rain. *What now?* A military Jeep approached them, its headlights shining bright. It stopped in front of the working crew, and four guards jumped out. Three men were armed with pistols, but one wasn't. While the unarmed man remained next to the Jeep, the armed ones each took a position, aiming their pistols toward the workers. It was like a scene from an action movie.

No, they didn't come for me, Miyong told herself. She had left the guest house only moments ago — ten minutes at the most — and the back door guard, without his uniform, had been sound asleep, on the floor, unaware of what he was losing.

"Don't move! Stay where you are!" one of the armed men, the tallest, shouted.

Miyong couldn't believe her eyes. It was the front sentry! She was lightheaded. *What if he sees me?* On second thought, finding her among this many people and in such weather wouldn't be easy. Thank God for the rain!

The tall guard turned to the man by the Jeep and asked, "Do you see the woman you let into the guest house?"

Wait, is that the back door guard?

"Yes, that's the bitch over there!" He pointed his hand directly at her.

The thunder roared louder than ever.

Chapter Twenty-Six

The Cage

IT WAS COMPLETELY DARK and very cold. The air was thick and heavy. And there was that smell, as though men had been urinating against those dark walls ahead of her. *Where am I? Why am I here?* Somewhere water seemed to be dripping, making musical sounds.

Her legs were achy when she accidentally stretched them. Something dull poked her belly. *The pistol!* She felt a current of electricity passing through her head. She remembered everything now: the Jeep coming toward the construction site in the pouring rain, and four guards jumping out; and her horror at seeing the back door guard from whom the prince had "borrowed" a guard's uniform, who identified her as the "whore". It had been the longest ride she could remember, the ride in the Jeep from the construction site and to this underground prison cell. She heard men's voices.

I must hide the pistol. But where? Now, the voices she had heard earlier were replaced by the sounds of feet on the dirt floor. She knew the prison guard would soon emerge from the darkness to take her for interrogation. Fumbling under the mat on which she lay, she learned

that underneath the straw mat was bare dirt, as damp as soft clay. She
sat up, carefully lifted one side of her mat, and poked the dirt with her
forefinger. It gave in. She began to dig, using all her ten fingers. Within
seconds, the hole was deep and large enough to bury the pistol, and she
laid it in the hole and covered it with clay-like dirt. *It will rust here,* she
thought, *and maybe never be discovered.* Who cared?

A bluish beam was coming in her direction, its light getting brighter
and brighter. She knew now where she was: she was in a wooden cage
with metal bars, the kind of cage for large dogs. It was about four feet
high and four feet wide.

"Lee Soonok, get up and follow me," a dark figure said as he
planted himself before the metal bars.

She saw dirty boots attached to khaki pants, but as she followed
her eyes up and up, she saw a man wearing a Mao-style uniform, and
holding a flashlight. Now the light was so bright in her eyes that she
automatically blocked it with her elbow. "Where are we going?" she
asked.

"You'll soon find out. I wouldn't ask too many questions, if I were
you." He unlocked the door with a key and opened it.

She had to bend low to get out. The light danced wildly on the
dirt as the guard led the way. The only sounds she heard now were the
guard's boots crunching against the dirt floor and his keys jingling on
his belt. *What time is it? Is it morning?* Turning twice, first to the right
and then to the left, they came to a brightly lit room similar to the CIC
Interrogation Room she had visited while attending The Pigeon's Nest
espionage school in the South. Though this room was smaller and had
a dirt floor instead of the concrete floor, they were built for the same
purpose — to break human bodies and spirits. On the wall facing her,
a poster hung with the inscription:

Answer all questions sincerely, truthfully, and in a timely manner
No arguments are allowed
Use proper language at all times
Anyone violating the above is subject to punishment.

With a coal burning stove crackling in the center, this room was warm and cozy, but Miyong couldn't stop shivering as she faced the middle-aged man and the young woman her age sitting at a square table. The woman wore the same uniform and the cap as the man, and seemed capable of cruelty.

The man spoke first. "Tell us why you're here!"

"I don't know why I am here, Comrades. Please tell me."

"What?" the woman shrieked, as if pricked by a needle. "You don't know why you're here?"

"No, Comrade!"

"Look here," the man said, trying to be gentle. "Do you think we have nothing better to do than waste time with an inmate who has no clue as to why she's locked up in the maximum security cell?"

Maximum security cell? Miyong didn't answer.

He pounded the table. "Answer! Where is Guest Number 18, whom you were with earlier today?"

Guest Number 18, the prince? He must have escaped, then. Otherwise, why would they ask me that? She felt better. She no longer shivered. "How am I supposed to know where he is?" she said. "I couldn't even get into the building this morning."

"Don't play games with us!" the woman snarled. "We have a witness who testified that he allowed you into the building around noon, and you lured him to Room 18 for a drink. When the witness passed out from drinking too much, you helped Guest Number 18 steal his uniform. Can you still claim your innocence?"

It was her word against the "witness," Miyong thought, which could be only the drunken guard himself. If she admitted what the woman just said, she'd rot here, in the *maximum security cell*. If she denied it, they would not believe her. *So why should I make life easier for them?* She dropped her gaze to her own hands. One of them was considerably dirtier than the other. She was glad that she had buried the gun in the dirt.

"Do you know what can happen to you," the woman said, "if we find you guilty of lying under oath? You can be hanged. You might think you can get away with this by not talking, but you'll regret it."

Still looking at her hands, she said, "Don't treat me as though I'm guilty of the charges you're building against me. Consider that your witness is a government employee who got drunk during his time on duty, and he'll say anything to save his neck. Again, I couldn't get into the building this morning, so I went back to the construction site. Call the guards there. They'll tell you."

There was a long moment of silence, and lifting her eyes, she saw the man looking directly at her, his eyes narrowed. "Then tell us why you were late returning to work after lunch? What's your excuse?"

Miyong repeated the same story she had given to the guard at work: that she had had abdominal pain which only women go through every month, and that she had needed to rest.

"Why should we believe you?" the man said. "You have records of improper sexual conduct with Chinese border patrolmen, and you ran away from the camp twice, didn't you?"

Miyong said nothing.

"You were caught for the third time near the Chinese border and brought back to the camp — can you deny it?"

"I didn't come here on my own to argue with your accusation. Whatever is on the paper is undeniable. So why do you even bother to ask me those questions?"

The man seemed to be losing his patience. He fidgeted. "Let's get back to Guest Number 18. How did you get acquainted with him?"

"I was one of the cleaning crew in the guest house."

"Were you…physically involved with Guest Number 18?"

"Comrade, how could you accuse me of such a thing? He's Japanese."

"Oh, you can fornicate with Chinese men, but not with Japanese? That's interesting! You have a conscience, I'd say."

Miyong saw her chance. "I want to speak to Lee *Depyo*!"

"Why do you need him?"

"Because he knows me, and he arranged for me to work at the guest house. If he thought I wasn't a decent girl, do you think he'd have arranged for me to work where important foreigners are staying? I think he should know what you are accusing me of."

He smiled, as if she were amusing. "We too know your case. If not, why do you think we're here? Look at all these papers. One more time: where is Guest Number 18?"

"I've already told you. I don't know."

The woman stood up. Taking a leather whip from a peg on the wall, she walked over and struck Miyong across her shoulders.

Miyong bit her lips to endure the pain.

The woman continued lashing her until Miyong let out a cry.

The man stood up, walked over, and took the whip from the woman. "That's all for now," he said.

*   *   *

Every day, it was the same ordeal. A guard would come to her cell and take her to a room, sometimes the same heated room, and other times a different room as cold as an igloo. The interrogators changed each day, but she heard the same questions over and over. It seemed that they expected her to reply, *Yes, Comrade, I am guilty of what you're accusing me of. Yes, I did have an intimate relationship with Guest Number 18. Oh, yes; I helped him as he forced the guard to drink and steal the uniform while the guard passed out. Yes, I told the guest to steal the scooter, too, and wished him good luck as he fled. I did everything you say.*

One day, two male interrogators she had never seen before presented another accusation against the prince: that he might have started the fire in the administration building.

Oh great, she thought.

One of them, with a dark bluish birth mark on his forehead, read a long statement, saying that if she admitted that she helped prince set the fire and helped him escape, they'd let her go free.

Miyong laughed. "I wish you could find him and bring him here so that I could ask him why he was causing me so much trouble, when I don't even know him, other than the fact that he was a guest. I am as tired of this as you are. Please let me go, and don't send another guard to bother me."

"You haven't learned your lesson yet, have you?" the same man said, abruptly rising. "Comrade Song," he called out toward the door.

The same woman who had beaten her with a whip earlier entered as if she had been waiting behind the door. After exchanging a few words in a whisper with the guards, the woman turned to Miyong. "Undress, Inmate Lee Soonok!"

"Pardon me?" Miyong said.

The woman stepped forward and slapped her. "Who said you could ask questions? Should I remind you that you're a criminal under suspicion of helping a criminal escape who might have set a fire?"

The woman ripped Miyong's inmate's coat, and the buttons flew off, despite the fact that Miyong held on to the front of it. The woman, who could have been a wrestler in her previous life, worked her way to her undergarments, slapping Miyong's arms to let go of her clothes. Miyong grabbed the woman's hands and twisted them as hard as she could. A sudden kick to her leg caused Miyong to lose her balance, and she was slammed into the wall.

"Raise your hands over your head," the woman ordered.

Miyong obeyed.

"Look at this, Comrades!" the woman said with an air of pride, as she picked Miyong's brassiere up from the ground with a stick. "She's wearing this filthy clothing called *braza* [brassiere] that doesn't exist here, not even in China. It came from Imperialist America! She's a South Korean spy!"

This is news, Miyong thought. In the South, all department stores carried women's brassieres. Like Samsung radios and Hyundai cars, South Korean textiles, men and women's garments, including women's lingerie, were now sold in the international markets. How strange that North Koreans couldn't produce such insignificant items as women's brassieres, and treated them as though they were from Mars? But realizing that the woman might accuse her of being a South Korean spy,

Miyong protested. "*Dongmu*, the filthy garment you're talking about is from China. They're available everywhere in China."

"You're lying. I never saw one in China," she snarled.

"When were you in China?" Miyong asked.

"That's none of your business," said the woman.

"Five years ago, they didn't have them," Miyong said. "I was in Dandong a few weeks ago, and I bought it in a department store there."

The woman haughtily walked over, forced Miyong's arms behind her back, and bound them with a scratchy rope. She then had Miyong kneel on the floor, placed something heavy and cold like a metal bar on her calves, and pushed her down. A crushing weight pressed on her calves and feet; at the same time, she had pain on the back of her upper thighs. Miyong heard her own wail of pain and felt sweat on her forehead. *This is how criminals are tortured,* she thought. She had read about how Japanese tortured Korean activists during their occupation of Korea years ago.

"Sit here until we return," the woman said. "In the meantime, think about these rules." She pointed at the poster. "This poster is here for a reason; it's not for decoration."

The woman and the two men left the room, closing the door behind them.

Dear God, help me! Miyong prayed. *With your powerful arms, gather me and carry me out of here, and to the South. I want to live, Lord…Oppa needs me when he comes back…*

*   *   *

Everything is white and sparkling in the brilliant morning sunlight. Miyong is running in the open field blanketed with thick snow, and her brother is behind her, holding a snowball in his gloved hand and yelling, "You'll be sorry for what you did, little rat!" She threw a snowball at him a moment earlier while he was talking to his pals, and he is now after her. She can hear the sound of snow crunching under his feet, getting closer and closer, but she can't run any faster. The wind laughs through the barren oak trees overhead, and she's filled with the anticipation of getting caught. A snowball whizzes by, barely missing her shoulder, and then another flies over her head. Her foot trips over the snow-covered tree roots, throwing her balance off, and she falls. But she feels no pain. She feels light and bouncy, like a feather riding the wind. A laugh bubbles up and she giggles.

"I got you," her brother says, slapping her back. The powdery snow jumps on her face and neck, tickling her, and she giggles more. Her brother laughs, too. "Let's do it again!" she says.

*   *   *

Something poked her arm, and Miyong jumped. It was dark, but she could still see the bars surrounding her, and there was still the offensive smell in the air. *I'm back in the cell*, she thought. Then, she saw a silhouette of a woman sitting in front of her. "Who's there?" she said.

"It's me, Yonhee!" the image whispered.

"Yonhee... How did you find me?"

"A wild guess. I'm sorry that you're locked in here. This is where the camp officials 'break' inmates until they lose their minds completely and say whatever they want them to say. I lived here, too, when I first came here. Remember? I was at the party and then got dropped here, on the cold floor. They call it 'the cooler.'"

"I didn't know that. How did you get in? Did the sentry let you in?"

"It's lunchtime, so guards are busy filling themselves and don't watch the gates too closely. I came in through the secret opening on the side that I found while I was locked in. Listen," Yonhee said, her voice dropping a notch. "I came to tell you two things: Your bag was taken away, but I'm keeping the money and the vitamins for you. I hope you don't mind."

"Of course not. The money is yours. What about the rest?"

"Soonyi took the camera and wigs, and Yongok has one of your sweaters and your cosmetics. What I'm saying is, the guards didn't find much when they turned your cot upside down, except some clothing and scarves. So don't worry."

"Good. What was the other thing you wanted to tell me?"

Yonhee came closer until her forehead touched the bars. "You and I should get out of here, with the money!"

"You can't be serious!"

"I *am* serious. We have enough money to bribe a guard, and once we're out, it's easy. We can find a smuggler who can take us to China. It's not hard to find one with this much money, I'm telling you."

"Then what? Going to China doesn't guarantee our way to the South."

"It does. First, we want to go to Vietnam, through China. In China, traveling is no problem because we look like Chinese. Vietnam is crying for help, I heard it from the secret radio station. There are a lot of nonprofit organizations using volunteers to help war refugees and to take care of the sick. There are all kinds of South Korean companies, entertainers, and nurses making money there. After a while, we can easily go to South Korea. All we need is guts to do it."

"Yonhee, I don't know if I can. They've been beating me, and…" A lump rising in her throat, she couldn't talk.

"*Shhh*, I know," Yonhee said, with a tinge of sympathy in her voice. "I've been there, as I said! But you have to get well fast. Here!" She slipped something through gaps between the bars and Miyong took it. It was her vitamin bottle.

"I brought them just in case."

"Thanks, Yonhee."

"Hey, they were yours."

Miyong took a few pills and swallowed them dry.

"I must go now, Soonok," said Yonhee. "But I'll be back tonight. In the meantime, don't think about anything other than the freedom on the other side of these fences. We can do it! Even if no one else in the camp can, you and I can!" She squeezed her hand in the gap between the bars and Miyong held it. Then she was gone.

Chapter Twenty-Seven

"GET UP!" A MAN'S voice awakened her.

By the sounds of boots and keys jingling, she knew the same old guard had come again to take her to the interrogation room.

She just lay there. The thought that they'd be asking her more of the same questions they had already asked made her hate her existence more than she hated the men she'd face soon. But Yonhee's words encouraged her. She must be in the South when her brother returned from Vietnam. He had no one else in the world but herself. No one!

The guard grunted, "Hurry, I don't have all day!"

In the same interrogation room she had been in last time, three strangers awaited her: two men and a woman at the table. Wearing a red star on each shoulder and sitting in the center, the woman appeared to outrank the men. The lightly tinted glasses she wore gave her a distinguished air.

"Your name?" one of the men wearing a bushy moustache asked in a square, unfriendly voice.

"Lee Soonok."

"Louder! We can barely hear you."

"Lee-Soon-ok!" she said, louder and slower.

"Why are you not cooperating with the camp officials?"

"I cannot confess to something I didn't do."

"But there's a witness who testified that you and Guest 18 forced him to drink and stole his uniform."

"That witness happened to be a guard who got drunk while on duty. He'd say anything. Why do you believe his story but not mine?"

"You're falsely accusing a government employee of lying. That's another violation of the law."

"Are you asking me to lie, *Dongmu*, to make your work easier?"

Suddenly pointing to the post on the wall, the interrogator said, "Read the first line!"

She read: "*Answer all questions sincerely, truthfully, and in a timely manner.*"

"How do you judge your conduct during the past sessions?"

"I answered all questions *sincerely, truthfully, and in a timely manner*, Comrades."

"Not according to this report." He shook the paper in the air. "You've argued with the officers and did not admit you're wrong, which tells me that you were *not* sincere and *not* truthful! Do you know what *sincere* and *truthful* mean?"

Miyong was suddenly very tired. Dropping her gaze to her dirty and coarse hands, she thought, *How many buckets have these hands filled with dirt? How many miles did I walk, carrying those heavy buckets?*

"Answer!" This time, the woman screeched like an angry bird.

Miyong was startled. "What do you want me to say, Officer *Dongmu*?" she asked incredulously. "I've already answered the same question dozens of times, but no one believed me. How many more times should I repeat the same answer?" Strangely, she wasn't afraid anymore.

"You're impossible!" The woman officer shook her head. Leaning over to the men, she spoke quietly. Then all three of them talked for a long moment, nodding, shaking their heads, and pointing at the papers in front of them.

Then the woman faced Miyong. "Comrade Lee Soonok, would you rather write down what's on your mind in a few words? Sometimes, thoughts flow better on paper. If your written confession is acceptable to the committee, you're free to return to your unit and there will be no more questioning sessions. We're here to help you. So far, you've not been cooperative with the officers."

"I have no confession to make, written or spoken."

The man sitting on the right side of the woman, who had not said a word yet, sprang to his feet. "If you don't cooperate," he said in a shaky, nervous voice, "we have no choice but to send you to another cell with murderers, rapists, and terrorists. Are you aware of that?"

Miyong looked at him, thinking, *Which guard will Yonhee bribe? How much will she give him?*

Surprisingly, the woman smiled. She leaned to her partners again.

"What? You want us to leave?" the man who had just spoken grumbled, loud enough for Miyong to hear.

The woman nodded and tilted her head toward the door at the same time. The two men looked at one another, but said nothing. They gathered their papers and walked out, saluting the woman.

The woman rose and locked the door behind them. Then she walked to the window on her right and pulled down the wooden blinds, turning the room as dark as an empty church in early morning.

An eerie feeling came over Miyong as she watched every move the woman was making. *Is she going to beat me like the other woman? Is she going to strip me?*

Slowly, the woman came over, her boot heels clicking on the floor, and planted herself before Miyong. The brass buckle on the woman's belt glowed maliciously in the dim light. Then, with a calculated motion, she seemed to be removing her glasses.

Why is she doing this? Miyong thought, her gaze on the floor.

"Look at me," the woman said in a strangely mellow voice.

Miyong did not look at her. "Officer *Dongmu*, it's a camp rule that an inmate shouldn't look at an officer. Are you asking me to break the rule?"

"Yes. Forget about any rule they taught you."

"I'm afraid I can't, Officer *Dongmu*. I'm already in trouble for something I didn't do, and now you're asking me to break another…"

"It's okay, Miyong. Look at me!"

Miyong didn't believe her ears. *How does she know my name?* Her gaze automatically lifted to the woman's face, and Miyong uttered, "Hyunja… how did you get here? I thought you were in Seoul."

Hyunja moved closer and talked fast in a tiny voice. "Major Min called me two nights ago to tell me about your arrest and what trouble Lee *Bujang* was in. He sounded desperate, which is unusual for him. He said, 'I know you still have connections with your old supervisors in the North. I need your help.' I told him I'd think about it and get back to him. The first person who came to my mind was Captain Ahn, our old director of the Youth Red Army. I've been informed that she has been recently promoted to Superintendent of National Security, a position rarely given to a woman. It was a lucky day for me, because her secretary said that Ahn was on leave for surgery. 'What kind of surgery?' I asked, and the secretary said she wasn't allowed to give out that information. 'How long will she out of the office?' I asked, and she said she couldn't tell me that either. It was an easy guess for me, Miyong. Ahn was either having a mastectomy or some other surgery people are reluctant to talk about. This told me that no one except her immediate family knew Ahn's whereabouts. I called Major Min and told him that I'd take a chance. He wired me the papers at three in the morning. I got here at six-thirty A.M., disguised as Ahn, in a black sedan driven by Red Snake. No sentry stopped me. Did I answer your question?"

"I don't know how to thank you."

"Thank me later. Our friends are waiting for us. Come!" She pulled Miyong's hand and walked to what looked like a closet door. Inside, many uniforms and jackets hung neatly in a row. Pushing them away, Hyunja revealed a small metal box the size of a pocketbook mounted on the wall. By pressing a button on the cover, she made a section of the wall move to the side. A long spiral staircase appeared in the floor. They descended two flights of stairs and passed through a doorway that led them into a warehouse-like structure with dusty windows in the concrete walls. Rows of metal lockers stood against one wall, like in a gym. Hyunja opened one in the middle.

Miyong suddenly remembered Yonhee coming to find her that night. "Hyunja, my roommate is coming to get me tonight and get out of here together. Is there any way we can take her with us?"

"Are you out of your mind?" she said, without even looking at Miyong. "We can't risk many lives for one inmate. Forget it!"

Miyong felt awful about Yonhee. *She was kind to me... At least she has enough money to bribe a guard who can take her to the border.* She now wished that she had given Yonhee her address on Kanghwa Island, but it was too late now.

Hyunja handed Miyong a Red Guard's uniform and ordered, "Put it on. It's the smallest one I can find. And we must go!"

Miyong wore it over her inmate's quilted coat. It was roomy but kept her warm.

Hyunja inspected her, like a mother inspecting her child's appearance on the first day of school. With an approving nod, she led Miyong to a window, where a thick rope hung down from the ceiling. She yanked on the rope. The windowpane moved up. Cold wind swept in.

A Red soldier looked in. "Come up!" he said.

Miyong was uneasy. Who was this man? But Hyunja wasted no time. She tied the rope around Miyong's waist and yanked it again, and Miyong found herself rising toward the ceiling, like a piece of furniture dangling from a crane.

The soldier grabbed her shoulder and eased her out of the open window.

Standing on a rooftop and feeling the cold wind on her face, she was dizzy with fear. About twenty feet below lay a gravel path next to a creek with ice around the edges.

The Red soldier untied the rope around her and said, "We'll make our way together to the edge of the roof and jump."

"Wait, I can't jump!" she cried, but he forced her to walk, his arm tightly wrapped around her. Standing on the edge, the gravel path below seemed further down than she had thought a moment ago.

"*Hana, dool…*" he counted, unaware of her fear.

Then it happened. The cold air numbed her sensations, and then a sharp agonizing pain pierced her left ankle. She must have rolled to her side because she was looking at the fiercely blue sky. A man's dark eyes peered into hers. "Are you all right, Miss Hahn?"

"I think so…" she said, trying hard not to cry from pain.

"You might not remember me," he said, pulling her up by the hand, "but we met last spring. I was in your community when they held a press conference after the commando incident. Call me Agent Bahn."

Hyunja rushed over, ordering, "Let's go."

With Agent Bahn holding her elbow, Miyong managed to walk. The pain in her ankle wasn't severe. Actually it didn't bother her too much, now that she knew she would soon be heading for the South. *It's only a matter of time! Thank God!*

Splashing, they crossed the shallow creek and entered into the woods before them. The sunlight was dimmer here than on the gravel path, and the air colder, too. Somewhere, a siren wailed, and she remembered the military Jeep appearing at Construction Site 12 with armed guards, to take her to the cage.

Turning to Hyunja, Bahn asked, "The camp interrogators didn't give you a hard time this morning, did they?"

"Not at all. Money helped. Even if they were suspicious of me, they have no one to report to now, since the big guys are all locked in."

"Good," said Agent Bahn. "Let's move out of here quickly before they find us."

After ten minutes of walking through thorny bushes and tangling vines in the icy temperature, they reached a clearing where everything was still and deadly silent. Agent Bahn picked up a stick from the ground and began hitting the trees as he moved on. *Tock, tock, tock…*

A bush in front of them with barren branches stirred. A boy about fourteen years old wearing a gray baseball cap jumped out of the bush and ran ahead of them, saying, "Follow me!" Two minutes later, they found an oval-shaped hole in the ground that seemed to be an entrance of a cave. Using a crudely built wooden ladder leaning against the cave wall, the boy descended quickly, and they followed him.

Miyong found herself in a dank and spooky space. A wooden door on her left indicated that there was another space behind it, a room or a passageway. A heap of rusted auto parts against one wall and dead wires hanging down from the dark ceiling told her that this space could have been used by the Red Army during the war.

Two Red soldiers emerged from the door on her left, came over, and shook hands with Hyunja and Agent Bahn. They seemed to be happy seeing one another like old pals. Unexpectedly one soldier turned to Miyong, acting surprised. "Miss Hahn, don't act like a stranger."

"Pardon me?"

"Don't you remember me?" he said. Then, to her shock, he rolled up his right sleeve, exposing his upper arm.

"Red Snake! What a surprise, sir!"

"Glad to see you," he said, beaming with a friendly smile. "Since I'm the one who brought you here, shouldn't I get you out, too?"

"Actually, I was expecting you sooner," Miyong joked.

Red Snake laughed. "I would have come sooner if it was my choice, but as you know, we're only cogs in a huge machine. At least we're going home together."

Home...? The word "home" had never sounded as sweet as it did now. She had had a vague, childish hope of finding *home* when she reunited with her father, but he mistrusted her. How did he know she was a spy? What was *home* anyway? How odd it was that Red Snake used that word when he meant to say "our country."

Red Snake said, "I know what you've gone through at Camp 14, but that's in the past. I congratulate you on your good work. Oh, you'll die when you hear this! Father Sohn said that shortly after you visited him that Friday at the graveyard, he saw two camp guards on scooters rushing to him and his helpers, one after another. No guard ever visited a graveyard on a scooter, he said. As they stood and watched, the first guard shouted, "Help! I am the prince you're waiting for!" The three men lurched onto the second guard, grabbed him, handcuffed him with the handcuffs that Father Sohn always carries with him, and dragged him to the tool shed, along with his scooter, and locked him up. Then, they left the cemetery quickly, with the prince in the guard's uniform, without waiting for you. I've talked to Fr. Sohn yesterday. He's glad that you're coming with us to the South today. Because of you, Miss Hahn, Father Sohn and Prince Koo are on their way to Dandong at this very moment."

A commotion erupted at the entrance. A woman in her forties, wearing a man's green sweater, and two small children—a boy about eight-years-old and a girl a bit younger— sat on the bare dirt under a rock wall, arguing. It seemed that the mother was crying and her daughter was trying to stop her. "*Omma*. I can't stand it when you cry!" she said in a whiny voice, leaning onto her mother.

The boy too was unhappy. "We're not going back, *Omma*, no matter how much you cry," he said. He seemed more mature than his age. "I'm tired of eating rats, grassroots, and insects, like animals. *Abuji* said that we should go to the South and live like people, didn't he? That's what we're gonna do! We should eat white rice, seaweed soup, and beef stew every day, three times a day!"

The girl said, "Me too!"

The mother yelled, lifting her head. "Shut up, you two! Can't you think of anything but filling your bellies when you'll never see your father again? Even dogs would behave better than that!"

"But *Abuji* said…" the boy said.

"Never mind what he said," the woman hushed her son. "A dying man can say anything to his kids he'll never see again. You're not puppies that only want to fill their tummies. Well, are you?"

The boy said nothing, his gaze dropped to the ground, but the girl began to sob. "I want *Abuji* to come with us. I miss him…"

As the mother reached for her daughter, she let out a loud cry. "How can we live without him?"

The boy leaned his head onto his mother's back and wiped his eyes.

"They're Lee *Bujang*'s wife and kids," Red Snake whispered, sadly. "His wife didn't want to come with us, but I forced her, for the kids' sake. She would have remained if it weren't for the children."

"What happened to Lee?" Miyong asked.

"Didn't you know?"

"All I know is that some top officers are locked up in connection to fire."

Red Snake paused for a moment, as if it was difficult to talk about. "He'll be hanged in a couple of days," he said in a grave voice. "After the prince's escape and your arrest, Lee's associate Kim Yongsoon saw her chance to promote herself. At their Struggle Meeting, she criticized Lee harshly about placing you in the guest house as maintenance crew, providing Lee's handwritten request. The rest is easy to imagine, isn't it? And the prince's release form from the clinic, bearing his signature played against him, too. I believe Lee knew that this would come someday, because he sent me a long letter asking me to help his family to move to the South and to take care of his kids as if they were my own. I said I would, of course. We've been close friends for a long time."

We were both in the Student Volunteer Army in Hamhung when the Chinese troops began to ambush the U. N. troops in late October, 1950. The Allied Forces had advanced to Pyongyang triumphantly a month earlier, after their successful amphibian landing on Inchon Harbor in September, turning the losing war to a winning one. But with the Chinese Volunteer Army unexpectedly stepping into the war, they had to retreat back to the South, in the freezing temperatures. Lee Bujang and I were lucky. The retreating American troops allowed North Korean refugees onto their troopships, and thousands came, including students. But when we found ourselves behind chain link fences on Koje Island, like prisoners, we were terrified. It got better, though. We were allowed three meals a day and were allowed to sleep on military cots with clean military blankets. In the North, we had been starving and sleeping on the hardwood floor, each of us sharing one blanket with another man. We had been singing Russian military hymns and North Korean National anthems, but now, in the refugee camp in the South, we were singing the American national anthem and military hymns every morning.

Not only did the Americans feed us three times daily, but they also handed out Hershey bars and canned snacks in between, and we began to respect our masters. When some kids sang the North Korean anthem when the Americans weren't around, we beat them up to show which side we were. As if they had noticed our loyalty toward them, an American Navy officer founded the Korean Labor Organization (KLO) that summer, and began to train us as spies against the North Koreans. We were so green and naïve that we didn't know we'd soon be fighting against our own families in the North. But at that time, all we cared about was doing what the Americans told us to do.

Our spymaster, named Nichols, treated us well. Besides three meals and snacks, they gave each of us one dollar a week to spend on anything we liked. Most importantly, the South Korean military or police couldn't touch us as long as we wore the greenish American military uniforms embroidered with "USA" on the breast. After three months of intensive training, which included investigative skills, physical soundness, and parachuting, the ten of us, Lee Bujang included, embarked to the North. We settled in the home of an old couple, whose son had been killed by the Communists earlier that year. As we were told by our masters, we contacted as many friends and relatives as we could to collect the information we needed, and told them to work with us, bribing them with money, chocolate bars, gum, and hard candy. What we didn't know was that Kim Il-sung had broadcast nationally, long before we got there, ordering citizens to report anyone suspicious, anyone showing up in the area after a long absence, and anyone handing out American goods. Within a week, secret police showed up, and we surrendered without even putting up a fight. The war ended while we were in prison. After my release two years later, I smuggled myself out of the North but Lee Bujang stayed, for the border security was extremely tight.

After I rejoined CIC, Lee and I connected again. That was ten years ago, and now I'm losing him.

Red Snake turned to the mother and her two kids, as if trying to find his old friend there.

More women had arrived by the time Red Snake's story ended, each with a small bag and a child or two, and the space was filled. Each of them had a story to tell. An old granny talked about her grandson who had died while crossing the Gobi Desert to find freedom, dabbing her eyes with a handkerchief; a middle-aged woman talked about her guilt at leaving her deceased husband's parents behind; a young, skinny woman hoped to find her father, who had moved to the South when she was only five. "Even if I find him, I'm not sure if he'll recognize me," she said.

When night fell, everyone slept like field animals, on the dirt. Lying on her back, her arms supporting her head like a pillow, Miyong finally realized that she was going home.

Chapter Twenty-Eight

THE BOAT LANDED ON Kanghwa Island on Friday afternoon around three. Miyong had been dozing in the warm sunlight coming through the window next to her, and when the boat's horn blared, she woke up. At first, she thought she was still in her underground cage in Camp 14 and shivered, but her fear vanished as soon as she saw the familiar signs that said *Pacific Seafood Trading Company, Choi's Soup Noodles, Kim's Barber Shop,* and men shuttling large crates back and forth. She wanted to rise and shout, *"I'm back! I'm back."*

The ocean surface sparkled brilliantly in the mid-afternoon sunlight as if welcoming her back. Beyond the familiar signs and huts and buildings, she saw a wide straight boulevard connecting the port and Hope Community sitting atop the hill, on which cars and trucks whizzed by, and she knew the new road had been completed while she was in the North. It was the fruit of the five-year New Village project the members of Hope Community had begun almost a year ago, in June. Major Min had been excited as he briefed her about the project, and with his order, she had made flyers for the villagers. She was a part of that project, although she had not touched a shovel or carried a bucket of dirt to actually build the road. If a dirt road could turn into such a sleek, straight boulevard like that before her eyes in a matter of a few months, it wasn't difficult to visualize for her modern homes or apartment complexes mushrooming everywhere on those hills in a few years.

It had been difficult for Miyong to part with Hyunja and Agent Bhang in Dandong, China, the border city between China and North Korea. She wished they were with her now. Hyunja had acted cheerful as she hugged her. "Good luck, kid. One of these days we'll run into one another again somewhere. Next time, our roles might be reversed." That was only hours ago, but it seemed as though an eternity had passed. She thought about Red Snake and Father Sohn, too. Red Snake had said he was coming "home" to the South with her, but where was he? Father Sohn would go back to the North and remain there.

The boat anchored with squeaky noises. Miyong followed the passengers to the waiting area, where a pool of people had gathered. She had a vague hope that she could find Min here, but instead, she saw his chauffeur, Private Kim, waiting for her near the parking lot.

Miyong ran to him as if she were seeing Major Min.

"Welcome!" he said, taking her bag. "You've changed, Miss Hahn."

"How?" she said.

"You look much thinner and…just different."

"How different?"

"Well, more mature, maybe."

"I'm glad. It's good to be back."

They walked to the Army Jeep parked in the shade of a spreading oak. Kim helped her get in the back seat.

"Major Min would have come himself to get you," the private said as he seated himself behind the steering wheel, "but he left for Seoul this morning for an urgent meeting at CIC. He was promoted to lieutenant colonel last month and will soon be replacing the director of Task Management Division at CIC Headquarters. The former director is retiring soon to take care of his son, who was badly injured in Vietnam."

"When is Major Min, I mean, Colonel Min coming back from Seoul?"

"Probably on Sunday evening, but I have a hunch that he'll begin his new job shortly."

Sunday evening? It was two long days away. *Who'll give me my brother's letters?*

When she was quiet, he said, "If you need to see him for some reason, maybe his secretary can help you."

Sunhee! Yes, she might know where Min kept my brother's letters. But there was more. She had anticipated a private meeting with Major Min upon her arrival, just the two of them. She had so much to tell him.

The private said, "There's good news for everyone at the Community."

"What good news?"

"The President designated Hope Community as a model community last month for its successful New Village Building Campaign. It was a big deal, I tell you. Three hundred fifty groups from all over the country gathered in the sports arena in Seoul, and Hope Community was one of the ten groups awarded with a trophy and a banner."

"How exciting!" she said unenthusiastically.

"The best part of the news is that the government set up a grant for each group for education. My understanding is that President Park wants to spend the money to educate those who participated in New Village Building Campaign. He sees something very positive about the way young people worked hard for the future of their country."

"Lucky for them!"

"What do you mean, *Lucky for them?*" He looked at her in the back mirror. "You're still registered here as a member, Miss Hahn. Your name was announced at the assembly."

"Are you serious?"

"If you don't believe me, go to the lobby and look at the list of the names yourself. It's still posted on the wall."

Can I go to college? It sounded too good to be true. Her brother would be glad to hear the news. In her bank account, she had the money her brother had given her the night he had shown up at The Pigeon's Nest, surprising her. Now with the grant, she might not have to touch her brother's money. On second thought, going to college didn't mean much when her brother might not be there to see her graduate.

"Oh, there's more news," Kim said eagerly. "You know Albert Boyles, the director of The Pigeon's Nest you went to? He has vanished."

"Who told you that I went *there*?" she asked stupidly.

"Everyone knows. You were gone for more than four months. There are no secrets around here. Anyway, that guy, Boyles, had been spying on the American Military intelligence network in Korea since the end of the war, sitting right there in Seoul, and then sold the information to Russia! He's a thief who steals from his own father."

"How did you find out?"

"It was in the paper." In the next few minutes, Miyong heard the whole story: Boyles was a heavy drinker, and had accidentally spilled the details of his own crimes at a bar in Itaewon that American soldiers frequented. A CIC agent heard him and reported to his American boss. Two weeks later, Boyles was spotted in a Berlin airport, disguised as a Russian tourist, wearing a fur hat, a fake moustache, and thick large sunglasses, waiting for a connecting plane to Moscow.

Miyong remembered Boyles as a strange character. On the first day at The Pigeon's Nest, he had introduced himself as "the mystery of the attic."

The Jeep swerved into the Community, passing the granite sign bearing Chinese letters. She suddenly remembered Jongmi. *Where is she now? Is she still in the North with Ho?*

"Mr. Kim, have you seen my friend Jongmi lately?" she asked casually, in case he knew about Jongmi's not-so-pristine record. "Do you know who I'm talking about?"

"I do. I heard some rumors," Private Kim said while parking at the curb.

"What rumors?"

"You know how women talk. It's not a pleasant story at all."

"Please tell me."

"It's obvious that someone made it up. It goes like this: a fisherman reeled in an unidentifiable woman's corpse with a rope tied around her neck, and the police were called in. The poor woman had lost some flesh here and there and was unidentifiable, so the police were about to close the case. But one of the girls at the Community volunteered to tell the police that it was Jongmi, because she had been dreaming about her. But of course, the police didn't believe anything she said. If I were you, I wouldn't pay any attention to it."

That evening, sitting at the corner table at the cafeteria, where she used to sit before she left for the North, Miyong noticed that one-third of the diners there were strangers. She felt as though she was a newcomer now, asking others why so-and-so wasn't there, and who was the girl next to this or that person.

Everyone talked about going to college. One girl with frizzy hair, on the opposite side of the table, said she was going to a women's college somewhere and another said she was going to a teacher's college in Seoul.

All Miyong wanted was her brother's letters, but Major Min was in Seoul and wouldn't be back until Sunday. *How is Oppa doing in Vietnam? Is he still alive?*

Something touched her shoulder, and turning, Miyong saw Sunhee with a manila envelope in her hand. "Welcome back, Miyong," she said.

"Sunhee…"

"Private Kim told me that you're back. Here's your mail."

"Thanks, Sunhee. It's so kind of you to bring my mail."

"Thank Major Min when you see him. Before leaving for Seoul this morning, he told me about your brother's letters and said that I should give them to you as soon as you got back. He felt bad that he couldn't see you when you got here."

"Thanks, Sunhee."

"When are you going to start working for Colonel Min?"

"I don't know. I just got here. Why do you ask?"

"*Why do I ask?* Isn't it obvious? When he moves to CIC Headquarters, you'll get paid better. I surely want to work for him, if I can."

"Does he know that you want the job, Sunhee?"

"Of course! He said I'm his second choice. Just between us, Miyong, we're rivals." Winking, she walked away.

His second choice? He must have promised her something; otherwise why would Sunhee behave like that, winking and talking as if the two of them were competitors? Noticing that everyone at the table was looking at her, Miyong left the table and headed for the courtyard, to read her brother's letters. No one was there. She seated herself in a bamboo armchair and carefully opened the manila envelope. To her surprise, she found only one letter and one postcard. There was no date on the letter, and the penciled note was sloppy, as if he wrote it in a hurry. She opened it.

> *Dear Sister,*
>
> *By the time this letter reaches you, you'll be in a labor camp in the North. I've been worrying about you more than you'd ever know. How unfair life is! You're in the North, working for CIC, and I'm here in this cursed land of rainforest and swamp, supposedly fighting for a better world. Actually I'm not fighting at the moment. You won't believe that I am such a coward, hiding from Vietcong with a bunch of Vietnamese women and their kids. It's irony that these women are protecting me, one of the Taihan soldiers known to them as invincible brutes. To make a long story short, my company was ambushed and I ended up here. I pray that someday I can tell you the whole story.*
>
> *How was your meeting with Father and Mother? I wish I can talk to you at this very moment. Know that I'm thinking of you.*
>
> *Love, your brother.*

She was worried that his company had been ambushed and he

was hiding somewhere with women and children. Was he safe? The postcard was not from him; it was from ROK (Republic of Korea) Army Headquarters in Yongsan District in Seoul. It read: "Dear Miss Hahn, Please contact the ROK Central Identification Division at your earliest convenience."

That night, her first night in the South, Miyong couldn't sleep. *Why would the Army headquarters ask me to contact them? Does it have something to do with him hiding?* She wished she could talk to Major Min about it.

Chapter Twenty-Nine

Vietnam

BARKING DOGS WERE AT his tail as Jinwoo waded through a swamp full of rope-like reeds. He knew that those dogs would shred him as soon as they could sink their teeth into his flesh. The fog was so thick that he couldn't see a foot ahead, and the swamp's bottom was gooey mud, which slowed his pace. He vigorously walked to gain some distance from the beasts, but it seemed he was going nowhere. Something sharp and painful pierced his left ankle, throwing him off balance. What was it? A stick? The dogs were getting closer and closer, so he kept on walking. Then, sickening orange flames leaped toward the sky. Red-hot flames were everywhere, singing and hissing, growing taller and wider by the second. A man was screaming, "Help me, help me, help me..."

"Papa, Papa!" A child's voice pierced Jinwoo's ears. He suddenly realized that it was he who had been screaming. *What happened to the dogs? Where am I?* His eyes were opened. At first, everything was blurry and he didn't know where he was. He was supposed to be hiding in a dirt hole in the thicket with four other guys. But this wasn't that dirt hole with a stink of something strong — maybe animal poop. *Where are the others? And why am I here?*

A brown fan made of large dried leaves was moving back and forth before his eyes. A small boy, as dark as a chestnut, was sitting next to him, on his right, fanning, and chewing something in his mouth. A pang of hunger stabbed his stomach, just seeing the boy chewing. He was hungry. He longed for steaming rice and a piece of pickled radish. The only things he had been eating for God knows how long were tender willow branches or tiny sweet yellow flowers that grew on vines or rubbery black mushrooms clinging on rotted tree trunks. But at least he was still alive! He was glad that he could someday go back to his sister.

A man was talking in Vietnamese. Turning to his left, Jinwoo found a dark, bony man with deep-set eyes babbling on. He wore strange clothes made of rough material. "You speak *Engrish?*" the man asked, switching to English.

"Yes, some…" Jinwoo answered in English.

"You Korean, no?"

Yes, I am. Jinwoo tried to sit up but the man waved his hand before him. "No!"

Jinwoo felt a sharp pain on his left foot. *God, what happened?* The pain was so intense that it took his breath away and he moaned. His bullet wound had finally healed after Hueh had washed it and applied some crushed leaves and bandaged it with a strip of cotton fabric. *What is it now? Why does it still hurt? And…where's Hueh? Where are the noisy women?*

The man switched back to Vietnamese. By the way he talked, touching his shoulder and looking into his eyes, Jinwoo understood that this man wanted to help him. *You injured but don't worry,* he seemed to be saying. *We'll take care of you. You're safe with us. Okay?*

Jinwoo was thirsty, too, but didn't have the strength to ask for water. His eyelids came down against his will and he saw the man's face losing its shape and then fading away. For a moment he felt no pain and was comfortable. All he could see were the tall columns of flames that had enveloped him earlier, squirming, hissing, twisting, and growing taller and taller. He didn't want to remember it, but it wasn't his choice. One thing was clear: if he fell asleep here now, he'd never wake up, never would see his sister again. He couldn't let that happen.

He bit his lips until he tasted something salty — his own blood. *I must stay awake in order to stay alive. Wait, how did I get here?* He remembered walking out of the ruined building Hueh had led him to. Unlike what he had anticipated, it was a noisy place with crying children and women yelling at them. There was no man other than himself. *How many nights did I stay there — two nights or three nights?* He wasn't sure. But he did remember writing to his sister on notebook paper with a stump of yellow pencil he had found in the debris and giving it to Hueh, to mail to his sister. But he had no way of finding out whether it'd reached her. The next morning, he left the place while everyone slept, leaving a note to Hueh. If he stayed there longer, he feared that he'd die with them sooner or later. After all, he was in their country for a purpose: to save people. And what was he doing there? Nothing! Women were protecting him, a *Taihan* soldier! He must find his company so that he could return to his country, to his sister, to the people he used to know.

He walked and walked, his uniform drenched by early-morning dew. He passed through a treed lot that had been devastated by bombs, black everywhere, and came to a narrow dirt path leading to a steep hill. He clambered up, skidding on the loose dirt and holding on to the uprooted tree stumps. When he reached the top, he knew exactly where he was. From the next hill, where his command post had been, he had gazed in this direction hundreds of times, looking for any sign of snipers. If he'd walk farther, probably a half mile, passing that mass of crippled field equipment and fallen trees and soot-covered building materials, he could get there in twenty minutes. If he were lucky, he might find some clue as to what might have happened to his company, maybe some Korean letters scribbled on a rock or on a tree trunk.

The sun came up from the hazy horizon ahead, coloring the fields and hills with its golden rays, revealing his ROK Army uniform. He couldn't believe his stupidity. If the enemy saw him walking like this, in the bright morning sun, he'd be cooked alive in two seconds. Seeing a puddle of muddy water in front of him, he took off his uniform top, and bending, he scooped up the mud from the bottom and smeared it on his face and his bare chest.

He felt a sudden chill all over him, but the sun was warm, so he continued his journey, carefully, looking around, making sure he wasn't a killer's target. About half way there, in the middle of the field, behind some tall trees, he saw something he didn't want to believe. The Korean flag, with a red/ blue circle in the middle, was dancing in the wind, and below it was what looked like a tank loaded with ROK soldiers. Shading his eyes against the shimmering sunlight, he tried to make sense of what he was seeing. He wasn't hallucinating! It was real. What else could it be? The next moment, he was running, shouting in Korean, "Don't shoot! I'm Korean!"

They didn't shoot. They waited, each soldier pointing his rifle at him. Some of them even waved. *God bless my Korean brothers!* Suddenly aware of his appearance, he shouted, "I took off my uniform in case the enemy might spot me. I'm glad to see you, Brothers."

A gunshot blasted, shattering his ears.

His arms flew up automatically. "Hey, I'm Korean! Can't you hear me?"

A voice responded in Korean, "Drop to your knees and put your hands behind your head!"

"Are you out of your mind? I'm Private Hahn Jinwoo, in the 29th Infantry, White Horse Division. Take me to Lieutenant Noh. He'll tell you."

Another shot rang, and then a volley of shots followed.

Jinwoo sank down to his knees, his hands behind his head.

Boots marched toward him. When they were near, he saw tan canvas boots, not the leather boots with ROK stamped on them. As they pulled him up, one on each side, the men babbled in Vietnamese. Jinwoo finally understood. *These are Vietcong. It was a set up.*

The Vietcong in South Korean Army uniforms captured four more Korean soldiers within an hour, while Jinwoo sat on his heels, his hands tied behind him. Then, quickly, two armed men escorted the prisoners to a straw-thatched hut standing in the muddy river a hundred yards away. It was a peaceful scene, like in a painting. Along the bank, a few women were beating laundry on flat rocks, and water buffalo were grazing on dried grass. Unaware of the terror Jinwoo felt, the women greeted the men with smiles.

How did I escape from them? It was unclear. He remembered an armed guard watching them through the tiny window at the door. He remembered hearing women's high-pitched laughs, too, but he must have fallen asleep at some point during the night because one of the Korean prisoners awakened him with a shove, and all four men walked out without even putting up a fight with the guard, who was no longer there. *What happened to him? Did someone kill him?*

A sharp pain blossomed in his upper arm, and he screamed. A pair of blue eyes was peering into his own. *An American doctor?*

"Are you a Korean soldier?" the owner of the blue eyes asked in English, pulling an empty syringe out of his arm. He had a silvery moustache and a few wrinkles around his eyes.

"Yes I am, Doctor… Please tell me why I am here."

"I'm Dr. Eric Palmer, a U.S. Army surgeon. How're you feeling young man?"

"Not too good. I'm nauseous, dizzy, and very, very tired."

"You stepped on a mine and lost a couple of your toes, but don't worry. We're taking you to our hospital in Hanoi by a chopper, and you'll be handed over to a Korean medical team there. Any question?"

"What happened to my buddies?"

He made a strange expression, wrinkling his forehead. "We'll talk about them later. Or, maybe Mr. Huong here can answer your question."

Jinwoo looked at the dark-skinned old man, but had no courage to ask.

As if he could read Jinwoo's mind, the old man patted his shoulder. "Go sleep! Don't worry nothing!"

Are they all dead? Fatigue crushed down on him, and he drifted fast to sleep.

Chapter Thirty

Kanghwa Island

"I AM LIEUTENANT WOO of the ROK Army Identification Division," Miyong heard a man's voice through the telephone receiver. "I am returning your call."

"Thank you, sir, for calling me back," Miyong said. "It's regarding the postcard, sir. Would you mind telling me what this is about? It doesn't say anything except to call the number on the card."

"I'd rather talk to you in person," the man said. "How soon can you get here?"

Miyong glanced at her watch. It was three p.m., the busiest time of the day in Seoul. "I'll get there in an hour, sir."

"Come to Room 225 on the second floor. See you then."

Lieutenant Woo was a short and stubby man in his early forties, with wrinkles on his forehead. "Thank you for coming, Miss Hahn," he said from behind his desk, without rising. "Please have a seat." He pointed to the chair in front of him.

She seated herself. An awkward moment passed between them as she waited for Woo to say something. She couldn't ask anything, afraid of what he might say.

"Let me get to the point," he said in a businesslike manner. "The ROK military intelligence has been trying to locate your brother for two months without success. He has been missing since late October, after an enemy ambush in Kahn Hoa Province."

Her mouth felt dry. *Is he still missing? In his letter, he was hiding with bunch of women and kids...*

"I wish I could tell you more," he said, leaning back in his armchair. "When a soldier is missing, there are only a few possibilities. He might have deserted the company of his own free will, or he might be locked up somewhere as a POW, or maybe he's been killed in combat but not discovered by the corpsmen."

She looked at him coldly. "Isn't it too early to presume that...?"

The lieutenant didn't flinch. "We're hoping to see him as much as you are, Miss Hahn. But it's fair to say that eighty percent of men missing in action never show up."

She didn't know whether to tell him about the letter. Before she could decide what to do, he continued:

"Some might show up within the first year and some within five years. In Vietnam, the odds are against us because of untamed rainforests, swampy jungles, and countless remote islands. Private Hahn could show up tomorrow, or he might never show up." Reaching inside his pocket, he produced a photo and pushed it toward her. "This photo was sent to us. Please tell me if the man in the photo is your brother."

An Oriental male wearing a cone-shaped bamboo hat over a long black Vietnamese garment stood before a straw-thatched hut under a palm tree. Although the image had lost some fine details due to exposure to the direct sunlight, the man in the print could be her brother, but she wasn't sure. *Why is he in these ridiculous clothes?* She had no clue. On second thought, how many Korean men wouldn't look like this man in the photo, had they worn the same outfit and hat? "I can't tell if he's my brother. This man could be any Vietnamese man," she said, pushing the photo back to him.

"I agree that it's not a quality photo. But the photographer who took that picture is our man in the same 29ᵗʰ Regiment who knows your brother well. He swore under oath that the man in that photo is Private Hahn Jinwoo hiding in a Vietnamese village, where the photographer himself had been hiding, too, for a short time before he rejoined his company. He said that your brother was in and out of that village with a Vietnamese woman, which isn't all that surprising, considering that a man will do anything to stay alive. What's surprising is — the photographer alleged that…" He stopped in mid-sentence and grabbed his half- burned cigarette from a brass ashtray.

"Alleged what, sir?"

"He alleged that…your brother might have had something to do with three Koreans killed in a cave."

"My brother wouldn't cast a stone even at a squirrel, sir," she said in a flat voice. "How could you say he was missing and then accuse him of murdering his own combat buddies? It's absurd."

"I didn't say he killed them, did I?" he said. "I said he *might* have had something to do with the killing. But there's no eyewitness. The only clue we have is this photo and what the photographer tells us. Our main focus is finding him, and we need your cooperation. Have you received any letters from him during the past two months?"

She shook her head, not looking at him. She wanted to end this agonizing conversation as soon as possible, for she wasn't good at lying.

"*Not a single one?*" he repeated.

She shook her head again. In the haze of smoke, the interrogator's face was slowly replaced by the one at Camp 14, and she shivered. *I'm not at Camp 14. I'm at the ROK Army Headquarters. But what's the difference? Men in uniforms are the same everywhere. If I let this man talk until he's satisfied, he'll gladly keep me here all day, torturing me with questions.*

Abruptly rising to her feet, she said, "Please find him, sir. Until I hear from my brother's own lips that he indeed killed someone, I'll refuse to believe what you've told me."

He awkwardly handed her his name card, but she didn't take it. He then rose and extended his hand to shake hers, but she ignored it. Without bowing to him, she turned and headed to the door.

"Thank you for coming," said the lieutenant, but she didn't respond.

Outside, the late-afternoon sun was warm and bright, but her mind was cloudy. She couldn't help but cry. Without her brother, she was an orphan all over again. More than anything, her brother was a murder suspect. *Who's building a false accusation against him? The lieutenant? The photographer?*

She wanted to talk to Major Min about this nonsense, but she didn't know how to find him. He was here in Seoul somewhere, without knowing what she was going through. Working for him again was out of the question now. *Give the job to Sunhee, Major Min! I don't care!* Finding a bench under a poplar tree, she sat and looked up at the sky. The blue expanse above seemed indifferent, distant and cold. *Where are you, Oppa?* A hawk flapped his wings from the light pole across the street, leaped to the sky, and flew west as if he'd go find him.

A bus approached and stopped in front of her. It was Bus #54, the bus heading toward the center of Seoul. She boarded it and got off on Jongno Second Avenue, one of the busiest streets of the capital. As she walked along the boulevard lined with tall buildings, many unfamiliar faces passed her in silence. She wasn't alone after all. They were strangers to her, whom she might never see again, yet she was one of them, sharing the same sidewalk, breathing the same spring air, and listening to the same car horns at this very moment. Some might even have a son or a brother or a cousin fighting in Vietnam, not knowing whether they were alive. Only lucky ones would come back, and if they did come back, who'd guarantee that they wouldn't die the next week or the next month? *But wait, are these people walking on this sidewalk with me in a better situation than the soldiers in Vietnam? Who can guarantee that a car or a truck wouldn't strike and kill me and them in the next five minutes?*

She felt as though she were awakening from a long dream, a dream that she hadn't known she was dreaming. She had lived through impossible times as a child without her parents, often hungry and cold, but compared to what she was going through now, it had been easier. At the stoplight ahead, an arrow sign that read "Vietnam War Veterans Clinic" caught her attention. Following the sign, she came to a one-story white building that stretched to the next block. On the front door hung a poster of a battle scene in which a Korean soldier was helping a tall, bleeding American soldier to walk, the injured man's long arm on his narrow shoulders.

She walked into the lobby, which had a light-blue carpet with dark stains here and there. On the facing wall, many handwritten notes and photos were thumb tacked under a sign that said "Looking for someone?" One of the notes, written on notebook paper, read, "A widow of Kim Iksoon, (34th Regiment, in Blue Dragon Division) is looking for anyone who served with her husband in Milai. Please contact…" Next to it was one written by a child: "Father, I miss you so much. The flowerbed along the fence that you and I made together before you left is colorful now, waiting for you to see it. When are you coming back?"

"May I help you?" a soldier at the desk asked, a phone receiver in his hand.

Incredibly, she heard herself asking, "Could you use a volunteer?"

While waiting for an interview, sitting on a wooden bench, she let her mind run in all directions. *College can wait. If I can get a room and board here, I want to help men returning from the battlefront of Vietnam. Every man entering that door is Oppa, in a wheelchair or on a cane, with an eye patch or an arm in a sling, crippled or not. By being here, listening to their nightmarish war stories or simply handing out some flyers about benefits or other information they might need, I'll be helping my own brother.*

Final Chapter

THE CLINIC WAS SERIOUSLY short-handed, and the volunteer coordinator, Kim Maria, an ex-Catholic nun in her early thirties, kept Miyong and a hundred other volunteers busy all day. After a week of training, Miyong was sent to different floors, one day in the emergency room to observe how to handle patients just flown in from Vietnam; another day a surgery room to watch the actual surgery in progress; and the next day, in the waiting room, answering questions. She worked a minimum of twelve hours a day. By the end of two weeks, she was doing a nurse's load, taking temperatures, administrating medications according to the doctor's specifications on the chart, and changing dressings of the patients with raw wounds.

By now most of the two-dozen nurses in the clinic knew about her: that she had a brother in Vietnam, that she was a hard-working individual with few words, and that she was considering a nursing career someday.

"Miyong, what's your brother's name?" Kim Maria asked one afternoon, while Miyong was writing on a chart what medication she had given to whom.

"Why do you ask?"

"Just curious."

"Private Hahn Jinwoo, 29th Regiment in the White Horse Division."

"What year was he born?"

"In 1944."

"At the Trauma Unit, I thought I read a name that sounded like your brother's. They have a few new patients just arrived from Saigon. If I were you, I would check him out."

"What does he look like?"

"His eyes were bandaged, and his head shaven, like most of the soldiers with a head injury. Other than that I can't tell you more."

Miyong left the nurse's station immediately. *His eyes were bandaged!* The doctors and nurses moved to one side to give her room to run. Stepping into the crowded Trauma Unit with rows and rows of men in identical white gowns lying on identical beds, she looked for her brother. *Any man could be him*, she thought. After making a full circle of the room, she remembered that the new arrivals were placed in the beds close to the door she had just passed and returned to that area. A man lying on his back, his eyes covered with white gauze, caught her attention. She got closer to him. He didn't stir. A wet spot on his white pillow under his cheek told her that this man drooled. Her brother never drooled, even when he was a small kid. She checked the chart taped on the wall above his pillow. Corporal Hahn Jinwook: 23.

It was as though she had been cheated. She had an urge to go back to the nurse station to vent her anger at Maria, but it wouldn't do her any good. Walking out to the courtyard through the side door, she looked for a bench to sit and calm herself, but all of the benches were occupied by men with walkers or bandages on their arms or heads. She stood there by the door and thought; *I shouldn't feel sorry for myself. Maria was kind to me, except that the man she had thought was my brother happened to be a stranger. Had she been right, I'd be crying by now. Maybe my brother will come back without a head injury. And soon!*

She checked herself, and seeing that she looked decent, she returned to the nurse's station.

Jin Ilsuk, the patient in Room 255 of the psychiatric clinic, suffered manic depression. On the door was a note addressed to the caregivers. "Patient is self destructive. Refuses to eat or drink or take medications. Severely depressed due to the amputation of arms. Often hostile. For further questions, consult with Dr. Ahn Nohyun."

On Miyong's first day in Room 255, she was careful, even nervous, because this man had only four-inch-long stumps for arms, which were covered with padded gauze soaked with blood and pus. He was a good-looking man with a light skin and dark eyes, which wandered about the ceiling while she introduced herself. He seemed far away, certainly not in this hospital room. Was he still on the battleground in Vietnam where he had lost his arms? Miyong didn't know. *What is he thinking about? Does he have a girlfriend waiting for him somewhere? How would his parents feel when they saw him like this?*

"Mr. Jin, I will re-dress your arms, okay?" she said cautiously. "Is there something I need to know before I begin? Have the wounds been bothering you?"

He ignored her, so she removed the dirty padding from his right stump with tweezers, carefully, but blood rushed out of the wounds, that reminded her of raw meat, and dripped onto the bed sheet. Panicked, she said, "I'm sorry for hurting you. I'm usually not this clumsy." She wiped the red fluid with clean gauze twice.

He didn't even wince, as though he had lost his ability to feel anything.

"You're very brave," she said, trying to get his response, any response. "Many patients complain when I remove the padding because it hurts. I suppose it doesn't bother you."

His eyes blinked slowly, but he still said nothing. She kept on talking while cleaning the wound with cotton balls soaked in alcohol. "I suppose men are braver than women, though some books say that women live longer and have more guts in handling life-threatening situations than men. But in my experience, men tolerate pain much better than women."

He stirred. She noticed that he was looking at her expressionlessly.

"You should tell me when it hurts, Mr. Jin. If you don't say anything, you're risking your chance of getting hurt even more."

"You didn't hurt me, Nurse," he said for the first time. His voice was coarse, probably because he had not been speaking to anyone for some time.

She wondered how long he had been in isolation like this. "Thank you for being kind to me. This is my first day in the psychiatry clinic. I'll try my best not to hurt you."

He made a soft noise through his nose. "Do you know what it's like waking up in a makeshift Army clinic in a Vietnam jungle?"

"No!"

"You feel as though you're in a slaughterhouse waiting for your turn: bombs explode somewhere, the wounded men scream their heads off, and the doctors and nurses curse at each other, making the situation far worse than it already is. That's where I found myself one evening, on a table surrounded by men wearing bloodstained white gowns. One of them said to me, 'Son, you're lucky. Eleven men died in that explosion, but you made it.' I felt like shooting him. I was well aware that my arms had been blown off, but these clowns were trying to keep me alive. Can you understand how I felt?"

"I do! It must have been terrifying, waking up in such a place."

"Actually, I can't tell you exactly how I felt. Angry, I suppose. The only thought I had was — Why didn't I die with the eleven others, God damn it! I've been thinking just that since you came in. I don't mind the pain, Nurse, not at all. It's such an inconvenience for everyone, including you, to keep me alive and trying not to hurt me, *ha*...I'll be happy if a gunman walks in here and shoots me. I mean it."

Stunned, Miyong muttered, "Listen to you! Do you know what you're saying?"

He shifted his gaze back to the ceiling. "It takes money to keep me alive, you know — government money that could be used for rebuilding our country or feeding the poor. I'm not the only one the government wastes money on. Hundreds of injured are flown out of the war zone daily and are taken to where they can be treated. In my case, the doctors at the front had no equipment to amputate, so they flew me to An Lac, the nearest town where a South Korean hospital was. After the amputation, they sent me here. All of the fussing and handling caused me much pain, besides being unnecessary."

"*Unnecessary?*" Miyong retorted. "It sounds like you have no concerns for your family or other people who care for you."

"My family? What do you know about my family?" he said angrily, the white in his eyes getting bigger. "My parents passed away during the war when I was seven, and I have two older brothers and two older sisters living in Seoul, but only one of them, my oldest sister, came to see me." A cynical smile came upon his lips. "Are you telling me that I should live for them? My sister wasn't at all glad to see me. To tell you the truth, I scared her."

"How? How can an injured man like yourself scare an uninjured person?"

"Can't you get the picture, Nurse? My sister worries that, if the hospital releases me, I might have to move in with her family since my other siblings don't even bother to come see me. She never came back after that first time! Now, tell me, Nurse, I have no concerns about my family. The problem with the folks at home is that they have no clue about how we fought in Vietnam or how we feel about coming back alive, some limbs missing or eyes blown away or head cut open, because they're too busy living their own lives. Look out the window! All those theaters, restaurants, bars, shops, and beauty salons along the street..." His right stump shook violently. "Who cares for us? The President? The American guys? The doctors and nurses here? Death is the only thing that guarantees our freedom!"

A strange thing happened before her eyes. The man lying before her wasn't the pale-looking patient she had just met but was her own brother talking about dying in an angry voice. The scene of the night at

The Pigeon's Nest, the night she had found him in the garden, standing like a statue under the moonlight, rushed back to her mind. It was the night he had told her that he would be leaving for Vietnam within six weeks and lectured her to be strong.

"Look at you," Miyong said angrily, "talking about dying. Didn't you say I should be strong? 'I can't protect you anymore the way I used to at the orphanage,' you said before you left for Vietnam. Now, you want to die, *Oppa,* so that your government can save money, and the doctors and nurses here don't have to work so hard to keep you alive. Tell the truth, *Oppa*! Tell everyone that you're scared to death to face the reality of your life as an invalid. It's true, isn't it? It doesn't take anything to give up, does it? So, go ahead! Be my guest! I'll bring flowers to your grave!"

Something touched her arm, and Miyong jolted. Instead of her brother, the patient was looking at her from his bed. "I'm sorry to upset you," he said in a calm, sympathetic voice.

Miyong didn't know what had just happened. Her mind was blank. The next moment, she found herself crying, covering her face.

He didn't say anything for a long moment and then asked, "Where is your brother, in Vietnam?"

"He's missing now, they say…" she said, wiping her eyes. "He was in Qui Nhon when their commanding post was bombed."

"Was he in the White Horse Division?"

"Yes."

"What's his name?"

"Hahn Jinwoo. A private in the 29th Army."

"The name doesn't sound familiar to me. There're four thousand men in that division. All I know is that they were hit hard while I served in the 9th Army west of Phan Rang. My very best wishes for your brother."

She didn't respond.

"Do you think I'm a coward, thinking about dying?"

"Yes," she said ruthlessly. "If you have any courage, you should think about what to do for the rest of your life with what you've got.

I'm sure it's not easy, but do you want to do only things that are easy? I'm sure fighting wasn't all that easy, was it?"

Jin's eyes blinked hard. "Actually, the doctors here have been talking about giving me artificial arms, saying that the prosthetic technologies have improved, but I'm not convinced that I want to live with artificial arms. I keep going to the same issue here: is life worth living as an invalid without arms and hands?"

An older volunteer lady wearing a white jacket over her blue dress walked in with a tray of food and set it on the bedside table. "How're you doing today, Mr. Jin?" she asked, faking her cheerfulness. "You're looking good today!"

He rolled his eyes. "Didn't I tell you not to bring me anything, lady?"

"Mr. Jin, that was yesterday," the woman said kindly. "You must eat. It's your doctor's orders."

"Take it back," Jin said. "I can't stand the smell of food, any food!"

The volunteer looked at Miyong for help. "He hasn't eaten anything for more than two days," she said, loudly enough for the patient to hear.

Miyong said to him, "If you can't eat regular food, Mr. Jin, maybe we can ask the kitchen crew to cook something special for you. Are you having problems with digestion?"

"I'm not hungry, that's all."

"If you don't eat, you'll die," the old woman said.

As if he had said all he wanted to say, the patient turned to the wall and closed his eyes.

The volunteer looked at Miyong again and shrugged.

"We should let Mr. Jin rest now," Miyong said and began packing the dressing materials she had brought with her.

The next day, Maria Kim assigned Miyong to the oncology clinic on the fourth floor, but all day Jin occupied her mind. As the old volunteer had said, if he kept refusing to eat, he'd certainly die. How could anyone make him eat?

Returning to the nurse's station at four, she was greeted by a slender white-haired doctor whom she had seen many times at the cafeteria or in the corridor. Rumor had it that this doctor had been born in Hawaii, and that his parents were pineapple growers who left the country during the Japanese control of Korea in the beginning of the century. But this man had been educated in New York City. His name tag read "Dr. Ahn Nohyun: Psychiatrist."

Noticing that Miyong was reading his name tag, he smiled. "I'm Mr. Jin's psychiatrist." Dr. Ahn had a gentle voice and spoke slowly in perfect Korean diction.

Miyong greeted him by bowing.

"My patient made a very unusual request yesterday, which is the reason I want to chat with you, if you have a moment."

"Most certainly, Doctor Ahn."

"May we go somewhere and talk privately?" He headed to the waiting area across the corridor and Miyong followed. Stopping by a wooden bench under the framed photos of President Park and President Johnson hung side by side on a wall, he motioned her to sit, and when she did, he sat next to her.

"Yesterday, Mr. Jin finally accepted our advice to get prosthetic arms and hands. He has been refusing to talk about it for weeks. In fact, he has been self- destructive, inflicting pain, not eating, and refusing counseling sessions. But yesterday, he was a different man. He sent a message that he needed to talk, and when I got there, his eyes were glowing with what we call positive energy. I'm very excited about this change. Would you please describe how he was when you saw him yesterday, and what might have changed his attitudes about getting prosthetic limbs?"

This was most unexpected for Miyong. She took a few seconds to gather her thoughts. "I can't tell you for sure, Doctor Ahn," she began. She related the dialogue she had had with him and summarized. "When he found out that my brother was in Vietnam but is reported as missing in action, his attitude changed. He was sympathetic. I might have given him a chance to think about his good fortune of being alive while others are still in Vietnam, missing or even dead. This was after he shared with me his doubts about life as a disabled man, and I couldn't help but tell him that he was a coward. Dr. Ahn, I really didn't mean to sound like a preacher, but I told him that if he had any courage, he'd not think about dying, but would do anything to live."

Dr. Ahn seemed pleased. "I am touched by your insight and compassion for men like Jin. Each of us needs someone to love and be loved by, but when we don't have anyone, we at least need someone to remind us how precious life is. And I think you did just that for him."

Miyong didn't know what to say. In fact, she was a bit embarrassed about confusing Jin with her own brother for a brief moment that day.

Dr. Ahn went on, "Most people would turn their heads away from men with serious physical handicaps or psychological symptoms, like Jin, but you talked to him, and gave him a piece of your mind, and the patient nevertheless felt that you cared for him. The Asian culture, including ours, is cruel toward people with physical imperfections or unsound minds, more than the Western ones. As you're well aware, here in our own country, even children born with some deformity are rejected by their own parents. Go to an orphanage; there are a lot of rejects from society."

I don't have to, Dr. Ahn, she wanted to say. She had seen such kids while she and her brother had lived in the Good Shepherd Orphanage in Seoul. Out of eighty children, about two dozen had been what Korean people called *Buyngshin*—deformed. Moonja, for instance, the girl Miyong had been close to before she was adopted by an American family and left the orphanage, rode a rolling wooden board fitted with a harness. Miyong never knew Moonja's age or how she ended up at the orphanage but admired her beautiful singing voice. And the boy with dark, curly hair named Tony. Everyone knew that his father was an African-American GI, but no one knew who his mother was. The story was that he had been rescued from a trash bin outside the U.S. Army base when he was barely a week old.

The doctor was talking again. "Unfortunately, Miss Hahn, many people, even the families and healthcare professionals, can't understand the depths of suffering that men like Jin are going through daily. To say the least, you gave Mr. Jin a ray of hope yesterday."

"Thank you," was all Miyong could manage. Compliments always made her uncomfortable.

"Let me ask you something," Dr. Ahn said. "How would you like to work with me in the mental health clinic?"

"I'd love to, Dr. Ahn. But it's up to Kim Maria, my supervisor."

"Actually, it's your decision. We're short of helping hands at the moment and a couple of positions are open. You see, in Korea, mental illness is regarded as the work of demons rather than a human condition, which is the reason we are seriously short-handed. You would be a valued employee for the hospital."

"I have no training in nursing, Doctor Ahn. I'm only a volunteer. But I've been thinking about going to school…"

"I know you are a volunteer," Ahn said. "But we can certainly use you if you're willing. I will arrange with the school where I teach, so you can take evening classes, too."

This was more than she had hoped for. "I will do my very best!" she said.

"Hahn Miyong, come to the lobby! You have a visitor," the receptionist's voice announced through the intercom one early afternoon. It was the beginning of her second week at the mental clinic as a trainee, and Miyong was in a conference room, listening to Dr. Ahn's lecture on basic patient care, with two other candidates. Miyong couldn't just get up and leave.

Dr. Ahn must have heard the message, for he stopped talking and said, "You may go!"

She ran to the lobby.

A short man in a light-gray summer suit stood in the lobby, looking out the window, his hands locked behind him. She immediately knew who it was. "Major Min," she called out.

He turned.

She immediately realized her mistake in calling him "Major," and apologized. "Congratulations on your promotion to Lieutenant Colonel."

Min smiled. "Don't worry about the promotion. I'm the same man."

She laughed. "So good to see you!"

"You look well," he said, trying to hide his gladness at seeing her. "The North Koreans must have treated you kindly," he joked.

"Yes, sir. They fed me meat, white rice, and fruit every day!"

He laughed a short quick laugh, but became serious. "Why didn't you let the people at the Community know where you were going? I had to do some investigation before I found out where you were."

She had something to say, too. "I had so much to tell you, Colonel, when I got back from the North, but you were nowhere to be found. There was no reason why I should stay there."

He blushed. "I'm sorry…I've been very busy. Anyway, we need to talk. Got a minute?"

Miyong wanted to ask, "How long would it have taken you to call me?" but she didn't. Seeing him blushing was enough. She led him to a square table in the corner by the window, and when Min seated himself, she sat too, facing him.

"You've heard about your brother missing, I assume?" Min asked.

"Yes," she said in a tiny voice. *God, don't let him give me bad news.*

"That's why I'm here. We know where he is, now."

She felt shivers down her spine. "Where is he?"

"He's in our military hospital in Saigon. The report says that he was transported from a U.S. Army hospital in Hanoi yesterday. I came as soon as I heard the news."

Her eyes were watery. And she had many questions to ask, but she restrained herself. She must take it one moment at a time. Knowing that her brother was alive and that she'd see him sooner or later was all she wanted to dwell on at this moment. The rest could wait. Too many things had happened during the past few days… Still, she asked "How is he?"

"He had an operation on one foot, but as far as I know, he's not in danger of any kind."

"So, he was injured!"

He looked at her for a long moment, which he had often done before lecturing. "Be glad that he has no head injury and wasn't exposed to Agent Orange, which is some herbicide Americans sprayed over jungles or villages to expose enemy guerrillas. Your brother's injury is minor."

"Thank God…!" Miyong remembered the unpleasant conversation she and Lieutenant Woo had had after her return from the North. "There's something I want to ask you…something I can't understand."

"Go on, ask me."

"Lieutenant Wood at Headquarters said that my brother is accused of killing someone. Do you know about that, Sir?"

Min's expression turned grave for a moment, but cleared as he spoke. "I heard it too. All I can say is that war is like a windstorm that raises dirt and debris from the earth and blurs man's vision and senses. I personally don't want to believe such a story. Even if it's true, a man like your brother wouldn't just shoot someone without a good reason. The military court of justice will make sure the accusation is solid and accurate, before sentencing. Does it make sense?"

"Yes, but…"

"If it's any comfort, worrying about it now will do you no good. My advice to you is worry about it when you need to. It's too early."

"Yes, sir."

Reaching into his coat pocket, he took out a neatly folded sheet of paper and laid it in front of her. "It's from the prince. He's at his home in California. Open it and read it."

She opened it carefully. It was written in English, in bold block letters.

Dear Miss Hahn,

    I hope you are back home safely by now. I cannot express how grateful I am for all you did to rescue me from the North Korean labor camp. I still wake up in the middle of the night sweating from the fear of death, only to remind myself that I'm free and I'm back home in peaceful Southern California. Every day, I thank God for you and all those who have given me my new life here with my family and my caring American neighbors. I will be returning to Seoul soon, perhaps in two weeks, to arrange my father's transfer to Johns Hopkins University Medical Center for further treatment, and I hope very much to see you again. In the meantime I want you to accept a small gift of money as a token of my appreciation for all you've gone through to get me out of the camp. Without you, I would have died there.

    I have secured a sum of $10,000 at my bank in Seoul in your name, which can be transferred to your account within 72 hours upon your approval. In addition, my wife and I would be honored to have you in our home here in Santa Barbara, California, as our guest, at your convenience, all travel expenses paid.

    I know one's kindness cannot be measured with any material means, but Miss Hahn, please understand my limitations and accept my small gift.

    May God be with you always!
    Edward Yi.

Miyong bit her upper lip as tears welled up in her eyes. She had never received any gifts except from her brother, but this was a large sum. *How much can $10,000 dollars buy in Korea?* She had seen advertisements for newly built apartments on billboards showing a number with many zeros. Maybe she could afford one now, with this much money? On second thought, she should save it for her brother's medical expenses, in case he needed long-term care.

"That isn't all," Min said eagerly. "He donated one million dollars to the Heritage Foundation for renovation of the palace where his father had been born and raised. He considers himself a part of Korea's past."

"One million dollars!"

"Today, an average Korean family lives on about ten dollars per month, and one million dollars can shelter, feed, and clothe a hundred thousand families comfortably for one month."

If Min's calculation was correct, Miyong thought, $10,000 would take care of one thousand families for a month. Miyong looked at Prince's Koo's letter in front of her and then the cluttered wall before her with hundreds of notes thumb tacked to it. Those notes were from people looking for their husbands or fathers or brothers missing or dead in Vietnam. Some of the note writers might have turned into the beggars she faced every day on the street, stretching their hands out to pedestrians, saying, *Please spare a coin, ma'am*, or *I've five mouths to feed*. Some children might have ended up in an orphanage, like she and her brother fifteen years earlier.

Min went on: "I suggested to the Heritage Foundation that they invite you as a guest of honor when they formally accept Prince Koo's gift in June. It's a good occasion to reveal the whole story: the prince's abduction to the North, and how he was rescued. It's about time the public should know that we have capable and courageous young women like you working in CIC."

"You're not serious!" Miyong said.

"I *am* serious!" Min said. "In fact, I've suggested to the sponsors that they should seat you next to the prince."

"Colonel, please…"

"What do you mean?"

"I will keep the prince's note, but I can't take the money." This surprised herself. She had thought about saving it for her bother in case he needed long term treatment. At the same time, she didn't regret saying it.

He stared at her coldly. "What are you talking about?"

How could he understand what's in my mind, even if I could explain? She swallowed a lump in her throat before she began: "These last few weeks have been trying for me, without any news from my brother. I've felt as though the world I've known all my life suddenly wasn't there anymore. I came back from the North alive, but no one was here to hear what I learned there and how I survived, without mentioning how people in the camp live. It was an eye-opening for me. Because of what I went through I am a different person today, Colonel. I don't need much money. I am very thankful that my brother will come back without a serious injury, and I can help injured men who need caring people. That's all I want to think about now."

"Good, I'm happy for you," Min said in a flat voice. "But why can't you accept Prince Koo's gift of appreciation and attend the reception as the guest of honor? You're not incarcerating yourself from the rest of the world, are you?"

"No, not at all. If I accept the gift, I'm afraid it might change me. It might sound stupid, but it'd be better if I donate the money to an organization in Prince Koo's name. That's better than spending it. About being invited as a guest to the reception…I really don't want to be away when my brother might show up here. I belong here, at the clinic, sir. And I see these men as my own brother; they need me. I can't be at any other place even for a short time until he gets here."

"But…you're missing a big opportunity," Min said, disappointed.

"I don't think so, sir. There are more important things in life than money or recognition. I want to be here, and that's all I want."

He said nothing, only chewing the inside of his mouth. He looked deflated and hurt. "I was about to tell you more exciting news, but maybe I shouldn't?"

"Please tell me!"

"Were you listening to the news this morning?"

"What news?"

"The Far East CIA clandestine director of operations, Joseph Taylor, announced yesterday that U.S. and South Korean officials will form an allied intelligence team strictly aimed at the North Korean terrorists sneaking into remote areas in the South. This is the first time the American CIA officials acknowledged us Koreans as their equal partners in the field of espionage. They were 'givers' until now; they not only saved us from our evil brothers in the North during the war, but also fed and clothed our poor and homeless. But their attitudes have changed. When they learned that we acted independently after the prince's abduction to the North, without even informing them, they were furious. But before they could even organize a rescue plan, the prince was out of the North and walked into the home of an American missionary couple in Dandong."

"Wait," Miyong interrupted. "I thought Father Sohn was going to hand the prince over to a CIC agent in Dandong and that agent will bring him back to the South. That's what Red Snake told me."

"That was the original plan, my friend," he said with good humor. "In this business, things can change at the last minute. According to the wired message he sent, Father Sohn followed the last minute instructions from his Heavenly Boss. I think he knew all along that he'd hand the prince to the American missionaries for safety reasons but told us a different story."

"Maybe it was best for the prince!" Miyong said. "Something could have happened to the prince on the way back here, with the agent."

"I couldn't agree more. But someday, that priest will get into serious trouble, acting independently like that. Anyway, going back to the CIA director's announcement — he appointed me the new director of The Pigeon's Nest, the espionage school Albert Boyle founded and managed until he disappeared. You know what happened to him, don't you?"

"Your chauffeur told me about it. It's true, then."

"Of course! CIA is quite embarrassed about the traitor and gave some serious thought about our abilities. Not only that our troops helped Americans in Vietnam, by fighting alongside their troops, our cars and other Korean products are showing up in the international markets. And Korean students in American universities and colleges are turning into professors, medical doctors, scientists, and lawyers. Appointing me as the director of Pigeon's Nest is only one example that Americans trust Korean people's ability."

"Maybe it's about time that they trust us," Miyong said. "I'm happy for your new position at the school, sir!"

Min sat quietly for two seconds before producing a name card from his coat pocket. "Call me if you ever decide to work for me again. I will make sure you have a job at Pigeon's Nest."

Miyong took the card and looked at it. It still read: Major Min Haksoon, Director of Hope Community: Kanghwa Island, Route 245. "You need to order new cards soon, sir," she said. For some strange reason, her voice quivered.

A hint of smile appeared on his lips but vanished quickly. "That's the secretary's job, not the director's!" he said. He then stood up. "See you soon!" With a quick military nod, he headed to the door.

Miyong wanted to say something but could not. Her throat was tight and her eyes were burning with hot tears. Holding the card tightly in her hand, she stood there and watched him until he was gone.

A few days later, the receptionist's voice pronounced her name once more: "Hahn Miyong, pick up the phone in the lobby and press Button No. 2. It's from Vietnam."

Vietnam? Miyong's hand shook violently as she approached the phone and picked up the receiver. "Yoboseyo?" she said.

"How's the weather in Seoul, Sis?"

It was a man's voice she had longed to hear for a long time.

The end